THE BLUES WALKED IN

THE
BLUES
WALKED
IN

KATHLEEN GEORGE

UNIVERSITY OF PITTSBURGH PRESS

This is a work of fiction. While the author has followed some of the key events in Lena Horne's life, she has freely invented a great deal to form the plot of this novel.

"Let's Fall in Love," by Ted Koehler and Harold Arlen, copyright © 1933 by Bourne Co. Copyright renewed, all rights reserved, international copyright secured, ASCAP.

Published by the University of Pittsburgh Press, Pittsburgh, Pa., 15260
Copyright © 2018, Kathleen George
All rights reserved
Manufactured in the United States of America
Printed on acid-free paper
10 9 8 7 6 5 4 3 2 1

ISBN 13: 978-0-8229-4524-6

Cataloging-in-Publication data is available from the Library of Congress

COVER PHOTO: *Lena Horne in Paris,* 1947. Copyright © Yale Joel / The LIFE Picture Collection / Getty Images
COVER DESIGN: Alex Wolfe
BOOK DESIGN: Joel W. Coggins

In memory of Richard, Catherine, Frieda, and Jenny

ACKNOWLEDGMENTS

LENA HORNE ALWAYS FASCINATED ME. SHE WAS BEAUTY, VULNER-ability, intelligence, and anger rolled into a package. And the anger was part of her fire.

This novel is an imagined life for Lena based on research. First capturing me were her recordings, especially the Tony-award winning *The Lady and Her Music*. This Broadway show was a stunner, partly for the music, but also for the wit with which she told bits of her life story. I played the CD often, aware of the ways she used and transformed anger.

And then I began to research. I am deeply indebted to the books that detail her life: her autobiography with Richard Schickel, *Lena*; James Gavin's *Stormy Weather*; and Gail Lumet Buckley's *The Hornes: An American Family* and *The Black Calhouns*. I was fascinated by the period in Pittsburgh's Hill District in which jazz flourished and European immigrants and Blacks lived in peace and with mutual respect if not full harmony. Information about the Hill came from Linda Haston, actress; from Eleanor Zacour, a Lebanese American woman who lived in the Hill during the 1930s and 1940s; and from the important African American newspaper the *Pittsburgh Courier*. With their permission I have quoted the ad for Fred Palmer's Skin Lightener and the review of *The Duke Is Tops*. Other *Courier* features in the novel are invented and are hopefully in the style of existing articles.

Beside needing to know about the Hill and Lena, I needed to look into Hollywood and MGM in the 1940s. I have to admit, that was a bit like playing. I watched movies and looked at pictures of the back lots.

Altogether a number of researchers aided me along the way. I would like to thank Maura Minteer, Amanda Olmstead, Kristin O'Malley,

Marilyn Holt, and Joanne Dunmyre for listening and figuring and cheerleading, not to mention helping with dates and other facts. I got invaluable information about police records and prisons in the 1940s from the late Commander Ronald B. Freeman.

I am lucky to have benefited from the kindnesses of family and friends. I am grateful for the wisdom of my late husband Hilary Masters and for the constant support of the University of Pittsburgh. Fellow writers Jane McCafferty and Meredith Cohen read versions of this manuscript and offered encouragement. Thanks again to Meredith who found my title in Lena's signature song "Stormy Weather." All in all, I am grateful for the help of so many.

THE BLUES WALKED IN

ONE

1936

WHEN SHE WALKED UP FULLERTON, EVERYBODY LOOKED. PARTLY it was the New York clothes, that suit with the little check pattern in brown and olive green, the olive-green shoes, the olive leather handbag, and the cocky little hat, a sort of brown disc, like an upside-down bowl with a sprig of green leaves bobbing out to the right. She carried a suitcase that hobbled her walk some—but it was of a good quality, straw and leather, and she didn't want to leave it anywhere. Two trunks would come later.

People looked. She was used to it. Those clubs she sang at, the Cotton Club especially, that's what she'd been on stage for—to be looked at—and then, even offstage, she couldn't help herself: she kept getting decked out so that when they did look, what they saw was good.

White and black, both looked at her. Her father hadn't come to the station—he'd told her in advance he probably couldn't, and if she didn't see him she should take a cab. But she didn't find a cab, not one that would take her, and there were no jitneys around, so she caught a streetcar partway and began walking.

She was thinking about getting married, learning humility, none of this sassiness of hers, wanting to be someone special. Her mother thought she should work to be famous, and it was tempting, but her father had made a serious speech the last time she saw him, saying life was about making breakfast, having kids, taking care of them. And there was the fact that she was not some Ethel Waters, not some Billie Holiday. They had style. Her own successes came from being pretty, and almost, almost white. The voices in her head included her grandmother saying, "You come from a family with class. Show business is low," while her mother (who didn't get along with her mother-in-law) was saying, "Nothing like it, glamor, show business," and her father was shaking his head, murmuring, "All that craziness. You could just stop and settle down."

She paused for a while, winded, put down the suitcase and sat on it. She'd sat on worse. On the last bus she and the musicians toured in the seats were so worn she'd gotten poked by rusty springs. She'd sat on a crate in a restaurant, one of the few that let her in, and she was grateful enough for the crate even though there were vacant chairs around. She'd sat in filth and washed her good clothes in rooms that stank of former occupants. She was not supposed to be tired at her age, a year shy of twenty, but she felt a bone-weariness from always trying so hard, adapting to things.

"Comfortable?" a man asked, passing her.

"If I work at it." She always tried hard, at everything.

Some fifty feet away, she saw what looked like an older and a younger teenager selling lemonade on the street, the one instructing the other. She squinted and hurried forward. Lemonade sounded mighty good to her. She wobbled a few steps and then found her swing again. The two girls were staring at her wide-eyed. "Is business good?" she asked them. The younger one—twelve, fourteen—shook her head and shifted position once. She was wearing a faded blue dress and shoes with socks. "Could I buy some of that cool drink?" *Please, God*, she thought, *don't let them refuse me.*

They had an assortment of glasses and chipped cups. Would they let her spend a nickel, then break the cup after? Did white kids with lemonade stands learn that lesson too?

The girls, both of them, had curly dark hair and they were fairly well suntanned, but she could tell they were white. And they surely had her categorized as Negro. It usually took a moment. Something about her confused people and then they looked again and made up their minds.

"Are you famous?" the older one asked.

"Slightly," she laughed. "Only slightly."

While the younger girl poured, the older one angled to take in her outfit, down to the shoes.

She put a nickel on the table. The little girl took it and carefully, balancing to avoid a spill, handed her a chipped cup that had a row of gray diamonds around the rim and a missing handle.

Lena drank thirstily.

"I love your shoes!" the older girl said. "And all your clothes."

"Thank you." The hat was slipping down toward her left eye, but she wasn't of a mind to take it off and reposition it.

The older girl asked timidly, "Are you a movie star?"

What an idea! Not that she hadn't had it herself. She shook her head, sorry to disappoint them.

"You have to be discovered. That's what they say."

"I suppose that's it."

Her father was only two blocks away. She couldn't wait to see him, so she hauled up the suitcase, which held as many pieces of clothing as it could bear without springing open. "Thank you, honey, for the cool drink." If she hurried, she wouldn't know if they broke the cup.

MARIE AND HER thirteen-year-old sister (the one with the lemonade business) had parents who'd come from Lebanon, though they mostly just said Syria because so few non–Middle Easterners made the distinction. The family had a grocery store, which they all worked. The girls also had cleaning jobs. Their father worked in the steel mill when he wasn't watching the store. Their brother, Freddie, was off in the army. Nobody in the family questioned the idea of working eighteen hours a day; it was simply what you did. Marie's family got up and smelled coffee, not roses, never would have thought to smell the latter.

Marie was a skinny thing, sixteen but often appeared younger. Her mother had chopped her hair awkwardly a year ago because she'd gotten lice—horrible lice, she shuddered to remember. The bugs must have gotten on her sweater when she cleaned a house where there were four little kids who were all infected. Her mother's ungentle hands got hold of Marie's head, chopped her hair, and doused her with a liquid she'd gotten from the hardware store. Marie was rid of bugs and eggs in a matter of hours, but also rid of a lot of her hair. Now the hair was grown in enough that Marie could work it to make the sections blend, although today she hadn't had time to do it before setting up the lemonade table.

She was considered the family beauty. It was funny the way people always talked about beauty and responded to it—she did too. It wasn't exactly fair. Her little sister was not pretty and it affected the way she did everything.

Marie's mother had told her that when she was a little girl, a married couple offered *money* for her, to take her away and raise her as their own.

"Why?"

"They say because you pretty."

Her parents had managed to say no.

As soon as she got home from helping Selma at the lemonade stand, Marie took her place behind the counter of the little store her family owned. "Everything all right, Ummah?" she asked. Her mother nodded curtly and went back to the kitchen. Marie looked at the clock they had hanging up in the store. Was her mother's nod a reprimand? She hadn't been gone long.

As soon as her mother passed through the beaded curtain, Marie slipped the one movie magazine they carried from its place on the counter and turned to the article she'd been reading. It was about why movie stars fell out of love so easily; it was called "Losing at Love." Loretta Young and Jean Harlow and all of the women who talked about their heartbreaks were *astoundingly beautiful*. And yet they claimed they had lost at love.

There was a string of customers that particular day just when she got to the part about how playing love scenes could be emotionally confusing—you could persuade yourself to fall in love with your costar and when the movie was over, so was the feeling.

One woman wanted two cans of kidney beans and a bag of penny candy. The store was down to the last three loaves of bread when another woman took two of them, saying she had relatives coming to visit the next day. She also bought most of the oranges and bananas and three cans of tuna for the lunch she had to make. Marie added up the purchases in her head. "A dollar seven cents," she said.

"How do you know? Would you write it down?"

"Sure." She tore off a strip of paper and detailed the items. The woman, not a regular customer, stretched to look at what Marie had written. "Oh. That's right," she said, surprised.

There were boys who, displaying nickels and pennies, wanted candy. "Saw you in school a couple of times," one boy said, hanging back after his friends had gone out to the street. "What's your name?"

"Marie."

"Italian?"

"No. Syrian."

"I thought Italian. That's what I am. What classes you have next year?"

"I quit."

"Quit school?"

She nodded. "My family needs me."

"Lucky you. I hate school." He paused at the door for a minute. "See you around."

She slipped a Tootsie Roll from the case and chewed. She was learning that Loretta Young had eloped when she was seventeen (one year older than Marie) but then had it annulled.

The articles were often about people who were doing something ordinary—changing a tire, hanging clothes on a line—when someone decided to put them in movies. It could happen to the beautiful woman she'd seen today even if she wasn't all dressed up. She could be taking off a shoe to rub a blister. Carole Lombard had been discovered playing baseball on the street.

The little bell on the door dinged. She looked up to see a person who looked familiar—from school, yes. He was a Negro boy.

"Sorry to disturb," he said, smiling,

"My mother doesn't like me reading in the store. She wants me to just stand here and keep dusting. This keeps me from going crazy."

He laughed and nodded toward her magazine. "I read about movies all the time. But I like to read about the directors. And the writers."

She hadn't thought about them.

"I need three cans of soup. Two tomato and one chicken noodle."

She put the Campbell's cans on the counter. They kept one of the ads for the soup tacked to the shelf. It showed tomato soup with crackers and the print said, A BOWLFUL OF GOODNESS.

"That's it. My father has soup for lunch every day—even in this weather. I don't understand, but that's what he likes."

"Some people do take them, even in summer."

Marie put the cans in a bag while the boy slid coins across the counter to her.

"Thank you," he said, and left. Josiah. Right. Josiah Conner. Nice kid.

It seemed forever until finally her older sister, Fran, got home to take her shift. Fran had spent the day cleaning a big house in the Oakland area, but that was only her summer job. Usually she worked at the high school, in the front office, but they didn't need her for a couple more weeks.

Fran was short. She had startling and memorable features. Black shiny hair, big brown eyes, sizable nose, full lips. And she was expressive. It was as if she needed a bigger body to fit all of her in. "What a house I cleaned!" she said now. "Some people are dirty." Her voice went up on "dirty." She dabbed at her forehead with her sleeve. "My turn. Anything good in the magazine?"

"Loretta Young."

"Where's Selma?"

"Ought to be coming home soon. She did lemonade today."

"In the heat. Not so easy."

Marie went up to the room Fran now slept in, little more than a closet, and she snitched Fran's lipstick and put it on before wiping it off. Then she went to the room she shared with Selma. She messed with her hair, this way and that, over the forehead, straight back. With a hand mirror she checked her profile from both sides. There was supposed to be a good side, the one you made people look at. Actresses in movies had a camera side and they could even have it written into *contracts* that that was the side to use.

ON THE THIRD night at her father's hotel, Lena looked at herself in the mirror of her room. She was wearing a slip, no skirt or blouse yet—it was too hot. She'd chosen a light red polish for her nails, a color that looked good with her skin, and now she was waiting for it to dry. When reviewers mentioned her they described her as chocolate cream, brown sugar and honey, café au lait—so often some kind of food.

She plopped on the bed, which creaked a little. There was hardly a breeze coming from the window. "I like this life," she practiced saying. "This is better."

The phone had rung earlier today at the hotel and it was for her. Why, she'd only been gone three days altogether and yet it was Sissle wanting her back on the bus, come autumn. "We're going to need you," he said. "Don't let this vacation stretch out past August."

She didn't tell him her father didn't want her to go back to singing, but she knew he sensed it.

She blew on her nails and tapped them to be sure they were dry enough, then got up and put on a shapeless printed dress she wore around the hotel, just a light cotton with tiny flowers, not her good clothes for tonight. Two hours from now she would be having a big meatloaf dinner at her father's house, a couple of doors down from the hotel. Her father was going to have her meet some people—one was a famous man, a baseball player. She was nervous about it, wondering what her father had in mind.

It was quiet and, she had to admit, boring, waiting for him to be done with all his commitments, and she was ravenous, so she left her room determined to feed one hunger or another.

"Do you know where my father is?" she asked at the desk downstairs where an old man, Pete, was sitting and half dozing.

"At the club, I think."

"Do you know much about Josh Gibson? We're having him to dinner tonight."

Pete straightened his suit coat, forcing himself to alertness. "I heard about that."

"What should I know about him? You know, to talk?"

"Hm. Your father hopes to hire him when he's done in the Caribbean. Um." Pete felt for and found his wire-rimmed glasses in his pocket.

"He's getting over a tragedy, losing his wife. Of course you know he's a great ballplayer."

"Tell me about that. Things I should say."

"Great player. Hits home runs. People love him. Catcher."

"Thanks!" Did her father have Gibson in mind for her? And if so, would she like him?

She started down the street to the club where her father spent a lot of time, meeting with people, playing cards with people who had some stake in the city and the music scene.

She opened the door to the bar and walked in nervously. Four men turned from their stools to stare at her. "Back room," she managed to say as she kept moving.

Her father looked up, his face registering surprise, anger, worry—in that order. "Something wrong?"

"Just visiting."

He frowned and went back to his hand, telling the other card players, "This is my daughter. She just came to tell me everything is going well back home." He laughed, then they laughed too.

He was the boss—well, second boss. Lena moved in behind him. Teddy Horne was holding three aces. Wow, she knew that was good. Her eyebrows went up. "Hey," he said, "go maybe help Irene and Elsie."

"I asked earlier. They don't need anything."

"Okay, then rest."

"All right."

Her father was dressed for dinner in a good clean shirt and pants; his coat with a bright white pocket handkerchief hung on the back of his chair. "You're changing clothes, right?" he asked Lena.

"Yes," she said. She made up an excuse for her visit. "I forgot the names for tonight."

"Mrs. White," he said quietly. "And Mr. Gibson."

It was well before five, and people weren't due at his house until six. She still had time to kill. She kissed him on the forehead and made her way slowly, walking backward to the door.

Man, she was hungry. Irene's meatloaf was supposed to be great, and tonight it would be served up with mashed potatoes, green beans cooked in ham, and ripe sliced tomatoes. And Irene was making biscuits. Her maid, Elsie, did the table settings earlier in the day and kept cleaning every dish and counter as she worked, telling Lena three times they didn't need her.

She quickly changed clothes, went downstairs, and asked Pete if he could find her something to eat, whereupon he took her into the hotel kitchen and showed her where some crackers were stashed in a box. From there she wandered outside, taking a few crackers with her, and settled herself on a creaky wicker rocker. She traced places where the wicker had split. Did her father notice? Everything in his mother's house in Brooklyn, where he'd grown up and where Lena had grown up too, had been of a high quality, perfectly maintained.

She sat, brushing cracker crumbs from her palm. She watched a man working in the yard. After a while a teenage boy brought the man a jug of water. They talked for a while, but she couldn't hear what they were saying. She felt . . . she felt it might be about her. The boy carried some pipes from one place to another. Minutes went by. She watched them talking, not talking, and for a while, the boy just standing around. She saw the man eventually wave the boy away. But the kid didn't leave, and a few minutes later he came up to her. "Excuse me. You're Mr. Horne's daughter?"

"Yes."

"You sing?"

"Sort of. Been told I do."

He grinned. "I've been hearing about you. Reading about you, too!"

"And you are?"

"Josiah Conner." He pointed to the yard. "He's my father. Same name."

"What's he doing?"

"Plumbing work for right now but he does just about everything." After a pause, he said, "When you have a hotel, lots of things need attention. My pop is good. Everybody says he's good."

"Is that what you're going to do?"

He shook his head, flushed, and said, "Maybe just for a while. I mean, when he needs me. Just while I'm in school." The boy was blushing so hard his eyes were red. "I plan to work in movies."

"Really? How? You know someone?"

"No. But I will."

"So you're an actor?"

She thought of the porters and waiters she'd seen in the movies and quickly imagined this kid Josiah in costume before he said, "Not acting. Unless it's the only way in. Someday I'm going to *direct* movies—as my work in life."

He had the most wonderful face—intelligent eyes that took in everything. He was nice-enough-looking, but it was a spirit of eagerness that defined him. For the first time since she landed at her father's place, she felt she was going to be okay.

"You want to sit down for a moment?"

He cast a glance toward his father, and then perched on the porch steps, more or less sitting at her feet.

"Well. That's fantastic. I never get tired of seeing movies."

"It's hard to break in. I know that. But man, if anyone ever should be *in* pictures, it's you."

A mother across the alley called her children to dinner in a shrill voice. Lena listened to the voice, thinking how awful it sounded. Her mother tried to *intone.*

"My mother is an actress," she said. "When she can get work. I think the problem is . . . she isn't very good."

Scrunching himself one inch to the left into a blade of shade, he said, "I think most people need some lessons and a little experience in front of a camera, and if they've got it, things click. I'd be one of those directors who takes care of every shot, every second. Like Frank Capra or George Cukor."

She leaned back, smiling. "Huh. You know some names."

"I see everything they make, those guys. Three times at least."

Three times!

A little silence settled over them, but it was pleasant.

Clunk, clunk, the sound of a pipe hitting a pipe. Josiah looked to his father, then back to her. He began to talk rapidly about Bert Williams and the need for all-Negro films.

Josiah interrupted himself, wincing apologetically, and went to the yard to say something to his father that, though she didn't hear, looked like, *If you need me, just call,* and his father said audibly, "Don't you bother that young lady." After murmuring something placating, Josiah came back. He explained, "I worry about him. I'm always checking on him. My mother died a couple of years ago and it's just him and me now, making do."

"I'm an only child," Lena said. "I wish I had a sibling."

"I have an older sister, but she's married and not around. So I know the feeling."

Suddenly Lena was aware of the door opening behind her. She turned to see her father.

"Lena! I've been looking everywhere for you."

"You come back and visit," she told Josiah, who got up carefully and nodded politely to Lena's father. She said, "I have to go for now. I hope you tell me more about your plans."

Josiah answered, as if donning five more years, "I'd like to. Thank you. Good day, Mr. Horne."

Teddy said tersely, "Our guests are over at the house. I thought you'd greet them for me."

She rose and brushed at her skirt. "I didn't know you wanted me to."

"Lena, were you flirting with that boy?"

"No. Just talking. Why? I mean, sometimes people think I'm flirting when I'm not."

"Well, think twice. He's just a young boy. And he's not our class. What kind of things did you pick up from your mother and that show business life, eh?"

"You look nice tonight, Daddy." She tapped his breastbone. "I like your shirt." It was an ice blue, so light you almost didn't see the blue but then you did.

"You're going to meet some fine people tonight. These are the Negroes you should be inspired by, not schoolboys, and definitely not road musicians."

Even though he was scolding her, even though he didn't understand how much she needed a friend, she got an overwhelming feeling of love for her father. She wrapped her arms around him. "My daddy," she said, planting a kiss on his neck. "Taking care of me."

Josh Gibson was far from the first famous person she had met. There were Joe Louis, Duke Ellington, and lots of others, and it seemed they liked her a lot.

Gibson and Lena were seated next to each other at the dining table.

He had a most serious furrowed brow and he lifted his knife twice and put it back down, distracted.

She sat up straight in the not-so-comfortable ladderback dining chair, aware again that her grandmother's furniture had been nicer, friendlier to the body. Whatever her father chose, however, was quality. The rug was one with an oriental pattern and the china had been made in England—gold scalloped edges. The linens were all white, soft and unwrinkled because Irene's Elsie ironed things into softness.

Gibson traced the edge of the tablecloth. He had circles under his eyes and seemed tired out.

"Tell me about baseball," she said brightly. "I always wonder how catchers *stay* in that position. Is it difficult?"

Gibson laughed and drummed his thighs. "It isn't easy."

She looked at his thick hands as he tried to figure out what to do with them. "I mostly know musicians. But I know you hit home runs all the time," she said, "and that you're famous for it."

He sat back a bit, looking at her. "People love the big stuff even if that's not what the game requires at the moment." A dish of greens came his way. He put some on her plate first, then on his.

"People like the extraordinary," she said.

He passed the greens on, smiling at Irene and at Mrs. White.

"Mrs. White," her father asked, "do you have everything you need?"

Mrs. White looked at her full plate. "Oh, my goodness, yes."

"Now, our Mrs. White reads about baseball all the time. She even wrote a letter to the *Courier* once, about how good it is for young boys to get interested in baseball. She knows Mr. Gibson works with young kids, to give them something to try for."

"Thank you," Gibson said.

Definitely a polite man.

"Mrs. White makes the best peach pie you ever tasted in your whole life," her father told everyone.

"I'll make you and Irene one of those pies next week," Mrs. White said to him.

He gave her a huge smile. "I can't say no." Then he added, "*And* she is a championship quilter. She makes big bed-sized quilts with the tiniest pieces of cloth, don't you, Adele? So tiny. Such patience."

Looking toward Gibson, Mrs. White said, "I love to make things from scratch. Beautiful things, I guess. And I always loved fabric."

Lena had the uncharitable thought that Mrs. White's blue skirt and white blouse didn't show a love of fabric at all.

Lena said, "This blouse I'm wearing is silk. I thought it had a good shine."

"Silk is very hot in summer," Mrs. White said.

Lena had been sweating profusely. "Well, yes it is," she admitted, suddenly realizing the truth of it.

"This food is wonderful," Gibson said, kindness in his eyes toward everyone.

"Isn't it!" Lena added.

"How do you like our city?" Mrs. White asked her.

"I like it fine but I haven't seen a lot yet. I've been begging for a tour."

"Lena's just settled in for a long summer's nap and now we're ready. I'm going to take her tomorrow daytime. And a few clubs tomorrow night."

"I'm holding you to that promise, Daddy." She turned to Mrs. White. "I'm sure I will like everything."

"I'm sure you will," said the respectable woman, but in a tone Lena knew was not exactly complimentary. Especially when Josh Gibson laughed.

By the time the evening was over, she was trying to figure out what her father wanted of her and if she'd failed or succeeded. Gibson appeared to find her entertaining, she thought, as she and her father stood at the door, bidding their guests goodnight. Her father said, as soon as the two were out of earshot, that he hoped Josh Gibson and Mrs. White liked each other enough to begin seeing each other.

Lena was surprised. Mrs. White seemed too boring for Gibson in her opinion, but she managed not to say that. Instead she poked at her father and teased him. "Are you really going to give me a tour tomorrow?"

"Of course. Tomorrow it is."

A COUPLE DAYS later, Marie was walking up the street from Aziz's butcher store where she bought boiled ham for her family to tuck into her mother's pita bread as soon as it came out of the oven, still hot enough to melt butter. She saw the beautiful woman, walking toward her, humming, her eyes cast upward, looking at something or dreaming of something. The woman was a Negro, Marie understood that, but what interested her was how she knew that exactly. It wasn't the skin, she thought. Hers and Selma's were almost as dark with the suntans they got each summer. Eyes, nose, mouth, hairline, hair? She wanted to understand.

This time the beautiful woman wore a light purple dress with white buttons and white shoes. Marie moved this way and that in her excitement and ended up right in the woman's way, practically tripping her up. The look on her face she hoped said *Hello* but she ended up saying, "Sorry."

"Oh, it's you!" the woman said.

"Yes. That's . . . that's another gorgeous outfit."

"Bought it yesterday! Here in town. It's cotton. Silk gets too hot." She shifted her stance, one toe pointed out. "You look a little different."

Marie hoped that meant better. She was wearing her good black skirt and white blouse with a necklace and the thick gold bracelet that came from the old country and was really her mother's. "I have to go to a wedding," Marie explained. "My friend's sister." She tried to study the woman's face, still not sure which part of it said *Negro*.

"And your hair is smoother," the woman went on. "It took me a moment to place you."

"It's very curly. It gets frizzy. In summer it's—"

The woman laughed, hands on hips. "You don't have to explain that to me." She moved closer to examine the bangs.

A man was passing them, a white man wearing overalls and carrying a drill and moving fast, and he said cheerfully, "Now you be nice to your little sister. I can see she's gonna look just like you."

They watched him continue up the street and both of them figured out what he'd just assumed.

That was exactly what Marie had been thinking about. Exactly. She thought maybe her family might be Negro from the old country.

"On my way," said the beautiful woman. For a moment she looked awkward and puzzled.

WHEN LENA GOT home from walking, she lay on top of the bedspread in her room and tried to cool off. Once again her father had been too busy to make time for her. She found herself longing for Josiah's company. But it was a Sunday afternoon and his father wasn't working. She'd been walking around the Hill so she didn't really need a tour so much as want one. She saw that it was an energetic place—that was to the good. The people were churchgoing; that was okay with her although she hadn't gone today. She tried not to miss New York, telling herself change was good for a person. And anyway, being on the road was mostly lousy.

She reminded herself about one of the nights in particular she and the band had had to sleep on the bus. It was the first time her mother didn't happen to be riding along with her, guarding her from men, and so the drummer sat beside her. First he curled his head onto her shoulder. She minded it, always angled to get a seat to herself when sleeping on the bus. But soon she began to feel his hot breath on her breast and the sensation was not at all unpleasant, and later when his head dropped toward her belly and she shifted, he curled up like a baby with his head in her lap. He was a little guy, kind of ugly, dark chocolate, and he had a wife and two babies somewhere in New York. Lena felt his breath on her thigh and the only problem was, sensations of pleasure notwithstanding, her imagination fired, so she didn't sleep well at all.

So when the bus, spewing fumes, finally slowed down outside Toledo at a little shack of a restaurant, she was sleep-deprived and ragged.

"We got to hope they have a bathroom," said Johnny, a small, tidy, mustachioed fellow; he was their organizer, so he sat up front. The bus heaved into the small lot, like a tired old man, panting. Johnny stood in a half crouch, then stretched himself up to a full standing position. "Should be okay," he said. This prediction came from the fact that they could see out the windows an old Negro man stooped on the pavement eating something off a napkin.

She wanted eggs and bacon. Something hearty. Even more, she wanted a bathroom where she could wash out her other blouse, the lilac one, and dry it in the wind of the bus so she could wear it that night. When she wore the lilac, the show was usually good.

At the counter stood a wizened small person, a flat board of a woman.

"Where is the bathroom, please?" Lena asked.

"Sorry. No Negroes allowed." The woman was looking next to Lena at Johnny, and then she shifted and looked at Lena. "But wait . . . no, not you either, not allowed."

Lena could taste her own hunger, the slightly roiling stomach prompted by the smell of something overcooked. Oil, grease, burnt hot dogs, burnt potatoes—whatever it was, the smell in the air was driving her crazy.

"We need food," Johnny said simply, no aggression. He'd had practice.

"No. See our sign." The woman pointed to a hand-printed sign on the wall and kept an arm outstretched toward the sign as if to say the sign was the enforcer. SERVING WHITES ONLY.

"What about that guy out front? He got food."

"He cleans here before we open."

Johnny's arms went out in easy supplication. "Right now you have no customers. We have money. We'll be in and out before you know it. Can you make us a classic breakfast?"

"I said no. You want me to call the police?"

Johnny's good spirits deflated. He turned back to the few who had straggled in behind him and he shook his head.

Lena stayed calm outwardly though inside she was shaking. She walked like royalty out the door to the back of the restaurant, where she stooped, head high, and relieved herself. She was wearing high heels. When she stood and walked to the bus, she saw the men in the band starting toward her spot, to add their urine to hers. The man eating the last of his payment breakfast for cleaning the shabby joint, had a hand over his face, saying something with that hand, like *I'm not here either*, or *Never saw you, so when the police come I can say I never did*, or maybe *This breakfast wasn't worth it, you're right*. Something.

It was better here at her father's place, she told herself. Only lonelier.

MARIE GOT HOME from the wedding at four. She changed clothes and worked in the kitchen, cleaning along with Selma while her mother made the bread.

Their father was asleep on the bench in the kitchen. It was his day off. Selma whispered that he'd snored through the afternoon, deeply asleep, but still his wife and daughters were afraid to talk or put a plate down too hard or let the screen door slam.

The kitchen must have hit a hundred degrees because of the bread— Ummah could only fit four or five in the oven at one time, and she had made twenty-five loaves. Marie had to slip outside to the garden in back for a little air.

Then it was time to wake Pap up to eat. Fran was in front, in the store. This was good because if anybody got Pap angry, it was Fran. Pap had often hit Freddie and also Fran, but *less often* Marie and *even less* Selma, as if, as the children came along, he got tired out, not necessarily less angry, just less able to raise his hand.

After they finished dinner, he went out to the backyard and sat with a cigar.

Selma and Marie washed and dried the dishes with the radio on. The music was wonderful—"Cheek to Cheek" and "Blue Moon" and "You're the Top" and "I Get a Kick Out of You."

Eventually their father came in from the yard. He shook his head and Marie turned the radio off. He liked Arabic music, couldn't see the charm in American tunes. Sometimes he went to the church basement to play the oud in a group of men. None of them were very skilled but they tried to keep the tradition going.

"Still tired, Pap?"

"Very tired."

After a while he wandered back outside.

Marie worried about her sister's looks. She offered to wash and style Selma's hair and finally Selma gave in.

Marie often wished she had ended up with light brown hair and blue eyes. Every once in a while somebody who was Lebanese *had* blue eyes and some of them had fair skin, too. People gave all kinds of reasons for the difference in looks, but one of them was about marauding Swedes in another century. Marie's family, all of them, had black hair and brown eyes.

Marie scrubbed at Selma's hair, which was even coarser than hers. Fran was the lucky one with smooth, wavy hair.

"Let's sit outside," Marie said. "I'll comb it and form curls."

"No. Pap's out there."

"He just took a walk down the alley."

Marie took the chair her father had been sitting on and Selma sat in front of her on a crate. She tapped Selma's shoulder and pointed next door. "Seen him lately?" she giggled, referring to Alberto, who was about twenty-five and so startlingly handsome that everyone talked about him and his looks. There it was again—beauty, the power of beauty. It was hard to actually catch a glimpse of Alberto because even though he was breathtaking, he was also, like Selma, afflicted with shyness.

Selma shook her head.

"I almost can't breathe when I see him."

"Good thing he's not out here, then."

A joke! Selma had made a joke.

As soon as their Pap came back into the yard, Selma went upstairs but Marie didn't want to go indoors or to bed. She wanted to smell the garden, pinch a leaf of spearmint and rub it on her wrists. She felt like a brave person trying to tame a mean dog. She shut the door quietly, moved the crate to beside her father.

She could hear neighborhood kids in the alley, playing—the sound of a ball, and she also heard shouts while some smaller kids tried to catch lightning bugs in jars.

"Pap, can I ask a question?"

He fetched a stubbed-out cigar from the ground beside him and struck a match and relit the cigar with several puffs.

"Your family was from Lebanon, right?"

"Kfarhazir."

"And Ummah?"

"Same. They matched us."

"But you always tell people we're Syrian."

"Same."

She'd heard people at the wedding saying the Lebanese were better than the Syrians. Fairer skin, smarter, gentler, and *cultured*. Then somebody else disagreed, saying, "We're peasants and farmers, all of us. Wherever we came from."

A picture of Marie's uncle in Lebanon, her father's brother, showed a man who looked, to Marie's mind, Negro. He had tight curly hair, dark skin.

"Was our family farmers?" Marie asked her father.

"Yes."

"And Ummah's too?"

He nodded.

The garden was flourishing. She supposed that was true, then. "Good farmers," she ventured.

He didn't appear to hear her. Finally he said, "Poor."

"I wonder if anybody ever thought some of them—like your brother—were Negro."

"Don't ever say that. We have enough trouble as it is, being what we are."

They sat quietly for a while, breathing in the neighborhood.

Tomorrow, laundry and sewing. She was making a rose-colored blouse, hand stitched from a dress a neighbor was throwing away. Once when she didn't have shoes and Pap bought her a pair of work boots, she cried for a day and then she cut the boots with a kitchen knife until they looked like shoes.

THREE DAYS AFTER the Josh Gibson dinner and the promise of a tour, Lena decided today was going to be the day. She waited for her father in her room, then on the back porch, then in the lobby, and finally she got some crackers and went out to the backyard hoping to see the Conners working but they weren't around. It was hot, so she came back in.

The old man at the desk, Pete, was asleep. After a while, Lena tapped him on the shoulder—scared the bejesus out of him—to ask when her father was due back.

"Don't know the answer to that. There's a game going down. Gus called and said your father had to be there."

"Busy."

"Always."

"I'll go down and find him."

She saw the old man hesitate and almost say, *Maybe you shouldn't,* but she went anyway.

When she got there she ran straight into her father's partner, Gus, who was so huge a man that he blocked her way with his big belly. "Have a seat. Let me get you a Coke."

"He promised me a tour," she said.

"Did he? I'm sure he will be out in a little while." Gus snapped his fingers and a waiter came running. "A Coca-Cola for her and a whiskey for me. You hungry?"

"Well, yes."

"How about get us two salami sandwiches," he called to the waiter, who had just moved off.

Lena knew Gus ordered her father around. They were partners but not exactly equal. Her father never said a word against Gus, always said instead that Gus was good to him. But Gus was in charge, maybe because he'd started the numbers-running business a good while before he let her father in.

Maybe some people snapped to attention around her father, but her father snapped to attention around Gus. He was about three hundred pounds of will. His hair was heavily pomaded and his suit, his very large pinstriped suit, wanted a trip to the dry cleaner. It was summer. She could smell a little sweat on Gus through the cologne or aftershave. She had never once detected anything but sweet smells on her father, who was fastidious.

"We have a good life, me and your dad," Gus said.

"I guess you do. If you're doing what you want."

"Always ask myself what I want to be doing. Answer is, taking in money. That's what I'm doing."

She could imagine her father's answer: *Going to sports events or playing poker or, for a change of pace, hitting the slot machines.* Gambling was in his blood. Even when she was a little girl, she could see he loved to use his manicured hands to crack and massage a stiff deck of cards. He loved games of any sort, period.

Her father was making a job out of doing what he wanted. He played cards just about every day, and went to ballgames and boxing matches almost as often.

"He calls your back room 'The Bucket of Blood,'" she told Gus. "What does that mean?"

Gus smiled. "We got us two Saint Louis boys playing cards back there today."

She was thinking about her need to do what *she wanted to do*, needed to do. She had to tell her father about the call from Sissle.

Lena drank her drink and ate her very good sandwich until she sensed Gus had relaxed his watchdog hold on her. Then, calling out a thank you, she slipped off the stool and went straight to the back room before Gus could get his big body in the way to stop her.

The two Saint Louis boys looked cocky—fedoras tipped back, chairs rocked back on their hind legs, jackets off. Both were chubby, their faces waxed with sweat.

Teddy saw her but kept his attention on his cards. The card players, meanwhile, saw Lena and their tipped-back chairs came forward, punctuating the silence with the sound of wood on wood.

"I'm his daughter," she said. "Go on, play your game. I don't mean to get in the way."

Her father played the next hand, and being a pro, he did what he did beautifully, watchably—easy and fluid in all his movements, but then he had to slide some bills over to one of the men, and he said, "That's it for me. I'm folding."

"No."

"Sorry. Date with my daughter. You guys need baseball tickets?"

"Good tickets?"

"Sure thing. The Crawfords."

"Did I hear you're an owner?"

Her father didn't answer, just made a face that meant *sort of yes*. Best Lena could figure, the answer was . . . *sort of*, compliments of Gus.

"Two good seats?" the second man asked.

Teddy said, "Of course."

"We would have liked to see Gibson."

"He'll be back. Mark my words."

The first man squinted at him. "How much?"

"Seats are on me."

Teddy told his waiter, "One more round for the visitors." And he told the visitors from Saint Louis, who had wiped him out, "My treat, too," he said, "the beer and the rye."

"Horne," they said when he got up to join his daughter. "We sure are happy to have met you. You had a big name in New York for a while, right?"

"Yes. My mother was pretty famous. She was very active in politics."

"No, it was you we heard about, in connection with gambling."

"Did a bit of that in the city, yes. Gotta go. Enjoy the game."

Out front he told Gus to give the Saint Louis guys ballgame tickets. "They weren't so dumb after all," he said.

"Sorry about that."

"You going to the game with me later?"

"Yeah, let's have a steak before we go. I'm buying."

"I thought you were going on about craving hot dogs."

"Steak first. I can always eat again at the ballpark," Gus laughed. "But you'd better give this beauty her tour. She's mighty restless."

Lena and her father left the club. She was worried he wouldn't recover from his bad day at the card table. She knew he joked about wanting to win 75 percent of the time with the 25 percent being just to keep it interesting. Same with baseball. He wanted an impossible .750 season.

He walked her out to the alley behind Gus's bar and used a key on a garage. There were few garages in the neighborhood, but he had apparently found one of them. Inside was a gleaming car, a Cadillac, brand-new, yellow, with very white wheels.

"What a beautiful car! It's yours?"

"Who else's would it be?"

"I thought maybe Gus's."

"No, it's mine. I do love it. Get in. Feel those seats."

It was all luxury, everything about it—leather seats, the clean dashboard, even its melodic hum.

Her father backed out of the garage and drove the Caddy with aplomb, leaning back, arm out the window.

"You look perfect in this, Daddy. Just simply elegant."

"You don't look so bad yourself."

There, he was cheerful again.

Some folks stopped walking to look at the Cadillac and several waved. Her father was well known here, that was clear.

"So your trunks haven't arrived," he said carefully. He cast her a quick glance to the side.

"I know." She took a deep breath and straightened her dress. "I held them up a little."

"I don't like what I'm hearing." He shook his head and sighed disappointment.

"I might need them in New York. Just for a bit."

"You're going back." Silence. "You were crying half the times I talked to you."

"Not half. Just Joe Louis." She had sobbed on the phone when Joe Louis lost the big fight. He was being beaten up and people were cheering. She and half of America listened on the radio that night. "It was like he stood for us and then he lost. He was us," she told her father.

Recovering his poise, her father said, "Sports. These things happen in sports. Don't be dramatic. That wasn't a good life for you on the road."

"It was *a* life. It had *some* good things. You loved it when I told you I palled around with Ellington and Cab and Kaye Thomson and Henderson."

The car hummed along. Her father had a flat hand on the steering wheel. Did he nod slightly?

"So it wasn't *nothing*," she continued. "People talk about me, they write about me. Just give me a little time to want the new me. I mean, I do want it. I just need a little time."

Her father said, "I can introduce you to lots of people, lots, everyone you just mentioned, easy, and more if that's what you want—hell, they all come through town. I know everyone."

He pulled over, looked toward a shop advertising cold drinks. "Hot as anything, isn't it? Well. Here's the thing. There's a band coming in in a couple of weeks. George Olsen. They called me asking could they play some music with you—have you sing with them. I said you weren't interested anymore—"

"I knew you would say that."

"But, you see, they were insistent." He smiled, nodding toward the little shop. Offhandedly, opening the driver's-side door, he said, "I have to keep them happy because, well, they'll stay at the hotel. It's good for my business if they feel treated well. Respected." And when he came to open her door, he offered what temptations he could to keep her. "I said maybe you could sing a little at the hotel with them. Messing around. After hours. Or at the club."

Her spirits quickened. "When?"

"Two weeks from now."

The way her heart leapt, she knew her decision. George Olsen, then back to Sissle and the road after.

"And we'll hit the Grill tonight," her father said. "We'll hear some jazz."

She stood from the car. The sun was high in the sky, the air was moist, things were growing, growing everywhere, even two plants outside the shop where they would get cold drinks. Her father was coming around.

As soon as she got home, she called Sissle back. "I'll come," she said. "September fifteenth, right?"

He said, "We have eleven bookings. It's looking good. People want to see you. And . . . I got you a coach."

"A coach?"

"Don't worry. You'll like him."

She went out to the porch, taking with her the book people were talking about; she had started it last night and ended up reading almost two hundred pages before falling asleep, then another hundred in the morning before her tour of the Hill. She leaned back in the creaky chair, reading, fanning herself.

Perhaps she'd go to a movie every afternoon until the Olsen band got in.

Yesterday she'd gone to see *Anthony Adverse*—all romance and fancy clothing. Josiah had come by and they'd talked again, even though she was nervous her father would see her and bother her about it.

They talked about every kind of thing. He told her how much his father had loved his mother and how devastated they both were when she died. He wanted to know about Lena's mother.

"That's a bad subject," she said. "I try to love her but it's hard."

"She's mean to you?"

"Well, sometimes. Pushy sometimes. And she got married again. I don't like him. At all."

"Ugh. That would be awful."

And after a silence in which she felt how sympathetic he was, she told him things she didn't much talk about—how her mother had once dumped her with strangers in the South, how scared she had been being with people she didn't know, going to a bad school, and all because her mother wanted some acting job.

"Ambitious," Josiah said thoughtfully, "and couldn't make it all work out."

"You understand things," she said.

"Sometimes," he laughed. He had talked about school. Many of his friends had quit or gone to Connelley Technical but he told her he was going back to high school.

She approved of that.

She talked through her dilemma about going back on the road, which if she did would disappoint her father. It was nice, having a person to talk to. A person who listened.

She hoped Josiah would come by today.

Late in the afternoon, as if wishing had made it so, Josiah and his father came back to do some work. Today they were painting the gate.

She tried to concentrate on her book, but when she looked up, she saw the father standing, rubbing his head as if to rub a thought in, and then when he walked down the alley, Josiah did a few quick swipes of the fence and came to her.

"Where's your father going?"

"To get a different brush. And lunch. Hmmm. What movie will you go to today?" he teased.

She laughed. "I *am* thinking of going."

She was the lesser student of movies. Josiah often took notes—he was trying to teach himself the rhythm of fadeouts and the use of calendars and such on screen.

"Did you make a decision?" he asked.

"Yes. I'm leaving in a few weeks. It won't be forever." They went silent for a few seconds. "You want a Coca-Cola?"

"I don't have any money today."

"No, I meant my father has some. I'm thirsty. I'll get you one."

She went into the hotel and asked Pete to fetch her two cold Coca-Colas. She hummed Cole Porter music and danced around the kitchen, so glad Josiah had come to see her. After all, she could only read so much of *Gone with the Wind* without wanting to throw something.

She carried the bottles of Coca-Cola outside. Josiah, who was sitting on the porch steps, stood to receive his. He tipped a head toward her copy of *Gone with the Wind*. "They're going to make a movie of that book. People are talking about how to cast it."

She turned the book over, thinking about how long it was, how large a project it would be. "Sit," she said. "Get comfortable."

He looked happy as he shifted the Coke from one hand to the other and scrunched down and planted himself on the steps again. He said, "When I'm a director, I'll put you in my movies. You're already cast."

"You are a brave soul."

"You have the actress look."

"Whatever that is."

"Liking being looked at."

"After this fall, I'm supposed to get out of show business and settle down." She stopped herself, revised. "I mean, I *want* to settle down. I just want one last . . . chance to perform."

"And do what then?"

"Regular life."

"I can't picture that. Not for you. I meant it about movies. I think you'd be good. Like Fredi Washington? In that movie where her mother was a maid. You should have roles like that."

"That's reaching pretty high."

"I wish I could write about you. Your story."

"Ha. Not much of one."

They sipped at their Cokes. He said, abruptly and out of the blue, "Did you see *The Emperor Jones*?"

"The movie and the play. I saw both. I think I was six."

"Wasn't he . . . ?"

"He was."

Somebody was sawing somewhere nearby. It reminded her of snoring that wouldn't stop.

She thought he looked at her too fondly. She sighed. "So I'm going to get married. Settle down."

His head jerked up. "Oh, I . . . I didn't know. Who are you marrying?"

"I don't have a clue yet. My father says this is the town to do it in."

Josiah drank the last of his Coca-Cola and looked out to the yard, where his father was back and darting angry glances at him. "I should help him."

"You should."

"I don't care what you think now. When I make the kind of movies I want to make, I'm going to call you wherever you are and offer you roles you won't be able to turn down."

He leapt off the porch steps and went to his father.

MARIE WAS MINDING the family grocery store. Fran had gotten called back in to work at the high school. The best office workers got summer preparatory work—counting textbooks, things like that, and dealing with the summer school students who had to do courses over. Fran's teachers had wanted her to go to business school or college because she was so smart, but there wasn't money for more school. She was lucky she got to finish high school.

Fran's limp went back to the time she was a girl of eleven and her father in his anger threw her down the steps and the fall broke her leg. She thought it just hurt like crazy, so she wrapped it up tight for a long time. Finally it was clear it had gone back together all the wrong way. But she moved quickly anyway, determinedly cheerful.

Marie thought Fran smiled too much and tried too hard to make people like her. She feared Fran might have a bad reputation. Her mother always said so, called her *sharmuta*, which was the swear word that meant a bad woman.

Lots of the Lebanese fathers were kind to their kids, but Marie's family got the bad luck of one they had to be afraid of.

The screen door opened and Fran pushed into the store with her lopsided walk. She put a magazine down in front of Marie, exclaiming, "I brought you a present," and then, catching her breath, said, "One of the summer school girls snuck it in. Anyway, we confiscated it and it was just sitting in the office so I took it, kind of put it under my blouse."

The magazine was called *Movie Stories*. It said on the cover, *You can read the stories of all the best movies.*

"Read them?" Marie frowned.

"It's a good magazine," Fran said, picking it up briefly to fan herself. "You can be prepared when you go to a movie, or *if* you go and don't understand something, you come home and read about the script. It's very informative."

Marie opened the magazine to peek at its contents.

Fran crossed to the fruit stand to get an orange. "You want me to watch the store?"

"Now?"

"Yeah. I'll take a turn. You could go to a movie today."

"But Ummah won't like it."

"Here's how you can do it. I heard the people who run the candy store on Fifth are looking to hire. I'll say you went to apply."

Marie ran for her sweater and her little pocketbook. The movie theater showing *Mr. Deeds* was advertised as scientifically air-cooled. She hurried down the steps and paused. "You really don't mind?"

Fran said, "Go on, pretty one."

The guilt over the fact that Fran sometimes embarrassed her plagued Marie as she made her way downtown. She wished Fran would figure out how to become more respectable.

Almost at the candy shop, only two blocks away, she saw a familiar silhouette ahead. She quickened her pace. This time the beautiful woman wore a stark white blouse and a pink skirt that moved side to side with each step. And white high heels. So elegant!

Marie caught up, breathless. "Hello! Hot day, isn't it?"

The woman turned but continued walking. "Oh. You must be following me!"

"No. Going to see about a job. Then the movies. I just saw you ahead." They passed one store after another, dodging other pedestrians. The sidewalks were crowded and there were a good many cars on the street, too, horns tooting. "That is a beautiful skirt."

They had to stop at a street corner. "What's that you're squashing in your hand? Reading about movies?"

Marie displayed the magazine. "It's something different. It's about the scripts."

"I know somebody who would love that. He probably knows about it. Let me look."

Marie handed it over. The woman looked for a minute and handed it back. She said, "I had a favorite skirt I stupidly wore going down to my father's basement and I ripped a hole in it right here." She touched her right thigh. "I ruined it."

"How big is the hole? Maybe it can be fixed."

"How?"

"Take an equal panel out of the other side. If there's enough cloth."

"I'm not good at that."

"I am. I would look at it for you."

"Really?"

"I remake clothes all the time."

"Come to the Belmont Hotel. After lunch? Tomorrow?"

"Yes. Here's where I'm going." They were almost right smack in front of the candy shop.

Suddenly a man and his wife stopped right in their path, arms out-stretched so Lena and Marie couldn't move on if they wanted to. The man cried, "Lena Horne! I heard you were in town. Your daddy says you're going to come live here."

"I don't know," the beautiful woman answered, then hurried to say, "I mean, yes, I am."

"You're going to keep singing, though?"

She waved the question aside. "Oh, I don't know. Yes."

Marie felt like she was watching a movie, trying to pick up on every line. She could tell Lena worried she would be a pest, so she said a quick, "Have to go," and opened the door to the shop. Before she was fully inside she heard the man mention a review in the *Pittsburgh Courier*, about a recording. So the beautiful woman *was* famous.

A woman emerged from the back of the shop.

Marie said, "May I see the manager?"

The woman behind the counter said warily, "I'm the owner. I'm Mrs. Kostopoulis. What is it?"

"I came to see about the job," she said.

The woman was tall and narrow with a high rooster's comb of black hair. "Are you Greek?"

"No."

"What are you? You look Greek."

"Syrian. Or rather Lebanese." People guessed every which thing. Italian, Hungarian, French.

"Can you add? Subtract? Make change?"

Marie looked to see if the group was still on the street talking, but they had moved on. "I do it all the time in our store. We have a grocery store."

"And you're pretty," Mrs. Kostopoulis observed. "Come back tomorrow. My husband will be here. I'll have him here to question you. Four o'clock."

"Oh. Yes. All right. I'll come tomorrow." Four o'clock meant she could still go look at the ruined skirt at one.

Just as Marie turned for the door, she heard, "Would you like to taste the chocolates?"

"Yes!"

"Choose."

Marie pointed to two pieces.

Mrs. Kostopoulis handed over the two pieces of candy in a piece of crisp paper.

Marie thanked her, thinking they were gifts.

"Twelve cents, please."

Stupid. She was stupid, she told herself. She paid with a nickel and seven pennies and had barely enough left to get into *Mr. Deed Goes to Town*.

Gary Cooper and Jean Arthur.

In this film, Longfellow Deeds, played by Cooper, had inherited twenty million dollars. Who could even imagine such an amount?

Marie carefully nipped bites of the two pieces of chocolate creams she'd gotten from the shop. One piece was filled with more chocolate and the other was filled with mint.

LENA HAD HER skirt on the chair next to her and ready in case the girl she had run into the day before came by. She fully expected to hear it could not be fixed. And that would be that. Since she wasn't that used to talking to white people, she would be relieved.

Honestly, the Hill was a small town. She kept running into the same people—not just this kid, but others, too, so that now people on the streets waved to her when she passed. The Hill was called a neighborhood, but it was a city in miniature. Within a few blocks you could buy anything you needed or wanted—a washing machine, a lamp, a blouse, a skewer of lamb.

She had extracted from her father a little history. This tower of Babel with lots of poor people, a good number of dilapidated houses, a multitude of accents, used to be where the rich white people lived. Then the immigrants came. Then the Negroes.

If she was going to give up her career, it was as good a place to live as any. The problem was replacing her career with something she could bear.

The day was hot, drowsy.

Pete came out back to tell her she had a guest.

"A white girl?"

"Yes."

"Could you ask her to come out here?"

She put aside her novel on a small wicker table and stood, then scooped up the skirt from the other chair.

The girl came out. She was wearing her black skirt again, and a plain cream-colored blouse.

"You're all dressed up."

"I have to be interviewed about that job."

"Oh, good, you want it, then?"

"I think so. All the jobs help."

"I don't know your name."

"Marie. Marie David."

"Would you sit for a moment?" Lena took her own seat again. "Here's the skirt. I think it might be hopeless." She watched Marie study it, measuring something fingernail to knuckle, folding fabric this way and that.

"I can do it so you can wear it again."

"Huh. Well, it's worth a try. How much?"

The girl was clearly taken by surprise. "I didn't think about that. I was just going to do it."

"You should always be paid. So long as the work is decent."

"Fifty cents?"

Lena wagged her head. "A dollar?"

Marie nodded.

"Would you like something to drink? I have iced tea."

"Okay."

Lena went inside to the kitchen she now used fairly often. She poured two glasses of iced tea and came outside just as Josiah, without his father, bounded into the yard.

"Josiah!" Marie said, and he said, "Marie!"

Lena felt a small disappointment. "Oh. You know each other?"

"From school," Josiah said. "And from her store. I'm going back to school, but she quit." He leveled an accusing look at Marie.

Lena handed one iced tea to Josiah, who seemed surprised and also grateful to get it, and the other to Marie. She said, "I'm going back inside for one more." She stopped long enough to ask Marie, "Why did you quit?"

"Oh, just to work. To help the family."

Lena said, "I'll be right back." Once more she stopped herself, to tell

Josiah, "She's the one who had the movie magazine I was telling you about this morning." She heard him say, "So you do really love the movies if you're reading about the scripts!"

Again a pang of jealousy. Would he now not need to talk to her? Would she lose her time with him? When she came back, Marie was saying, "I saw *Mr. Deeds* last night."

"What did you think?"

"I liked it. I wonder why so many scripts have rich people in them, though. The writers really like to write about people with money."

Josiah nodded and bit his lip, thinking. "It's what people like to see."

"But Deeds had millions."

"I know. I saw it."

Lena said, "He sees everything. I saw it too, a couple of days ago. Last night I went to *Anything Goes*. The songs are still in my head. Even when I'm reading."

Josiah looked at her copy of *Gone with the Wind*, eyeing the thick side and the thin side around her bookmark. "You're almost done!"

"Almost. Still makes me mad. Those southerners!"

"My mother was from North Carolina and she was wonderful."

"White southerners."

"That book is going to be some huge movie," Josiah told Marie. "Did you read it?"

"No."

Lena said, "Well, I'm taking this back to the library tomorrow or the next day. You could swoop and get it before somebody else does." Lena thought suddenly from the look on Marie's face that she probably didn't read, didn't go to the library.

"You could try," Josiah said.

"I might try," Marie said quietly. "Maybe. I'm almost always working."

"Are you sure you have time to do my skirt?"

"Mornings, I'll do it. I can fit it in. I should go."

The girl was nervous, uncomfortable, and Lena was too. But Josiah appeared to be enjoying the three-way conversation. She felt like a high schooler again, with friends and all the complications that came with them.

"Can you remember the songs from the movie?" Josiah asked.

"I knew them before."

"Of course," he said. "You would!"

She started to sing the crazy lyrics already seared into her brain. The rhymes were amazing—Coliseum and museum! But just as she got going, the faces of the other two told her to look behind her.

"Hello," her father said. "Hello, all. It's a little party."

"Hello, sir."

"Where's your father?"

"He had an emergency today. A bust. He's coming back later."

"Good."

Lena said, "Daddy, this is Marie David, a young woman who sews."

"Ah. Yes, nice to meet you." He stretched as if he had just wakened from sleep and went back inside.

Josiah said, "I'll come back when my pop is working."

Marie said, "I'm leaving. But could I ask . . . I heard the man on the street yesterday say you made a recording. Is that true?"

Lena said, "It's in the shops. My father's business partner apparently called the radio stations about playing it more often. I haven't heard it on the radio yet. I keep missing it."

"I'll listen for it," Marie said.

Lena began reading after they left, waiting out her father, who had scared them off. He appeared, finally.

"Who was that girl?"

"She seems nice enough. Her family owns a grocery store."

"You should talk to Irene. She can get you a seamstress. I can see you're lonely here. You haven't found your crowd."

"I know."

"And the boy . . . as I said, don't lead him on. Sure he wants to climb up, but you have better things to do."

After that day, Teddy instructed Irene to take Lena shopping and to have a party with people she knew from a charitable organization at the church. He took her to the clubs to hear music three times in the next week and let her go three other times with some of Irene's acquaintances. She sang in her room at the hotel, practicing. She added "You're the Top" to the songs she knew. The Olsen band came in, thrilled to be working with her, and that made her happy. Her father, who didn't want her to want a career, sat listening to the Olsen band at a front table of the club with his chin in his hands, looking proud.

MARIE HAD WORKED on Lena's bright yellow skirt for three days. The cotton was of a very fine quality, she could see that. Marie cut carefully into the section with the tear and cut just as carefully into a balancing section that would hit the left leg. She had to make two fine seams and make them look purposeful. Since she had no sewing machine, she did this project, as she did everything, by hand, and though she was careful, she was also fast. When she thought the skirt looked good, she took it back to the Belmont. She understood that Lena's father had wanted to sit outdoors that day and hadn't much liked the company his daughter was keeping. She understood his point of view, but she felt angry anyway, knowing she was considered unworthy. The reasons were—she could tick them off—she had few changes of clothing, the clothing she had was inexpensive, she didn't read fast, and around people who had money she got tongue-tied. Somehow he knew these things about her.

Sewing and counting, math of all sorts, were her strengths.

When she told Lena on the day she returned the skirt that she would be happy to take on more work, mending or remaking clothing, Lena thanked her but said her father and his wife wanted her to use the tailor and seamstress they used for such jobs.

She felt the dismissal in her gut. She received the dollar and Lena's compliment about how the yellow skirt was now saved and usable again. Her face got hot with embarrassment that she had wanted to be friends with a famous person when she had nothing but sewing skills to offer.

The candy shop owners, however, liked her for her looks and her quickness making change, so she'd gotten the job.

ONE AFTERNOON LENA, after the Olsen band came and went and just before she was going to meet Sissle's coach, settled on the old wicker chair to read. She saw a movement, looked up, and found Josiah passing in the alley, but just passing, not coming in. It had just started to sprinkle rain. The air had been wet, threatening rain all day.

She just wanted to see him, that's all she knew. He'd stayed away except for a couple of times he worked with his father, but they only talked very briefly on those days in little snippets, about what she was singing, what she was reading, and which movies he had seen.

She waved him in. Her father was out of town.

Oh, what a smile.

"Do you have time to talk? Sit."

He looked worried but took his usual spot on the steps before she could invite him to sit in the other wicker chair.

Josiah had several books in a paper bag, which was speckled with rain.

"May I?" He moved the bag further onto the porch.

She had always wanted a sibling, she told herself, a sister, a brother, either would do, someone to argue with, tease.

Josiah had a particularly serious look on his face. "Can I ask you something?"

"Sure."

"I know you've been in the *Courier* a lot, but it's an ad from over a year ago."

"Oh, yes. I know what you mean."

"I clipped the picture way back when I saw it."

She hated that picture. The newspaper had printed a cutout of her head, but the cutout ended at the chin, no neck. It looked as if she'd been decapitated, and all the while there she was, smiling about it.

"In the quote, you said everybody could benefit from Dr. Fred Palmer's skin lightener. My sister was visiting once and she said she wondered if you used it. This is my chance to ask."

There were to be no secrets from Josiah. The rain had started up again. Laughing, she said, "You'd better come on in. Did your books get wet?"

"No, they're okay."

They entered the hotel kitchen. "I made my father stock a few things. He's out of town. Would you like cookies and tea?"

"Yes!"

"I thought so. I'm not proud about that ad. It's just how things are done—it's a way to get known." She went about heating water in the kettle. The kitchen had two stoves, cast-iron, both yellow and green, like twins. The room also held both a small round table with two chairs and a larger rectangular table where her father gave orders to a cook when they absolutely had to come up with food for residents, which was rare because people who stayed at the Belmont ate in the neighborhood restaurants, a pattern that made her father popular with other business owners.

They chose the smaller of the two tables.

Josiah removed his books from the paper bag. His worn brown pants and lighter brown shirt were dotted with rain.

She saw that Josiah was using the *Courier* ad about the skin lightener as a bookmark. She couldn't be completely sorry for it, could she? The ad had helped to make her a bit of a celebrity.

While she waited for the kettle to whistle, she took the ad out of his book and looked at the headline and her endorsement.

READ WHAT LENA HORNE SAYS

Lena Horne of the New York stage is one of the most beautiful, talented, and famous actresses of today. Miss Horne's wonderful successes have made her name known in thousands of homes. Her startling beauty holds her audiences entranced. She is one of many prominent theatrical personages who endorse Dr. Fred Palmer Skin Beautifiers.

"They called you an actress," Josiah said.

"Oh, they just say that. They don't try to be accurate."

"*Did* you ever use the skin paste?"

She shook her head. "Never did." She went to a cupboard and came back with a plate and a package of cookies as she digested his criticism.

His gray eyes flickered and picked up light.

"You are just like having a little brother. Making me answer to you. Scamp!" She slid the clipping back to him and pulled at the cellophane on the package of cookies.

He placed the clipping back in the book, which he had kept open, and when she looked, he lifted the book to show her. "Miss Hurston? Her essays about Negroes? You probably know them."

She perched on the seat across from him at the round table, waiting for the water to boil. "I should. I know I should. My grandmother used to talk about her."

"It's pretty interesting."

The kettle finally whistled and she got up.

"It helps me think about movies in a way. She says the Negro is naturally dramatic . . . we like action . . . we're physical and visual; she says we like metaphors."

"You must have a decent school, talking metaphors," she teased while pouring water into the teapot. Her Brooklyn school had been very strong in language and literature. "So, metaphors, huh?"

"She also says we make up words. We like to say *ain't* because it's softer than *aren't*. That shows—well, she thinks it shows—creativity. Do you think that's true?"

"You shouldn't say *ain't* no matter what. It's not correct. This tea needs to steep. Don't pour it yet." She put the teapot and two cups on the table.

"It's nice being in here."

"You're my little brother."

His face betrayed a momentary disappointment, but he went on, "You want to look? She says we like angularity and asymmetry. I think that's true. I do."

"I'll maybe take a peek." She put the cookies on a plate and moved the plate toward him. The rain started to beat at the windows. "Don't go home in this. You'll be soaked." He didn't protest. "We can have a study hall."

They drank tea for a while and ate Fig Newtons. Josiah ate a good half dozen of them. He opened one of the books from his bag and when he did she took her peek at the Hurston book. The rain coming down made a wonderful rhythmic sound because it had not only a steady beat but also an occasional accent that came when it gathered for a splash at one leaky downspout. She heard it all as . . . music.

She skimmed the book Josiah was enchanted by, reading a little bit about African heritages like trickery and folklore and friendship with the devil. It all seemed to her to be more about poor Negroes or southern Negroes than about her. Was she wrong? Was there a "we?" The theories didn't sound like her grandmother, who was stiff and political and precisely verbal—and awfully symmetrical, come to think of it.

She looked up. Josiah was studying her.

"My sister wanted to change her skin to lighter. She said if you used it, she would buy it."

Lena held back her hair, which felt like rough cotton today from all the humidity. "Truly, I came into the world this way, lighter-skinned than some."

He nodded slightly. "You can borrow the book. I've read it. I have time on my card."

"Go on, have another couple of cookies."

When he left, Lena wandered the hotel, itchy for more talk. There was nobody around today, so she just walked the hallways. When she finally came back to the kitchen to slog away at Zora Neale Hurston, she saw that Josiah had left the *Courier* ad as a bookmark.

> "*I cannot praise Dr. Fred Palmer's Skin Whitener Ointment enough. I am always particular about my complexion, especially in the summer, because every actress must always look her best. Naturally I depend on Dr. Fred Palmer's Skin Whitener Ointment because of its extra-strength action and lovely results. I recommend it to all my friends.*" (Signed) *Lena Horne, New York City.*

So she was a liar. She had that part of her heritage down.

She was getting too close to Josiah. In a little while she would be on her way back to New York and he could forget about her.

HAVING PASSED INSPECTION with the Greek husband of the woman who had first interviewed her, Marie was firmly ensconced in the candy shop. She was due downtown three to nine every day except Sunday. Her pay and the four chocolates she was allowed per day whenever she worked were the benefits. She dressed at 11:30 for the day and worked the grocery store until almost three and then hurried to the candy shop in time for her shift. The hours she worked were the ones with customers going to and coming from the movies. They bought boxes of assorted candies to take into the theaters or to take home.

At first she was terrified, but when she figured out that most of the customers were moviegoers, she began to ask them about what they were seeing. It became clear to her that she liked meeting people.

She said to a young romantic couple, "I hope you enjoy the movie."

"As much of it as we see," the man joked, and the woman pretended to hit his arm. "But it's a good one, I hear. *The Petrified Forest*. Scary."

They waved at her as they left. She promised herself she would see that one.

"You're doing very well!" Mrs. Kostopoulis said one day when she came to check on things. "Business is good."

Mrs. K tended to wear stiff-looking but good-quality dresses and everything she added was clearly thought out—earrings, scarf, etc. The stiffness extended to her hair, which looked molded, every day exactly the same.

One day, only three weeks into the job, the doorbell sounded and Marie looked up from straightening the candy in the cases to find Mrs. K., stiff hair and all, at a time she didn't usually come in. The owner went into the back room for a moment and came out, saying, "I've watched you. You're quick at math and making change. My husband is opening another shop and he wants me *there*. If I do that, I can't come back to close up here. Or work on the accounts. I'm wondering if you think you could do the books after closing, clean the shop, list the orders, and close up."

So she wasn't being fired. The opposite. Marie squared her shoulders. "I think so."

"Could we try it? Starting next week? That would extend your hours to, say, ten thirty. Is that all right?"

"Yes."

"All right, let me show you." Then Marie's boss began to explain the columns that specified what had been sold, where they were running low, what should go on the order sheet. She showed Marie the cleaning materials, which hadn't been hidden at all, since they were in the small room in back with a toilet and a tiny table.

With great solemnity, Mrs. K handed over a key to the front door.

"Do you get hungry? The hours you're here."

"I eat before I come. My mother makes me bring a sandwich. I keep it in back. Just so you know, I only eat when there are no customers."

"Very wise, very wise."

The next week, it was definitely autumn, chilly, the smell of dry leaves and cold in the air. Mrs. K kept popping back in the afternoons, checking the books, over and over. It was clear she was amazed that the money kept coming in, every piece of chocolate was accounted for, and the pretty skinny thing she'd hired was apparently honest as the day was long.

TWO

1936, 1937

LENA EYED THE TUNA SALAD SANDWICH AND MILKSHAKE SHE'D sent the stagehand for an hour ago. He had put them on a stool near the stage door.

Sissle had indeed hired a coach to rehearse her in a falling-apart theater in Harlem before the others got there. The coach was a grumpy composer/piano player named Skeetie. He was fat, tired, and all his facial hairs, like his body, were out of control. He ran his fingers over the keys of the piano, looking thoughtful as Lena stood up on the stage singing out this phrase or that, waiting for him to tell her what to do.

Some of the auditorium chairs were broken, tipping over dangerously. Skeetie had put hardly any lights on. And the place smelled like dust that had been warmed by hot light for decades, then left to settle.

"No, move this way, elbows out." He stood up, demonstrating, looking ridiculous. "Right. Goes with the songs better."

Lena wanted to cry. She could tell she was all wrong.

"Your smile is too bright. Can you make it more sultry?"

"What does sultry look like?"

"Sultry, smoky, you know, a 'come hither' glance."

"My grandmother only let me learn go-away glances," she joked. The laughter she hoped for from Skeetie didn't come, but the stagehand guffawed once and tried to stifle it.

Skeetie plopped at the piano again and began playing. Lena tapped her foot, found her note, and sang a few bars of "Pennies from Heaven," trying to come up with a come-hither expression, which made no sense with the song.

"That's a little better. Come on down. We'll try something else."

"Like what?"

"First off, what are you thinking? Let's get into those thoughts of yours."

"I'm thinking, 'Did I get the notes right?'"

Skeetie heaved himself into a broken auditorium chair, which sagged dangerously low under his weight. "Of course. You always do. Lyrics are perfect too. You get an A-plus on learning the songs. You must know that. Sit."

"But my singing . . . is lousy?" She sat beside him, waiting for him to say yes.

"Well. You're in tune. And most audiences are happy with that. But—"

"You want me to go back to Pittsburgh," she said. Afternoons on the back porch again, not so bad.

"The opposite. We want you to take the band up to the next level. We want you to free up the feelings inside you."

Audiences had *always* been happy with her. Bad as she apparently was, the more time she got on stage, the better the reviews the band got. But this hairy guy was saying perfect diction, perfect notes, perfect timing wasn't very interesting.

Her stomach growled loudly. The stagehand lifted the bag of food. Skeetie said, "Go. Eat."

The rest of the musicians would be there soon.

She sat on the tiny low stool near the stage door, her knees knocking together.

"Why do you always do things for me?" she asked the stagehand.

The light from the open door caught some gray in his hair. His faded blue shirt and pants looked like a uniform, though they were just ordinary clothes. He was about forty. His name was Martin.

"You have that way about you."

"What way?" She unwrapped the sandwich greedily and offered him half.

He shook his head. "Famous."

She ate two bites quickly, trying to swallow so she wouldn't speak with food in her mouth.

"You've got, you know, that thing they call *it*." He chuckled softly.

"I never know what that is. Heard of it. *It*."

"Appeal."

She sighed. "It's just my looks, right?" Unfortunately, the good reviews mostly talked about her beauty.

"No. Your looks are good, they're great, my wife would die for your looks, but that's not the magic."

She became alert. "It isn't?"

"It's how angry you are. It pops out of your eyes."

I'm not angry, she thought. *Well, perhaps a little*. She said, "I'm just hungry and confused and figuring I shouldn't have come, even for a few months and a few bucks."

She concentrated on eating and drinking and going over her songs.

She was supposed to add "That's What Love Did to Me" to the program because that was the song she had on the radio. Suddenly, as she went over the notes and lyrics, she understood something. Outside herself, looking at herself, she heard her neatly well-behaved rendition.

She finished the sandwich in record time and was about to have the last tiny bit of milkshake when Skeetie called. She put everything down and climbed up onto the stage, all the while thinking, *Anger?* Martin made it sound like a good thing. Why would people like anger?

Skeetie had ditched "My Man's Gone Now," because he said she couldn't for the world sound Negro enough or convince anyone that she was poor and bereft or that anybody had left her.

He played her the intro to the damned "Pennies from Heaven." She thought, *What the heck, why not sing angry?* She sang "Pennies" in a way that suggested she didn't expect any pennies, and then launched into "I've Got You under My Skin," with a little of the leftover bitter energy she'd summoned up.

Skeetie's eyes were alert. He said, "Can you go beat something up—like a trash can or something? Let more of that out?"

"You want me to get rid of my bite on a trash can?"

"No, the opposite, sweetheart. Find it, use it, and *keep it*."

"Makes no sense."

"Try it."

Skeetie unwrapped a sandwich he'd carried in his pocket all this time while she did the assignment with the trash can. Martin had climbed the steps to bring one to her. The dust in the theater seemed to kick up. She looked back to Skeetie, who nodded, *do it*.

"Don't want to be famous," she said over and over again as she got down on her knees. She felt her stockings pop and begin to run. But she beat the trash can until she was sweating and laughing at the ridiculousness of her kneeling in her ruined stockings, and then ruining a perfectly good metal can with a piece of broken broom. *Who am I so mad at, anyway?* she asked herself. Mother. Father. The world. "I just want to be *good*," she whispered, banging on "good." "I just want to *be* somebody," banging hard on "be." Skeetie didn't stop her, so she said it over and over, a hundred times, getting the fury out.

AFTER CHURCH, ON a Sunday in early October, Marie sat in the tiny patch of land that was their backyard, where they were still harvesting the last of the green beans, tomatoes, cauliflower, zucchini, and green peppers. There was a chicken coop out back, too, green wire and weathered wood. Her mother would choose one of the chickens, wring its neck, pluck it, and roast it tonight.

Anya, the little girl who lived next door, still all dressed up in her churchgoing clothes—a white dress and a pair of patent leather shoes—came over with a ball and jacks. "Will you play me a game?"

Marie, who was a failure at anything athletic or physical or anything demanding eye-hand coordination was, against all odds, excellent at jacks. She could beat almost anyone. But when she played with Anya she pretended to miss a few jacks, letting the child win.

There appeared to be a lot of activity in Anya's household. People in their best clothes kept looking into the yard. Marie tossed the ball up and then picked up a few jacks. "What's going on?"

"Wedding," Anya said.

"Who?"

"My big sister."

"Who is she marrying?"

Anya pointed to the house on the other side of Marie's, where the beautiful man lived with his parents, quietly, almost invisibly. Today, however, there were now shouts coming from that house.

Something dramatic was afoot. Was he really getting married? To Helena, older than he.

Everybody in the neighborhood swooned for Alberto in his white shirts and neat dark pants. He had wavy brown hair and the largest brown eyes she had ever seen. And he apparently played piano and sang. He was a combination of Italian and Hungarian. His family told people to call him Albert, more American.

"Marie! You come. I need you clean while I roll out bread."

"Coming!" she called back to her mother, but she was riveted by the scene out in the alley. There were four men now—Anya's relatives—carrying Alberto out his back door. Two were lifting him from under his arms, two were holding up his legs. He wore a suit and tie and he looked as good as ever, but apparently he couldn't quite walk on his own. The men were shouting cheers at first and then they broke into song and stamped their feet at some of the lyrics. They put a bottle to Alberto's lips. Coming behind the group were Alberto's parents, dressed in their Sunday mass clothes.

"Marie!"

"I'm coming!"

Anya picked up her jacks and ran toward her yard, where she opened the back gate for the party of men.

Marie could hear Alberto's voice, quiet but insistent. "Priest. I want a priest, you understand."

"The priest is in the house. We got Father Joseph. He's Catholic, don't worry. We'll bring him out. You'll see him. We got everything. Food. Drinks. Come on, man."

They were forcing him! Or were they?

Marie insisted, "Ummah, Mom? Come out for a second."

"You come. I call you."

"Please."

A few people from around the neighborhood had heard the ruckus and were lining up in the alley. The men let Alberto's legs down and he stood in the yard of the house where Helena lived.

"You can't change your mind," one of the men muttered.

"No." He stood straighter.

In a few moments Helena came out of the house with her mother and the priest. Helena was wearing a blue suit and carrying flowers that drooped and that an uncle had brought from somewhere—maybe a church, maybe the funeral home. She wore a blue-and-white veil that reminded Marie of a Madonna painting.

The men held Alberto up. The mother and Anya held Helena up. Father Joseph made quick work of it—perhaps five minutes of what sounded like rapid Latin.

Marie's mother had finally come out to the yard too. Once Helena lifted her veil, family members pushed her and Alberto toward each other and they kissed. The neighbors applauded enthusiastically. Helena had tears in her eyes. Alberto was crying too, and he . . . looked happy.

"Ummah, capture one like him for me!"

Her mother looked at her, puzzled, then, shaking her head, said, "Tell them I send bread later."

Marie ran over to tell them there was bread coming and to congratulate the couple. Helena, beaming, did not try at all to hide her awkward shuffle. Alberto was transformed. His eyes lifted from the ground. They met Marie's eyes as if he had always been able to look at people. "Your mother's bread," he said, "is the best gift we could receive. Thank you."

How amazing. He even had words at his command. How did a person *get* this magic? From being loved? From feeling love.

LENA HAD SUNG (sometimes with the anger that gave a bite to the songs) all over the Eastern seaboard and the Midwest for the best part of three months. It was just after Thanksgiving and she had finished up in Cleveland. She was leaning against a wall, her bags packed, when the yellow Caddy pulled up. In the big yellow car her father had a passenger, a man. They opened both front doors and got out, leaving the car doors ajar.

"There's my lovely daughter," Teddy said.

Lena hugged him, holding on hard.

"This is Louis Jones," her father said when she let him go. "He went with me to the fights last night."

"You were here in town yesterday?"

"Just overnight."

He could have come to hear her sing. Fifteen minutes. She'd wanted him to hear her with the new, tougher voice she was using. "Hello," she said vaguely to Louis. "Happy to meet you."

Her father tapped Louis lightly on the arm and said, "Louis here is going to make us proud. This fellow has brains. He went to West Virginia State College."

"Took exams, too," Louis added, smiling. "Yes, I even passed a few." He moved back a step, hand on the open passenger door, to let Lena in.

Lena liked his spirited reply. She looked at him then. A pleasant fellow, he was smartly dressed in a wool suit of light gray; he was light-skinned and barbered to a T, though Lena was not sure what a T was. He said, "You can sit in front. I'll take the back unless your father wants me to drive."

"I do. I would like that," her father said. "It's getting dark and you'll get us home safely." He came around to the front and climbed in. Lena slid into the back seat, not sorry to have room to herself. "My daughter is coming home!" her father sang.

Lena understood, years later, when she thought back to this moment, that this outburst of feeling was her father wanting to make up for the eighteen years he hadn't taken care of her. He'd sent gifts, and letters, yes, but she rarely saw him.

On the phone about a month ago, he'd said, "Have you had enough yet? Are you ready to quit?"

She was still sending her mother money, and she didn't know why she kept doing so. It confused her. But she didn't tell him.

He'd said, not even knowing she supported her mother, "Slavery is done. Quit that band. That life is not good enough for you."

She knew he was at least half right. She wasn't twenty yet and she was down in the dumps some days from working all the time at a job that dished out as many insults as compliments.

Her father turned around from the passenger seat. He pointed to the well-barbered college graduate he'd brought along to fetch her home, to show her somebody who was not in show business and who was doing fine. "Louis Jones's father is a minister. Louis and I played cards together a couple of times back home."

"And yesterday," Louis said.

So cards *and* the fights.

Louis slowly and methodically checked everything before starting her father's Caddy. She couldn't picture him in a back room playing skin or poker.

Right now, as the car moved, she just wanted to sleep. "It's cold," she said, wrapping her coat more tightly around her.

"We'll make good time," her father assured her. "Home in a couple of hours."

As she drifted into sleep, she thought, *Did my daddy bring this man to me?* She embraced herself and slept.

In a couple of hours Lena was walking into the Belmont Hotel again and everything felt familiar if not homey. The wood floors had a smell—maybe the wax Pete used.

She'd told Josiah last summer about all the places she'd lived. She said she was trying to imagine what it would be like to grow up in *one* place, a place you loved, with a wonderful mother, like he had.

She went straight to the kitchen, opening cabinets to see if her father had stocked cookies.

Practically sleepwalking, she made herself a cup of tea and all the while she could hear her father and Louis talking in the other room. She was glad they were busy, because she felt too scattered to get to know Louis tonight. She wanted to do her hair and feel good about herself and . . .

Louis wandered in as she, having found a loaf of bread and some butter, was just putting a piece of bread in the toaster. "Needed that nap," he said.

"Yes. Sorry."

"Well, I won't bother you." He paced to a window and back. "This is a great city. I know your father has taken you to see the nightspots—"

"Oh, I've been to the clubs, yes, Daddy knows where to go."

Louis cocked his head and smiled at her. "You look like him."

"I guess that's lucky. I'm having tea. I could make you some," she offered. "Toast?"

"No, no. I'll be going." But he didn't sit or leave. "We have fantastic music here."

Had her father asked him to sell her on the city? She was already committed to being here. "New York, New Orleans, Chicago, Kansas City, Pittsburgh. The big five," he continued. "I hope you want to go to the clubs again. I'd love to take you."

The clubs were her favorite part of the city, music being as necessary as food.

"Maybe tomorrow?" he said.

"Oh. Yes. All right." She came to the table, carrying the teapot and the butter dish. A lock of hair fell over her eye. He came up to her and gently moved it back.

"There. I can see you're in need of a little bite. I'll come by at around one to see how you feel. If you want, I'll give you an afternoon ride and we can still go out later in the night. Is that okay?"

"Yes." She knew little about him and, coming out of her fog, asked, "Are you a musician?"

"No. My real work is politics. I'm an organizer right now."

"I'm not sure what that is."

"Oh, well, I go to meetings a lot of days and nights a week. It's completely necessary to getting things done. And getting known. I'll run for office soon, so I need the connections. I'm a natural politician."

She had not known any politicians close-up, or what they actually did in meetings.

"However," he smiled, "I do make a living. I file papers at the county coroner's office."

She moved to sit down but paused to ask, "Are you sure you don't want tea?"

"No, no, but thank you. Of course, I'll do better eventually when the jobs start opening up. I'm talking too much. Your eyes are closing."

"Sorry."

"I'll see you tomorrow afternoon, then." Louis hesitated at the door, then left.

It was happening so fast. Her father must have told this Louis Jones to start courting her. He was a very respectable guy and his touch was gentle. After she had tea and toast, she went to her old room upstairs, thinking about a marriage, babies, a family, all those normal things. Her body hummed like a string on a bass, vibrating.

Louis Jones. He seemed very nice.

Her father came up to say good night, something he rarely did.

She told him, "Louis is taking me for a ride tomorrow, another little tour."

Her father looked surprised. "Really? How did that happen?"

She watched her father's face for a smile of approval, but he was cocking his ear at the door, listening to something happening down at the front desk.

"I'd better get some rest," she said, finally.

Louis came back the next day with a borrowed car, a Packard. The first place he drove was right down to Fifth. "This is the best place to buy furniture when the time comes."

Her head spun at his phrasing. Had something already been decided?

"You've seen some of this?"

"Some. In the summer. I walked around a lot."

There were people everywhere—clerks, lawyers, secretaries, government officials, politicians, and bureaucrats, just every kind of person coming from lunch or running home to change clothes. "Don't you have to be at work?"

"I took the afternoon off so we could do this."

"Oh, I'm honored."

Louis began pointing out "excellent buildings" by significant architects.

He's a man who likes architecture, she told herself. *So notice buildings.*

He turned up Centre to give her a view of the Gulf Building and the Koppers Building.

"They *are* impressive."

"Aren't they?"

When they got to the poorer parts of the Hill, she said, "These sections remind me of parts of Brooklyn. I loved it there. I miss it."

She kept studying the houses, imagining the lives within. "The buildings are so gray, black almost," she observed.

"It's the price of steel," he explained, "which we need. It's the identity of our city. In politics, we try to preserve that."

Studying him, she realized he must have gone home to change clothes or taken a fresh shirt to the office, because he wasn't dusty. Even his shoes were buffed. He was slender and bookish-looking, partly because he wore glasses and had a habitually serious expression.

He pointed out the Connelley Technical Institute and Miller Elementary and then more churches and schools.

Buildings, churches and schools, she told herself. *Like them.*

When they passed the New Granada, the movie theater she sometimes went to when she didn't go downtown, he pointed upward. "Doctors and such above. Offices. All kinds."

He was cute. A little stiff. They passed shoe stores and funeral homes, all of which she knew. He stopped in front of the New Rome Coffee Shop. "A big murder was committed here. Did you know?"

She hadn't.

"Some streets are more Negro than others. Anyway, anybody bothers you, you tell me."

She laughed out loud this time to think of lean and bookish Louis, polite Louis, in his perfectly pressed suit and his little red tie, punching someone who had offended her. He took her hand.

She liked his name. *Louis.* She'd adored the boxer Joe Louis from the start the time her father introduced him. And there was famous Louis Armstrong, whom she also adored.

So the name was a good sign.

She was growing up. She was taking on adult life.

What she didn't admit to herself that day or that evening at the Grill, though the thought flashed by more than once, was that her future husband who naturally took on a teacher-preacher role was going to be trouble.

Two days after her first date with Louis, she got up at ten, grabbed her winter coat and her handbag, and went down to the kitchen for a quick late-morning coffee. Drop cloths covered the tables; two men were painting. They turned. She was delighted to discover the two men were Josiah and his father. "Oh, hello!" she greeted both.

"Ma'am," said the father.

Josiah said, "Hello there. Been wondering about you."

"I didn't know my father was getting the place painted. I was just going to have a coffee and then go shopping. I have to buy Christmas presents. It's hard to believe it's in a couple of weeks. . . . I'm sorry. I'm in your way."

The elder Conner was moving his ladder from in front of the stove. He said, "You can make your coffee. I can do the border over the other way."

Josiah was looking at her with great affection. "Welcome home. Was it wonderful? The Sissle tour?"

"Terrible and wonderful. Both." She tried to be quick about getting the percolator going. "I do think I'm in your way."

"You go ahead," Mr. Conner said.

She stood at the stove, urging the pot to boil. "My father is hard to shop for. I have to find something special for him. Though I have a knack for that. I think I do, anyway."

"Did you get homesick?" Josiah asked.

"I did, sometimes. Other times I was too busy. I wrote letters to my father. He wrote back, kept me posted—which bands were here, all that. He's a great letter writer, I mean, *great*. I keep one of his old letters in my wallet all the time." Since she had her handbag with her, she took out the letter in illustration. She practically knew it by heart. She kept it with her because of the last two lines.

Before she handed it over to Josiah, who was plenty curious, she read it again, smiling, saying, "This was in my Cotton Club days and I was in a show on Broadway—they sort of lent me out—but anyway, I was very young. Very young." Then she held it out so Josiah could read. "It's about Louis Armstrong."

Armstrong came to town the other day. He is quite a personality. It's no secret he was born poor and brought up rough in New Orleans. He has come a long way and I don't mean to dismiss that, but he brought this woman Mae along on this trip and her voice still screeches in my ears. Alpha was nowhere in sight at this point. Louis and Mae argued a lot and one of their tiffs happened on the street. Now, Lena, I'm not a stranger to tiffs with a woman, God knows, but Louis is completely unembarrassed. Here he is famous around the world, but this wildness of his worries me. The upshot was Alpha showed up and Mae took a train and things calmed down some.

And on top of that it cost me. His band was wearing suits and ties, all matching. The ties were plain charcoal gray. The suits were a lighter gray. Louis lost his tie somewhere in the travels and he was just going to put any old thing on. He didn't care about the color at all. They were running late, just having something to eat and by then the stores were closed. I ran home and got my best tie, which was a navy blue silk. I loved that tie. I said, Louie, I would be honored if you would wear this. It makes sense to be just one little bit different from the rest of the band. That's what I told him.

Alpha told him the tie was quality, so he said he would wear it. So I solved that problem and then we had the concert at the Stanley.

He was brilliant. He played Hot Five and Hot Seven songs and then Stardust and Lazy River. I think he grins too much. Still, he just gets you going with him, wanting to be where he is. Is it joy? I don't know how it can be when he's had it so damn hard, and now he has Mae on his hands, some of the time anyway, and she's a handful. So is he just a great faker? His trumpet is like a voice yelling hallelujah. It's like a person deciding to believe in heaven and then deciding heaven is really close.

He left with my tie. Not so much a thief as a man in another world, not thinking. He doesn't have class. Some of us keep wanting him to be like Duke, just elegant and brainy. But without class, he gets colored people some credit.

What do you think, Lena? What do you hear about him?

I am proud of you, my daughter. I love you. You have class and talent, always have and always will.

Love, Daddy

P.S. I miss that tie.

Suddenly she was self-conscious about the fact that the letter referred to class. She searched Josiah's face to see if he was offended. She thought maybe he was, a little.

She poured a coffee before it was quite ready. She said in a bright voice, "See what a long, chatty letter it is? When I got it, I had the most horrible schedule, almost no time away from the theater, and my salary was tiny and I was just a kid in New York, but I ran out on a break and bought my father the best dark blue silk tie I could find. And it made him happy."

She drank her coffee, folded up her letter, thanked Josiah and his father for what a good job they were doing, and went to look for a special gift for her father and something for Irene, and perhaps a little something for Louis, though it was too early to be sure they would be exchanging gifts.

IN EARLY DECEMBER the candy shop was busier than usual because Christmas made people want to treat themselves and others. Marie ate her four pieces of allotted candy per day, bought four more out of her own money, and had those as well as the large Syrian bread sandwich she carried to work.

Each day went by without a glimmer of what her future life was supposed to be. The most exciting thing that had happened lately was that she had heard Alberto bursting with song in the morning as she stepped out back—and it was *opera*. She'd thought it was a record at first, but then he came out to put out the garbage and he was still singing. He waved at her. He said, "We're going to sell the old phonograph. Let me know if your family is interested."

Then that afternoon Josiah came into the shop. He'd come once before. Neither time did he buy anything. He appeared to be more interested in talking, which was fine with Marie. He talked at first about school and about the movies.

She said, "You know, I get four chocolates a day, free, can't eat them all, so pick two."

"I couldn't."

"No, seriously. Do. Never mind, I'll just give you two."

He took them, looking pretty happy about the tiny gift. "Thank you!"

Finally she asked if he'd seen Lena and he shifted and brightened, clearly glad that she'd asked.

"She's back from her tour. When I'm not in school and I'm working over there, I sometimes see her. You?"

"I haven't seen her at all."

"That's a shame. Do you do any more sewing for her?"

Marie, unable to hide her disappointment, shook her head. "Do you think of her as . . . kind of conceited?"

"No. No, I don't."

"Maybe it's just, I guess, that she's rich."

He paced a few steps. "I don't think she is, not really wealthy. She has a lot of . . ."

"Money?"

He laughed. "No. No, no. She always wants to make a living. Even her father agrees she should make money singing. He just wants her to do it here, not anywhere else."

"Oh. She looks rich."

"She does. I wonder if she's ever had a white friend. I think she's a little afraid."

"Oh."

"She's . . . in some way she's delicate. She didn't have a good child-hood, not like I did. I had a great mother. Lena's mother just left her places or sometimes used her. I always thought I wanted to write about that one day. You know, a movie script."

"Where did her mother go?"

"Off to be an actress. Lena told me she was put here and there, sometimes at a horrible school."

One thing about Ummah, Marie thought, she never went anywhere, which was both bad and good.

Josiah was full with things he wanted to say. "And then when she works with the band, like she just did, the conditions are really rough. *Really* rough. No. I mean, she's lucky she came from a family with lots of education. Political people, doctors, teachers. They're smart and re-spected. So that's lucky. It's just . . . her life is harder than it looks. I un-derstand her." He shrugged.

Josiah's eyes looked moist. Marie felt bad for him, for whatever he was feeling, and she said, "You really worry about her."

"I do. I understand her."

"Do you know about music? My family might get a phonograph. What records should I buy?"

"I could make a list. I'll even ask her, if I see her."

"That would be great."

"Don't say bad things about her."

"I never say *anything* about her. Except to you. It's just that she looks so strong, like everything comes her way."

"Aw. It doesn't."

THERE WERE CHRISTMAS decorations everywhere; the Kaufmann's windows Lena could see were thrilling—as good as anything in New York, she thought as she and Irene got out of the Caddy. They were being dropped off by her father to go shopping for dresses and shoes for Lena, her reward for coming home. He told them to take their time and get something to eat, too, to enjoy themselves. He would pick them up in five hours.

Partway through that day, they left Kaufmann's and were walking down Fifth. And it happened that they were passing the candy shop where Marie worked. Now it had occurred several times to Lena to go in and say a quick hello to Marie since Josiah had let her know that Marie felt the sting of being rejected after doing good work on the skirt. It seemed easier to do this task while Irene was with her. They could buy chocolates (that was an advantage) and not need to stay long.

Marie came from the back room when they entered. She was swallowing something, and from the look of it, too fast. She coughed once. "Sorry."

"*I'm* sorry. You were taking your dinner break."

"It doesn't matter. I eat when I can. I hope you like being back here," Marie said. "I knew you were with a band for a while. Touring and everything. I mean, Josiah told me."

Again Lena felt irritation that this white girl could be friends with Josiah when she got into trouble over it.

Lena said, "This is Irene Horne, my father's wife," and added, "We're having a nice long shopping day."

It was good that more customers came into the shop, meaning Marie wouldn't be able to talk after she served Lena and her stepmother. Irene had taken some cash from her purse. Lena said, "If it's your treat, Irene, you choose, then." But as Irene pointed and chose, the silence seemed awkward, so Lena asked Marie, "Do you like this work?"

"Yes. The people who come in are nice."

Irene chose mostly mints, saying, "My weakness. My weakness."

Lena left before any more conversation could get under way.

THE BELL RANG and a man came in, a person Marie recognized as having come in before. He was tall and thin with flat combed light hair, and he had a beaky nose. He was smoking. Somehow he looked like a character in the movies. She said, "May I help you?"

"A little something to take to the movies." He pointed out six choco-lates, then upped it to eight.

"What are you going to see tonight?"

He said, "*A Woman Rebels*."

"Oh, I hear that's interesting. I love Katharine Hepburn. Do you?"

"Well, she does tend to play the rebel," the man said. "They have her typecast." He laughed.

"So you like her?"

"I guess, yes I do. She's a corker."

"Me too. I don't understand people who don't." Reading magazines as she did, Marie was up on all the stars. Some people thought Hep-burn wasn't pretty, some thought she couldn't act or shouldn't wear pants. One writer complained she was small-breasted, as if she could help that.

The man touched the counter for a moment, coming a bit closer. "We should go to a movie sometime, you and me. What do you say?"

She hadn't ever had a date. Her only experience of men proposing a date was on the screen. "I'll ask at home."

"Ask what?'

"If I can."

"You have to ask? I don't get it."

"I come from a strict family."

He hummed with a downward sliding sound. "Well, ask your strict family about Saturday night." He took out a small notebook and wrote down his phone number.

"It would have to be Sunday, because of my work hours."

"Oh. Ask about Sunday, then. Will somebody be sending a detective to check me out?"

"Probably," Marie quipped, proud of herself that she was coming up with words. "You? What do you do? Where do you come from? I'll need to give the detectives a hint."

"I come from Highland Park. I'm an insurance man. I dunno, does that sound sketchy?" He tore out a page from his notebook and handed it to her.

"I meant, what country do you come from?"

"Country? Born right here. Is *that* suspicious?"

"I suppose not." She saw from the paper he'd given her that his name was Keith Lofton. He seemed like an actor who would play the best friend of the hero, or a lawyer or a theatrical agent.

"Well, let's see. What else? My parents were born here and so were theirs. They came from England. Back a ways."

"There are lots of English people in the movies," she offered. "You remind me of them."

"Yes. Land of stories."

Marie felt relief when two women came in to buy candy. The women were a mother and daughter who looked alike, one in a beige coat with a beige hat sporting a feather and one in a dark green coat with a similar hat, feather included. They ordered a large box of chocolates to take to the movies, carefully choosing each treat. As Marie rang them up, she noted that they were whispering intently to each other. She also saw her Mr. Lofton standing near the door, waiting.

"We think . . . do we have this right? You are the David daughter?" the older of the women asked.

"One of them," Marie answered.

"Your father has a little store in the Hill?"

"Yes."

"We are the Elias family," the woman continued. It was likely from her appearance that she was from Syria or Lebanon.

"It's very nice to meet you," Marie said. She handed them their box, all the while thinking they were like her imaginary detectives, because they appeared to be scrutinizing not only her but also Mr. Lofton.

After they left, Lofton loitered for a moment and then said his goodbyes.

Marie asked her mother that night what she thought of a date with Mr. Lofton. "He's of English background. Works in insurance."

She had gotten her mother to sit down (which was rare) at the dressing table, and she unbraided her mother's long gray hair and brushed it. "Why you want to do this on me?" her mother fretted.

"I've been thinking how it would look cut. In a style."

"No, no."

"And your dresses." She pointed to the cotton housedress. Her mother had only three. Each one was in a tiny print: flowers, diamonds, and dots. Marie had made them, sewing by hand. Her mother washed one out every day, hung it to dry near the kitchen stove, alternated wearing them, covered over in winter, as now, with the large navy-blue sweater. "Ummah. I want to buy you a beautiful dress for Christmas."

"No, no."

"You're still very pretty," Marie insisted.

Her mother reached back and began working the braid back into her hair. She'd done it so often her wavy gray hair simply knew where to bend this way and that to practically braid itself. She touched Marie's face—an alarming and tear-producing move. She never touched or hugged her daughters. She said in a quiet voice, "Not with the man from the shop."

"Mr. Lofton. I didn't tell you much about him."

Her mother shook her head. Marie realized she'd asked permission with a lack of information and an intonation that invited the answer no.

She'd likely done Mrs. K out of a customer. She wondered where Mr. Lofton would buy his chocolates now.

IRENE PUT A piece of pie in front of Lena. Her kitchen smelled wonderful, with pre-Christmas foods—sugar cookies, apple pies, a chocolate cake (which had nothing to do with Christmas, but Teddy Horne loved his chocolate cake). There was a roast beef in the oven.

Lena had bought and wrapped an imported cardigan for her father and a very soft cashmere pullover for Irene. She had bought a sweater vest for Louis, and a tie—two things she was pretty sure he was going to like. She'd sent a check to her mother.

"And so," Irene said, "you wanted to see me." She raised her eyebrows, waiting.

"Louis asked me to marry him."

"And will you?"

"I said yes. I mean I think that was in the cards all along." Louis had been borrowing his friend's Packard as often as he could; they always drove around for a while, and then parked and steamed up the windows. Lena had not kissed before or touched before. She liked that physical stuff fine, as she had always known she would.

"You can't keep seeing each other and not get married," Irene said. "Your father wants you to be respectable."

"I know that. I just . . . he said—Louis said, 'Why not a small wedding?' He wants just a minister to say a few words. Is that what I should do?" She thought her father might want a big production to show her off.

"I think small is very wise. It's just a day. You just dress nicely and make your vows. From what you say, Louis is very busy. So I think something simple is just fine."

"What would I wear?"

"It should be something you love. Do you want to go shopping? I'd go with you but I'll bet your father would love to go instead."

"Oh, you come too, but he's so brilliant with clothes."

"He is. And, all right, after the wedding we'll come back here. I'll make a nice dinner."

"Louis said we can live with his brother for a while—the one in Herron Hill. I can't stay in the hotel forever." She waited for Irene to say they would make room for her in their house, but Irene did not say it. The house was nice but small, and Lena supposed her father and stepmother wanted their privacy. Lena wasn't thrilled about living with in-laws, but the in-laws had room and it meant Louis could save money.

Lena said, "I want to make some money, too, to help out. If I sing, I can. I've had a couple of invitations, all here in town."

Irene said, "Yes, I've heard. I talked it over with your father. He thinks those engagements are all right. Are you going to eat any pie?"

"Of course. I was teasing myself." Lena picked up the fork and had her first bite. It was a spectacular apple pie.

"Your father worries that you don't know your effect on people. He said you were talking the other day to the boy, the son of Mr. Conner he hires, and that the boy is too interested in you."

"We're friends. He's crazy about books and movies. If I'm over at the hotel and he's there, it's hard not to talk."

"You have to watch who you choose to be friends with. Your father says you're breaking this fellow's heart."

"No, no, he's just a young boy. All right, he has a tiny crush but he understands I'm getting married."

"I hope so. It isn't nice to break hearts, you know."

So it was settled. She would go to live in her husband's brother's house in an adjacent section of the city, Herron Hill, and she would learn to make biscuits.

Louis was invited for Christmas dinner. The ham was delicious and the gifts were a success. Teddy Horne gave Lena money in an envelope. She made him promise to take her shopping.

"Just a good dress, one you can use again," Irene said.

The one she liked best was a black dress, long and shimmery. The clerks fell over in admiration when she put it on. "Is it bad luck," she asked, "wearing black to get married?"

Her father said, "You look wonderful. I don't hold with nonsense." And he bought her the dress out of his own pocket.

The wedding happened in January. The dinner at Irene's dining room was exceptionally good, another roast with plenty of sides.

"I'm a grown-up now," Lena told herself.

THREE

1937

MARIE THOUGHT AT FIRST IT WAS AN OLD MAN LEANING AGAINST the wind and carrying a newspaper under his arm until the man came into the shop. It was Josiah, almost hidden under a knit cap.

"Brrr," he said, making it a word, not a sound. "Cold today. I got some extra money in my pocket. The last of my bonus money from my pop. How about some candies, whatever this buys?"

He put down fifteen cents and she chose for him, putting the candies in a bag. "I hope you like them."

"Oh, I will. Going to see *Tarzan Escapes*." His eye went to the little clock on the wall. "Oh, no. I'm late. It's starting!"

"Ah."

"So, well, bye."

After he was gone, she saw that he'd left his paper. It was the *Pittsburgh Courier*, which she read sometimes when she found a discarded copy. Business being slow because of the cold and the after-Christmas slump, she had time to read the whole thing that night. There were letters this way and that about intermarriage—her parents were against it even though they knew of a terrific woman in her neighborhood, a white nurse, married to a Negro and both seemed happy. There were political articles she didn't quite follow, but she read them anyway. And finally, she turned the last page and Lena was in the paper again.

> *Our informants tell us that the beautiful Lena Horne has just married the politician Louis Jones and they will continue to live in Pittsburgh. It was a quiet wedding with little fanfare. The bride reportedly wore a dazzling black dress. Rumor has it that she has agreed to sing at private events throughout the city when the Mellons or Fricks call. She was last with the Sissle orchestra in New York City and on tour.*

Josiah hadn't said this was happening. Lena had fallen in love!

When would it happen to her? Would it ever happen?

She'd probably have to sneak out if she had a date. Her mother had said it was good she hadn't mentioned Mr. Lofton to her father, who would have become crazy with anger that she so much as asked.

Pap was hard, so hard. When he came home from the steel mill, the women hopped around him, serving him. Whatever he wanted was his in an instant: an ashtray, a dish of rice, a song, a radio program, an hour's *quiet*, anything.

Ummah was beaten down. Back when Marie was three and four years old, her mother had worn fashionable clothes and styled her hair and made lace and gone out to other neighborhoods to sell it. Now she seldom spoke and her hair hung in a long gray braid straight down her back.

When Marie finished the *Courier*, she turned to the movie magazine she had already read several times.

Later in the evening, the doorbell chimed and she was surprised to see Josiah again. He said, "Sorry to bother you, but I think I left my newspaper. If you threw it away, that's all right."

"No. I have it. I read it. Lena got married. Just like that."

"I know. It was very quick." He took his paper from her and tapped it against his hand.

"How was the movie?"

"Great. Silly, but great. Do you watch the Tarzan movies?"

"I haven't yet, but I read something about this one. It said the story is that Jane inherits a half-million dollars, right? Why is everybody so rich in the movie stories?"

"You asked that before. It's a good question. I mean, a really good question. Somebody should write an article about that."

It was lonely and quiet after he left. She realized she could do what her sister Fran did, join the library and read something—slowly if she had to, but something.

LIVING WITH LIONEL and Marian saved everybody money, of course, though Lena did not like spending so much of her day on the third floor.

Even though it was cold and sometimes blustery she went out and walked over to the club to see her father playing cards, other times just walked, often down to Centre Avenue to look into the shops. She visited the lumber company, the Home Drug store, just to get out of the house. She just felt . . . in the way.

Although Lena was allowed to use the kitchen, so long as she coordinated with Marian (and most nights she cooked something or the two couples ate together), tonight was different. The in-laws were going out. Lena had been thinking to serve soup and a pastrami sandwich tonight (what Louis had asked for), but she realized the food could hold for a day. She hoped to talk Louis into a dinner out, maybe a movie, maybe a chance to rekindle those evenings in the car when they first held each other.

Tonight was the rare night with Louis having no political meeting after work, so she had dressed in her best skirt and sweater, hoping for some fun and romance.

She had thought, before getting married, that married people kissed and made love every night. Louis told her that just wasn't so, that she was foolishly and naively romantic. "What's wrong with that?" she asked.

He said, "Are you serious?"

Louis was smart, for sure; while she combed and pinned her hair, she enumerated his virtues: he was clean and well dressed—shined shoes, not a spot on his shirts. Loved his widowed father. Loved his brother. Came home every night—did not gallivant. Liked good music. Read books when he had a chance. She had to get used to the idea that he was not a constantly delighted lover, but she also wondered what things she could do to make herself more appealing.

She heard him come in.

"Hello? Where is everybody?" he called.

"Coming." She met him at the bottom of the stairs.

"You're all dressed up?" he said, puzzled.

"Yes!"

"On such a bitter day."

She took his coat from him because he already had it off, but she held it, smoothed her hand over it. "We could go out, maybe, for a little dinner—just something different."

"Out? Oh, not today. Why today?"

"Well, you're home early."

"I can't do it today. What were you thinking?"

"Dinner and a movie?"

"I'm sorry. I'm much too tired. Take my shoes. They need to be shined."

She removed his shoes as soon as he seated himself.

"I have slippers in the closet, don't I?"

"Yes." She fetched them for him, examining herself. Why did it bother her so? Wouldn't she do this for her father without complaint? Why did she feel like a servant?

"You do have the vegetable soup, right?"

"Yes."

"Good. Where are the others?"

"They're eating out. I think they knew you had a night off and they wanted to give us some privacy."

She went to the kitchen and got the vegetable soup heating and made two luxurious sandwiches while she worked to reframe her thinking. She served this simple dinner in the dining room, moving as prettily as she knew how, but he didn't seem to notice and he didn't make love to her that night.

It took her a long time to get to sleep. In her head, she talked and talked, but she had no one to tell her worries to.

Her father came by with a letter for her the next afternoon. She saw that it was from one of the Cotton Club girls and she put it aside for the moment, excited to have her father as a visitor. She urged him toward the sofa, poured him a whiskey, and begged him to stay a bit.

"Sure, okay," he said. He kept his coat on and perched on the end of the sofa.

They could both hear Marian in the kitchen washing dishes. Lena and Marian did all sorts of tricks to stay out of each other's way.

Lena whispered to her father, "Things are kind of rough, Daddy."

"What's rough?"

"Marriage."

"Well, it's not the easiest thing in the world."

"Louis isn't like I thought he'd be. I don't know how it happened, but he thinks of me as a servant. I didn't go through all I went through to end up a slave."

Her father shook his head, saying, "No, no. Don't tell me things like that. I don't want to hear that."

She added, with a little more heat, "Daddy, you can't just abandon me. You chose him for me. Help me through this. Say what I should do."

They both looked toward the kitchen.

Her father protested in an intense whisper that threatened to be voiced, and too loud, "Never. I never chose him for you. Lena, I'm get-ting angry here. Listen to me. I always wanted you to make up your *own* mind . . . on feelings . . . on love. Nobody else can know those things." His rising voice made Lena jump nervously. "You want to know the *truth*? I didn't think Louis was right for you from the very beginning. I was surprised by it, but you fell in love. What could I do? Now you have to make it work. That's life." He downed the whiskey she'd poured him.

Lena got a sinking feeling in her chest. "You didn't choose him for me?"

"No! Why did you think so? You *thought* that?"

"Why did you bring him to Cleveland?"

"I wanted someone to ride with me, share the driving, go to the fight. That was all." He took up the bottle and poured himself another shot.

Was that true? She began to cry while he sipped, then downed his second drink. She wiped at her eyes and said angrily, "I should have listened to Mama. She was against him. She's still mad at me."

Her father plunked his glass down. "But your mother is so crazy, how do you ever know what she's really mad about? Half the time it's jealousy."

"I do know one thing." Lena forced herself to whisper because she no longer heard the clanking and clunking pot and plate noises in the kitchen. "Mama wanted me to have a career. She thought I could have a good one. Now here I am, sitting around, being told, 'Do this, do that.'"

"Well, I think you're having a problem with your memory. You're forgetting you were working sixteen, eighteen hours a day. And half the time no place to lay your head. So now you have a bed, you have food, you have respectability, right, but, yes, you have to make breakfast and dinner. Is that so terrible?" His face, though, showed that he might not be fully convinced about what he was saying. He concluded, almost ministerial. "You now have a different job—and that's to make the marriage work."

"You and Mama didn't stay together."

Her father took several deep breaths and buttoned his lips to keep from answering right away. She saw, under his coat, that he was wearing the Christmas sweater. Finally he said, "Just think about these things calmly." The kiss he brushed on her forehead was barely a kiss. He left the house in Herron Hill, looking as wounded as she felt. He was her favorite man in the world and she never wanted to hurt him, but today she allowed herself to remember the story of how he missed her birth because he was off gambling the hospital money.

An hour later she got her time in the kitchen and made biscuits to go along with a dinner of greens and pork. She invited her sister-in-law to eat dinner with her and Louis but Marian said she and Louis's brother wanted to eat earlier because Louis got home so late.

When Louis arrived at nine, Lena was desperately hungry, but she smiled and flashed her eyes. It was a performance, like being a chorine again. Cheerful and pretty, that's who she needed to be. An undaunted spirit, no matter what; that's what people wanted to see, even husbands.

FRAN, GRINNING RIDICULOUSLY, showed Marie a front door key she had had made. She leaned against Marie's dresser, whispering. "When they're asleep," she said, "I'll leave. There's a dance. It goes on until one."

Marie got a sick feeling inside. "Please don't."

Selma, who was sleeping, stirred. Fran pulled the blanket up over Selma's head.

Marie pulled it back down. "Don't smother her."

"It's just . . . somebody should know where I am. Do you want to come with me?"

"No!"

When there were snores coming from their parents' room, Fran made her way down the steps, which made a creak every time her right foot hit.

Marie couldn't sleep, at least not until after two, when the stairs creaked again with Fran's return.

All Marie learned in the morning was that Fran had walked around with a guy and messed around a little bit but decided she didn't like him. Fran said, "I guess it's spring fever. The weather is warming up."

When it was time for Marie to go to work, she grabbed the sandwich her mother had made for her. She would put on makeup when she got to the shop so there would be no argument with her mother about it.

"Wait," Ummah said. She went to the cup in the cupboard where she kept cash and she removed several bills. "You need new coat. You think stores still have for winter?"

Marie was amazed. Her mother was returning a good portion of her pay envelope—something she had never done. Maybe it was because Fran had talked at dinner last night about how clever and thrifty Marie was, the way she stitched a braid to the places on her coat where it was frayed and worn. She *did* need a new coat, but a brand-new store-bought coat was something she hadn't imagined.

"Ummah, thank you."

The weather was breaking. Sunlight streamed into the windows. She donned a sweater to wear under a light spring coat that once was Fran's and hurried downtown in the hopes of getting to Gimbels before she was due at work.

People moved more rapidly on the streets than they had two days ago, birds sang, and Marie felt happy. She practically ran up the stairs at Gimbels. When she got to the second floor, she found only one small rack with a big SALE sign.

While she stood, catching her breath, a saleswoman approached her, asking, "What can I show you?"

"I'm looking for a winter coat."

"You came to the right place. Here's our rack."

The woman moved things along, displaying each. There wasn't a lot to choose from. There was a red plaid coat that didn't appeal to Marie but it was small, her size. There was a green coat, sort of startling, but she'd never worn green, having been told by Fran that green was especially bad for her coloring. And another twenty coats but they were either too big or just not right.

Suddenly the saleswoman said, "Oh, I have an idea. I have a great idea." And she disappeared to a back room.

When she returned she was carrying a coat of brilliant blue wool with a fox-fur collar. Even draped over the woman's arm, Marie could see it was a wonderful coat.

"A woman brought this back after a year! We weren't supposed to take it back but she fought so hard, we did. She swore she never wore it. I don't know. It's gorgeous, merino, fancier than these others. Do you want to try it? I'd give you a great price. Lower than the regular wool coats."

Marie knew this was the one. She almost wished spring weren't coming so she could wear the coat every day.

FOUR

1937

FOR THE LAST SEVERAL WEEKS LENA HAD HUDDLED IN BED UNTIL ten or eleven, trying not to throw up when Marian made breakfast downstairs. She certainly did not want an egg. She cried upstairs, in that room, as she lay there, worrying.

One day she became aware that spring had arrived and things were perking up: flowers, kids on the streets, people talking about baseball, even her own appetite, and she, too, was perking up, just like that, coming around to accepting the thing going on in her belly.

She stood, she combed her hair, she buttoned and rebuttoned a sweater. She would go for a walk.

Marian called out that she was wanted on the phone. She went downstairs and took the receiver. "Busy tonight?" her father asked.

"Don't joke. Busy throwing up."

"Would you like to go to the Savoy Ballroom with me to hear Count Basie?"

"Would I!"

He chuckled. "Wear your best."

That night she dressed eagerly, wearing her new white wool suit, which *just* fit. Her father fetched her in the Caddy and off they went.

Basie didn't have Billie Holiday with him on this trip, alas. The singer and the band had an off-and-on relationship; the people in the audience probably longed to hear Billie. After all, Lena did, too.

She and her father were late arrivals, though they were treated as important personages and seated even while the band was playing.

Basie looked good. He was heavy, but he knew how to dress himself. He wore a dark suit and tie, not a tux, and that looked just right on him. She liked his mustache, which was full, not one of those little spindly ones.

She was out in the world again where music was being made!

When the band took a break, Basie greeted Lena warmly at her table—by now it was commonplace with bandleaders to know about Lena holing up in Pittsburgh—and asked her to sing a few songs that evening and she, now ready for such invitations, asked him which he would like. He mentioned one of Billie's standards, "Now or Never," and said the next song after that could be something Lena chose so long as he knew it. She said, "What about 'What Is This Thing Called Love?'"

Basie said, "Yes, that's a good one, honey, and why not add 'Stormy Weather' while we're at it?"

She hesitated. "I'm always afraid to sing that one. I always think Ethel is going to hear about me singing her song and come from somewhere and kick me off the stage."

"Oh, let her try," he laughed. "She's bigger but you're probably tougher."

"I don't think so," she said gravely.

Basie winked at her. "I think you are."

Her father chuckled, liking that compliment.

When Basie went back to the stage, she said, "Hope I can still sing up to his expectations."

"You're going to be okay," her father told her.

She kissed her daddy hard on the cheek, grateful for that rare compliment.

He said to her, "I have to tell you something. I was planning to tell you tonight. Should I tell you before you sing?"

Basie was tuning up his bass player. The crowd broke into animated conversation as they waited.

"Don't know," she answered, worried because whatever he said might shake her and get in the way of her performance.

"Well, Louis came to me. He's right. I see his point. You need to have your own place, you two. We've pooled our resources, me and Irene and a couple of people, and you're going to move. We'll move you. Next week."

"Oh. You mean back to the hotel?"

"No, no, we've found a small house."

"Did you say . . ." There was so much conversation rising up in the club that she wasn't sure she'd heard him.

"Small. Not fancy. You'll make it look good, make it a home."

Her own place. "Oh! A house!"

"It's the right thing," he said.

How did that make her feel?

Happy. Trapped.

"Thank you, Daddy."

Basie beckoned her up to the stage. Applause carried her up there. She sang at first tremulously, then, remembering her lesson with the wastebasket, tougher, biting out the words. The *Courier* wrote in a piece that came out the next weekend about how well she sang but more about how beautiful she was in her white suit.

She sang informally with three more bands in April and May. She got six invitations to sing at rich people's houses after their dinner parties. She said yes to everything and knew that singing made her feel like herself, no matter the situation. She sang until she looked too pregnant to hide it.

ONE WEDNESDAY IN mid-July Marie discovered a note in Fran's handwriting left on her dressing table. *I'm okay. Don't worry. Tell them not to worry. I won't be home tonight.* Marie panicked. What lie was she supposed to tell her parents?

She buttonholed Selma in the little bathroom. "Fran told me she can't get home this evening. Tell Ummah and Pap not to worry."

"But why?"

"She has business."

Marie hid the note in her purse. She felt aware of it all morning and early afternoon while she watched the store. Then she brushed her hair and added earrings for the candy shop, and left.

The day wore on, long and torturous, as she tried to rehearse answers for the coming inquisition. But when she got home, Selma was sobbing. "Why didn't you tell me anything? They've been quizzing me."

"I don't really know anything. Just that Fran goes her own way."

"But you got a note."

Marie relented and showed her sister the note in all its vagueness only to have Selma run to tell her mother before Marie could stop her. She gritted her teeth and went to face them. Their mother let out a wail and collapsed into a kitchen chair. Marie's father had one glass of whiskey for courage and went out into the neighborhood to look for Fran.

Selma and Marie managed to stay awake until one thirty in the morning by eating candy from the cases, then pie, then drinking coffee, but finally they couldn't sit up anymore.

Their mother apparently sat up all night, waiting, because at nine in the morning she still sat in the kitchen, on the same chair, with the same crossed arms.

Marie poured herself a coffee and went to work the grocery store. Selma followed, poured herself a cup of coffee, and went out to the store, too, declaring she would not go to school. Marie shifted items around on the counter, wondering if they should have called the police. Selma dusted everything madly though she'd done so only hours earlier. And then the door suddenly opened, the bell sounded, and Fran came in, pulling in a dark, heavyset man by the hand. "I'm married," she announced.

"My God, Fran, they're going to kill you."

"Yesterday. It's done." Fran was happy, victorious. "I'm living in his apartment. Is Pap at work?"

"Yes." Marie couldn't quite see the odd little man standing behind Fran. She could see that Selma had hidden herself in the hallway near the stairs, as if marriage were a communicable disease.

Fran cocked a head toward the kitchen. "Go get Ummah. Okay?"

Marie hesitated. She asked, "But the priest—he let you?"

"We went to city hall. Go get Ummah, please. I'll watch the counter. Help me break it to her. She likes you better."

With a heavy heart, Marie went through the beaded curtains to her mother, who was no longer sitting but was up, kneading dough. "Fran is back," she said as brightly as she could. "You don't need to worry."

Her mother punched the dough hard. "Sharmuta, sharmuta. She was with a man. I know."

"She got married. She should have told us, but she got married. So it's not a bad thing."

Her mother stopped kneading the dough. "You knew this?"

"No! Just now. She came in with him."

Her mother never liked surprises. Her face was stone when she said, "Tell her leave the house." She resumed kneading.

Marie blurted, "You should meet him. We should at least meet him." At her mother's silence, she began to cry. "She's your daughter. Ummah . . ." It was so easy to be abandoned here, there were different ways of being left on the doorstep. Marie untied her mother's apron and lifted it over her head. "Come. At least for a minute."

Fran looked terrified when Marie brought her mother in, but she said to her new husband, "This is Ummah." And then she took a step toward her mother and said, "Ummah! This is Harry Lesoon! He used to live in Cleveland but he came to live here in Pittsburgh. He got a job as a salesman for cars. Harry Lesoon."

Marie finally had a moment to study the man. He had almost no forehead; it was only a slight exaggeration to say there was a mere inch between brow and hairline, so he was one of theirs—Marie had seen plenty of low foreheads at church. He had a large nose and eye bags. He was a funny combination: extremely short and fierce-looking but also heavyset and timid. She almost laughed, trying to think what had attracted Fran to him.

"How do you do?" Harry said mechanically to Ummah.

Fran nudged her new husband. "And of course these are my sisters. Selma and Marie." She had to point across the room to the hallway to introduce Selma, who was still hiding.

"How do you do?" Harry said.

Marie thought he might not be too good at selling cars.

"You can't come here now," Ummah told Fran. "No more."

"I know. We are going to live in his place. It's only four streets away. I'll still work the store, the hours you need me on the weekends and after school."

"No. You go."

"Go? You don't want me to work the store?"

"I do it."

Fran paused for a moment, breathed deeply. "Ummah, come to dinner at our apartment. I'll cook."

Their mother shook her head. "Go now."

For the first time, Fran looked stuck for words. She watched her mother make her way back to the kitchen. Finally she said, "I should get my clothes."

"Watch the store," Marie ordered Selma. She ran up behind Fran, asking, "What's the address? We should have it in case we need to bring something you forgot."

"Thirty Davenport."

"Not far."

They went into the tiny room that Fran had chosen for herself, what used to be their brother's room. It was hardly a room, just enough for a single bed and a dresser, but Marie's sister actually liked it because she could read into the night. With a sigh, Fran began to assemble a few pieces of underwear on the bed while Marie ran to her parents' room for the only suitcase they owned.

"You'll have to bring the suitcase back," Marie warned as she opened it for her sister.

"You can bring it back here today."

"Give her some time and . . . maybe she'll change her mind."

Fran shook her head. "She'll tell him and it will be worse—for a while, anyway, maybe forever. I knew it. I had to get out."

"Is it legal? City hall?"

"Yes. Lots of people do it that way."

Fran was wearing her only suit, brown. She owned two good dresses, both black. She threw them into the suitcase, then two blouses and two skirts. That was about it.

Marie straightened the rumpled and worn blue chenille bedspread, wondering what would become of this room. She looked up to see Fran fighting off tears. "Oh, Fran!" she blurted, because Fran never cried.

"Come to dinner? Someday soon?"

"I'd have to ask for a specific day off, but I guess I could. If I didn't tell Ummah and Pap." Lying was infectious.

"You tell me when."

"Next Thursday. Do you know how to cook now?"

"I have to learn."

"If they find out, I'm dead," Marie murmured.

"Will you come anyway?"

"Yes."

Fran with her big smile and frightened eyes and awkward limp bumped down the stairs, dragging the suitcase. Marie caught herself thinking, *Sharmuta, sharmuta.* But she didn't want to become her mother. She hurried after Fran and hugged her.

As the household tried to recover, Selma took the little room Fran had vacated so that Marie, who liked makeup and fashion, could spread out and admire herself.

LENA WAS NOT feeling very pretty. Her hair had lost its luster. Her belly was so big she didn't go out much. All in all, it was a time of being on hold.

At five o'clock, she opened the package of chicken she was about to season and fry; she was trying to decide on grits or potatoes, salad or not, kale cooked in onions or boiled, when there was a knock at the door of her new house and she opened the door to find herself facing Josiah.

"Ah, I can't believe it! You're what they call a sight for sore eyes."

He was carrying books. "Been reading a lot," he said. "I thought I would lend you some if you want."

"Come in, sit down!" She began in a rush to evaluate whether there was enough food to invite him to dinner, though there was still the problem of her father defining him as an employee, never to be treated as a guest.

Her belly—there it was in an unflattering plaid maternity top. Josiah glanced quickly, then looked to his armful of books.

"I'm going to get you iced tea," she said, escaping to the kitchen.

As she took two glasses from the cupboard, she hoped—Josiah looked healthy and energetic—that the year had been good to him.

How quickly both of them had grown up. Ah, but she could return them to the past. She had sugar cookies! So . . . she put a dozen on a plate and took them, along with the iced tea, to the living room and Josiah gratified her with a laugh.

"You know me," he said.

Her facial muscles felt different. She was smiling. "Catch me up. School. Anything else you're doing."

"Reading a lot, a whole lot. More than before."

"That's wonderful. Me? I'm going to have a baby."

"I know. I heard people saying you stopped taking singing jobs for a while. So you must . . . miss it."

"I do."

"Hollywood hasn't called yet?"

She laughed. "No."

"Darn. Anyway, I knew you always read a lot and I figured you might get frustrated staying home so much. So—" He sat forward but adjusted his long legs one over the other and gestured to the books. "I've read them but I renewed them. In case you're interested."

"Film books?"

"No, novels. Because I was studying articles about how novels get made into film. So I was trying to figure out how to do it."

"Wow. I'm impressed. What's the answer?"

"From what I hear, it's pretty tough, all kinds of people fighting about the script, writers getting fired, getting rehired. Quite a business."

"You're sounding awfully smart, Josiah."

He laughed. "One teacher thinks so. One, anyway."

How wonderful it was to talk again. "Can you . . . stay for dinner?"

"Oh, no, no. I just wanted to say hi." He shifted forward once more on the sofa to signal that he was just about ready to leave but he stayed for the moment and took a cookie.

She asked, "Is everything okay? Is your father all right?"

"He's the same." He broke the cookie in half, letting the crumbs fall to the plate. "He never liked me bothering you."

"I know. I saw that. But I never thought of it as a bother."

"I know you didn't. I understand a lot of things. I understand your father and my father, how they think."

A long silence took over. "Still seeing movies?"

"All the time."

"That's . . . terrific."

"Are there girls after you?"

"Not too many. One in particular."

"You like her?"

"Yes. I do. Yvonne."

"Good for you." Her eye went to the pile of books. "What did you bring me?" She lifted one. *Steppenwolf.*

"Maybe you already read these? *The Sun Also Rises*, *The Trial*, and *Nicholas Nickelby*—that's older. The librarian recommends things to me."

The sound of a cough, then the sound of a key, made Lena pause. She put down the Dickens she was holding. "That'll be Louis. This is his early night."

Her husband came in. "Oh," he said. "What's happened? Is everything okay?"

"You remember Josiah. You met him over at the hotel. He and his father work for my father. Josiah Conner," she said.

Josiah stood, extending his hand. "Sir, how do you do?"

"I do okay." He did not take Josiah's hand, pretending to fuss with his coat, which, for a change, he hung up himself.

Lena said, "I told you Josiah made last summer lovely for me. We talked about movies most of the time. But books, too."

Louis could not erase the scowl on his face. Lena sighed impatiently at how quickly Louis resorted to impoliteness when he was surprised at all.

Josiah said, "I brought . . . Mrs. Jones some books."

"She has a library card. Special delivery, huh?"

"No, sir, just things I thought she'd like."

Should she tell Josiah to take the books away? And what was she facing either way tonight? She could see the glare in Louis's eyes, the start of a rage coming on.

Josiah said, holding steady eye contact with Louis, "I've read them, thought they were good." To Lena he said, "There's two weeks' time on my card if you're interested."

"I am. Should I just take them back when I'm done?"

"That would be fine." He turned back to Louis, bristling slightly. "Pleased to meet you again."

Again. Good, Lena thought, it's good to be angry when somebody freezes you. She walked Josiah out the front door. "I'm sorry he wasn't very friendly."

His smile faltered and he swallowed hard. "I don't want to cause you trouble. Ever."

"I'll talk to him." She watched Josiah leave. For a while she just leaned against the house, watching people walk down the street. She didn't want to spend the evening with Louis, so she was glad she had that pile of books. She could read again, she could disappear into the books piled up on her coffee table.

Her back ached. It had been aching for days and now tension with Louis didn't help.

She went inside and to the kitchen, where she hid out and made dinner. When she finally had to go to the dining table, she did, quietly. Louis talked about city politics the whole time they ate.

He didn't say anything about Josiah for days.

She read one book after the other. He noted what she was reading, she knew that, because she twice caught him checking her bookmarks.

Finally he said, "A visit from a boy. I hope you know it isn't seemly. People will say terrible things about you. They'll call me a dupe."

She rehearsed for the next confrontation but she didn't need the practice. Josiah didn't return.

MARIE THOUGHT LOVE was everywhere and just about everyone was married except her. Her friend Eleanor's sister. Helena next door. Lena Horne. Fran.

She hurried through the streets to where Fran now lived.

Harry Lesoon's apartment was on the second floor of a building on Davenport. It was just a bedroom, a kitchen, and a living room squashed together. When Marie arrived, Harry was sitting on a small worn green sofa that looked scratchy. His hands were folded and he waited for dinner while he listened to the radio, tuned to news and music.

Fran, wearing an apron and a crazy too-big grin, said proudly, "Come, see what I made!" The aromas coming out of her kitchen were impressive.

"The salad is almost done, just needs lemon. I have a whole chicken in the oven, stuffed." That meant with rice and lamb, of course.

"I'm frying some cauliflower. I started it because I have to make more than one batch in my little pan." Then Fran chuckled and took Marie by the arm. She led her to the iron stove, where there was a pot on the burner with water in it. "I still have to cook the chicken parts. So they don't spoil. But look!" She held up a chicken neck and whispered, "Guess what that looks like!" Fran wiggled the chicken neck and Marie gasped in shock.

"Quit it! Don't do that!"

"That's what it looks like. A lot bigger in Harry's case." Eyebrows up, a giddy and gleeful look in her eyes—this was Fran, this was who Fran always had been. Embarrassing, awkward, unstoppable. Fran whispered, "I like it. But don't ever tell Ummah. I'm sure she wants to believe I'm suffering." Then she left giddiness aside and sighed. "Life should be freer. Better than what we learned at home."

"I know."

Fran had pointed out on other occasions that all the old Lebanese women who thought sex was dangerous and horrible and not to be spoken of spent all day cooking and when they formed food, especially sweets, they chose two shapes: elongated rolls and mounds with a nut on the top. "Penises and breasts," Fran said. "They can't help themselves."

Marie squirmed, caught halfway between her Ummah and her grinning sister.

FIVE

1937

MARIE QUICKLY SWALLOWED THE CHOCOLATE SHE HAD BEEN
eating. The boy who'd come into the shop wore frayed work clothes. He
said, "My name is Federico. I been in before. . . . Maybe you remember
me?"

"I'm not sure."

"I remembered you. You had a movie magazine one time, a lot of
customers the other time."

"I follow the pictures."

"What I mean is, I been thinking about asking, would you maybe . . .
go out with me?"

She liked Federico a lot better than she did Mr. Lofton. His nervousness had the effect of calming her. "To a movie?" she asked.

"Pictures are okay," he said, "but I like to look at a woman, not at a
screen." He had an appealing face, no meanness in it; he was perhaps
twenty-five or twenty-six. He was saying, "Besides, I love to eat. So I'm
asking, you know, for dinner."

"I don't get many days off. Sometimes a Thursday when the boss asks me if I want to take a day and she comes in to do the shift."

"A Thursday then. That's good. This week?"

"Well, it just so happens . . ." She had already asked her boss for Thursday because Fran wanted her for dinner at the apartment again. "I do have that night off . . ."

He beamed. "That works out, then. So, this Thursday. It was meant to be. Where's your house—"

"No, no," she said. "I'll meet you here." Then she realized that might not make sense. "Where is the restaurant you have in mind?"

"Down here. Downtown."

"Good then. I'll meet you out there, in front of the shop."

"You're not married, are you?" he asked with a nervous chuckle. "I mean, I'm willing to fight, but I'd want to see what he looks like before I get into a battle."

She burst into laughter at the image of herself not only married but sneaking out. "Not married. Just not allowed to date."

"That's hard. You must have men climbing to your window or getting ready to mug your father and brothers."

"Just one brother. He's away."

"Okay, I'll come down here to meet you if that's what you want. Oh, I don't even know your name."

"Marie." She took in the fact that he was tall, had a good mop of hair and a very good forehead.

"Federico. So here then?"

"Yes," she said definitely. "Here."

He lingered a bit, pretending to look at the cases. "You like movies, huh?"

"I love movies. Who doesn't?"

"I guess. You look like a movie star. You probably know that."

She could feel the blush rising. "I'm never sure what that means."

"It's just a look. Maybe the way you stand. Your hair." Suddenly he seemed even more jittery, out of courage. "See you right out front on Thursday. Two days from now. God, I hope it isn't raining."

For the first time in a long time she felt she might one day be like other lucky women. She wrote a note to Fran and hand-carried it to Davenport Street.

And on Thursday night she stood outside the candy store, realizing too late that she should have chosen another place because her boss, who was working for her, was watching her from inside the shop, probably miffed that Marie had taken the night off. Finally Mrs. K came outside to ask, "What are you doing here?"

"Just meeting a friend."

"Oh. Don't you want to come in to wait?"

"That's okay. He should be here soon." And then she saw him bounding down the street.

"Him?"

"Yes."

Did Mrs. K seem disapproving? Since she shook her head and went back inside, Marie worried that her boss had some parental insight. It didn't matter, though. Marie was playing a rebellious part tonight and was determined to see it through.

Federico said, "Who were you talking to?"

"My boss. The owner."

"Ugh. I hate bosses. Anyway, you look very pretty. Let's go. It's three blocks from here. I never asked what was your favorite restaurant. I just picked mine."

The truth was she hadn't been to a restaurant downtown in all this time and only to the Kaufmann's Tic Toc coffee shop before this. Her family was frightened about poverty and so they didn't go out, and to be safe, they stored any cash they had in a metal box under the bed.

"I think you should order a steak," Federico said as they walked. "I think that's their best item."

Marie sneaked sidelong glances at him. He had the blossom of a breakout on one cheek, almost-black hair that grew slightly wavy and was not fully tamped down, blue eyes; his suit, blue with a gray stripe, was close to threadbare. She saw a telltale nick on his neck from shaving. The smell of aftershave, or maybe it was cologne—something sweet and acidic—wafted toward her as they walked. He was excited and that was nice to know.

The restaurant had waiters and menus and cloth napkins. It seemed terribly exciting and very much like what she'd seen in movies. She felt she was *in* a movie. *Katharine Hepburn. Erect posture. Queenly manner. A kind of distance in her gaze.*

"Wow."

"What?"

"Whatever you were just thinking. You scared the waiter. You look like you're going to send the steak back the minute it gets here just for the heck of it. Or the wine."

"We're having wine?"

"Of course. Here it is."

The waiter brought two glasses of wine to the table. She stared at her glass, then took a sip, then another.

"Okay?"

"Um, yes." She had never had wine outside of church communion. She took another sip. "I just realized you never told me where you work."

"I'm trained as a bricklayer but I do some 'this and that' for a guy I know and he makes sure I always have money in my pocket."

She drank. "I don't get it—'this and that?'"

He winked.

This and that. Ah. So, something illegal. She found she didn't care, really, everything was fine with her—the wine was perhaps part of the reason—and she concluded that cheerfulness was the most important quality in a man. Federico had that for sure.

Federico told her about friends he'd valued at one point but who were not worth his time anymore. Then came a complicated story about a car and some pistons and an engine and a former friend who had cheated him.

"Terrible," she said in a sweet haze.

The steak went down fine. Just cutting into a whole steak made her feel special. She finished her wine.

It turned out they lived not far from each other in the Hill, so they began walking toward their homes. The autumn air nipped at them. He took her hand as they walked and the most amazing feeling went straight through her. How could the touch of a hand possibly undo her this way, changing her very breathing?

"Come to my place first. We could have another glass of wine—"

"Oh, no. I think I'm weaving."

"How about a whiskey?" he laughed.

"Please, no."

"I could make you a cup of tea."

"That might be better." She was excited to meet his parents. Her mind leapt ahead to introducing his parents to her parents.

However, when they got to Roberts Street, there was only a dark little house. No lights. He opened the door, proudly ushering her in. Did he live alone? Nobody she knew lived alone except Harry Lesoon—before he met Fran.

The living room she entered was tidy, with lace doilies on the backs and arms of the sofas and chairs. Two rosaries curled on top of the large wooden radio console. The smells of tomato sauce and onions hung in the air. "It smells great in here. Where is everyone?"

"Out of town. Funeral," he announced triumphantly.

"Oh, how sad."

"But good for us, right?"

The first kiss was a surprise. Awfully sloppy, she thought, but after a few seconds she got used to it and began to understand Fran's insistence that mess could be a good thing. He pulled her to the sofa and said, "Now relax."

Tea, she thought for a moment, *he promised tea*, and then she forgot about it. At one point she surfaced, trying to get her bearings, afraid of what she might do if he kept kissing her.

The house was dark and she didn't even know his last name. Finally she found a little voice, a tiny screeching thing, not worthy of the movie she thought she was in. "I have to go."

"No. Please. Aren't we having fun?"

"I shouldn't be here."

"Why not?"

"I shouldn't even have gone to dinner on a lie. I've been bad."

"And it felt good, right? Bad is good."

He had a point there, but she summoned strength enough to straighten her sweater and find her handbag. "You don't have to walk me home."

"Are you kidding? I'm not going to abandon you."

"Okay, well, I have to go."

"Waste of a funeral," he said.

He took her hand as they walked and the sensations began again.

As soon as they came within sight of her family's store, she pointed to its front windows, saying, "That's it. There," and he said, "Yeah, I know that store. Too bad it's so damned close," and began kissing her as they walked.

Her parents had a sixth sense—where they got it she didn't know—but they opened the door to the store just as she was thinking, *I am on a date, I am kissing on the street.* She surfaced from the kiss to see them step out to the sidewalk, arms folded.

"I'm in trouble."

Even Federico knew it. "I'll come visit again."

"No!"

"Downtown, the candy store, I mean, not here," he murmured before looking indecisive and then running off.

Her father grabbed her and pushed her into the store. Her mother didn't hit, but she didn't intervene either when Marie's father pushed and pulled and smacked Marie for twenty minutes, calling her names.

Selma stood on the stairway, watching.

WHEN LENA'S LABOR pains began—they were expected, it was December—Louis was at work. She called the hotel but Pete didn't know for sure where her father was. She called Irene, who said she would come but that she would call Lena's doctor first and maybe would meet up at the hospital.

Lena stood in the kitchen drinking water, thinking maybe she had panicked too early. But another wave of pain told her she was right, this was it. The pain made her collapse on a kitchen chair. Then she hauled herself up again because standing felt better, and that was the clincher for her—her water broke, and she tried to remember everything she had learned thus far about what to do and how she should not panic. Finally there was a knock at the door.

Her doctor said, "Aha. It's time. You're right."

She'd always loved him and she loved him more on this day, for the way he held her under the arms and guided her to the car, saying, "Easy, easy, this will be fine."

"Is the baby all right?"

"Oh, yes. Sing something."

"Sing?"

"Deep breath. Sing."

What came to her, unbidden, when she started to sing was "Pennies from Heaven." Stupid song. Damn, she hated it. But he sang along with her as he moved expertly through traffic and soon enough pulled up at the hospital. "I have to leave you for a minute. Sit tight."

He went inside but she screamed out for him the next time a pain hit, hating more than anything to be alone.

When he came back it was with an orderly pushing a gurney. They got Lena onto it and before she knew it she was in a hospital hallway. She twisted, looking backward. "Where's my doctor?"

"We'll take you from here. Try to relax. Breathe. We'll get someone to look at you."

"But my own doctor brought me in." Still she couldn't see him anywhere.

"He's gone," a nurse told her.

She had trusted him, loved him, *loved* him, and always told herself he was the best and would never, ever let her down in any way.

How could he abandon her?

White nurses wearing starched uniforms wheeled her into a room that smelled of alcohol, bandages, peroxide, cleaning materials. They told her to relax because it would be a while until the baby came, and then they left her alone. An old white doctor came in eventually, touched her belly, and said the same thing. "Relax. Gonna be a while."

A different nurse poked her head into the room to say a woman named Irene had come by but went out again for a while.

The same pains, the same questions, and the feeling of fear that nobody would help her, went on for hours and hours until the white doctor came in again and said, "She's close now. Okay."

"Where is *my* doctor?" she asked between ragged breaths. "Did someone call for him?"

The nurse who was taking her blood pressure looked at her with a frown. "Why do you keep asking? You know he's not allowed in here, don't you? He's Negro."

Lena tried to sit up. "I'm Negro."

The nurse said, "Please lie down. It's just policy. We're allowed to deliver your baby, don't worry about that. Get ready and breathe. It's time now."

"Push," said the doctor.

The wrong doctor, the wrong voice, said, "Push, push, come on, you're strong now."

"Why didn't he tell me?" she gasped.

With something close to a laugh, the nurse said, "Well, I'm sure he thought you knew."

Lena pushed hard. She used her trash can anger to push and hoped that her anger would not hurt the child who entered the world.

"A girl."

Lena heard crying, but it was a quiet, modest cry.

"Does she have a name?" the nurse asked.

"Gail."

SIX

1938

ONE DAY IN JANUARY AFTER CHRISTMAS, WHEN MARIE WAS WORK-ing and business was slow, Josiah brought a copy of the *Courier* to the candy shop. "I want to keep the paper but I thought you would want to read this. I was passing by."

"How's school?"

"It's good. I'm doing better than I used to."

She looked quickly at the page he had opened to. Ah. Lena had had a baby girl! "I see. How great for her."

"It is. I always thought she was going to end up in the movies. It's not too likely for a while."

"She's lucky, though. To have a baby."

He looked at her with an air of putting something together. "I also wanted to buy you two chocolates. I owe you for that time you gave me two of your chocolate pay. Now you choose."

"You don't have to."

"I want to. I really want to."

"Okay." She chose what she had chosen for him that day, two peppermints. "And for you?"

"Nothing today. I'm coming back for a whole box on Valentine's Day."

"Are you going to a movie today?"

"Yes. Always."

"Which one?"

"Not even sure." He paced for a few seconds. "I told my father I'd work with him for two or three more years, then that's it—out to Hollywood. That's my future."

Wow, she thought, that was brave, so brave.

"Did you have a good Christmas?" he asked.

"Sort of. But ours hasn't happened yet. January 7 is ours."

He tapped his temple. "That's right. I heard about that." And, smiling, he left, remembering this time to take his paper.

When the evening of January 6 came, Marie and Selma made their way through the snow and slippery sidewalks up to Saint George for midnight mass.

The service was in Arabic—a minor, keening sound. So sad, too sad. Marie studied the grimacing altar boys, who for a moment's entertainment in her mind transformed themselves to child laborers who whipped donkeys and tilled fields.

Selma whispered, "What are you staring at?"

"Kids. Wondering how my baby will look if I ever have one."

The next day was Christmas. But it was just an ordinary Friday workday for the Davids.

About one o'clock, when Marie was still in the grocery store, a customer came in, a Negro man with two little boys dressed in heavy coats and hats. The three were very handsome. She'd been thinking a lot still about looks—who got beautiful faces and who didn't and how that affected them in the world.

"Choose now," said the man. "Tell her how much you have."

"Five cents each," one boy reported. "What can we get?"

Marie took out two paper sacks and helped them choose. Sourballs and Tootsie Rolls and caramels. She thought, *Candy, that's my life.*

"Very well done," the man proclaimed, "so now you can go ahead and have your treats." Marie watched them move over the sidewalks, which had some new snow today. She liked the way the father guided his boys and the way the boys beamed and dug into their paper bags. She thought a good father was an amazing thing, just amazing.

LENA WALKED BACK and forth at the Herron Hill house, dusting this, checking Gail, dusting that, trying to get a routine going.

She made tea, came back to see how Gail was doing, made biscuits and just got them in the oven, thought about getting herself to the library, looked at the winter weather and, instead, paced the house.

She had Gail's bassinet parked by the phone because she often called her father or Irene. Her daughter was sleeping so peacefully when the phone rang that it didn't even wake her.

"Harold Gumm here. Is this Lena?"

"This is Lena."

"Listen, Lena, dear. We got some folks going to make a musical movie—very very quick, almost no shooting time. We want the best talent for this thing. That'll help make it go fast. Ralph Cooper is going to be in it."

"Cooper! Wonderful that you got him."

"And we want you. He wants you."

She could hear the tick of the mantel clock in the silence. "You're kidding, right?"

"Not at all. We want you to come out to Hollywood."

The whole way out to California? Was he nuts? The biscuits were done; she could smell them. She needed to put the phone down.

"It's called *The Duke Is Tops*," he said.

Of course she had to say no, but she couldn't help being curious. "Who is coming up with the money?"

"Popkin Brothers."

"I never heard of them."

"Shoestring, but it's a movie. With colored people."

"It's sad, but I can't, Harold. Don't you know I can't? I mean, I'm married now. I have a baby daughter."

"Think about it. This is a big chance."

When Louis came home she put a basket of brown biscuits and two plates of pork chops on the table and told him about the call.

"Hmmm," he said.

She had been completely ready for scorn, so she ate carefully, waiting for him to hit the ceiling. They made it through the whole meal with no explosion, which completely surprised her. Was he considering it? Impossible.

She told her baby Gail all about the Hollywood offer as she dressed her to go out the next day.

She got to her father's hotel without slipping or falling and, miracle of miracles, found him there instead of at the club. When she told *him* about the offer, he made a face and said it was sad that the timing was bad, but that of course she really couldn't travel at this point in her life.

She sat in his office and, holding Gail, went through his papers until she found what she wanted, an address for Josiah Conner Sr. His son was the one she really wanted to tell. It was only a little after noon, so she stayed for a while, reading her father's journals, nursing Gail, waiting for school to let out. She would walk by Josiah's house to tell him it had *almost* happened. That would probably make him *almost* happy. Oh, she didn't think she would really see him—he might not go straight home right after school, but she could walk by his house, in case. She picked up Gail and started out at three.

Throngs of kids were coming up the street; she was thinking how easily she could miss him when she saw him, solo, walking home. He saw her.

Needing a prop, she lifted Gail.

"Hello!" he said. "I . . . you're here! Is everything okay?"

"Yes, fine."

"And this is your daughter!" He went around to look at Gail's face. "Aw, she looks like you. Aw." He came around to her to say, "You look happy, too."

"Do I? Well, I wanted to tell you something. I was going to write a note but I was taking a walk. I mean, I can't say yes, but I want you to know I got a call about being in a movie. Can you imagine!"

He almost leaped up. His grin said, *yes*, he could imagine. "I *always* thought it. You can't do it?"

"Not now. No."

He got very sober, nodding like an older man. "I understand. You should keep it in your mind, though, as something that will happen again. When you need courage, remember it. I think it's something you want."

"I *do* want it. I feel silly, but I do, and I can't even explain why."

"Almost everybody wants it. The difference is, you have a chance to have it. I'm excited you told me."

"I had to." She understood he was trying to stay away from her so she wouldn't anger her husband or her father and *he* understood it was a kind of bravery to walk to his house.

"I should get her home," she said. "It's been a long day."

The phone rang in her house as soon as she entered and it was Gumm again. "What is this? You don't want fame? You don't want money?"

"Money is always nice," she said. "Okay, give me another day."

At dinner she waited Louis out for as long as she could. "Tell me the truth, don't you think we could use the money?" she tried hesitantly. "It's not for long."

Louis kept buying himself expensive clothes—ties, suits, shoes— saying he needed to look right in political circles. His political pals had told him they didn't want him to run for office just yet, that they were still training him, telling him what to say, how to be. He got angry but he didn't let up one bit, trying. His look, according to him, was a part of it. He had big clothing bills, bigger than hers. She could help.

"I'm thinking."

He didn't say no! Ah! To be on a movie screen! To be seen by so many people in far-flung places. Her mind wouldn't stop. Wasn't Josiah right from the beginning? Negroes had to make these chances for themselves and for each other and if they didn't grab when they could . . .

When she went upstairs and saw herself in the mirror, she thought, *No, I'm dreaming.* Her hair no longer looked healthy or strong. Gumm remembered her as a skinny hoofer and sometime singer who worked hard. She was different now, a boring biscuit maker, a gravy maker, a mother.

Despondent, she sat on the edge of the bed with two of her favorite dresses on her lap—a feathery light gray wool with a plunging neckline and a fitted royal-blue dress. The last time she'd tried them they'd hardly fit—baby weight.

Louis came into the room and sat beside her, "You're right. We could use the money. We'll get you some clothes. I know you need new things. You have to dress like they do out there, movie star clothes. I just called Woogie. He said you can borrow his wife's fur."

She couldn't believe what she was hearing. Louis was saying yes! She threw her arms around him and planted kisses on his face everywhere she could reach.

This was just what they needed, a couple of weeks away from each other—a break, a longing for each other, and a fresh path back into the marriage.

Louis surprised her the next day with clothes he'd chosen for her on a shopping spree, clothes that were so expensive she wondered how her movie pay was going to get them ahead. He, like her father, knew how to buy women's clothes. He'd chosen two beautiful dresses, one blue dress, one black, two skirts, two silk blouses, and even new shoes.

Gumm said she was to take a plane to California. They wanted her right away.

She slipped out of the house and mailed a letter to Josiah to tell him she was going after all and that she didn't want to bother him but would send a short report by mail if she could.

A whole coterie took her to the airport. She had never flown before and now she would be up in the air in under an hour. It frightened her to think of it. She hadn't slept for two nights, but she did what she could with makeup. The *Courier* photographer, Mr. Harris, who arrived only minutes after she did, took a dozen pictures of her. Meanwhile, Woogie, part of the group seeing her off, was saying, "Go ahead, smile, look like a movie star. Yes, that's the way. Great outfit." She was wearing a stylish white peaked hat and carrying the borrowed Persian lamb coat over her arm.

And then a stewardess told her she had to get on the plane. An airplane was a terrifying thing. She climbed up the stairs to the body of it, the metal pod that would soon be up in the sky.

A half day later, when the plane was grounded in Arizona and she, lugging luggage, had to transfer to a train to finish the trip, she felt more like herself, her real self. Hardship was her familiar.

She made her Hollywood entrance, frantic and bedraggled, clutching the borrowed fur, with a thin line of sweat at her brow. The whole thing made her laugh. "Going to be in pictures," she told herself.

JOSIAH HAD TOLD Marie that Lena was going to be in a movie, so she bought the *Courier* at the newsstand near the candy shop, where the man looked at her questioningly but took her money. She sat in the back room of the candy shop, turning the pages. There were articles about the South and about famous Negro personalities and some about politics before she got to a picture of Lena wearing a white hat and carrying a fur coat. The caption said, *Lena Horne Jones on her way to Hollywood a week ago to make "The Duke Is Tops."*

Customers arrived in the shop when she least wanted them. She came to the front room to serve the couple, the paper still in hand. She put it on the counter, folded open. They paid no attention, bought their candy, and left, but just as she was going back to the paper a man came in.

"I'd like to buy a little something for my girlfriend," he said.

"Certainly."

"She's angry with me."

"Oh, dear."

"What would she like?"

"Lots of candy."

So he chose lots of candy and she boxed it. As she took his cash, she said, "There's my picture in the paper!"

"Really?" He looked. "Is that you?"

"No. Just kidding. Somebody told me I look like her."

He left without looking at the paper again and she went back to reading it.

> *This reporter got to visit the studio where "The Duke Is Tops" has been shooting for three days. This is a movie starring the great Ralph Cooper, who plays a stage show impresario who is in love with one of his singers—Ethel Andrews—and the role of Ethel is played by Pittsburgh resident Lena Horne. It's a love story about how Ethel is offered big-time fame in New York City but she doesn't take it because she is loyal to Duke and she loves him. The plot thickens when he figures out a way to trick her into thinking she has to go to New York. So she does. And his company falls apart.*
>
> *Don't worry, readers. The story turns out very well.*
>
> *I was allowed to witness a rehearsal and a bit of the shooting. When Ralph Cooper wasn't on camera, he talked to me. "Did I ever tell you I can cry on cue? I can. Gonna do it today."*

I told him I would be happy to see that. He was very amusing and is a great entertainer in general. He is famous for certain things—his hangdog face, his famous gasp, all of which he will need when the beautiful Lena Horne breaks his heart in the movie.

Miss Horne sings, "I Know You Remember," all about the beginning of love and also she sings a song titled, "Don't Let Our Love Song Turn Me Blue."

Late in the day when I got to interview her, I asked if the plot frightened her at all about her own life. After all, she was away from her new husband, Louis Jones, away from home. Here is the interview.

How do you like Hollywood?

Well, I like it fine but I haven't seen much of it because we're on set all the time.

Is it hard being away from home?

Very hard. I get horribly lonely and I miss my family.

It sounds like you like marriage.

It's a wonderful institution and I am very lucky. Love and a child, it's what life is all about.

Will you make more movies?

Well, the fact is, it's not up to me.

I think it is. I'll bet it is.

Let's see how I do on this one. Then, yes, in a few years. I'm a new mother right now.

This reporter thinks she was excited by the idea of more movies. She was also close to tears when she talked about her family. And all in all, every expression only made her more beautiful.

What a life! Marie thought, folding the paper. *What a life! Everything* does *come to her.*

IT WAS EIGHT, almost nine in the evening in California when Lena asked the hotel operator to ring her father's house, then the Crawford Grill, then the Belmont Hotel—and she finally found him there.

"Doing my books."

"No letter from you yet," she said, trying to keep it light. From the small window of her very small room everything was dark, only a few lights twinkling.

"I wrote one, sent it. I wrote another one tonight. What's going on?"

"It's too early to go to bed. I didn't sleep well last night."

"Call room service. See if they can get you a cup of tea."

She didn't tell him there wasn't room service at this hotel or that she was in a room with a single bed covered in a threadbare bedspread or that the towels were undersized and worn as well. She'd tried a nip of whiskey earlier, which had done nothing. She'd have to try another.

"I sent Louis some money for the gas bill if that's what you're calling about. Buying your clothes cleaned out his account."

"Oh, I never asked for those things. And nobody dresses like that here. We just work."

"He meant well."

She plopped back down on the bed and reached to open the small bottle. "I think when I get back home, I have to hire a babysitter sometimes and get more club work, Daddy. The one thing it's teaching me here is that I'm a singer and I've gotta be around music. They're telling me I'm 'in voice.'"

"Hm."

She waited for him to tell her she was good at singing.

"Ah, well," he hummed. "I have to get to bed."

The liquor didn't quite work. She didn't get to sleep until three.

The next day the first letter from her father caught up with her, mostly telling her about a young guy who had played at the club and how many college students came to hear him because the boy was so good at publicizing the event.

A day later, she got a letter from Josiah.

Thank you for telling me. I saw in the paper it's working out. I know you will be wonderful. I always knew it and I will always be your biggest fan. I won't write to you at home unless you ask me to. I can understand that your husband is nervous about public opinion. Enjoy everything. I knew Hollywood would find you.

Under all that gangly youth, he had years on everyone.

A few days after that, she and the actors were filming late. It was getting on toward nine at night, and Lena was lying on a rug in the studio between takes, trying to do what the director had asked her to do, to remember what it felt like to be in love. She was supposed to summon her memories like a movie in her mind in order to feel those things again. The director told her to think about the rush of romance she experienced when she first met her husband.

The floor was hard—she was aware of that. Her reverie, such as it was—the night in her father's kitchen, the way Louis touched her hair—was interrupted by the director's voice, saying, "That's all for today. We're shutting down." Anyway, the reverie, or exercise, wasn't working too well.

She pushed herself up off the floor and practically fell to the space behind the curtain where she changed clothes. She loved joking that the little curtained space was her dressing room. It was all pretty amateurish, she had to admit.

The scene paint was still damp but earlier in the day it had been messily wet, and she'd had to play the scene of tearful leave-taking from her lover all the while worried about bumping her clothes against the muck. She'd never liked the pungent, earthy, vinegary smell of scene paint—not at the Cotton Club, not anywhere on the road. Still, what they were using on this set was clearly bargain stuff. "Hey, this odor is tough on a singer's pipes," she said as merrily as she could. A few boys tried to find a fan, but they came back saying they didn't have one and there was no money to buy one. So she did all the acting tricks she had heard about, imagining she was at Coney Island smelling salt breezes instead of paint.

They kept saying she had talent.

If she had persuaded them that her character was lovestruck and stagestruck while she worked to avoid the scenery and choked on the fumes of scene paint, well, maybe she did have talent. Dear God, she wanted it to be so.

Finally back in her own street clothes, she decided to take the director up on an offer to use the studio wall phone to call Louis, who was staying up to get a report from her. It would save her paying for a call at the hotel. There wasn't money for anything, not . . . *anything*. The producers had managed to secure only three-quarters of their tiny budget, but they forged onward. "We'll get the money down the line," they assured everyone. "We know you all need to be paid."

Louis answered right away. "You called," he said, "which I thought was not going to happen. It's midnight."

"I know, but I'm still at the studio using their phone. Saves money, sweetheart, but I don't have long, they need to lock up. And, I need some air. Is Gail awake, by chance?"

"No, of course not, she's sleeping. Wait a minute. What are you saying? Aren't they paying your hotel bills?"

"Well, there's a money situation, Louis. In a word."

She watched two boys sweeping up, listening in. She wondered if those two would get paid anything at all. Her stomach growled with a headache-making hunger. The only good thing about having so little money was that she might finally lose some of the baby weight.

"I want you to define *situation*."

She leaned against the wall in spite of the fact that she didn't want to get dust on her black sweater. "The definition. . . . Well, there isn't any money. At the moment. Could you wire me a little something?"

"They didn't pay you." He said this evenly.

"They can't yet. They don't have it."

"Damn it! Listen to me. Listen. I want you to leave that ridiculous operation right now. Forget the plane, get on a train and get back here where we need you."

"Well, I don't exactly have train fare and we only have three more days of shooting. So that's not a good idea."

"It would show you have some standards and won't put up with being treated like a tramp who would do anything to—"

"Louis. I have to go. Others need the phone." The two boys were hanging around, watching out for her, and the director was still sitting on a chair in the midst of the smelly flats with his head in his hands, perhaps problem solving, perhaps not.

"Just come home. This whole thing is a disaster."

It *was* a disaster. A cheap film she would probably not be proud of, but she couldn't just leave. There were other people involved. How could he not understand that? "Louis. I have to go. I'll call you tomorrow. I'll try to call earlier."

She heard something crash and the sound went straight through her stomach to her heart. She said, "Please try to be calm and wire me a loan until they can pay me. Bye, honey," she said, trying not to cry.

"Everything all right?" one of the boys asked.

"Just tired and hungry. You think that sandwich shop is still open?"

"They close something like eleven."

"You two want to come have a sandwich with me? My treat."

How grateful they looked. How nice to see somebody happy about something.

They walked to the dinky diner, so unlike anything she thought she would see in Hollywood: stained stucco walls, a drooping roof, and inside, cigarette burns on the chipped counter and tables. It was clear the boys were even hungrier than she was. They could hardly control their faces as they stretched to look at the smeared green chalkboard behind the counter. She calculated what was in her purse. Six dollars? She ordered six ham sandwiches and three cups of coffee.

They told her about their families, they admitted they never finished school, they talked about loving movies, and she felt good being around them, like a kid again herself.

Back at the hotel, she slept for a mere six hours and then called her father, this time from the hotel.

"Oh, man," her father said, "I really don't want to be awake yet."

"But you are." After all, it was nine in the morning. "I hear music." Ellington, "Mood Indigo."

"I was trying to get back to sleep on the couch. Your husband was banging at my door early this morning. I took him in the kitchen, made him sit and have a coffee with me."

"Daddy, I don't know what he told you . . ."

"Oh, just about everything he could dredge up about the movie. Sounds like a bad deal. So, you need money."

"I asked *him* to send it."

"Says he doesn't have it. From the jacket and shoes he was wearing for church, I thought maybe he spent it all on his duds," her father muttered, but tried to pretend it was half a joke. "Look, tell me, are they paying anybody?"

"I don't know. I doubt it. They really don't have it."

"Uh-huh. How much do you need?"

"I should have a hundred to get me through three days and then back home."

"I'll go get it from Gus later today. I'll wire it to you."

"Thank you."

"Your husband said he wanted to redo your kitchen to make it more like ours. Where's he going to get the money for that?"

"I'd better earn some," she said whimsically.

She knew what Louis envied about her father's new kitchen with diamond-shaped black-and-white tiles on the floor and counters that were sparkling white. The stove was not cast iron but modern, white, and, yes, clean, too. The breadbox and toaster shone so brightly they could have served as mirrors. Irene kept it up, or rather had Elsie do so. The checked yellow curtains were laundered every week. Apparently Elsie washed them with the sheets and ironed them to crispness.

Louis wanted that clean and moneyed domestic life.

She filmed for three more days and then went out with most of the company to celebrate the shooting being done.

The cast *liked* her. They thought everything she said was fascinating. All through the evening they asked about the musicians she knew and the ones she didn't. What fun it was to be with a group of people and to talk and talk.

She had a bourbon and then another and then another. She felt her legs relax.

Had she met Earl Hines? Yes. Did she know Armstrong? Yes. Wasn't he great? Yes.

And they gossiped, of course, for a while about Ethel Waters—bitchy, sexy, bitchy, everyone throwing in an opinion.

The gossip made her nervous. What would people say about her if she ever came up in conversation? If only she could have predicted.

And yet she loved all the people she'd worked with and wanted to be one of them. At the evening's end—what was more like four in the morning—she threw her arm around Ina, the costumer, and said drunkenly, "You ever need a job, you call me."

"You have one to give?"

"No! Not a penny to my name!"

They all laughed and slapped at the table and ordered another round.

So the first day on the train back to Pittsburgh was given to a pretty bad hangover, the second and third days to thinking about her life as she watched America pass by. She felt that somehow she was meant for this—travel, a big world.

And then she was in a jitney going back to her house. She opened the front door, let go of her suitcase, and dropped into a chair with her coat and her hat still on, wanting very much to feel joy, but tugged instead by a great sadness. She managed to get her gloves off. She had an hour or two to pull herself together before Louis got home.

Only seconds later Minnie came running, bringing Gail to her. Elderly and thin, Minnie, Louis's aunt, thrived on tasks—cleaning, cooking, handling the baby, doing everything almost at a trot. She had short, nappy hair and wore beige dresses with a tight belt. An excellent worker, good at every task around the house—indispensable, really, but she was also completely devoted to her half nephew, Louis. It tipped the balance more than a bit in his direction.

"There you are!" Lena cried, grabbing at her daughter. She nuzzled into the child's neck, smelling powder, shampoo. "I'm home. Mama's home."

Gail stretched away in order to get a better view.

"It's only been a couple weeks. You don't know me?"

"She knows your voice."

"Maybe the hat bothers her." Lena put her daughter over her lap, supporting her head on one of her knees. "Let's get this off!" she said energetically. She plucked out the hatpin and removed the little black felt with feathers, letting it drop to the floor. Minnie picked it up. "Better? Does Mama look like Mama?"

Gail began to cry, just a brief shout of a cry, before resuming the work of studying her mother.

What went through a baby's head? Lena didn't remember her early years. She only remembered feelings she'd had after the age of six—how ecstatic she was when her father visited and how disturbed she was when her mother came for a visit.

"I was off being an actress," she whispered to her daughter. "I think I'm pretty darned good. That's what they said."

Gail closed her eyes.

"Time for her nap," said Minnie.

Minnie held the baby while Lena stood to get her coat off and then tossed it to the old blue brocade chair. They needed furniture. If only she'd been paid.

"We kept every notice," Minnie told her. "Louis clipped every one. You're in the papers more than anybody I know." Then Minnie brought over the sheaf of clippings. "See? Your husband is very proud. Clipped all these."

"Did he? Really?" She took the baby back.

Minnie picked up the coat and hung it while Lena quickly shuffled the papers and then sang nonsense syllables to her child.

"How was it?" Minnie asked.

"Awful. Worth it. A foot in the door. I don't know." She found herself shivering. "Can we get more heat in here?"

"Louis worries about the cost."

"Just for today, till I get my Pittsburgh blood back."

Minnie lit a gas fire in the fireplace and soon the room was warmer. "You're tired. That makes a person cold."

"It was a cheap movie, not too fabulous." She laughed. "I think the whole thing cost sixty bucks. I'm exaggerating—a little. I just hope it goes over okay."

"Maybe you want a hot bath."

"That sounds like what I need. And maybe a cup of hot chocolate or tea. Then I'll be right as rain."

She handed the baby over once again and shambled to the kitchen to make herself a warming tea and then she went upstairs and ran a hot bath and even put on stockings and a good dress, the soft gray one that she now fit into a bit better, and because she was still not warm enough, she added her black sweater with embroidery at the collar.

Smells came up from the kitchen—ah, the beef roast Minnie had started for her. She only needed to add some potatoes and then cook up some green beans.

Minnie was in the living room, holding Gail and giving her a bottle when Lena came down. "I'll do that."

"Are you sure? In that dress?"

"Yes."

"You have the most beautiful clothes. Expensive."

"Some are—what Louis buys, what my father buys. But I look for sales. Still, I got my daddy's eye for color, for fabric." Jiggling Gail, she added, "Once when I was just a little kid, my father sent me the most gorgeous coat—royal blue with gold buttons. Another time he sent me a fur coat! I used to want to take it to bed, like a pet. So, anyway, clothes are in my blood, from my papa."

When everything was neat and dinner was well along, Minnie went to the front door, saying, "Give Louis my love."

"Minnie, I don't know what I would do without you."

"I had a good time with the baby. It was a pleasure."

She left and there was quiet in the house until Lena heard the rattle of the doorknob and Louis was home.

"At last!" Lena said, her most cheerful voice dredged up.

"So," he stomped slush from his shoes. "Did they pay you?"

MARIE WENT TO dinner at Fran's, an American meal, sort of, hamburgers on pita bread and a salad. She told her sister excitedly, "Lena Horne is in a movie. They keep writing about it."

"Oh, yes, I've heard people talking at school about some write-up."

"I'm still trying to figure out if she's terribly conceited or just scared. I tried to be her friend but she was sort of snotty."

"Huh," Fran said, a little distracted, listening to footsteps on the stairs, then focusing. "I thought that might be Harry at first, but it's the neighbor. You were saying 'conceited or scared.' I heard. People say she's so beautiful, so I guess she has a right to be conceited. I don't know. What would she be scared of?"

"Me, maybe. One of her friends, a boy I know, said she's a little afraid of white people."

Fran nodded, thinking about that emotion. "It's hard to be scared. I try not to be."

"I'll go see her movie anyway. Curiosity."

Fran said, "You sit. I'll do the dishes. Did you like the hamburger?'

"It was delicious."

"The trick is to not cook it too much. Then it has taste."

For the first time in memory Fran's spirits were not high. She was trying for her old self but she was preoccupied. Marie suspected it had something to do with Harry but she didn't ask. She liked the quieter Fran. It was a shame that sadness made her more likable.

"Does Ummah ever talk about me?"

"No."

"She's tough!"

"I know."

"I don't care! So what! So *what*!" Fran began dancing around on her bad leg and pretty soon she was the old Fran, too cheerful.

Marie stayed a little while, then went home when she could pretend she was coming from the candy shop.

SEVEN

1938

LENA GOT A LETTER FROM INA SAYING THERE WAS A RUMOR THE
Courier review was going to be a rave.

She made cornbread for dinner. And fried chicken. She played with
Gail all day in a high mood. And when Louis got home, she kissed him
and teased him about the tired-old-man look on his face. As they sat
over dessert—and she made that, too, apple turnover—she told him,
"Good news. I got a letter telling me the review of the movie is maybe
going to be a rave."

His face changed immediately. "We will not talk about that movie."

"But it's over. I'm home. And they set the date for opening. And
there is a big fundraiser here at New Granada for the premiere."

He shoved his plate of turnover away from him. "You didn't make a
buck. It put us in debt."

She paused. It was always good to pause with Louis. "Right now it's
rough. Money might come after it opens."

"I said I didn't want to talk about it."

"Okay." She picked up their dessert plates, trying to think of how to calm him down.

But he continued in spite of what he'd said about shutting down the subject. "You didn't stand up for yourself once you got there. You were as much a victim as any slave I ever heard of."

Not quite, not quite—she'd gone voluntarily, stayed voluntarily, got to practice acting and singing and learn something about herself. She breathed in deeply, began to clear the rest of the table, humming inside her head. For some reason it was "Minnie the Moocher" that came to her, a song that usually cheered her, even though she hated the way Cab jumped around and threw his head back, as if he were trying to be southern, some happy innocent slave, which he wasn't and never had been, and he was a good-looking man, too, so why didn't he shut his damned mouth some?

People couldn't see themselves. Was she all wrong, too, and just couldn't see it?

And her husband? Wrong, and he for sure didn't know it. She wanted to tell him he should never lean forward like that and lecture, that he would never be elected to *anything* with that mean face of his.

She turned to the kitchen and went dizzy, just like that, because of his attitude. She lurched forward. In the kitchen she grabbed hold of the cast-iron sink, then leaned over the draining ribs to steady herself.

Whatever a hoochie-coocher was, she wanted to be one. If she could be a low-down something she might have the guts of Louis Armstrong, Ethel Waters, and the rest of those entertainers who got toughness from living at the very edge.

The *tap tap* of Louis's excellently made shoes, the smell of his Bay Rum, warned her he was behind her. "We aren't going to let them use you—not the politicians, not even the NAACP. Understand?"

She stayed quiet, deciding he needed a week to calm down.

Somehow she made it to bed, curled into herself. She talked to Gail during the days. She cooked. Several cornbreads and biscuits and desserts later, she was still not engaging Louis in a fight. The *Courier* came out a week later with a big announcement about the world premiere in Pittsburgh. Louis never mentioned it. So Lena didn't. *How are you, dear? How was your day?*

MARIE SAW THE notice about the NAACP fundraiser.

> *Pittsburgh, however, is proud of the fact that one of its houses will be included in the world premiere showing. This is because Lena Horne is a Pittsburgher, and the management of the theater is making every possible effort to have the affair featured with all the fanfare of a typical Hollywood premiere.*
>
> *In connection with the effort to make Negroes fully cognizant of the rapid progress the race has made in providing high-class all-sepia productions, the company has also shown its other two great pictures in many cities throughout the country.*

She wasn't sure what a fundraiser was or how it worked. But she wanted to go. She clipped the notice and showed it to Selma. "I'll ask for the night off work. It will be like a party."

Before she went to the candy shop, Marie stopped at the New Granada to ask about tickets. The man said, "Well, people give a lot of money to come to it. We have some important contributors. It's not regular tickets that night, it's a matter of patrons." Embarrassed, reminded once more that the world held many things she couldn't be a part of, she told the man she would see the movie another time.

THE DAY FINALLY came and Lena dug at the back of the wardrobe where she had stashed a brand-new floor-length gown, bias cut, bronze and sequined. The saleswoman had told her she looked like a mermaid in it with the sequins sparkly like scales. Lena climbed into it, zippered carefully, and turned to the mirror. She looked at first glance almost nude. Nude and shiny. It made her feel sexual, alluring, and daring. She dabbed a little Kobako behind her ears, then worked on her hair by pulling the mass of it up and slightly to one side, then she fastened it and decorated it with a gigantic white artificial flower that looked so real she could almost smell it. Holy Moses, but she looked exactly as she intended: like a Hollywood starlet.

She stood in the living room, waiting for her husband, knowing he would be irritable, but thinking she could remind him of all the money-eyed people he would be able to mix with tonight. She'd had his tux brushed; it was hanging and ready.

The door opened. He came in. He was very quiet. He sat and loosened his shoes. "What is that getup all about?"

"You know what it's about. The premiere. Tonight." She could hear Minnie upstairs singing to Gail.

"Take it off. You're not going. Let's have some supper and let them rot in hell." He eased off his shoes and sat back in one of the two old upholstered chairs.

"Louis, you don't have to go. I do. I have to go."

"There is no such thing as *have to*."

"I'm expected."

"Not going will send them a message. You are not willing to be their monkey."

"But if I choose—"

"No. You have to be treated with dignity. As a professional. Period. Are we having dinner?"

She caught a glimpse of herself in the mirror near the door. She hated that she looked scared, uncertain. "There are leftovers. Minnie can put something together for you."

"You are not going."

"Louis, this is—people will come to the door for me if I don't show up. They'll be looking for me."

"Ah. Then we won't be here. Put on some regular clothes. Tell Minnie not to answer their questions. We're going out. Downtown. They won't be able to find you."

"Louis, I'm begging you to understand."

"Please. Do not embarrass me."

Lena was never sure, looking back, why running away with Louis had been a solution she accepted. Maybe she thought she could get back the Louis she first met—when he was cheerful and wanted to please her. She flew up the stairs and put on street clothes. She didn't have time to undo her hair, so she left it as it was and hurried down to her husband. She tried to avoid the eyes of passersby as the two of them walked to the streetcar and then as they rode downtown, where, to make the statement Louis had in mind, they went to a movie. He chose *Boys Town*, with Spencer Tracy. What was he saying—and making her say—to the world? *We'd rather watch a white film?* She didn't challenge him with that question.

For the first half hour of the film Lena was on the verge of furious tears, but eventually she started to care about the people depicted in the movie, and she had enough brainpower left to realize that she was witnessing the very miracle of movies, the way they could give you an alternate life when you couldn't stand your own.

She knew her movie was no good. She knew she'd made trouble for herself by missing the gala. People would call her a diva and not want to work with her.

And poor Louis. Stretching toward dignity, stretching, stretching, almost to the point of breaking. She felt terrible for him and told him she would practice speeches with him so the other politicos would let him run for office.

MARIE AND SELMA had walked over to the New Granada that night. They saw soon enough that they weren't the only oglers. A few hundred people, white and black, who hadn't been able to afford entrance, milled about.

It was wonderful to see all the splendid outfits of the people who *had* been able to afford tickets. Some women wore beautiful street-length dresses or fancy suits, but there were plenty of long gowns.

"I can't wait to see what Lena is wearing. It ought to be better than everything else."

They took a place in the middle of the crowd, but they were jostled badly. Marie grabbed Selma's hand and they pushed their way to the front.

"Oh. Look. There's Josiah." She pointed out to Selma the tall boy in a suit walking eagerly toward the door. He looked very grown-up. He sensed something, looked toward Marie, and when he saw her, smiled and waved.

But something was wrong. They could hear muttering in the crowd. "Where is Lena? Why is she not here yet?" Somebody behind Marie theorized that Lena was being slipped in through a back door. And how frustrating that would be if it were true. Lena was the one the crowd wanted to see. Some fans had bouquets of flowers to give her.

After a while they could hear that the program was starting inside. It was a warm and glorious June night. People didn't want to stand around forever. Although some sat on the ground, waiting to catch a glimpse of the star at the end of the evening, most went home.

Marie and Selma decided to go home.

"I still want to see the movie," Marie said. "I mean, I met her and she's famous, so you have to go with me some Sunday." Selma never said no to her about anything, so that was fixed.

THE EARL MORRIS review in the *Courier* was a wild rave.

> *"The Duke Is Tops," starring Ralph Cooper and beautiful Lena Horne, is the tops. It is the best colored motion picture I have ever seen. And I am screaming it from the housetops. GO and SEE this picture. It is the first serious attempt by a colored film company to make a musical. It is definitely BOX OFFICE.*
>
> *This picture should be most important to the sepia theatergoing public. It contains no "Uncle Tom" bandana or calico sequences. It is definitely a racial achievement.*
>
> *The story deals with a beautiful sacrificing love tale. The hero, portrayed by Ralph Cooper, submerges his ambition, his ideals, rather than to hold back his sweetheart, played by Lena Horne, who is undoubtedly one of the most beautiful girls I have even seen on the screen, colored or white.*
>
> *The picture is important first because it is the first serious attempt by Negroes to produce a feature-length swing musical. Secondly because it is highly entertaining, contains nothing which would reflect on the Negro.*

To herself, correcting the prose, she said, *reflect* badly *on the Negro*. She clipped the article and put it safely with her papers, away from Louis.

However, that good review was upstaged a week later by articles in several Negro papers about how the star hadn't attended her own premiere. All kinds of reasons were given, most amounting to her being too haughty to attend.

THERE WERE ONLY four other white people in the whole New Granada Theater by the time Marie and Selma were able to take a day to see it.

Marie watched the screen intently, studying Lena, who, as far as Marie was concerned, was the best thing about the film. It was different from other movies she'd seen, unfinished in some way, but she was unable to pinpoint all the reasons.

Patrons in the theater talked and although Selma showed no interest in listening in, Marie tried to hear, to gauge her own experience against others.

"She's good."

"She's pretty."

"She never attended her own premiere, thinks she's too good for us."

The *Courier* had also written that Lena was having significant marriage problems.

EIGHT

1938, 1939

SUMMER LEFT AND AUTUMN CAME AGAIN. THE LAST THING LENA expected in her life was another offer from Gumm. She also never expected Louis to consider the request, but she reported dutifully what Gumm had asked of her. And he didn't scream. He said, "Let me think."

Lena's father was sitting in the back room with a couple of guys, playing cards, when Louis dragged her in to report about the offer. She mouthed to her father, *Not my fault.*

Teddy looked up and said, "Fellows. You know my son-in-law, Louis Jones? This is Louis Jones. And my daughter, Lena." He frowned a question at her—*what's up?* "Louis? Would you mind getting us each a beer? Lena, just, just sit."

Louis went off to fetch glasses of beer and when he returned with a tray, he sat a little apart from everyone else and tapped his foot.

Oh, God, Lena thought. *The man is smart but stupid.*

When the game ended and the men left, Teddy went to get himself another beer. He came back to the table and, taking his former seat, waited, drinking thoughtfully.

Louis finally said, "You'll never guess. She got a call from this guy Gumm. Again."

"Gumm, yes."

"He wants her for the revue they're doing. New York this time. *Blackbirds of 1939*."

Teddy sipped, doing everything he did slowly.

"The other *Blackbirds* revues have been successful," Lena offered.

"I know," her father said. "Saw half of them."

Two men at another table laughed raucously about some private joke of their own.

Louis waited out the interruption and then said, "It's working for a white guy. How is that going to be?"

Is? Oh, my God, he was looking for a way to say yes.

Her father made a show of mulling things over before he said, "Lew Leslie—has a decent reputation."

"So I hear," Louis grumbled.

"Why don't you talk to him on the phone about what the arrangements are, you know, so he knows you care how our Lena is going to be treated. Don't you think?"

"I could try."

"What do you think?" he asked Lena, playing each card slowly enough to let Louis catch up.

"My singing would benefit. All that practice."

"Always good to improve," Teddy said sagely, avoiding any talk of money, but his eyes told Lena he heard Louis's need as well as her own.

Some weeks later, Lena and Gail got themselves to New York, to a small rented place. They were met there by a cousin from Lena's side of the family, Edwina, who had come in from Chicago to take care of Gail. Lena felt happy that the new nanny was a Horne and not a Jones.

Lew Leslie was not like anybody else Lena had ever worked with. He was just different. Kind—yes, even though he made her rehearse until she dropped. She worshipped him by day three because he asked things like, *Did you have breakfast? Are you feeling okay? What's for dinner? How is your daughter? Do you want to have the sitter bring her to a rehearsal?*

He was like that with everyone, not just her.

"Do you need to call and check on Gail?" Lew asked one afternoon. He even knew her daughter's name.

When she called the apartment, she asked Edwina to put the phone to Gail's ear. Lena said, "I'm here, baby, I'm here. Be right home."

Lew smiled, nodding. He liked families, personal lives. He was very pale, very white, a Jewish man. At first she had thought, *How can a person be that pale*, but now she was used to him. No, more than that, she adored him.

Later in the day when the rehearsal room was filled with tired performers and musicians, he put up his hands. "Listen, everybody, let's go get something to eat. You must all be completely starved. We can have our notes over dinner."

They went to a little Jewish restaurant they frequented where white Lew and a slew of black people were served happily and without question.

Jewish food. Matzo ball soup, latkes, blintzes, briskets. She found the food warm and tasty, tangy sometimes.

And there was always wine and lively conversation.

"Look," Lew said after notes. "I have to be straight with you. I'm not going to be able to pay you your full salaries. My wife is pawning everything we don't need. But this I can promise you: I will bring in food for lunch and take you to dinner every day."

The cast took it in and several nodded.

"Thank you," one guy said.

This was love—nothing carnal, just family love, family feeling. All the performers and Lew were pals, in it together.

Even when the cast suspected the show would not survive, let alone be a hit, there was a crazy feeling of happiness backstage.

Three days before opening, Lena warned Louis. "Don't come up. It's not the best show, it's got problems and . . . we have to hope for something to help it along."

But opening night arrived and so did Louis, wanting to be the guy in charge of Lena's career. The performers gave it their best, as Lew hoped they would, but they could feel the death throes all the while. The reviewers would kill the show off by morning.

Backstage, when the rest of the cast was sniffling and hugging and joking about their failure, Lena wanted to hug with the rest of them but she got out of costume hurriedly because Louis was pacing the hall. The only thing he'd said was, "Big surprise, you were used again."

The stage manager announced he was locking up in five. So the whole group grabbed bags, purses, and coats and scurried out to walk to the restaurant they'd all agreed on.

Louis spoke in Lena's ear as they walked behind the others. "Dignity. Remember. That's what I ask of you. Dignity." She looked longingly at the knot of cast members just up ahead, arms around each other, heads leaning toward each other.

One man turned and called back, "Coming, Lena?"

"We can't!" Louis shouted. "You all go on."

"I need to get some rest," she said in a voice hardly loud enough to carry. "Have a good time."

At the apartment, she went straight to the bathroom, where she locked the door and wept until morning.

NINE

1939

ONE SATURDAY IN SPRING MARIE WAS TAKING ONE OF HER WALKS when she saw Federico coming down the street, looking at a piece of paper, frowning. When he looked up and saw her, he smiled. "Oh. It's you. Marie."

"Yes."

"Still at the candy shop?"

"Yes. For life, I think."

"Aw. Are your parents still strict?"

"The same."

"Did I get you in trouble?"

"Yes."

"Hm." He looked down at the paper in his hand, creased it, and put it in his pocket. "You ought to run away."

"I can't. What were you studying so hard?"

"Oh, a shopping list. My wife moved in with my family. She's always sending me for something."

"You got married!"

"Yes, I did. I was ready."

"An Italian girl," she guessed.

"No, Irish. My parents practically fainted but now they love her. The Irish are lousy cooks except for soda bread. So she keeps making soda bread. Can you walk? I'm going to Delillo's."

"Sure," she said.

"You should get married. It's fun."

"Not always. Some people have a hard marriage, from what I've heard." Josiah had indicated the last time she saw him—a long time ago now—that Lena's marriage was not a happy one.

"That's too bad. I wish you the opposite."

When they parted she thought with amazement that she had once been in a swoon, kissing him.

By midsummer there was an article about Lena that gave Marie more questions than answers about marriages and love. Marriages, she supposed, repaired themselves. Or, like her mother's, simply survived.

Lena Horne is Expecting Second Child

The beautiful Lena Horne, married to Louis Jones of Pittsburgh, has just announced that she will live in Pittsburgh again. She and her husband are expecting a second child. She and Louis have already chosen names. If it's a girl, they will name her Corrine. If it's a boy they will name him Teddy after Miss Horne's father. When asked how she felt, Miss Horne said she felt just fine and happy to be back in the city. Asked when she will get back to work, she answered, "Well, I doubt if I will ever stop singing somewhere. The where is the question I don't have an answer to just yet."

Marie took many walks around the neighborhood she loved without once spying Lena out on a walk. There was a notice in March about the birth of a boy named Teddy, the second child of the "happy couple," Lena and Louis Jones.

TEN

1940

LENA QUICKLY FILLED A SUITCASE AND THEN PULLED THE TWO traveling trunks from the crawl space off the bedroom. She filled the first one with her best clothes—coats and suits and hats. Something about looking at the clothes, lying there like corpses, reminded her of a death. It *was* a death; her old self was gone and she didn't know where to find a new Lena who could deal with a botched career, a failed marriage, and two children. She let out a cry.

"What, Mommy?" Gail asked.

"Nothing. I'm being silly. I'm just crying and singing a silly *sentimental lullaby*." She sang the last two words to the tune of the introduction to "Let's Fall in Love."

"Lullaby. Sing."

"It's supposed to be *alibi*," she said vaguely, distracted by the fact that she had packed badly. "I was making a joke." But Gail looked so sad, she said, "All right. I'll sing it."

Her brain, her whole mind, tried for a first word, a first note, but she wasn't thinking right and couldn't remember how the song started, so, to calm her daughter, she did a verbal time step. "Harold Arlen wrote it. You remember that name, little button. Once you come live with me people will ask you all about the songs I sing and you'll know *all* the answers, okay?"

Gail's face told Lena she was terrified of what was happening, though she didn't know what it was.

"I'm coming back for you," she whispered to both her children. "Don't you worry. I'll come get you."

Little Teddy in his bassinet slept through the promise, but Gail, who sat on the bed, watching her mother closely, reached out for Lena's dress and held on.

Lena couldn't move. Teddy let out a small murmur in his sleep. He was such a good baby, and so far it seemed he was going to look like his grandfather—which was the idea, the magic, of choosing a name.

"How about you sing me 'Blue Skies?'" Lena suggested. Gail sang nervously, her little piping voice repeating the first two words of "Blue Skies" over and over, but she let go of the dress.

Lena placed nightgowns and underthings in the second trunk, and even though she knew she should split things up differently, she was in a hurry. Irene's workers were coming for the trunks at noon and she had to be ready. She had written a note for Louis but it was hidden in her purse and she wasn't sure she should leave it. Oh, she'd wanted to do it more civilly, had considered packing her clothes and talking to Louis while he was home, but she couldn't shake a terrible fear of Louis's temper. What if he started tearing or cutting or burning her clothes to prevent her from going? They were almost all she had in the way of goods. The little bit of travel money in her purse came from her stepmother, a loan, so Lena simply had to get work right away in New York; the clothes were needed for that endeavor.

The opening words of the song came to her at last. She sang to Gail, who listened with great seriousness as if the words held a code.

> We might have been meant for each other
> To be or not to be, let our hearts discover
> I have a feelin,' it's a feelin' I'm concealin,' I don't know why
> It's just a mental, incidental, sentimental, alibi

"Alibi, not lullaby!" she said. She tapped her daughter's nose with the jumpy rhythm of the next lines, but Gail's laughter was forced, and she looked like a child crying instead.

> *But I adore you, so strong for you*
> *Why go on stallin,' I'm fallin,' love is callin,' why be shy?*

> *Let's fall in love*
> *Why shouldn't we fall in love?*
> *Our hearts are made of it*
> *Let's take a chance, why be afraid of it?*

The second verse she sang to her baby, Teddy, pouring out conviction that she would have her son and daughter with her as soon as she got settled.

> *Let's close our eyes*
> *And make our own paradise*
> *Little we know of it*
> *Still we can try to make a go of it.*

The door slammed downstairs. Surely, surely, *surely* not Louis. Was it Louis, in the middle of the day? Her heart sank. Again. His whole being was tuned to finding her weaknesses. He knew just when to pounce, how to catch her.

Someone had told him. Minnie? Had Minnie seen the signs that Lena was going? Yes, it was probably Minnie.

The sound of his footsteps coming up the stairs practically broke her. Shaking, she dumped a last handful of sweaters and blouses, unfolded, into the trunk. There was no disguising what she was doing.

He stood at the door, taking in the packing, nodding. In the long silence, Gail hummed nervously.

"You're ridiculous," Louis said. "Completely ridiculous."

"I'm going. You know I am."

"What? Your European tour? Following the greats out there to the French and English? Do you think they'll like you?"

"Don't be cruel. I'm going to New York. I just need to make a living. *We* need it, the children need it, and I need to be away. You know we aren't good together."

He stood, feet planted, arms crossed. "Divorce is not acceptable. My father will have a heart attack."

"Or I will."

"There you are again, selfish, ridiculous." He eyed the trunks, his lips tightening. She moved in front of them. "What trunk were you thinking of putting our children in?" he said.

She hated when he couldn't just talk straight. "I'll send for them. As soon as I'm settled." She was banking on the fact that he would realize he couldn't take care of them. He was terrible at it.

"You won't get jobs. You make more singing here for dinner parties than you will ever make in New York."

Her body sank with the fear that he was right. Her name was golden in Pittsburgh. Mellons, Fricks, everybody who had money seemed to want her to slip into their houses, sit in a bedroom or some side room until called, appear in a shimmery dress, sing a few songs and eat a bit of dessert as if they were all just friends, and then go home. The cash came into her hand a day later through a third party, all very . . . discreet, all very racist.

"I have to try . . ." She let out a strangled laugh and could not come up with the words for what she wanted.

Louis said sadly, "I should have known from the start you didn't want marriage. You have your mother's disease—that show business disease, thinking you can be somebody."

"I just want to make a simple living. Be able to give things to our kids and maybe to my father and mother."

"The great earning queen."

"Please, Louis, you're nicer than this. I know you are. You were so sweet when we met."

"Go. You'll be back."

She waited for him to say *begging* or *crying* or *and I won't have you.* He looked away from her but didn't say those things.

Teddy started to wail suddenly and Louis picked him up before she could get to him. He found words again and they were words that seared her. "You're never taking Teddy. Never. He's a Jones. He's going to be great in some way someday, I'm going to make sure of that."

Downstairs there was a pounding at the door. It would surely be Irene's helpers, come to take the trunks. Hurriedly she clasped the trunks shut, afraid to leave Louis in the room with them, but what choice did she have? She brushed past him and down the stairs to the front door. Two hefty men stood there. "We're supposed to pick up two trunks."

"Yes, this way." She led them upstairs and then turned to them. The men's eyes took in the empty closet, the drawers hanging open, the man clutching his infant to his chest. "These two trunks," she said.

"To Mrs. Horne?"

"Yes."

Under the shuffle of the scraping trunks, Louis muttered, "You got her to help you?"

Lena didn't answer. Now he would hate Irene.

The men carried the first trunk down the stairs. Gail clutched at Lena's dress. "No, don't go, Mama."

"Just for a little. I'll come back to get you."

Louis said mildly, "I'm putting down a bet that you'll come back in record time. Remember I said it."

"I can't live like this."

"In a house, with a husband, with two lovely children? How very special you must be!"

The men came back for the second trunk, bumping into each other in their hurry to get away from the tension.

Louis watched them go. Lena pulled out of the closet her good straw suitcase that was already packed with the things that would get her through until the trunks arrived. Her father had found someone to drive her to the train station. He didn't want to be the one to do it— that was too much siding with one of them for him.

Gail now hung on to her mother's leg.

"You can have Gail," Louis said. "Not Teddy. Never. He's mine. Whether you come back or not."

ONCE, JOSIAH CAME to the grocery story on a Saturday morning for soup. He took down two cans of chicken noodle. "How you been?" he asked Marie.

"Okay, I guess. You?"

"Okay. Nothing much changing."

A woman who was browsing the shelves looked at him and inched away.

"Lena went to New York," she said, taking his money. "I know you must know that. Is she . . . is she going to be . . . ?"

The woman turned to watch the conversation.

"Alone? I don't know. She's married still, officially. But hopefully New York is the next right thing. Gotta go, my father is waiting for me to help with a wall. Still at the candy shop?"

"Yes."

"I'll stop by when I can. Okay?"

"Oh, yes."

The other customer left without buying anything, looking miffed at their little bit of conversation.

LENA, ALONE IN New York, counted forty-six rejections. She wanted to give up, but how could she? Then, when she was about ready to take some other job, waitressing or anything that paid, she got another tour with a white bandleader, Charlie Barnet—for which she felt very lucky, even though her father was furious that she was working for a white man again. She tried to tell him about all the other singers and musicians who had done so. But of course he knew that perfectly well.

But the miracle was, she was working again. Then Barney Josephson, another white man, offered her what turned out to be the best job she ever had.

Café Society Downtown was *the* place to be—any musician who was anybody played there: Mary Lou Williams, Art Tatum, Billie Holiday, and a hundred others. The tiny tables with their white tablecloths could squeeze two to four people each and you'd surely bump into the people behind you, black or white, because it was *the* club that catered to both equally. Hitherto unheard of and downright fantastic! The walls were covered with satirical murals; one of Lena's favorites was of patrons, black and white, at a crowded place, getting their drinks mixed up. The expressions on the faces of the cartooned customers were hilarious.

She didn't usually go on until nine thirty. Comedians entertained the crowd before the music started. The drinks were strong there and she was learning to get them down. You could get bread and cheese and potatoes and beef to soak up the booze. The best part of the place, to many minds, was the logo printed on everything, napkins included, that said THE WRONG PLACE FOR THE RIGHT PEOPLE. Sometimes Lena felt she was living in the *New Yorker* magazine come to life. It was a glorious job, a pure blessing.

Everybody who was anybody also ended up in the audience. If she tried to move through the room, she came face to face with other musicians, actors, journalists (though she didn't always recognize them), painters—and the best part was that they were of a mind politically. It was a very Left place. Maybe even her grandmother would have accepted the whites who loved the place.

And Barney knew everybody. He hadn't started out that way. He'd been a shoe salesman back before all this, but the *everybodys* gravitated to him and to the statement about equality he was making with his club.

One day while sitting with Lena he told her he remained good friends with Billie Holiday, who was performing at Kelly's Stable these days, and that Lena should get to know her.

"I don't want to push myself on her."

"Go. She's great. And smart." The next week Lena had a night off when there was a private party in the club. Barney urged again, "Go see Billie. Go on. Go see her."

So Lena went to Kelly's Stable. The bar was crowded but she managed to get a chair at a tiny table in the back. And soon enough the room hushed and the famous singer with the famous small voice stood in a pool of light and began. There was no one like her. She took a person's breath away. Lena had heard her live before, and she'd listened to records, of course, but watching her made Lena want to change everything about herself. Here was a singer who let her emotions show. Meanness, pain, right there, just right there to touch.

Lena stilled herself, a hand in front of her face as she watched. One of the staff had recognized Lena when she first came in, so she told him she hoped to say a quick hello to their star at the evening's end. It turned out, however, there was to be no waiting until the end of the second set. At intermission a man came to her and said Billie wanted to see her.

Lena followed the man through a curtain to the backstage, which was very hot, and to the doorway of a small room, maybe eight by eight, with an open door. The dressing room was crowded with the materials of show business—dresses and shawls on hooks, a rack of clothing, a suitcase, a small table with a mirror and an assortment of puffs and powders, lipsticks and pencils.

Lena dabbed at her throat for a second before she slipped into the tiny space to the only spot big enough to stand in.

Billie looked up from where she sat on a stool. "Hello, hello," she said, using her almost squeaky voice. She swatted at her hairline with a scarf, then fanned with her hand, saying, "Damned heat. Take a seat, honey." Absently, she took a jeweled clip out of her hair and put it right back in. "I get so hot."

"I do, too." The broken ladderback chair was the only place to sit but it had a bunch of flowers on it, which Lena lifted and held in order to sit down. Her demure little sweat was nothing, completely inferior to the perspiration pouring out of Billie Holiday. Lena said, "I've been want-ing to meet you. We've been in the same clubs from time to time but we never got to speak. Once I was sitting in the back, just listening. Admir-ing, of course. And tonight—"

"But honey, you're a singer. You don't have to be humble. We both have the same job."

Lena let out a big breath, relieved at the tone. Everybody said Billie was really nice.

"You want a drink? It's just whiskey. Plain old." Billie reached for a bottle on the floor amid pairs of shoes.

"All right."

"I've got to go on again. Dull audience tonight. I hate when they look cross-eyed."

"I understand."

"They make the night long, don't they?" From an open drawer at her table Billie lifted a glass and poured. After she handed that glass to Lena, she poured a triple shot into her own glass on the table.

Lena didn't drink right away. She plunged into an issue that had been making her nervous. "The thing is, I've been singing some of your songs—like 'Fine and Mellow'—pretty regularly. And I never got to clear it with you. That's partly why I'm here."

"No need, honey. Just sing what you like. Songs are like stars. We can't have 'em for ourselves but we pluck them down anyway, borrow them. You sing fine. I like your singing."

"You've heard me?"

"Sure. Don't downplay yourself. You like your job?"

"I love it."

"Glad you're happy there. Barney's a good man."

Lena had some of her drink then, and breathed even more freely. Generosity. What an amazing thing.

Billie said, "You've had the good ones. Lew Leslie, Sissle, Charlie Barnet, now Barney. Best in the business. Be grateful." She nodded. "And you have kids."

"Girl and a boy."

"Big interruptions." Billie applied lipstick, saying through the maneuver, "I never wanted kids myself. They get in the way of drinking and card games."

"Well, I don't play cards much."

Billie chuckled at that.

Lena said, even more comfortable, "I actually allowed myself to go to Charlie Barnet's band because you paved the way—my family was very upset about the idea of a white band."

"It's about the music."

When Billie poured again, Lena put a hand over her own glass even though every month she was a better and better drinker.

For a few moments they just sat there, instant old friends. Both women had been refused admittance to hotels. They had had to dress on the musicians' bus, they had had to have food brought to them when restaurants wouldn't serve them, and both of them even had times when the white band was allowed to play so long as the Negro singers stayed out of sight—in many cases sitting on the bus in the cold or heat. Maybe the silence in which they sipped whiskey was a way of acknowledging that.

Lena wanted to give Billie advice. *Let your eyebrows and hair grow in more,* she wanted to say. But she implicitly understood that Billie wanted her body to quit asking to be cared for. Billie grumbled, "I got to change gowns. This one is too sweaty. You can stay."

The blue sequined gown came off and dropped to the floor. Lena tried to look aside. Billie turned to the clothing rack, exposing battered-up skin, marks and scars, and she chose a red dress without sequins. Billie was only two years older than Lena but her body was already tired. Signs of poverty and tragedy came off her skin. Whiskey and resignation did, too. Her whole being said, *Take me as I am.*

"You should come visit me again," Billie offered, pulling up a side zipper.

"Really? I would love to."

"You have a good man with you these days?"

"I'm separated from my husband."

Billie laughed. "Didn't mean him. You left him, you had a reason. You take care you find another man, a good one. If there is such a thing."

"I don't really want any of that."

Billie's eyes said she knew this was a lie, that Lena had been known to see other men, but she said, "Well, when you do, don't *blame* yourself for it. And if you're hiding somebody under your skirts, you just bring that person along when you visit, 'cause I don't get shocked—black, white, whatever—and I also know how to quiz a man. I could make him shake. I'll look out for you."

"My kids are enough for me right now."

"Then . . . use the loneliness. Loneliness works some kind of magic when we stand up to sing. Don't you think?"

Billie slugged the rest of her whiskey, tugging at the red dress, and hummed three notes, back and forth, the same three notes. She slapped the jewel back in her hair and mopped her brow. "Time to sing."

The man who had let Lena in came to the door to return Billie to the stage.

As Billie exited, hunkered over like someone who'd been punched in the stomach, she called back to Lena, "You keep singing. Come back to see me."

She told Ina, her assistant, about the visit with Billie. True to her word, Lena had brought the costumer from *The Duke Is Tops* to New York, for which Ina was ecstatic. She loved the bustle of the city, the huge stores, the small stores, the food.

She loved the parade of well-known people who came to hear Lena sing.

One night, not long after the visit to Kelly's Stable, Ina rushed back to the dressing room, starstruck as usual, saying, "You won't believe who's out there."

"Billie!" Lena guessed.

"More famous than Billie Holiday. Guess again."

Lena was trying to get some cool water down. *Louis Armstrong? Count Basie?* No, she knew they were playing in other cities at the moment. And she'd already met them.

"Robeson!" Ina said triumphantly, unable to wait.

"Oh, God."

"Maybe I shouldn't have told you."

Knowing was better than casting her eye out at the audience and seeing him while she was in the middle of a song. Paul Robeson was a god, plain and simple, a god and a genius, brilliant at everything he touched—sports, music, writing, acting. Lena had not met him, only seen him, as she'd told Josiah, on stage and on film. But she knew he'd acted in London with the best English actors. Even white people put him on a pedestal. When it came to respect, some put him before Ellington.

She left her dressing room and stood backstage, where she could hear her name being announced, then applause mounting. For a moment she imagined herself running out the stage door and to the subway. Instead, she sailed out to the stage, head higher than usual.

The club was so crowded she couldn't see the white tablecloths. The lights were low, people were squeezed in and leaning toward each other, but she saw him anyway. Who could miss his large, vibrating presence? She took in the familiar smells of cigarettes and whiskey. And then she began.

She tried not to sing straight to him. "The Man I Love" suffered from lack of focus as a result, but "Blue Skies" worked okay, even though she detached and began noticing those open gestures she did with her right arm. She got through "Once in a While" and "It Looks Like Rain," both songs new to her repertoire. At the end of her performance, she raced to her dressing room and collapsed.

Ina was there seconds later. "Lena? He's coming back."

He stood in her doorway, tall, broad, and with a personality bigger than his physique. He was very dark and had a bit of woolly gray coming into his hair.

"Lena Horne. I've wanted to meet you." His voice rumbled and at the same time hit notes like music.

"I am honored," she said.

He chuckled. "Likewise. What do you say? Shall we be friends?"

"I think that would be . . . wonderful." She slipped her hands under her thighs as if to warm them.

"Why don't we start by going to a late supper some night—tonight, if you can. Are you hungry?"

"Always."

"Good. You see, I almost feel I know you. I mean, I knew your grandmother. She was a fine woman."

Lena tried to revise her memory of the woman who was always whipping her into shape and who thought singing and dancing brought shame on the race, on the family. Other people remembered her grandmother as *fine, dignified*. To her own surprise, she blurted to Robeson, "*Fine*, I know she was, but the truth is, I was afraid of her a lot of the time. She'd be rolling in her grave at what I'm doing."

"Fierce woman."

"Fierce! Yes."

"Quietly so." He grinned, eyebrows raised.

Lena was already in love with Paul Robeson in her stupid way. Another father. How many did she need? But she couldn't help her feelings. Josiah Conner and those sweet stagehands in California were like the brothers she never had. She'd tried to explain how much she needed that family feeling to Irene once, back in Pittsburgh, when Irene fretted about how much time she'd given Josiah. Irene said, "I don't understand. You must be so lonely. He's just a poor boy from the neighborhood. Common."

"So let's have our late supper tonight," Robeson was saying. "Right? You can eat?"

"I'm always starved."

"Good to hear it."

"I need to change first." She released her hands from under her thighs.

He stood and almost bowed. "I will excuse myself."

That voice. It went right through her body.

She changed out of her long black dress to what she'd worn to the club that day, a fitted wool burgundy dress. She left on the stockings and the good shoes, even though there was snow and slush on the streets; she added a necklace of tiny pearls and matching earrings, and Ina helped her into her current winter coat, black wool with a lambswool collar.

Paul Robeson waited outside her dressing room, hat in hand, as if she were the more famous one.

He took her to a small place that seated them immediately and willingly though there were no other Negroes in sight. Lena watched the waiter and the host inclining their bodies forward as they served him.

"The beef stew is very good here," he whispered.

"I'll have it."

"Two beef stews. With lots of bread to sop it up. And your hot mustard. And a bottle of Burgundy." He held up a hand and turned to Lena. "Do you want a salad or an appetizer? Just name it."

"No, I think meat and bread will do it."

He smiled. "Good. Like the Elizabethans. So now, now we can talk. Do you have any fight in you?"

"Fight?"

"You're going to be important."

"How do you mean that?"

"In our fight."

Fight. She'd only hoped for some compliments about her performance and a good meal. "I like the way they treat you here. Is that what you mean?"

"I'm talking about getting treated that way all the time—in business, in schools, in shops, in hotels, in restaurants. All places."

"That's a tall order."

"That's what we need."

They were interrupted by the arrival of the wine. He clinked her glass. "Mr. Robeson—" she began.

"Paul, please."

"What did you think of the show? Don't worry about offending me. I'd be honored to have your notes."

He stopped moving and concentrated as if working to put words together. There were other conversations going on throughout the restaurant. She could hear, "want to see it" and "worth the cost."

Paul spread his hands, palms down. "I loved it. I'm sorry I forgot to say. You have incredible appeal. People simply want to know you, to know what is behind your eyes." Then, making beautiful, stage-worthy hand gestures, he added, "You sing and they are hanging on to find out what you think, what you like, who you are . . . where to find the crack in your poise." He let his hands rest. "You're a stylist. A personality. And I guess you know you're beautiful."

"So I hear."

"People are going to seek you." He tipped his head toward other diners. "They already do. And critics, reviewers—they're already in your pocket." Then he leaned forward and said more quietly, "People sometimes take you for white, I know."

"Some do."

"They tell you to pass."

"Some, yes. Used to."

"I don't have that particular battle. Nobody doubts I'm a Negro." He smiled.

She could sense his will, his *willfulness*; it pressed against the air around him.

"I work hard," he said, as if to answer her. "But lots of other people work hard too. I think what I have is anger and also *lust* for all the good things. It's a pretty good combination, anger and lust. When you want the best of life. Do you have that determination?"

"I don't know that I do," she answered honestly.

The stew arrived. Both of them dug in, and it *was* delicious.

"You have been doing well, don't get me wrong. You do it by being a silvery mermaid in the waters, so elusive, so appealing, so . . . *safe* might be the word I want."

She stopped to take in what he said. Damn. *Safe*, again. Safe.

"If only you could do it as a Negro. I want you to fight."

"How? Fight where?"

"Anywhere. For the rights of our people. Speak out. Keep speaking out. People will listen to you."

She said, "I'll try."

"Are you happy here in New York?"

She nodded. "Everything is wonderful right now. I love Café Society. I'm back in Brooklyn, living in the house I grew up in."

"That grand house!" He squashed the last of his bread in the juice of the stew.

"My father let me rent it from him. My children are wonderful. I've had my son with me for the last month. Oh, God, that's the *most* wonderful thing. It's only a loan, that's what Louis says, but . . . I keep thinking surely he'll change his mind. I can't wait to have Teddy all the time."

Robeson listened. He seemed to understand.

When they finished eating, he told her he wanted her to come to a meeting of the NAACP the next day. "In time we'll make you bolder."

"I'm actually shy," Lena said.

"I know."

"Oh."

"And afraid of fights," he added with a raise of the eyebrows. "But we can change that. Lust and anger. Remember that."

He paid for their meal, helped her into her warm coat, and whistled for a taxi.

A taxi stopped immediately in front of him while two more screeched in behind it.

ELEVEN

1941

THERE HAD BEEN FEW CUSTOMERS TONIGHT, AND NOW NOTHING.
Outside it was snowing so heavily Marie could hardly see anything, and
the snow was inching up fast. She had wanted to leave earlier but was
too afraid her employers would get angry, and now she was stuck. All
evening as she watched the snow swirling crazily she wished her father
would call some Lebanese man with a car to come and pick her up. But
it hadn't happened. And after a while, she became aware she hadn't
seen a streetcar going past. The few automobiles that were out earlier
had skidded this way and that, sometimes hitting each other or the curb
or a pole. The streetcars were probably stranded.

The size of her plight became more and more clear to her. She didn't
have boots with her; it was going to be a horrible walk home. She went
to the front window, leaned hard against the glass, and saw, way, way up
the street, just what she had feared: a streetcar off its tracks. It looked
lonely and strange, like a huge abandoned carcass.

Would Fran or Selma come find her, carrying boots? Someone?

For a while she considered curling up on the floor of the back room with her beautiful coat over her, but that meant being alone all night in the shop, which was fairly cold. So she tried to persuade herself the streets weren't as bad as they looked.

Finally, at ten thirty, she emerged from the shop, determined to get home, knowing full well her only decent shoes were going to be totally ruined in the walk and that she would have to work hard not to fall. She turned to close the door of the candy shop but stopped when a sound pierced the air—a car backfiring, she thought. Then again. Twice. Then she heard a shout, followed by another shout. She was pressed against the door of the shop to keep it from blowing open, but she turned enough to see a car moving fast through the white haze, skittering so wildly she thought it was going to jump the curb and hit her. She stayed tight against the door and turned to see the car finally gaining traction and driving off. Up the other way was another car sitting right in the middle of the street. The driver in that car sounded his horn once, brief- ly, and, she thought the weak sound was probably a call for help. There must have been an accident. Or was the car stalled? A man was running toward the car. *Good,* she thought. Help was coming. The wind whipped blades of snow at her.

A piece of paper soared down the street and toward her face, and at the last second slapped against the window of the shop and fell. She looked back up the street. It appeared the man who had approached the car was saying something to the driver and the driver was saying some- thing to him. The man on the street looked frantic; he looked about— up and down the street—perhaps trying to find someone else. Did he see her? He started to move in her direction.

From Wood Street a police car appeared, siren blaring. Then a sec- ond police car came up the street from Stanwix.

By that time the two cops from the first car had accosted the pedes- trian and slammed him against a building and begun handcuffing him. It was hard for her to see much more. She was at the wrong angle. She opened the shop again and went back in. Her good coat was covered with snow, half an inch thick. She sat in the dark watching the street, and the snow kept coming down. At one point two men from the sec- ond vehicle carried a stretcher to the man in the car and got him onto it. The pedestrian had been put into the first cop car, which she saw starting off.

She tried to think, to understand what she had just seen. She wasn't sure of parts of it. Was the pedestrian a killer who threatened the people in the car that had driven off so wildly? And then assaulted the man in the stalled car? She felt she'd been watching a film and somehow missed some crucial frame that would explain it all and that she would have to read *Movie Stories* after the fact to find out what her eyes didn't catch.

Her heart pounded for a long time, especially when she thought of that crazy car, sliding, going fast. If she'd tried to cross the street as it careened, she'd probably have been killed.

Later, after the street cleared of police and she had sat miserably in the back room, in the dark, still wearing her coat, she decided to risk going home, and so she set out. The piece of paper that hit her was outside the door, now stuck to it. She looked at the soggy paper for only a second. Handwritten was *Jean Arthur . . .* and then she couldn't make out the rest. She let go and the paper flew away on the wind. She began walking home.

She could barely step through the deep snow, and got stuck several times. Her soaked shoes kept threatening to come off. For a while a man walked behind her, then beside her. He was young and not particularly clean-looking, dressed only in a thin coat, and she couldn't think what help to ask him for. Suddenly he bounded ahead—or tried to, sliding once, placing his legs more carefully after, perhaps fearing she might ask something of him and hold up his progress.

One car came by later—drifting dangerously toward her before the driver got it under control. He rolled down his window. "You want to get in?"

Marie shook her head and the driver moved on.

When she was three-quarters of the way home a full hour later, she saw Fran with her bad walk dragging toward her. Fran had not thought to bring boots.

"Oh, poor honey. I *made* Ummah talk to me. I asked if you came home and she said no. Did you think of staying?"

Marie's teeth were chattering so badly she could hardly answer. "I thought of it."

"I tried to figure what you would do. On the radio they're calling it a terrible blizzard and saying it's a disaster. Nobody should be out, they said."

It took a long time, but Fran got her home. The next day Marie, who had always been frail, was so clearly ill with a high fever that neither of her parents balked at paying the cost to call a doctor to the house. The doctor diagnosed pneumonia and insisted she not get out of bed for a full week.

Her family piled all the covers they could find on her. They forced her to take in warm liquids. She shook with chills. Once she was warm enough, she slept fitfully through the night and morning, tossing, lost in the illness.

Downstairs at the store they stocked the *Pittsburgh Post-Gazette* and the *Sun-Telegraph*. When Marie was alert enough to think, she asked for a newspaper. Fran had simply forced her presence in the house to take care of Marie. She brought hot broth and hot tea, and she fetched the newspaper when Marie asked for it. All the while, Ummah and Pap refused to talk to Fran and moved past her as if she weren't there at all.

Marie learned the following facts. The man she saw in the car in the middle of the street had died. He was a businessman named Klein. He supplied restaurants with cash registers, cigarette machines, and jukeboxes. He died of a gunshot wound—the sound she heard—from an assailant who shot into his automobile. Oh, she had known something was wrong, she had felt her heart stop at the sound and yet tried to tell herself it was nothing. She read that a young man who was a resident of the Lower Hill had been apprehended at the scene and had been arrested for the murder.

Then she read his name.

Josiah Conner. Josiah Conner! How could that be. . . . She fought a deadening fatigue to remember the sequence of events—the shot, then . . . then, the pedestrian beside the car.

She tried to read the article again from the start, but her illness won and she fell into sleep and later drifted back up to consciousness, feeling confused, knowing there was something important she had to do. What was it? She could hear squeals of joy on the street—kids who didn't have school, playing in the deep snow.

The newspaper was gone. Her mother must have taken it. She managed to sit up; as she came more and more out of sleep, she realized she needed to talk to someone.

After sliding out of bed she grabbed onto furniture to support herself as she stumbled toward the stairs, only to find her mother ascending with another bowl of broth. "Y'allah!" Her mother indicated with pushing gestures that Marie should go back to bed.

Marie retreated. That small exertion had already made it hard to breathe, let alone speak. She climbed back into bed and in a muted, raspy voice said, "Ummah, I think I should talk to the police. Will you call them? Uh, about . . . it's in the paper . . . a *murder*." She slowed herself down more so her mother would understand. "They arrested . . . a man. I think the man they arrested was . . . trying to help."

"What you talk about?" Her mother pulled the covers up over her.

Oh, it felt good to lie down. She said weakly, "The night I stayed late. I saw something."

Her mother put the bowl down on the bureau, and in clear exasperation, said, "You no talk to police."

Marie got a coughing spell but managed to say, "I think they made a mistake." She raised herself up as well as she could, and, conserving breath, explained, "They arrested a Negro boy I know. But I saw what happened. There was another car on the street."

"You talk, somebody shoot you." With all the certainty in the world, her mother announced, "The boy is bad if they write it."

Boy? Man? The room spun. Marie wanted to describe what she'd seen but telling it to her mother was hopeless.

Her mother looked frightened. "You very sick."

Marie, shivering again, let her mother tuck the blankets tight.

LENA WAS IN town to return Teddy to her husband. To do so, she had caught a train to Pittsburgh, where Louis, feeling his power, insisted she leave Gail with him for as long as she was in town. She was miserable. A huge snow had begun and Louis wouldn't let Lena sleep at his house, so she'd made it to her father's hotel just in time to be trapped by the blizzard. She missed her babies desperately but she hadn't even tried to go out last night. Now she could see through the window the result—

deep snow everywhere. Almost nothing was operating. A new problem: How would she get Gail and herself back to New York?

She lay in bed until afternoon, trying to ignore her hunger.

When she came down to the ground floor, she found her father shoving advertisements about a concert into cubbyholes. *Bad night at the card table?* she almost joked, but she stopped herself. His face . . . he was terribly agitated.

The hotel was quiet, almost empty. She could smell something from the kitchen, a burnt-coffee smell.

She put her arms around her father and could feel his muscles tensing. "Daddy? What? What's the matter?"

He pulled away from her and collapsed into the only chair behind the counter—the rolling chair that was too short for the height of the front desk and was where Pete sat when he was in charge. Then her father reached to a pocket under the desk and took out his copy of the daily newspaper. "You don't know, I guess."

"Know what?"

"Bad news. The kid you talked to out back all those times? Conner's son."

"Josiah?"

He looked up at her, handed the paper over like he might a court summons, levelly, carefully. "Read. Go on. Read. He's arrested for murder."

"Not Josiah." She searched her father's face, and when he nodded, she grabbed the paper and tried to read.

"What kind of things did he say to you?"

She didn't answer because she was desperate to read.

When she looked up her father looked small in the chair, almost frail. His voice was hoarse when he asked, "Were you still in touch with him? I hope you weren't still in touch with him."

"Daddy. This makes no sense. Something is wrong. . . . It can't be Josiah. He's maybe the kindest person I ever met." Her stomach was instantly sick, her heart erratic. "I don't believe it." Her father shook his head. She said impatiently, "Someone must have attacked him."

"Read the paper. He was robbing some white guy. That's what they say."

The paper said there was a gun involved, a driver killed. She lowered the paper, repeating, "He wouldn't do that."

"We never know people, do we? Louis wasn't who you thought he was."

"That's different. Daddy. Where is Josiah's father?"

"I don't know. I'm sure he doesn't want to lift his head up."

"I hope he's fighting. I hope to hell he's fighting."

Lena took the paper to one of the four chairs in the small lobby. She began to read the article in earnest from the start again.

MAN ARRESTED IN BLIZZARD ROBBERY
BUSINESSMAN SHOT ON FIFTH AVENUE

Joseph Arthur Klein, co-owner of K & K Business Machines, was pronounced dead at Pittsburgh Hospital after a shooting late on Tuesday night. He was in his car alone when accosted by a 21-year-old youth in an apparent hold-up. The gunshot was from close range and Klein died on the way to the hospital.

There were no witnesses. The city was in the grip of the snowstorm that had emptied the streets. It was only by chance that a patrol car driving the city streets in expectation of auto accidents happened upon the victim and his assailant. The assailant was Josiah Conner, a recent graduate of Fifth Avenue High School. He claimed he was in the downtown area to see a movie. He is being held in the Allegheny County Jail. Bond has been denied.

Klein founded the business with his brother Howard in 1927. They built it from a small store that repaired typewriters and other machines used in businesses and expanded over the years to include large machines used by restaurants. Once Prohibition ended, their customers numbered many owners of bars in the Tri-State area.

Joseph Klein lived in Squirrel Hill with his wife, Madeline, and two sons, Michael and David.

The article was hardly about Josiah at all. "Where's the *Courier*?"

"Not out yet. Anyway, everything is held up. I guess you want coffee."

"I wouldn't mind."

"I'll start a fresh pot. I could make you toast."

"I'll come help. Can I take the paper?"

"Take it."

If she read it a hundred times it would not make sense of the boy she knew.

They went into the kitchen.

"I was heating up some coffee earlier, forgot it," he said.

"I smelled it." She now saw a burnt saucepan.

She let her father make her toast and a fresh cup of coffee. She asked him about the game of cards he'd played the afternoon before and about the two current guests at the hotel, quiet people in to visit relatives. She understood that he thought Josiah's arrest reflected on him and her and their whole race.

When the breakfast was finished, she went upstairs for her coat and came down and told her father she was going to visit her kids. Instead, she started through the snow to downtown, to the jail.

She prepared herself to be very polite, calm, and even-tempered. The sidewalks were slippery and unshoveled in many places. She moved from sidewalk to street and back as she could, slowly, wondering if she could have been wrong about Josiah, but her heart kept renewing her faith in him. She needed to speak to him.

Finally she got to the jail.

The desk sergeant at first brightened at her approach. "Yes, ma'am?" Behind him three officers worked at file cabinets or desks, but did not look up.

"I came to visit Josiah Conner—you've just arrested him. I'm concerned."

"I'm sorry you came all this way in the weather. He is not allowed visitors."

"No one?"

"His lawyer."

"Does he have a lawyer?"

"He'll get one eventually."

The desk sergeant paused, looking harder at her, working out that she was Negro. He took a big breath.

"Can I help to hire him one?"

His eyebrows went up. People offering money was not so usual. "I suppose we could send that message on to him. You want to write down your name?"

"Yes."

"Are you family?"

"No. A friend. Who *can* I talk to? I know this boy. He's ambitious, a wonderful, smart boy." The officer stared at her, eyes glazing over. She continued in spite of the boredom he was showing her. "I just know there is some big mistake being made."

Now his eyes focused sharply. "You saying we don't know what we're doing?"

"No. Just . . . something is wrong. I feel it."

There was the *rat-tat-tat* of a typewriter then, and the whoosh of papers being filed. And she could hear voices rising in contention in a hallway behind the office area.

The desk sergeant studied her, making a sort of chewing motion. "Women get feelings. They aren't always right. I'll pass on your name when the time comes to figure out who will represent him, unless he doesn't want someone."

"Surely he needs a lawyer. He's smart but not, you know, showy. He's interested in making movies and getting out to Hollywood."

"Maybe he was looking for money for a train ticket to get him there," the man said with a forced grin.

"Is there some way I can talk to him, even briefly?"

The desk sergeant shook his head. "We don't run things like that. This is jail. He already walked the Bridge of Sighs. He knows he did a crime and he has to be locked up. He's not a boy, either, by the way. He's fully adult."

Lena dashed at tears. "Please tell him I want to help. Tell him I'll help in any way I can."

He handed her a piece of paper. She wrote her name and address.

Another officer came up behind the desk sergeant. He had been half listening in these last moments and not much continuing to write whatever report he had been engaged in writing. The desk sergeant handed this man the paper with Lena's name and address on it. "Give this to someone," he said.

To someone. Did that mean it was going into the wastebasket?

Lena left, shaken, not wanting in the least to learn what Louis would say once he knew Josiah had been jailed.

When she found a *Courier* the next day, she read it hungrily. At least this one was about Josiah.

LOCAL MAN ACCUSED OF MURDER

Josiah S. Conner, 21, has been accused of killing businessman Joseph Klein on Monday night around 10 p.m. when the city streets were nearly empty because of the blizzard. Conner was found at the car where Klein was bleeding badly of a gunshot wound.

Conner, who had blood on his hands, said he was trying to help the wounded man. When questioned about what he was doing downtown, he said he had been to a movie. He was unable to produce a ticket stub. He said he often saved them but that he must have lost this one.

He has been jailed without bail. A trial is estimated to be scheduled in 6 months. No gun was found at the scene.

The accused has insisted there were occupants of another car nearby at the time of the killing. Police are hoping if there was another car in the vicinity that the occupants will come forward if they have information. No other witnesses were present.

Conner is the son of plumber Josiah Conner, Sr. Mr. Conner states that his son has been wrongfully jailed and that he will work to make sure the investigation proceeds fairly.

Lena took out a piece of her father's stationery and began a letter to the jail, to Josiah, trying to explain she had to get back to her job at Café Society but that she would do whatever she could for him, that she would keep tabs from New York by calling her father to find out what was going on.

She mailed the letter herself, not wanting to trust it to anyone else. She was furious with the system. The anger Robeson had insisted she needed was there in her, of course it was there, and it frightened her.

A day later she gathered her bits of clothing and the gift of a scarf from her father and Irene, and she got herself and her daughter on the train for New York.

A WEEK AND a day after Marie fell ill, she insisted on going back to work. Selma was nervous about it. "But you aren't even better yet," she agonized. "What's Ummah going to say?"

"Tell Ummah the owner wants me to do something special with the candy orders." Mrs. K had actually told Marie to take her time to get fully better.

"I hate to lie."

"I know." She patted her little sister on the head. "Hey. It's okay."

Selma offered, "You look nice, though."

"Do I?"

Selma arranged and rearranged candy bars. "Want something?"

"Yes—candy, sugar." She already had her little supper of bologna on pita bread in her handbag, a package she'd made Selma prepare for her so she didn't have to get into an argument with her mother. She was using the little mirror she kept in her purse, applying rouge and lipstick before leaving because she didn't want to wait until she got to the candy store. She had a stop to make.

Selma finished counting the pennies in the drawer, then cupped a palm full of penny candy for herself and another for Marie's outstretched hand. "For while you walk."

Marie slipped on her good coat, which was three years old but still looked new. It had survived the snow.

Selma carefully unwrapped one of her candies. "When you wear that coat you look like a rich person."

"Good."

"Are you meeting a man?"

"No. I wish, but no."

Selma followed Marie to the door. "You're buying something?"

"Yes," Marie said decisively.

Outside she pulled the coat more tightly around her and detoured a few blocks over to a police station, where she hoped nobody she knew would see her.

Finally an officer emerged from a back room.

"Yes?"

"I have information about the murder of that man Klein."

"What information? You knew him?"

"Oh, no. It's just that I was downtown and the behavior of that boy Conner was not like a person who did a shooting. Or a robbery. So I want to explain—"

"Ma'am. That's all long past. It's going to trial."

"I know. I saw the paper."

"You're saying you want to be a witness?"

"I guess so."

"I don't know why you would want that, but you probably need his lawyer. You need to tell somebody who could do something."

"How do I do that? Where should I go?"

"You know how to get to the jail down on Ross? They might know who his lawyer is going to be."

A lawyer. She hadn't thought of it that way. She'd imagined talking to a detective. But maybe that was just in the movies. She thanked the policeman and started out again, warmed a little from being indoors for a moment, and she made the familiar walk to the downtown, ending with an unfamiliar jog over to the county jail, which was in the court-house, a big, impressive stone building. The place was from another world, where people who knew about crimes and law dashed back and forth, making momentous decisions. The edifice itself was huge and there were, even now, probably, trials going on inside.

It took several attempts, asking directions, to get to the section that housed the jail. Her footsteps echoed in the cavernous hallways.

Finally she found the right office. Nobody paid her any mind. Men in uniforms talked on phones and another officer angrily slammed a file cabinet shut and in the corner, halfway out in the hallway, a young offi-cer appeared to berate an old officer. She waited, standing, then sank to a wooden bench. The young officer who was giving the old one a hard time glanced over at her but went back to his task.

Finally a more senior-looking officer came to the desk. "What is it this time?"

His question puzzled her, but she managed to rise and say, "I wanted to talk to someone about the murder of that man, Mr. Klein. I was told I need the boy's lawyer."

"We handed your name over to our legal guy. No word yet about what's happening. You didn't need to come back."

"I was never here," she said. "You don't have my name."

"You were here."

"No, no, that can't be. I work in the York Candy Shop. I was working that night—when it happened. I think I saw something."

"What are you trying to say?"

"Just . . . I saw a car on the street. Another car. After the shot, the other car left. Really fast."

"Wouldn't you leave? If some kid was shooting up the street?"

She took a deep breath. "I think it wasn't Josiah . . . shooting. That's what I want to explain to someone. Can you tell me who the detective is on the case? Or the lawyer? If I could talk to someone, anyone—"

"Lady . . ."

She waited, but there was nothing coming from him except irritation. She forged ahead. "What I need to report is that it was more likely . . . somebody in the other car. So shouldn't I tell someone? What I saw?"

"Please. I know you're concerned. I understand." He stared at her. He spoke again but with less certainty now, as if her face didn't quite look right or make sense to him. "Once again, we are doing our best. And there are rules. And once again, you cannot go back to see him."

Dizzy with confusion, she crumpled onto the bench again.

She'd been talking in a dream and nothing in the dream world was making sense.

"Are you all right?"

"I had pneumonia. Maybe that's it."

"You take it easy. We'll make sure he gets a lawyer."

"I came the whole way down here to—"

"We'll look into it. You can leave now. We're busy."

She got up from the bench.

A young man came and asked, "Anything I need to do?"

"Nothing," said the middle-aged one, "except maybe log it in the book that Mrs. Jones came back."

The younger man walked away. The older man nodded her a dismissal and went back to his work.

Walking out of the building, she heard in her head, *Mrs. Jones*, and she realized who they thought she was.

THEY SAT AT a small bar near Café Society.

Robeson listened.

Lena had met him to tell him she couldn't speak at an event he wanted her for because her life was upside-down.

"And I'm going to have to let down Barney Josephson—oh, he doesn't deserve it, he's been wonderful to me, wonderful, but the thing is, well, I have another offer and it's for a club in LA."

Robeson's lips tightened. He put his hands up as if to say he was still listening.

"*And* the divorce is dragging on and on and it's really . . . ugly. I try everything to see my son. On top of all this I have a friend accused of murder. Josiah. A boy I've been friends with for a long time. I know the police have to be wrong."

Robeson finally nodded. "Many things," he said.

"Why does everything happen at once?" she asked.

"It's always that way. I take comfort from the writers."

"I don't understand."

"I played Claudius once. 'When sorrows come, they come not single spies / But in battalions. First, her father slain: / Next, your son gone; and he most violent author / Of his own just remove: the people muddied . . . ' et cetera."

"You're showing off."

"Yes. Or Shaw. I always think of the cavalry charge he describes. First one pea hits the window, then a couple more, then the rest rain down like crazy."

"Showoff."

"Yes. I know what you're thinking. I see you. I see what you're running *to*. Dreams of Hollywood, huh?"

Embarrassed that he'd seen through her, she looked away. If she got to LA—everyone said it—maybe she'd be discovered for a movie.

"Stay here. The divorce will do whatever it does, not in your control. Work to help your friend. Speak up."

"I will. I do. I did. I went to the jail to see about a lawyer for him."

"Write letters, go to the jail again, talk about it. See? Be noisy. Another drink?"

"Yes."

"You're going to California, aren't you?"

"I think I am."

When Joe Samuels from the *Courier* came to interview Lena on a Friday afternoon in late January about the rumors that she had been offered a job in California, she decided she would manipulate the conversation to fit in what she had to say about Josiah.

They were in her Brooklyn house for the interview.

Edwina, good as always, brought tea and cookies. Samuels, fastidious and slightly pudgy, took one bite of one cookie, looked at the crumbs on his tie, brushed them into his hand, and never took another bite.

Lena said, "I want to tell you about something in Pittsburgh where I was just visiting. A young man I know is in jail. It's surely a wrongful arrest—"

"Could we save that for later? Your other news is why they sent me. Is it definite you're going to California? Eyes set on Hollywood?"

She recited the speech she'd rehearsed. "It's true that I am going to California, but it's to sing at a new club they're building out there. It's called the Trocadero. I mean, I love Café Society here; it's been wonderful to me, but entertainers are more national these days and California wants entertainment like what we have in the East. So a new nightclub out there, with music that people want to hear—it's exciting. A new enterprise."

She watched him writing fast.

"You have nothing to report about movies?"

"Nothing at all."

He changed tack. "Is there a man in your life?" Samuels examined his tie for further crumbs, but only briefly. He mostly looked up and then down to write.

Now, what the heck did that have to do with Hollywood? She'd rehearsed. She answered, "No. I'm too busy."

"Are you divorcing your husband?"

"I have no such plans." Of course, any day now someone would leak the court documents but until then she would downplay the ugliness. Her face got hot. In spite of the blush she could feel the whole way up to her eyes, she added, "Louis and I are working long-distance to be good to each other and good parents to our children. A career performing has all kinds of challenges."

"I'm sure it does. But you meet important people every day. You know the major big band leaders."

"Yes, many of them."

"And Paul Robeson."

"He's like another father to me here in New York."

"And he's a wonderful actor. Has he given you advice about Hollywood?"

"No, not at all." A complete lie! Said smoothly.

"Are you tempted by Hollywood?"

"Who isn't? I don't know what it takes to break in in a serious way. There was this boy in Pittsburgh, the one I was telling you about, the one who was arrested, and he studied movies all the time. He knew how hard it was. I do want to tell you about him. You see, he—"

"Just a sec. Acting lessons, then? From Robeson?"

She was able to laugh at that question. "He's much too busy. He's political. Involved in the NAACP."

"Is that what you meet about?"

"Yes."

"Are *you* political?"

"Not quite full-time, but I'm starting to learn what I can do. For instance—"

"Why the NAACP in particular?"

"It's a very good organization. My family helped found it, in fact."

"So when you spend time with Robeson, it's political?"

"Yes."

"What will happen, out in California, when—notice I am saying *when* and not if—Hollywood comes calling you? You'll be singing. Someone will discover you, surely, if that hasn't already happened. 'I want to put you in movies,' that person will say. 'You are a natural.'"

"Is that what they'll say?" she tried to tease.

"I'm sure of it."

"I think many women have heard that line. I'll have to be the judge of the speaker."

"And?"

"Who knows? Perhaps it will happen. I don't say yes to things easily, you know."

"You're hard to get."

"Very."

When he left, Edwina said they should go upstairs to see which clothes would be suitable for when she made the trip to Los Angeles.

She followed Edwina, complaining that she hadn't been able to talk about Josiah. On the other hand, it would help if Josiah would write back to her and tell her what was happening. Did they give him paper, stamps? She wasn't sure how those things worked.

Edwina held up items, judging them, checking for unraveling threads. Meanwhile Lena studied herself in the full-length mirror of the bedroom, wondering if she was ready for her California days. She was thinner—to the good, people said. It was torture being slender. She loved to eat.

Hollywood. Robeson hated it and she wanted it, just like any other dumb kid thinking about big-screen fame.

THE FIRST THING Marie did after her visit to the jail was to write a letter to Lena. The Davids didn't have real stationery in their house, so notebook paper would have to do. She used the Belmont Hotel address because she wasn't sure where Lena was from week to week.

> *I know this is not good stationery but I am not good at letters and I want to get this in the mail and not go to the store for real paper. You know me from when I worked on your skirt. I wish you luck in your career. But I want to tell you about a strange thing that happened. I was working in the downtown the night that Josiah Conner was arrested. I could see that he was the person trying to help. I think I saw the car of the person who shot Mr. Klein. I tried to tell the police but they didn't want to listen to me. Also when I went to the jail they thought at first I was you coming back a second time. I know that's crazy but they got us mixed up. Anyway, so that is how I learned that we were both trying to do something for him. So if you have a way of getting them to listen, do it and I will tell what I saw. I will try again with them.*

She sealed and sent the letter before she could feel too foolish.

Then she wrote to Josiah in jail and said pretty much the same thing. At least he could tell his lawyer there was a witness willing to come forward.

A few weeks later she wrote a second letter to Josiah. She did not get a letter back from him and that at first irritated her, and then it saddened her. For a while she gave up. But then she told herself it was possible these things took time. She even allowed herself the question: Had Josiah avoided writing because he did the deed? She couldn't make the idea stick.

She thought he might be despondent, maybe even sick.

So, one day in May she went back to the jail. She'd been counting months and the trial was supposed to happen in June or July. When she stood before the desk sergeant, she asked, "With the trial for Josiah Conner coming soon, I thought I should come back. If you could give me the name of his lawyer—"

"Does he have a lawyer? I don't know. Maybe the warden would be up on this. Were you one of his girlfriends?"

"No. We went to Fifth Avenue."

"School buddy?"

"Yes."

He shook his head. His expression completely communicated that he found her of questionable morals and wanting in sense. "Let me see if the warden is around. He keeps track of things."

She sat on the bench for almost an hour. She thought she would finally have to leave when a man opened the gate and sat down beside her. He puffed a little because he wore significant weight. "I don't have long. I'm the warden. Schmidt. You the one asking about the Conner fellow?"

"Yes. His trial—"

"Oh, they put that off."

"Until when?"

"That's a good question. We have some that get put off for six years or thereabouts."

Six *years.* "I have information. I need to tell his lawyer. But I don't have a name."

"Barney McKenna, the lawyer."

"Would I find him in the phone book?"

"Think so. Not that I have anything to do with it, but . . ." he asked in a low voice, "what kind of information do you have?"

"I wrote to Josiah. Three times, offering my help."

"He doesn't get any letters. Sure you wrote?"

"Yes. Are you saying he doesn't know I was downtown that night? I mean, I saw . . . sort of saw . . ." The warden made a face Marie could not interpret. She explained, "I was working. I saw another car leaving after the shot. When I put the whole picture together, you know, it seems Josiah went to where the man was shot to help."

The warden rubbed at his jaw. "Brave of you. Coming forward. That's not much to go on . . ."

"I guess not."

"Barney McKenna. Tell him you'd come forward. He's been stalling. Who knows how long? Sometimes, like I say, they put it off for a long, long time."

"That's awful. And letters aren't allowed?"

He looked at her kindly. "Allowed, yes. Maybe something went lost in the mailroom."

"Is Josiah all right?"

He waited to answer. "For a long time, I'd say no. Almost didn't eat. I thought . . . he wasn't going to make it." The warden tapped his head. "I put him as my assistant. Gave him library work. And he started reading. He's our biggest reader. Reads everything in sight. It took a while but he woke up to wanting a lawyer."

So she had to do something; she was right.

The warden took a small notebook out of his shirt pocket. "I should maybe get your name for myself." He handed her the notebook and pen.

She wrote her name and address. "Thank you," she managed to say as she handed it back, but she was tearing up and couldn't say the rest. *For talking to me.*

Only a couple of days later, Marie dredged up her courage once more and composed a letter to Barney McKenna, whose name she found in the phone directory.

TWELVE

1941

LONELY, WHO COULD GUESS HOW LONELY SHE WAS, HOW SHE missed her father, her children. But she was in California and waiting, waiting for the club to open, tuning up her pipes every morning, and tonight she was sitting in a theater seat, seeing *Jump for Joy*—an Ellington show, and her ticket had come from the Duke himself. The second act was about to begin when suddenly the seat next to her was no longer vacant. She turned to see a slim, bespectacled man smiling at her. "I'm Swee' Pea," he said. "Been dying to meet you."

"Swee' Pea! You're Billy?"

"Duke wanted us to meet."

"He did. I know he did! He talks about you all the time."

Billy Strayhorn had the friendliest face she had ever seen. She'd never met him until now, even though he was from Pittsburgh. He gave her a warm smile and grasped her hand as if they had known each other all their lives.

The boy genius was a musician, a composer, a lyricist; he could do it all. "How is it for you out here?" he asked.

"Hard. The Trocadero hasn't opened yet. There's nothing for me to do."

"I heard that. Waiting is the hardest thing."

And then the Ellington orchestra began to play again, and it felt as if the two of them were being lifted on a balloon of good feeling. The whole way through the second half of *Jump for Joy*, Billy Strayhorn held Lena's hand.

Quietly, people always dropped the fact that his relationships were with men. Lena wasn't shocked by that.

"We'll do things together," he said when the show ended. "We'll kill time by using it."

That night they went to an after-hours club. She told him her whole life story—New York, the South, Pittsburgh, her mother, her father, her love for movies, Josiah, her husband, her children. He told her about his high school days, his love of music, the prizes he won (though she'd heard about them) and about a man he was often with. They talked for three hours.

The next day they went to a little restaurant and talked again. Swee' Pea looked up at the waitress and ordered two pieces of apple pie.

Lena started. "How did you know what I wanted?"

"It was what I wanted, so I figured . . . I'm sorry if—"

"No! I've been dreaming about apple pie!"

That's how it was with them. Happy. They might have been five-year-olds, playing, loving life. She thought, *If only I could marry* him *and be with him all the time. Bliss.*

MARIE NEVER GOT a letter back from the lawyer. She felt invisible once more. In July and August she made four calls from the newly installed phone in the candy shop to his office, leaving messages. It wasn't until September that she got a call back from his secretary and got an appointment.

McKenna was a large, craggy man with bloodshot eyes. By the time Marie got to him she felt beaten, silly. Nobody *wanted* her testimony. And her parents would kill her if they knew she was getting herself involved.

In fact, the first thing McKenna asked was, "Why do you want to put yourself forward?"

She couldn't think what to say, except, "I thought I should."

McKenna had a heavy look. Not weight, but manner, bogged him down. "What do you know about the justice system?"

"Nothing."

"Nothing?"

"What I see in the movies? Trials, people coming forward."

He fidgeted, rubbing at one eyebrow. "So you want to be a heroine?"

"I don't know about that, no."

"Tell me what you think you saw."

She talked. He wrote it down, at least. That made her feel somewhat useful. "Will you tell him I came here?"

"I . . . can do that."

"Do you know when the trial will be?"

"It's indefinite."

"How awful."

"Sometimes that's better. Things change, people change, don't try to push it."

She left. She had had to beg Mrs. K to stay in the shop until four so she could get to this appointment. Hurrying down the street, she realized she had done all she could and she felt empty now, both lightened and without the preciousness of a secret courage.

Done. The end of something bigger than her small life.

One Tuesday in early October a man came into the shop and she noticed him at first standing politely near the doorway, opening the door for others. The shop was unusually busy, customers streaming in before the start of the fall movies that had hit town. It was just cold enough that people's breaths were making brief cloudy puffs in the air outside. Soon it would be very cold.

Finally the shop was empty and the man was still there. He approached the counter. "Hello. I . . . You don't know me, but my mother and sister used to come in here. Regularly. Going to the movies, you know. They would always talk about you."

She knew immediately somehow that he meant the two women who had appeared to be scrutinizing Mr. Lofton. They hadn't been in for a while. "I can guess who you mean. Movies? Tuesday nights?" she asked.

He nodded.

"Very nice people."

"Many times they said they wanted me to come meet you. I've been busy. But here I am."

"And they? Are they coming tonight?"

"My mother died. Three months ago."

"Oh. Oh, I'm sorry."

"Yes." Now that she could see him clearly, he looked a little like his mother and sister. He was one of her people, Arabic, but he also had blue eyes and light skin—very light, actually. Perhaps the marauding Swedes had happened upon his family.

He appeared to study the chocolates for a long time. She tried to determine what he might like but he didn't say anything for a while.

Finally he looked up and added, "My sister knew your sister a little, too, I think from church."

He meant Fran, then. Did he know the worst? Harry Lesoon had gotten Fran pregnant and then deserted her, just run off to another city, and now Fran was alone, nearly divorced, and on the way to being broke. Marie's parents would never get over it.

"Would you like me to package some candy?" she asked.

"I'm George, by the way. George Elias. Oh, yes, choose whatever you think is good. I was hoping to talk with you. Could I offer to walk you home when you're done?"

"I might get in trouble."

He frowned. "I wouldn't want anything like that."

This man was different from Federico, not dashing, just polite, fedora off and held lightly in one hand. So just talk. And walking. And maybe some candy.

Three giggling women came in, interrupting her answer. She served the women, aware that George buttoned a button on his overcoat and then unbuttoned it again.

When the women left, he said, "I have a restaurant. I just opened it—last month. I bought it five months ago and got it ready."

"Oh, that must be exciting."

"Exciting, yes. Also a worry. I'm afraid to leave it for long."

"There, I've chosen a half pound for you." She showed him.

"My mother liked you very much."

A duty call, a fix-up. "Oh, and I liked her."

He wasn't somebody she could get interested in, but she hoped to be civil. "What did you do before you bought the restaurant?"

"Everything. Worked for other people, tended bar, hauled lumber. Delivered newspapers when I was a boy."

"Our people always have jobs."

"I know. Do you work many hours here?"

"Just usually a bit over forty. I could get more but I work in our store at home, too."

"Are you warm enough in here?"

She had been tugging her cardigan about her. "Never. I put my coat on when there are no customers."

"They should raise the temperature. Or buy a heater."

"Maybe if I told them to, they would."

He paid for the candy. "Have you decided? About letting me walk you home tonight?"

"All right." It came out of her so suddenly she didn't feel herself deciding. "My name is Marie David."

"Oh, yes, well, I knew your name." He smiled.

He left for a bit and came back an hour later.

"Did you check on the restaurant?"

"Yes, I'd love to show it to you sometime."

On the way to her house, he told her about buying the business. It had been a tough decision; with the country coming out of the Depression, financial decisions had to be good ones. His mother told him she would tell him what to do in the morning, after she dreamed an answer. She woke up telling him yes, buy it. Also, she said, he should go to the candy shop to meet the beautiful woman who worked there if he were lucky enough to find her still there. "That's how she referred to you."

"Oh, well, thank you. And . . . she died three months ago?"

"Yes. It was sudden. My brother, my sisters, none of us expected it. The heart. She had a bad heart."

"I'm sorry."

"If you come to the restaurant—if you're willing, it's not terribly far—you can have whatever you'd like to eat. It's not a fancy place, but I try to make it good. It's just in Oakland. We live near there."

We. She wasn't sure what that meant.

"I almost never leave the business except to run to the liquor store to put in an order. I have a guy named Emil working it tonight. He's a third cousin."

Marie thought it was such a shame that this George was shy and had pushed himself to do this thing his mother wanted him to do and that she would not be able to love him even if he wanted it and her parents allowed it.

HER PARENTS WERE not at the window.

She did not get a beating.

George came calling the next Sunday and asked Marie's parents if he could take her on a date. "I'd like to take her to my restaurant when she has a night off."

Ummah and Pap asked about his family and about the restaurant. Finally they said yes.

He suggested a brief walk in the neighborhood that same afternoon, and her parents gave him a nod of approval.

The next Thursday George and Marie took a streetcar partway and walked the rest of the way to his restaurant, which was situated in a row of businesses on hilly Oakland Avenue. It held a counter and twelve booths. He brought her a menu. Hot Meatloaf Dinner Special and Chicken Pot Pie appealed to her because they were things she hadn't had, but they weren't the cheapest items on the menu. He watched her and said, "Anything." He joked, "Order two meals. Check things out."

Finally she chose a simple hamburger with French fries.

"That's what you truly want?"

"Yes."

It was a pleasant enough evening. They took the trolley back to her house.

A soda shop and another restaurant and several movies later and she did not have any idea how to let George down. Or how to let her parents down. She began to feel very nervous.

One morning Marie's mother said, "Sit. Watch me make bread."

Her mother's hands flew quickly, mixing the yeast with water, everything in the same pot—well, Ummah had done it a million times, almost a million. Marie, good with numbers, began to multiply: if her mother made bread every other day at least, that came to almost two hundred batches of dough a year times roughly twenty loaves each baking, times almost fifty years . . . well, okay, not a million.

Her mother said carefully, "I think George ask you marry him."

The flour, as her mother worked it, went from light powder to paste to wet dough so quickly. Marie loved when the smell of yeast pinched the air. Her mother nodded toward the pot. "Not too much water. Have to make fast."

Then a silence.

Marie broke the silence by saying, "I don't know what to do."

"You learn to love him."

"That's what happened with you and Pap?"

"Man and woman get to know each other and then forget everything else. So."

Marie got up and put an egg on to boil. Her mother looked irritated by that show of independence. Ummah wanted all cooking to come from her.

Marie slumped, waiting for her egg to boil.

George was quiet and kind. It was impossible not to *like* him. But love—well, that was another matter. Love caused some sort of wonderful craziness, didn't it? Not that she could ask her mother.

Ummah took the egg out of the pan and broke it open over a small bowl and scooped it out of its shell. She salted it and handed it to Marie, going back to her bread.

Marie ate quickly, got up from the table, and walked outside. She thought of all she would lose if she married. She would have to move from home—from the familiar sights and sounds. On the verge of tears, she began walking fast, first down to Washington Park, where she had played as a little girl, and, because nobody was on the swings, she went up to them and touched them, almost sitting down, almost letting herself sit and swing, but she stopped short. A few older boys were playing basketball today—they'd no doubt quit school as she had. She walked up to Cliff Street, where she used to roller-skate because it was smooth there, macadam, not cobblestone. When she got back to the streetcar tracks at Fullerton, she thought about the fun she and her friend Eleanor used to have putting caps on the tracks to make explosions.

Well, all right, she wanted to be a child forever.

If she did leave this place, she would come back often. Every other day.

She didn't know how to cook. George liked food, and what's more, knew more about it than she did. Her mother had invited him one evening to eat with them; he was crazy about her mother's bread, everybody was, but he traded ideas about the best ways to do the lamb and rice and yogurt and salad.

One night George came to the candy shop just to spend time with her. There were no customers, so they talked for quite a while and she used the time to straighten things in the cases. He told her he had to go to a meeting of the Moose Club the next night because his friend Howard Klein had put him up for membership. She didn't know what the Moose Club was.

"Routines, rituals, but also just friendship, drinking, jokes. A private club. And secret. I'm not supposed to talk about it."

"You shouldn't, then."

He laughed. "I don't care so much about it but Klein is a good guy. He's going through a lot. His brother was murdered."

Suddenly she stopped, all attention. "The Klein who was murdered?"

"Sure. You followed that story?"

She told him about the night she had been caught downtown in a blizzard and what she saw. Or thought she saw. And how she offered herself as witness, for the defendant. The opposition.

"You did?" He seemed disturbed by the news.

"I had to. I knew him. We would talk when we passed or he came into the shop. And the thing is, I don't think he could ever have done it."

"I don't think I'll mention this to Klein," he said with a trace of something like whimsy. "I didn't know you were so brave."

"Does he think they got the right man? Does he think the man they arrested is guilty?"

"I think he assumes so." George looked thoughtful. "You *are* kind of brave."

In mid-November, when George and Marie had taken the streetcar from downtown after her work because it was too cold to walk and she had invited him in, she sensed something different between them. His arms lingered at her shoulders as he helped her remove her coat. He whispered, "You are very beautiful."

She usually hung up their coats in the closet next to the small parlor off the grocery store and then they would go to the kitchen for a cup of tea.

But, removing his own coat, George asked, "Can we sit for a moment? In there?"

"Oh. Yes."

She couldn't hear her parents. They had not poked their heads out of the kitchen.

She and George sat on the brown short sofa Fran liked to call a loveseat. George produced the requisite small box, but did not go down on a knee, which Marie decided wouldn't have looked right. He was large, almost kingly. He said, "I know how lucky I'll be if you say yes. I want to marry you and I hope . . . you will say yes."

"Oh, dear." She had told herself she would not have to decide so soon.

His face and body sank.

Enormous sympathy washed over her. She reached out and touched his face. "It's all right. I mean, well, yes."

"Are you saying yes?"

"Yes."

Her mother and father were prepared for her answer, it turned out, because they appeared seconds later with a bottle of whiskey.

FRAN, ECSTATIC ABOUT Marie's upcoming wedding, insisted on using her own savings to buy Marie a dress. At the shop, Marie winced to have Fran's enthusiasms vocalized, but Marie loved the white gown "with a train!" that Fran got excited about, and so she accepted the gift.

George still lived in the house his whole family had once lived in, but now there was just George and his brother, Philip, who would be his best man. When Marie managed to say something at the dress shop to the effect that Selma would be her maid of honor, Fran's face dropped.

"I'm sorry. It's just . . ."

"I'm pregnant and abandoned," Fran murmured. After a few minutes, her smile, faltering at first, returned, then caught.

They began the walk toward the candy shop where Marie would start her day's work. George wanted her to quit at the candy shop (and at the store), to simply quit work altogether and be taken care of, but she agreed with Mrs. K to work up until the wedding.

Fran had many worries now, so her good spirits were all the more impressive. She expected to lose her job at the school once they realized she was pregnant. Ummah wouldn't let her come home. So she had begun making lace, sewing for people, all the while trying to locate her husband to formalize a divorce. She still lived in the apartment she had shared with Lesoon and would have to find ways to make the rent when the school system dropped her.

"You're so pretty," Fran said, outside the candy shop, before Marie went in for her shift.

"Am I? I wish I were good at things."

Fran frowned. "What do you want to be good at?"

"Anything. Something. I used to think I wanted to be discovered and be an actress. Stupid, huh? I'm only good at sewing and making change at a shop."

"Well, you—you *were* discovered, by George."

"Ha. Yes."

Marie loved her dress, but on the day of the wedding—a cold November Tuesday—there weren't many guests to admire it. The small affair was held at George's house, as some church weddings were in cold weather.

Altar cloths draped the dining room table, which was dotted with icons. George's two local sisters and their husbands were present, and his brother Philip stood as his best man. Selma and Fran were the only representatives for Marie. Ummah and Pap were working—his shift at the mill, hers at the store.

Old Father Malouf did not stint on one bit of ritual. He did not do a quick ceremony as the priest who had joined Alberto and Helena had that day in the yard. He chanted and keened his minor notes in Arabic for ninety minutes, at one point banging crowns back and forth on George's and Marie's heads so hard that he pushed Marie's hair down into her eyes.

Marie cried pretty much the whole way through the ceremony.

A maddening smell of kibbee and lamb roast and *loobyeh* and bread and spinach pies crept toward them from the kitchen—the bread from Ummah, the pies from Fran, the loobyeh and kibbee from the sisters-in-law. George himself had put the lamb leg in the oven.

Finally the priest removed the altar cloths. George kissed Marie briefly and hugged her, whispering, "We did it."

The husband of one of George's sisters took photographs while the sisters hurried to replace the altar cloths with table linens, plates, and serving dishes, the priest sat silently in a corner, and the brothers-in-law poured red wine. Marie, who had only ever tasted wine during communion and on her date with Federico, felt it go right to her knees again.

"A toast to Marie," George said, lifting his glass. "I am very lucky."

"You are lucky too," Fran whispered as everyone cheered and raised glasses. "So lucky," Fran repeated. "He's handsome."

"Is he?"

"Of course. Lots of women at church talked about him. They all wanted him."

"Sit, sit," the sisters-in-law said. "It's time for cake and coffee."

When Marie sat, George's brother took the seat beside her. The white cake was foamy with sweetness, the coffee good and strong. Marie told Philip, "I love coffee. I had it when I was twelve and I could never get enough."

"It's in our blood," he said. He winked at her. "You're a beauty. You make a good bride."

Sarah and Evelyn, the sisters-in-law, sat across from Marie. Sarah, the one she didn't know at all, asked for paper and wrote out recipes for chipped beef on toast and for something called salmon patties. Marie read the directions, frowning. "And meatloaf and macaroni and cheese are in the cookbook we gave you," Sarah said. "You can call if you have questions."

"Shame your parents couldn't come," Philip said quietly to Marie.

She felt herself flush. "They're always working." She'd been comforting herself with the memory of the newspaper report about Lena Horne's mother and stepfather and father-in-law not attending *her* wedding.

She said goodbye to the guests and closed the front door. *I'm going to live here,* she thought. She felt the strangest combination of happiness and sadness.

"TRY IT AGAIN in G," Lena told the practice accompanist she had hired. They were in a small studio he'd borrowed. It was Sunday night. She'd figured, why not work? Nothing else going on. She preferred working with Swee' Pea but he wasn't available, alas. He always knew what key she needed. He always knew when to take a break if she drove herself too hard. But today she had Robert—nice enough, fairly competent, just not Swee' Pea.

Today, every time she sang the high notes her voice got tremulous. She couldn't figure out what was going on. She was okay with the smokier part of her voice on "What Is This Thing Called Love," but when she got halfway through the stanza and had to change the tone she felt shaky. Robert said she was fine, so they moved on to "I'm Mad about the Boy."

He transposed to G, but she still didn't like the sound she was producing, didn't like thinking how much the song made her think of Swee' Pea. "Stop," she said. "Let me regather my wits"—suggesting that she'd had them not long ago. Ha. Lessons. Head position up, up, open the throat. Confidence, and, all right, remember anger. Anger and lust, anger and lust.

She'd done these songs for RCA records; why was it so hard?

"Want a drink?" Robert asked. He removed a bottle from a satchel.

"You come prepared." *I want to be good, I want to be good,* she thought.

Oddly, Robert said, "You are very good."

She beat up the trash can in her mind. *I want love. I want people to answer my letters and my phone calls.*

Robert stayed in his own world and poured the whiskey and eventually went back to the piano.

AFTER everyone left, Philip said he would stay downstairs listening to the radio, which George and Marie understood to mean they deserved a wee bit of time on their wedding night. It was strange—the bedroom reminded her of Ummah and Pap's because it seemed everyone chose the same kind of bedroom set: heavy mahogany furniture, horizontal bureau, upright dresser, vanity, headboard and footboard, all matching.

When George embraced her, Marie was struck by how firm his embrace was without its feeling wrong. He told her she was beautiful and kept contact with her hand, then her arm, then her back while she took off her shoes and stockings. Then he fumbled with the buttons of her dress, but managed to get them undone. "Which one of us goes to the bathroom to change?"

She asked if he would. She said, "I'm a little bit afraid."

He said, "There's no rule. We can wait."

They didn't wait.

So long as he kept holding her tight, she was all right.

At three they heard Philip climb the stairs to go to bed.

The next morning she went downstairs in her new dwelling place to make breakfast, which she did determinedly. It looked unappetizing: dry eggs, bread. She made dinner that night, too. She tried the chipped beef and hated it. Thank heavens they were invited to Evelyn's for Thanksgiving, because she wasn't ready to make a turkey. To Marie, American cooking seemed to need something. She eventually would decide it was salt and butter. Also onions and garlic. Also oil.

Her kitchen hands were unskilled.

"I'm not good at this," she told George.

"I'm sure you will be. You just haven't developed a pattern yet."

On subsequent days the breakfast eggs were hard discs, the toast and bacon burned, the meatloaf didn't hang together, the hamburgers were like little baby saucers. Still she cooked for the three of them every day the first week.

Philip laughed at her failures. "At least George gets to eat at the restaurant," he said. George told her everything was tasty even when it wasn't. In the next week he turned over a salmon patty or a chop long before she would have, thus giving a cooking lesson without calling attention to it.

Marie was used to working, so she worked. She cleaned the sink, scrubbed the stove, studied cookbooks, remade a few of the dresses she found in the attic.

Life was surprising.

She noticed she couldn't wait until George got home for dinner and for her time with him in the evening; she was eager to touch him, to feel his warmth and strength. When he was at work, she longed for him.

It turned out that George—the two of them together—was what she wanted, what she had been longing for all her life.

LENA HAD BEEN instructed by Gumm to say yes to all cocktail parties, and there were plenty of them in LA. She was supposed to be *getting known*. Some mornings she could hardly lift her head off the pillow. She was a novelty. *Oh, we have a singer here. Lena. Look at her. Isn't she smashing? Isn't she downright gorgeous? Perhaps she'll sing something later.*

And if she refused to sing, of course she would not be invited again. That's how it was. A Negro got to perform for nothing—free entertainment.

Swee' Pea did it too when he was not needed for a real job.

The upside was that it got her out of the tiny apartment in which she felt trapped—perhaps she was simply awkward, but her elbows bumped into the walls of that apartment when she moved. She quivered to think what Louis would say if he saw it. The bedroom was also the living room; the kitchen doubled as her dressing room because it had a mirror.

The place had a phone, anyway, and the phone rang.

It was Robeson. "Okay out there in movieland?"

"Not okay. No peas are hitting the window out here. The Trocadero is nowhere near opening yet." She saw herself in the mirror as she spoke and God, she looked awful. Her eyes were puffy. Too much booze. Tonight she would say no to the martinis.

"You should come back to New York where you have work. Are you writing letters about that boy who's in jail?"

"I wrote to him several times. He never answered."

"Must be a reason."

"Must be." *But what?* she often wondered. Did he hate her now?

When she hung up with Robeson, a little irritated that he was always pushing her, she dug out a long red dress, thinking of it as her Billie Holliday dress, but this one was less worn. She had agreed to attend another party tonight and looked forward to it this time because Swee' Pea would be there.

Sitting on the kitchen stool, applying eyeshadow and mascara, she thought Robeson was right. What was she doing here? Without her kids, without . . . anything.

Her girdle pinched at the waist, her high heels pinched her feet—thematic, the pinching—and by now lots of people had seen the red dress. She needed new duds. But she lunged forward, onward, getting out the door, finding a taxi, thinking about how her agents said she should enter parties with a look of gratitude and amazement, *oh so happy to be here*—the humble act—and she'd gotten terribly good at it.

Soon enough she was there, at a mansion.

But then there was also Swee' Pea. They grabbed their martinis and went out onto a balcony where they held hands and drank.

"They'll ask me to sing."

"Sure they will."

"It's wrong."

"It is wrong. Only I like to play a good piano and you like to sing. So here we are."

She put on a British accent. "'Oh, my dear. So charming of you to come.' That Diane woman actually said that. Just like that. And she's from West Virginia."

Swee' Pea laughed.

"Why do they want to be English?"

He appeared to think about it. "Maybe because the English seem to be so sure of themselves and their place in the world."

"Well, okay, explain the fake southern accents, then. Did you see our hostess? She grew up in New York! She tiptoes around and says, all soft, all drawling, 'Why, hello, honey, I've heard of you, yes, I certainly have.'"

Swee' Pea laughed agreeably again. "Isn't she silly? Aren't they all silly? They all just want to be somebody."

"You're very nice. I'm not so nice." She sipped slowly, trying to make the martini last.

Swee' Pea's eyes wandered over the balcony. What was he looking

at? The sky? The blond man who came to the railing and threw a cigarette over?

"What's happening?" She touched his ear delicately.

"I'm hearing a melody I don't want to forget."

"Ah. I'll let you be."

He took her hand. "Shhh. Just let me sing it to myself."

They stood there for a long time, Lena sensing the thrum of his
blood, wondering what kind of song he heard, and whether his musical
idea had been prompted by her anger.

At about ten o'clock, the hostess, of the newly acquired southern
background, approached them and with a soft hand on Lena's shoulder,
asked, "Honey, would you do us the honor of singing a song? People
inside keep telling me I have to hear you sing 'Stormy Weather.' But also
whatever else you want to sing. You are so beautiful, honey. They're all
saying you are so gorgeous and so sexy."

Lena went inside, where a man she didn't know played runs on the
piano. "'Stormy Weather,'" she said.

He tried a few keys. "Good?"

"Yes. And how about 'Imagination' after that. You know it?"

"Sure."

Martini glasses held aloft, people began to gather 'round. Lena gave
them what they wanted, a long drawn-out wail of pain as she sang about
lost love and the stormy weather it brought. Her listeners loved her. But
she was distracted, lost her concentration, and wondered where Swee'
Pea was and if he could hear her.

"I'm going to sing one more. I don't know why exactly I keep singing
about the weather! But somehow I do! How about this one? It's called
'Imagination.'" She heard her own voice—suddenly slightly southern,
slightly Negro. She was saying, Um for I'm and dropping her g's. Where
had that come from? She winked at her audience. "You know, about the
sun breaking through the gray, right? Right? That's what you call a met-
aphor." Then she sang "Imagination" for them.

The hostess told her, "Honey, you were marvelous. I wish I could be
like you, so . . . sultry, sexy. Excuse me, I'm a little drunk. Whoops. I'd
better get back there and have something to eat."

"Oh, it was my pleasure."

When she rejoined Swee' Pea, she said, "I suddenly got more Negro tonight."

"I heard that."

"Because I'm miffed?"

"Probably."

She thought about this.

"Sexy and sultry, too," he teased.

"Anger," she said sadly, "my little professional secret."

"I adore you," he said. She felt her spirits lift.

THIRTEEN

1941, 1942

GEORGE WAS JUST PULLING THE BEDCOVERS UP TO HIS SHOUL-
ders when he stopped. "Oh. I forgot to say earlier. There's a big dinner
dance New Year's Eve at the Moose Club. Howard wants us to double
date."

"You mean Klein?"

He reached to switch off the light beside the bed and leaned over
and kissed her on the forehead.

She shifted and sat up. "I've never been to a dinner dance."

"Kind of fancy. People get dressed up."

"Gowns?"

"I don't know about gowns. Maybe. Whatever you need. Howard
has been seeing his sister-in-law for months. They just made it legal at a
JP."

"Married and going to a dance? Doesn't it seem too soon after being
widowed?"

"She told Howard she wanted to."

After a while, Marie said, "I think maybe I want a black dress."

"We'll get you the finest, whatever it is." Soon after that his hand let go of hers and he was asleep.

Marie, restless, relived the night of the murder all over again. She didn't much like having it come back to haunt her but now that she was going to meet the brother she was likely to think of it much more often.

She tried to concentrate on the upcoming dance instead. She wanted a black gown because of a picture of Lena Horne in the *Courier* a couple of months back. Lena's hair was up and there was a flower in it. The writer described her as totally elegant in her black dress. And Marie remembered Lena had also worn a black dress for her wedding. So she wanted something like that, something classy.

Two days later Madeline called her. "I heard you wanted to know what people wear. Last year I wore a white suit," she told Marie. "This year I'm wearing white again, a dress."

Last year would have been just before the murder.

"Floor length?" Marie asked.

"No. I always think the three people in floor length look cheap, like they think they're movie stars. But suit yourself. That's just my opinion."

When Marie went shopping a few days later with the cash in hand that George had given her, she found herself studying red, pink, gold, blue dresses, and still definitely wanting black.

There was a black chiffon, but it was floor length. Then she found a black velvet suit, darted in at the waist, low cut.

In the dressing room she got the skinny skirt on and zipped. But the jacket was the main feature, the way it hugged her shape. She buttoned the two buttons.

"Wow," said the saleswoman. "That is one gorgeous outfit."

"What would I wear with it?"

"Really good shoes. You'll have to get those on your own. But I'll bring you some jewelry. That suit is just fantastic on you."

The woman came back with a set of rhinestones—a necklace that graduated downward like a cathedral in reverse, following the shape of the plunging neckline. It came with a set of matching earrings and a bracelet. "You'd better buy this. I've never seen anything so perfect."

Feeling giddy, Marie handed the cash over.

She might have to wear this suit for the next twenty years, for every event she would ever attend, but she didn't mind. She loved it. Married three weeks and all seemed right.

ON THE FIRST Sunday in December, Marie came home from church and put a chicken in the oven. George beamed. "I love roast chicken." She was determined to become good in the kitchen. Each day's food was a little better than the last.

He settled into a chair in the living room, almost dozing. He'd gone to the restaurant in the morning to work on the books and the orders. They'd had a small ham sandwich on Lebanese bread for lunch. Philip was out somewhere; that was a blessing.

She had what she most wanted: more of George, a Sunday at home, calm.

She switched the radio on. At first they heard the music of big bands, music she liked. She hummed along a little and George's upper body moved rhythmically, keeping time. "We should practice dancing," Marie said. "For New Year's Eve. Fran taught me."

"You're going to be disappointed. I can't do dips. I can't do swing. I can do a couple of slow dance steps, that's about—"

"Oh, come on." She hauled him up.

"You're going to find out how clumsy I am."

"I'll lead!"

Head cocked toward the radio, he said, "This song is too fast." But then he swept her up and did a fairly credible swift foxtrot, at least for a few bars.

She was holding him tight and loving her life when the music stopped suddenly and a voice broke in after a brief crackling pause. "We interrupt programming for a special bulletin. News is coming in that the Japanese have struck American ships in Oahu, Hawaii, this morning. They have attacked without declaring war and the attack is ongoing."

Marie and George stood in their living room, just looking at the radio. There was a pause and a rustle of paper from the broadcaster.

For the rest of the afternoon they listened to the news. Everyone they knew called them and vice versa. Men were going to be lost. It was coming, war had been coming all along, and now it was here.

"You have a business. They count that."

"Yes . . ."

Philip came home full of the news. He was drunk from wherever he'd been and seemed ecstatic. "We're going to war! Finally!"

SITTING AT THE piano with Swee' Pea on that same Sunday in December, what felt like a *regular* Sunday because she had Swee' Pea and not Robert playing for her today, Lena was working on her phrasing. She had to return to New York for an engagement at the Savoy all through the Christmas and New Year season. She and Swee' Pea heard raised voices on the street, voices that were disturbing enough that they disrupted his timing, and then the phone rang. When he answered and listened, his face told her it was bad news.

"What is it?" she asked.

Swee' Pea put on the radio. "This is the horrible thing we've been eating with our breakfasts."

They listened to the report.

"I can't believe it." Lena walked back and forth, hunched over, sick. "War. It means war, doesn't it?"

"We don't have a choice," he said. He went to a window and pulled the drape aside, just looking out. People on the streets were talking to each other intensely, some giving the message, some first hearing it. "I might be drafted."

He was five foot two and delicate. He was a genius. Could he survive such a fate?

As the day went on, as words became concepts and were repeated, one of the big fears being bandied about was that California was the next place to be bombed. She held on to Swee' Pea's elbow. "Maybe you should come with me to New York. Maybe we should get married. I mean . . . I would."

He looked at her, his eyes sad behind large-framed glasses. "Are you proposing?" he teased.

"Why not? I am. I don't care about the other thing."

"You would care," he said kindly. "You would."

"Is there a way to keep all that separate?"

"I wouldn't want to. And you're not divorced, so this is just war talk making us scared. And you're nervous about New York."

"I'm happiest with you."

"We are best friends. You're going to be fine. It's the Savoy, honey. But come back here when you're done."

"I have to. I signed for a house."

EVERYBODY TALKED ABOUT nothing else but Pearl Harbor for days. And yet . . . and yet stores opened in the mornings and people bought gifts and went about the business of the holiday. As week turned to week, they sang carols and made dinners and talked about war as they sat down to meals, slowly accepting the fact of it, and when New Year's Eve finally arrived, people kept to their plans.

Marie had the bedroom to herself as she got ready for the big dance. She'd used Ellis Wave Set, a green gel, on her hair to get a pompadour like the ones in magazines. She dabbed Coty Echoes of Paris, a Christmas gift from George, behind her ears and the smell of flowers aroused her. She was falling in love with herself. Then the girdle, the bra, the stockings that made her legs feel smooth and silky, the black slip, and finally the suit and the rhinestone jewelry. A tap of her fingers on the necklace, a smoothing of her hands over the suit jacket, made her feel utterly daring, appealing.

She heard the shower water stop. George always said it took him exactly six minutes to get dressed completely, hair combed, the whole bit. And she timed him once. He was right.

A moment later he stood at the bedroom doorway, looking stunned. He was wrapped in a towel with a robe over it. "I feel like you're somebody else," he said. "Like I don't know you."

"You like it?"

"Yes!"

Even that temporary anonymity thrilled her. She slipped out of the bedroom and sailed down the stairs. Philip, sitting on the sofa, reading the newspaper, looked up once but didn't say anything at all. Marie paced a little in the kitchen, holding her clutch bag this way and that. It was the only thing that didn't totally fit—just plain black leather.

George bounded down the steps six minutes later, saying "Isn't she spectacular?"

Philip looked up. "She looks nice."

And then a car horn told them Howard Klein and Madeline were outside to pick them up. Howard had just bought a new car. "One day we'll have a car," George promised. Marie always told him she never felt the need for one. She walked most places and there were trolleys for everywhere else.

From the moment she saw the blonde woman, head erect, in the front passenger seat, Marie was a little afraid of her.

"Hello there?" Madeline said in greeting. "I see you found something to wear that is not hanging below your coat."

George and Marie sat in the back seat of the Chrysler. "How do you like the car?" George asked.

"We like it," Howard said. "We looked at a lot of cars."

"It's fine," Madeline said. "I'm getting used to it." Her exotic and no doubt expensive perfume filled the car.

When they pulled up to the club building, Howard angled the car to get his passengers as close to the door as possible before he drove off to park. "How thoughtful he is," Marie said.

"Oh, yes," Madeline said. "He *is*."

They moved to just inside the door. Madeline was wearing a fur coat, something almost white and beautiful. Her hair was in an updo with sausage curls at the front—very much in style, but it reminded Marie of food falling off a plate.

"You're looking at my hair."

"Oh, uh, trying to figure out how you *do* it."

"You go to a beauty shop, that's how!"

George helped Madeline out of her fur. Madeline's white dress was very elegant, with jewels that came down like fingers on one side and pulled the cloth to asymmetrical pleats. When Howard came in, he took the fur from George so George could take off Marie's coat. "Are we the two luckiest men at this dance?" Howard exclaimed. "Look at them together! Both beautiful."

Madeline was all white, even to her very light blonde hair and her shoes. Marie was all black.

"Gorgeous," George agreed.

The dance hall was a huge room decorated with red, white, and blue balloons hung from the ceiling every two feet and crepe paper streamers in the same colors linked one balloon to another. A live band on the stage was playing "All of Me." In her mind Marie could hear the recording of Billie Holiday singing it with that small hard voice.

George whispered in her ear, "You're the gorgeous one."

Marie wagged her head to deflect the praise.

"You look like somebody," Madeline said, squinting. "I can't think who."

Marie looked to George, who didn't suggest anyone, so she said, "Are you maybe thinking of Lena Horne?"

"No, my dear, that's not it."

Then Howard was soon dancing his wife off to the music and George, a bit less showily, guided Marie to the floor.

"Does he love her madly?" Marie asked.

"Madly? Probably not madly."

"Huh. She seems snobbish."

"He's a good guy. She has two kids. I think he wants to be able to provide for them. I think it's even in his tradition, stepping in to take his brother's place."

"Oh." She nuzzled her head against George's cheek and they danced.

"She was with another fellow for a while," George continued. "Howard told me this confidentially. So it's not something to ever bring up."

"After the death?"

"Yes."

Marie's experience of widowhood was only of witnessing Lebanese women who mourned for life. Some never wore anything but black, ever, for as long as they lived. "Madeline was quick about it," she said, immediately regretting her tone.

"It might be a form of mourning."

"What?"

"Recklessness might be. Kind of like a craziness is what I mean. The guy she was with was a lowlife. According to Howard, anyway. Finally she gave him up. Howard was in his cups when he told me. I'm sorry to disappoint you in her. She's probably okay. I guess he hopes we do things together."

"What if I don't get comfortable with her?"

"Howard and I will survive. You don't have to like her for my sake."

Marie decided to let things be. She'd had more to drink than she was used to, and that helped her let go.

The next morning she felt the effect of those whiskey cocktails. As she turned over resolutions, she decided to go visit her mother even though she still held a grudge that her mother hadn't come to the wedding.

She dressed, walked up to Centre, and took the 85 Bedford the rest of the way to the Hill, then walked to her old home, which she'd now been away from for more than six weeks. At least it wasn't terribly cold out as it had been last year when the blizzard hit. After spending last night with the Kleins, the memory of that awful night was close. She arranged the scarf she wore over her chest. No more pneumonia. She was in love. She wanted to live a long, healthy life.

Her mother had closed the store for the holiday but customers knew they only had to knock if they needed something; her mother would open up for them.

Ummah didn't even ask if Marie was hungry, but put before her a plate of food, a mixture of canned spinach and canned beans cooked with garlic in oil (in summer it might have been dandelion) and handed over a triangle of bread to sop it up. The lunch was tasty and gave Marie an idea of something she might make one day when she was out of fresh ingredients.

Marie tried to hug her mother, but her mother moved away as if irritated by the touch. Marie almost gave up, but she tried, "Why don't you drop everything and come to dinner with me today, see the house, let me serve you?"

Her mother shook her head slightly, and said softly, "Not today."

"You were right," Marie said as brightly as she could. "I do love George. It happened all at once. Isn't that strange?"

Her mother made a face that meant either yes or no, it was not clear.

"He's putting in a big ham today, it's probably already in the oven. His sisters are coming. So if you would maybe just think about it—"

"No, no, I need stay here."

A weight of sadness dropped from Marie's heart to her stomach, but she couldn't stop herself, "We could take a walk, you and me, it's not bad out. I'd love to be in the neighborhood."

With a slight shake of the head, her mother shuffled toward a pot with something she rarely made, meat dumplings in yogurt, though Marie suspected the pot didn't need stirring.

"You go," her mother said, and not meanly, but with a tone that was absolute. "You walk. Selma maybe go with you."

"Have I done something? Are you angry?"

"No. No, no, not angry."

Marie went upstairs and found Selma, who was washing out two blouses. "Let's get out of here." And once they were on the street, she exclaimed, "What's the matter with Ummah? Does she hate me?"

"No, she loves you best."

"Why can't she move?"

But Marie was asking the wrong person. It hit Marie that Selma was like their mother, a person who did not want to shift even a minute from routine, *could* not.

Selma managed to say the truth of the matter. "She likes her life the way it is. Everything else makes her nervous."

And that was Selma, too. Of course. Marie had to quit trying to change them.

Marie went back to her Ummah's kitchen and more quietly accepted a cup of tea.

Frightened, both of them, mother and sister.

As she was leaving, there was a knock at the door and the newsboy handed her two copies of the *Sun-Telegraph*. Before she could say they probably didn't need the papers today because the store was closed, she saw the headline, and as she read, the boy ran off. By the end of the first sentence she stood there reading, unbelieving.

She couldn't breathe. She couldn't think. She took both copies inside, praying that she had seen mistakenly, read wrongly. But there it was in the paper, in print. All her trying had been for nothing.

ACCUSED MAN KILLED IN PRISON

Police and security guards say they have no suspects as yet in the killing of Josiah Conner in the Allegheny County Jail. Conner was arrested in connection with the murder at gunpoint of businessman Joseph Klein a year ago. Klein was driving his Buick on Fifth Avenue, downtown, when he was accosted in an apparent robbery and shot at close range. He died before reaching the hospital.

Conner had been assigned an attorney, Barney McKenna, who claimed the youth was going to plead not guilty. No gun was found at the scene of the crime but there was deep snow that had not been cleared. There were no witnesses to question about the incident.

Conner had attended Fifth Avenue High School. Teachers report that he was a good student. He worked with his father, Josiah Conner, Sr., of the Hill District, a plumber and painter.

An investigation of the jail killing is in process. Another man was wounded. Officials did not reveal the name of the second victim. Because of the holiday there were fewer guards on duty New Year's Eve.

Marie stared at the floor of the store, remembering Josiah's voice, his face. Memory provided something like little bits of film—a smile, a hello, the times he bought soup, the time at the candy store he forgot his newspaper.

After she took her leave from her mother and sister, she retraced her path back to her new home, walking, streetcar, more walking. George looked up from the newspaper, worried, when she came in. He thought he was going to tell her about something she didn't know. He had the paper on the hassock, front page showing. He said, "That boy who was accused of killing—"

"I know. I saw."

"It must have happened while we were at the dance. How terrible."

She let him hold her. "I tried so hard."

He continued to hold her. "You tried very hard. Nobody could have done better."

"We understood each other, I think. *He* understood everybody."

What she wanted was to go to bed for the rest of the day, but the smell of baking ham filled the air, reminding her she couldn't. She was supposed to make potato salad and set the table and be ready to greet his sisters and their husbands.

When the phone rang an hour later, George said, "It's for you. The man didn't say who. Not your father. No accent."

Marie went to the living room and lifted the phone with wet hands. "Yes? Hello?"

The man with no accent said he was Schmidt, the warden she had spoken to at the jail. He said he needed her help and asked if he could come by to speak to her.

"I have people coming for dinner."

"When?"

"Six."

"I'll be there right away."

"Is this about—"

He had already hung up.

WHEN LENA CALLED her father on New Year's Day, she said, "Happy New Year, Daddy," and was about to tell him about her holiday show the night before at the Savoy, but he was saying, "I have to tell you something. Important." He paused. "That boy Josiah . . ."

"Josiah," she repeated. *Called, wrote, a trial set . . .* were the words she expected to hear.

"He was killed in jail."

She made him repeat it and then sank onto the bed. She tried to ask her father how and who and why but he didn't know those answers and nothing helped her accept the news.

"There is always a mess in jail," her father said. "People you don't want to know. It's crazy there."

Trembling, she called Robeson and told him what had just happened. "I wrote those letters. Did I do harm?"

"I doubt it. What did you say?"

"That I wanted him to have a good defense. That I simply knew he was innocent. That I would help pay for a lawyer. He never wrote back. Didn't care that I wanted to help, I guess. That hurt."

"Tell me what you said."

"That I believed he had to be innocent. No gun was found. I emphasized that. Said I believed he was downtown because he'd been to a movie. He had no motive to kill a motorist. No robbery actually took place. Those are the things I said."

"You did no wrong. I'm glad you tried."

"I'll go to Pittsburgh. I want to be at the funeral."

"Yes. You can still speak out."

All right. Unsmudge his name. All the good it did now. Wasn't life in any form better?

The manager of the Savoy was furious when she called him to say she was taking three days off. She didn't care. She'd been angry with the manager for weeks. Even though she was the *headliner* at the Savoy, they wouldn't let her sleep there. She had to taxi every night to Harlem, no matter how late it was.

Three days was all she asked. She would get to see Teddy, she would go to the funeral. She still felt pain that Josiah, who had been the sweetest human being she had ever met other than Swee' Pea, had not returned her letters. But funerals were for acceptance, forgiveness. To see the face in the casket, to believe in repose, to tell yourself that the end of a life was in some way the end of trouble.

WARDEN SCHMIDT ARRIVED at Marie's door, looking frantic. He said, "May I come in? Could I have ten minutes?"

"Of course."

George stood from where he'd been sitting and introduced himself.

Marie said, "Can I get you coffee?"

Schmidt shook his head. "Please. Sit. I don't have much time. This is going to be hard to explain."

"Something about Josiah?"

"I'm here to ask for your help."

"All right," Marie said.

"Suppose. What if I went into work at seven this morning and they told me Conner was killed. Right? Are you with me? And they had a guy named Lucas Findlay in a holding cell because they were going to transfer him to another jail, out of town, for safety. Suppose I go look at the body—my assistant, Conner was my assistant for four months. And it isn't the right man. And I go to the holding cell and it is . . . the right man. The one who is supposed to be dead. Are you with me?"

Marie couldn't breathe. She grabbed George's hand.

"I need help. He needs clothes. He needs to get out of town. I can't go to his house. His father is surrounded by mourners."

"His father—"

"He knows. He came to the jail for the formal release of the body. I had a hard time telling him what to do. But he's doing it, I hope. Pretending. The story is he's shipping the body to relatives in North Carolina. I stopped at home to get some money. Now the next trick is to get Conner out of town. I have to make a show of getting back to the jail, getting the other body shipped out. Questions are flying." He looked at his watch and up at them. "I've maybe asked too much of you. I had your name. I told him you'd been writing to him. He said you were good."

George said, "You want us to bring Conner into the house, then? Where is he?"

Schmidt said, "The car I'm using. The trunk. I parked a block away. I can drive around back. You'll do this?"

George looked at Marie. "You want to help him, don't you?"

"Yes."

Schmidt said, "I knew you cared about him. Hide him for tonight. For a couple of days if you could. Do you have a car?"

"I'll borrow one," George said.

Marie touched George's arm. They were so new, only six weeks married, they'd hardly had a chance to know each other. Were they crazy to do this? She asked Schmidt, "Do you believe he's innocent?"

"Yes. I do. I got to know him. I completely believe it."

"I do too," she said.

George said, "All right, then."

Marie started toward the kitchen. "I'll get the basement door open."

Schmidt took off. Since it was a holiday the streets were almost empty. Only one car went by as Schmidt hurried to his.

Marie didn't bother with a coat or a sweater, but went out back, making a show of putting out garbage and then going down the three steps to the wooden door, which she unlocked from the outside. She couldn't sense reality through any of this, just movement, just doing things, like a person in a war zone, though all she knew of that stunned state was what she saw in the movies.

A gray car pulled up close to the fence. Schmidt opened the trunk and acted busy, moving a lot. He took off his coat and tossed it in. Then after seconds of some fuss, Schmidt and Josiah, wearing the warden's coat, walked steadily, carrying a toolbox and a pipe, as if they were workmen coming to fix the furnace. When they were closer, Marie saw that Josiah looked older, sadder, but . . . not afraid to meet her eyes.

Once they were in the basement Schmidt said, "He needs clothes, like I said. I understand you sew a little."

Josiah took off the coat and handed it to Schmidt. "Maybe you should keep it," Schmidt said.

Marie told Schmidt, "Take it. I'll find something." She was already thinking how to alter Philip's clothes, because he was smaller than George.

"The train station might be a good bet by Sunday morning, early. A train to somewhere. To buy time." He said most of this to Josiah. "The thing is to not be seen."

"Shouldn't I just go? Take the chance now?" Josiah asked. His fists clenched. He moved toward the basement door.

"No." Schmidt said it again. "If you're recognized, it's over. Somebody will blab."

"This way I'm causing trouble for all of you."

"Do you want to live?" Schmidt demanded.

"Yes."

"This is your best chance. I'm leaving now because I have to. I have to get myself back to the jail. I was never here. Right?"

There was a sound of the laundry sink dripping. Marie, dazed, went over to tighten the faucet. They were criminals, all of them. She watched George open up the basement door and tell Schmidt, "We'll try to do right. We'll take it from here."

Schmidt murmured, "Try to keep him calm. He's not thinking straight. He's got a cut, too. Ribs. But he's alive."

"I'll get him out of town," George said.

"That would be his best chance. But give it a few days."

Marie and George walked Schmidt to his car. Marie asked, "There was a fight? Is that how . . ."

"What happened in jail—that was ordered. Lucas Findlay didn't know him at all. I told Josiah to use Findlay's name for a week or so just to get away, but then he has to drop it because whoever hired Findlay is going to want to know how he disappeared. I think he might be able to pick a name and get through at a recruiting station where they're desperate for anybody. Or a job in manufacturing. They need men badly. Tell him to try Detroit, where they need workers. I have to go. I was never here, okay?"

Schmidt slid into his car and took off. As soon as Marie and George got back into the basement they heard a sound upstairs. Philip. They gestured an apology to Josiah, and, telling him they'd be back when they could, they hurried up the stairs to the kitchen.

There was the familiar sound of the closet door opening and a hanger scraping the bar, no doubt Philip hanging up his coat. He called out, "The ham smells great."

Marie carefully closed the kitchen door that led to the basement. "Where did you go?" she heard George ask his brother.

"Out and about, seeing people."

They might have to tell Philip what was happening, but her gut told her it was a bad idea and should not be done unless necessary. George's conversation in the next room suggested the same decision from him.

Her mind clicked through what she would need to do. There was a primitive toilet in the basement, and a laundry sink. One broken kitchen chair. And there was enough food in the house for an extra person. She would have to make up a bed of sorts . . .

When she stopped thinking of tasks to be done she got frightened.

Alive. Josiah was alive. She almost missed her grief. It was easier, certainly, than what lay ahead.

Potato salad and the table preparation were tasks, and tasks helped her to be ordinary. She chopped celery and called out to George to help cube potatoes. She told Philip to set the table.

"The good plates in the dining room cupboard?" Philip called back.

"Those," she directed. "And everybody gets a fork on the left and a knife and spoon on the right."

"I know that much," Philip muttered. "I'm putting out wineglasses." She heard the glasses being plunked on the table. He came into the kitchen with a plain glass and poured water in it, and whiskey. "To get the party started."

The relatives arrived in one car a bit before six.

"Aha, she's cooking," Sarah said.

"I'm starving," Evelyn said. "Potato salad looks great."

"George told me how he likes it."

Sarah and Evelyn tasted the potato salad, each with a clean fork, before it ever made it to the table. Evelyn said, "Not bad."

All the while Marie hoped the activity upstairs was a clear indication to Josiah downstairs why she couldn't get there to see him.

All through the serving and eating she planned each thing she needed to do.

"The house looks very clean and orderly," Sarah said. "So, you've made your mark. Soon you'll be making the ham too."

"I want to learn everything about food I can."

Sarah approved, lifting her glass.

George kept catching her eyes. *What have we done? Are you all right?*

"She's just thriving," Evelyn said.

It wasn't until eleven when the relatives had all gone and Marie insisted on doing the dishes herself that she filled a plate with some of everything, covered it with a napkin, and piled all the table linens on top of it while George distracted Philip with talk of the war.

Josiah sat on the lone chair, shivering in front of the furnace. Since it wasn't cold in the basement, the shivering was from fear. "I can't stay long," she whispered. "I'll make all this better tomorrow. I have a brother-in-law in the house. It's best he doesn't know. Let me see the cut."

He pulled up his prison shirt, which was light blue with a lighter blue vertical stripe. The shirt had a cut in it and a maroon line of blood. The slice across his ribs was still seeping.

Alcohol, peroxide, iodine, she could bring them down. "Eat. You need food." She took a rag rug from the clothesline. "Lie on this for tonight. Cover yourself with the table cloth. I'll bring something else as soon as I can."

She put only the napkins in the washing machine.

"I don't want to do this to you," he said.

"Shh. We'll talk tomorrow."

She had a great curiosity about everything—the year in jail, what he had thought, felt, why the warden was so helpful to him. It was hard to put off knowing the answers. But she climbed the stairs and shut the door.

She stood at the entrance to the living room. "Just tossed the laundry in. Let's get some sleep."

George was up, with an arm around her, squeezing. "You did great. At everything. Thriving, my sister said!" Marie turned, worried that

Philip would stay up, that Josiah would cough or sneeze. "Come on, Philip," George said. "Hit the hay. A new year begins. Got to get it right."

Philip grumbled something and followed them.

Two hours later Marie tiptoed to the bathroom. After waiting a few minutes and hearing no change in breathing from either her room or Philip's, she gathered peroxide and iodine. She grabbed a washcloth. Holding the things she'd found, she crept into the spare room for the two single bed blankets at the foot of each bed. Would Philip notice they were missing? She had to hope not.

Each step creaked as she tiptoed down and down. She grabbed a towel from the kitchen and kept going.

Josiah got up as soon as he heard her. "Shh." She folded one blanket into thirds and put it over the rug.

Then she indicated that he should take off his shirt. Using the washcloth, she swabbed the cut with peroxide as he hissed in air, then with iodine, finally dressing it with the only thing she had, a kitchen towel. She had never touched him before. It was strange how the people in her life didn't touch, didn't embrace, until George. She hoped she was gentle.

"Thank you."

The tablecloth went back as the first cover and the blanket as the second. "I'll keep doing better," she said, and then crept back upstairs.

George left the house in the morning for work, telling her, "Call me, call for anything. I'll get here if you need me."

While Philip slept she took an egg and bread and coffee down to Josiah, and during that time she found a long clean rag to make a proper bandage. For three hours Marie did laundry that didn't need to be done so Philip didn't wonder why she kept going to the basement.

Philip and the unused bedroom were subjects she hurried to explain. "He doesn't hold his tongue," she said. "And there's the attic to consider, too, but no water, no toilet."

"I'm okay here. Every minute I think I should leave and leave you in peace, but I don't."

"Don't."

Josiah smiled for a moment, almost an image of his old self. "Did you ever think you would be this person?"

"No! I thought I was a candy shop girl for the rest of my life."

"I never thought I'd be this person either. I fought. I fought with that man who wanted to kill me. He didn't expect it, the way I fought, and neither did I."

"I'm glad you did."

"Yeah. I don't think I'll ever get over it. I . . . tried to revive him."

"Warden said it was planned."

He dropped his shoulders and his head. "I wish I could be myself. My old self. I killed someone and I wish I could undo it."

"You can't."

"I don't know how to . . . think. I can't think right."

Marie went to the stairs to listen for Philip.

"Did you ever read *Tom Sawyer*?" he asked, suddenly with a glimmer of his old spirit.

"No."

"He went to his own funeral. He wasn't dead, but people thought he was. He went to see people cry for him. My poor father has to fake it. He's not good at faking anything."

"What do you think of Schmidt?"

Tears filled his eyes. Then he managed, "Took care of me. I don't even know why."

"I hear Philip getting up. Next I get you clothing. When I can."

She went back upstairs and made breakfast and waited for what seemed forever for Philip to leave the house. Then she rattled around in the attic for old clothing of Philip's but her best bet was a pinstriped, old-fashioned suit that must have belonged to George's father. She grabbed a shirt that might have been George's. It had two tears at the seams. It would have to do. She took those things to the basement with her sewing materials.

She cut the shirt to a smaller size and stitched as fast as she could. Josiah was looking at the suit. "I really will be someone else," he said.

"That's the idea."

She sewed recklessly fast. "You had a lot of time to think. Did you think who killed Joseph Klein?"

Josiah said, "I didn't know him. I only knew it had nothing to do with me. Everything from hearing the shots was . . . like a bad dream."

"You could write a movie about it one day."

He shook his head slightly, then more firmly.

WHEN LENA GOT to Pittsburgh her father told her the service was to be a coming together, not a full funeral, because the body had already been shipped to North Carolina to be buried in a family plot. Old Conner was going down there as soon as the Pittsburgh memorial was done.

The event took place on a Saturday, two days after New Year's in West's Funeral Home. Family and friends paid their respects to a high school photo of the boy.

A *Courier* photographer, a man subbing for Teenie Harris at the wake, was more excited about Lena's celebrity than about the Conner family, so he kept snapping her picture.

She wept, more than Josiah's father and sister did. Sadness filled her, for lost youth, lost dreams. And Louis was still so angry with her that she got only a brief glimpse of her son before she had to go back to New York.

GEORGE SAT ON a stool at the Moose Club bar, having just told Krieger and Donnelly that he was looking to borrow a car to take Marie on an excursion Sunday morning. Krieger was saying he'd see at home about their car and Donnelly said his wife hated to miss church, but Howard Klein had come in behind them and must have overheard, because he said, "Take mine!"

George shook his head. "No, no, no. Your new car. Don't be silly. I'll rent one. It's just for a couple of hours is all. A cousin of Marie's wrote us a note. She owes a visit."

"Take mine," Klein insisted. "Shame it's not for something more exciting."

"Go ahead," Krieger said. "But he's right. Go to lunch or something. Or go to a hotel Saturday night. Make it fun."

George told Marie all this in all its strangeness. They were going to transport Josiah in the car of the man who thought Josiah had murdered his brother.

Marie asked, "You can't tell him you don't need it?"

He said it was too complicated and would cause more questions. So late Saturday night he took a streetcar to Squirrel Hill and got the car, and not much experienced as a driver, shaking the whole time, he drove it back to Oakland.

It was dark on Sunday morning—Philip was still in bed—when Marie carried two blankets from the basement and they brought Josiah up to the kitchen, quickly handed him a large packed lunch, and went out the back door, closing it carefully. "Back seat," Marie said, "and then soon as you can, lie down. Pull the blankets the whole way over you."

Josiah kept his head down and did what she said.

Marie looked up at the house—knew to look up, somehow—and saw Philip in his bedroom window, watching. After all their care! She gasped once and thought about what she would say to him.

But the motor started and they were moving.

She didn't tell George at that point about Philip because he was already nervous enough driving Howard's car. Every time he braked, the car stopped too abruptly.

"I'm sorry to have dragged you into this," came a voice from the back seat.

"This may be the most exciting thing that's ever happened to me," George said, finding his driving rhythm.

After a long silence, George asked, "Where will you go?"

"Any place I can get a ticket to. Then I'll figure it out from there. Warden told me not to call my father, not to write. For a long time, anyway."

Marie had been thinking that when he felt safe he would go to Hollywood. He'd always wanted to. Nobody would know him out there. "Will you go find Lena?"

"No," he said. "That was a long time ago. She has a new life, a career. No. I'll leave her be."

"But I should write to her to tell her you're alive, right?"

He said, "Let her be. If she asks you, if she comes to town and you talk, if she asks you about me, then tell her. Otherwise, no."

He was done with her. A broken heart, then.

The train station in Johnstown was nearly empty. The board told Marie there was a train to New York City in fifteen minutes. From there a person could go anywhere. Marie bought the ticket and came back to the car, handing it over. "You're going to New York."

"I will figure out a way to repay you."

"No," George said. "No. Not necessary."

They each shook his hand and he was gone, wearing a pinstriped suit, George's large overcoat, and a battered fedora.

"Now for us," George said. "Now to breathe."

He had given her a lot of trust. She touched his arm, leaned over and kissed his cheek. "You are the most wonderful—"

"Nah." He started up the beautiful car. "You maybe are."

Then he began the drive back to Pittsburgh. He would have time to spare and easily be able to give Howard his car back by eleven. Accelerating rapidly, he started to get the feel of the car, what it could do.

FOURTEEN

1942

SHE SIZZLES AND SHE'S BEAUTIFUL.

The reviews were glowing.

She felt reckless. She was in mourning. She was angry, hungry, confused. And she sang all of that out at the Savoy and again when she got a few weeks, after the Savoy, at Café Society.

One gossip rag said Lena Horne only slept with famous men and suggested she'd abandoned her husband because he was not famous enough. She didn't care what they said about her. She loved men. She couldn't help herself. She was aroused by men pursuing her and they pursued her and so she was aroused. She knew what Negro women always said: if you married white guys, you married up. And if you just slept with them, you were a tramp. So . . . there was always a need for a bottle of scotch.

Tonight she stayed late after the show at Café Society and drank. There was no Artie Shaw to drive her home, no Jack Gilford to walk her to his place, and she told a lot of people, half of them strangers, after more than a few drinks that she really really wanted to be alone. She was tired of all of them, the people sitting at the bar, the ones in her head.

Cab Calloway always told her to go back to LA and set her sights on Hollywood. Robeson constantly said the opposite. Everybody had an opinion about her; everybody wanted her to be a person she probably couldn't be.

Now, on a chilly night, at three in the morning she weaved down the street in Brooklyn, aiming for home, her silk shawl dragging.

Finally she was getting close to her house, with half a bottle of whiskey in her belly.

If she fell and cut up her face, she wouldn't be pretty anymore. Then what?

She let out a cry when she arrived at her house because she'd dropped her silk shawl. It slithered down the steps like something alive, while she tried to right herself on the stoop.

Edwina came to the door. "It's four a.m."

"So?"

"Don't let the neighbors hear you this way."

"Who cares about neighbors!"

Edwina just stood there at first, then after a few moments tried to lift her. Lena scrambled up, brushed past her, and watched as Edwina went outdoors to rescue the shawl, which was now wet and muddy. "What happened?" Edwina asked when she came back in.

Lena swayed unsteadily. "Bad review. Of the recording. I'm not good outside a club." She lowered herself to the sofa.

"It will pass."

"I heard someone laughing about it. I hate everybody."

"I'm going to bed. I'm glad you're safe."

"Am I safe? Men say I'm a tease."

"I know. I see all that. Believe me, I see." Edwina hesitated at the stairway. "Three men called here today. I wanted to hang up on them, but I took messages."

"Eh—"

"I know what they want. You don't have to give it."

"Oh, really? And you know this, do you?"

"I'll talk to you in the morning when you're sober. And a couple letters came for you. Your father sent them. Some are old, one from some woman in Pittsburgh."

Edwina handed her a letter.

Lena squinted at the name. Marie Elias? "Don't know her." She ripped up the letter and tossed it to an end table.

Edwina went up to bed and Lena rolled down into a ball on the sofa and wept until she was asleep.

ABOUT A WEEK after Marie and George had taken Josiah to the train, Philip, who lay on the sofa much of every day watching Marie, asked, "Who was your boyfriend? The guy you snuck to the car, crack of dawn?"

"You must never ever talk about that. We needed to do a favor for a friend of your brother's. It's important. I'm not kidding."

He looked at her as if he didn't believe her, but he didn't ask anything else.

Marie could not abide the fact that Philip was almost never out of the house. And the way he looked at her. She hated to think of him in the next room at night.

Philip had told her not to clean his room but she kept everything spotless, so having a room off-limits bothered her. That day when he finally went out to see about a job, she opened the door to his room, curious. The first thing that caught her attention was a pile of cash on the dresser top, weighed down by a saucer. She'd wondered where that saucer had gotten to and she'd thought perhaps Philip had broken it and hidden it in the garbage. But there it was, a paperweight. The second thing that caught her attention was a deck of playing cards on his bedside table with a lewd picture on the back of each card. The room was otherwise moderately neat. She left it.

When Philip returned home he said he wanted a ham sandwich.

Irritated that he ordered her around, she paused, but she made the sandwich anyway. "How was the job interview?" she asked, handing over the plate.

"They didn't keep me. Asked me two questions. But who'd want to do that job?"

"What kind of job was it?"

"Sweep their floors, load their shelves." He'd brought the mail in and was sorting through it as he took up the sandwich.

"Oh. That wouldn't be *hard*, anyway. What were the questions?"

"'Where do you live? Have you ever worked before?'" He let out a quick laugh and began eating.

Among the immigrants she knew, when there was a business, family members worked it. They didn't go out looking for other work or sit around all day. "Why aren't you working for George, then? I don't get it."

"Big brother doesn't want me there. Thinks I'll embarrass him."

"How?"

He winked. "Winking and drinking. And maybe arguing. And alienating people."

"You wouldn't do that."

"Wouldn't I?" He sat back, the sandwich plate almost balanced on his chest, the mail still in his hand.

"Don't even joke about it."

"I'm not joking." Watching her, he tossed the mail to the coffee table.

She lifted it and looked quickly. Her early letter to Lena had gone astray. She'd never had an answer—Josiah was in jail then—and now so much had happened that she couldn't talk about or write another letter about.

Philip said, "No letter from your boyfriend. I looked."

To get away from him, she went out. It was odd weather, an almost-warm winter day. At first she walked without a destination. When she ended up on Atwood Street in front of Cantor's, she stopped. Last week, because of what George pronounced a good week between Christmas and New Year, he'd taken her out to dinner here. She loved everything about it. The clean white tablecloths and napkins. The smell of the foods being served. That night she'd had Matzo ball soup and brisket even though the smell of roast chicken made her want to order that, too.

George loved to see how much she enjoyed herself. "You are awfully easy to please," he said. "So we'll definitely have to do this again."

As soon as she poked her head inside, a waiter in a crisp white jacket

with a white towel over his arm said she should follow him and he began to lead her to a table.

She'd already eaten lunch and told herself she was just coming to
look. "Is it all right to get just a bowl of soup?"

"Certainly."

Today the same glorious aroma of roast chicken hit her. To be out
like this—oh, it was wonderful. She saw what looked like university
people at the other tables—they leaned forward, smart and intense,
probably arguing a point.

Suddenly she missed the candy shop and the fact of *seeing* people all
day.

The waiter presented her soup with a flourish. And he used the same
gesture for a basket of bread. And then for a plate with a pickle. The
events of a week before seemed unreal.

After she finished her second lunch of the day, she felt a sense of
purpose and walked to her husband's restaurant. George jumped when
he saw her. "Is something wrong?"

"I missed you."

"Oh." His face flushed. "Just a sec." He hurried two menus to one of
the booths and came back to her. "Sit. Let's sit. Nothing is wrong, then?
Nothing about—"

"No, no."

They took an empty booth. "I want to help you here," she told him,
taking his hand. "I'm a good worker."

"Oh. I know you are, but . . . no, I want to give you things, make you
comfortable. That's the whole idea."

That was his goal. How could she tell him she didn't want it? She
watched the single waitress, a stolid woman, bussing tables. She whispered, "I could do her job."

He looked upset. "She needs the work. She has children."

"Oh."

"You got restless today."

She said steadily, "Very restless. The house is clean. It's not time to
make dinner."

"Could you . . . go to a movie?"

How funny—the thing she used to always want to do and now she
wasn't even thinking about it.

"It's because of what we did. You're nervous."

It *was* because of what they'd done, a reminder that she could solve problems, make things happen. She drummed the table. Plates and utensils clattered in the kitchen.

He had to get up to take an order. She heard him tell Emil, "Two grilled cheese." He came back to her.

"Tell me about Philip."

George looked surprised. "What?"

"He went to try for a job today. He came home soon enough. He thought it was beneath him."

"Not a surprise," George said sadly. "He's very smart."

"Is he? I can't tell. How does he earn his money?"

"Earn? He doesn't."

"Well, there was a pile of money on his dresser. I hope he didn't steal it."

"He's not a thief," George murmured.

"A gambler?"

"That money was from me." He blushed deeply. "It's his allowance."

"For what?"

"This is not the time—"

The word *allowance* was ringing in her head. Didn't it mean the nickels parents gave children?

"Why isn't he helping you here?"

"Because . . . you've seen why. He drinks. He's not okay when he drinks."

How stupid she'd been. Of course he drank. She saw now what had been right in front of her. "It makes no sense to give him money for liquor."

"Then he *would* be a thief. It's the one thing he's definite about—loving whiskey and wanting it." George stood reluctantly. "We'll talk about this later. I thought you knew why I never ask anything of him."

She walked home slowly, unwilling to lose the feeling of being out in the world.

Philip looked at her when she got into the house, as if he knew she'd been talking about him.

LENA WAS BACK in LA when one day without warning she answered the phone and heard a man say he was calling from MGM. "Lena Horne? I'm calling for Mr. Mayer. He wants you to come in and talk about a possible movie contract."

"For what movie?"

"Nothing specific yet. To be one of ours."

She just about fainted with excitement as the man talked, hardly able to take in what he was saying.

Stunned, she called her father and told him the man had said something about a seven-year contract. Her heart beat so fast and hard as she reported the talk she could feel her pulse pounding at her throat. *Hollywood, movies.*

Her father said, "I'll be right there. Don't sign *anything*."

"Okay. I'll put them off."

And he did come. For a blissful period while the negotiations were under way, she had her father and Gail and Teddy with her. Her father had known to bring Teddy with him, telling Louis it was a vacation.

As soon as Lena got her father's okay and signed the contract, the word was out, not just in the *Courier*. Everywhere.

Now she sat in a breakfast diner in LA, sunshine streaming through the window, as she ate her eggs and bacon and toast and fruit compote. She was reading the *Courier* to find out if she sounded okay in the last interview.

The *Courier* journalist—not Samuels this time, another guy—wrote that when he talked to her she was "startlingly gorgeous." He wrote that she was a lucky woman to have a life on both coasts (this she disagreed with).

> Q. *Ah, a colleague tells me you were recently seen at nightspots in L.A. with a most handsome fellow a week ago, drinking champagne and dancing. It sounds romantic. Who is the lucky fellow?*
>
> A. *My father! At Martin's, on the water? That was my father.*
>
> Q. *Oh. Yes, indeed, that was it. You get along well by all appearances.*
>
> A. *He's the best. He came out here to negotiate my contract with Mr. Mayer. He wants to be sure I get the right kinds of parts.*
>
> Q. *And that's what I wanted to talk to you about. This amazing movie contract.*

A. *I thought so.*

Q. *So you'll be in movies now? I saw your first one. That little one you did.* The Duke Is Tops.

A. *My practice run. Yes.*

Q. *What's next, then?*

A. *I don't know.*

Q. *But you signed on the dotted line?*

A. *Well, yes. They're going to write parts for me. I have conditions. My contract spells them out. M.G.M. had to agree to the conditions— that means the kinds of things I'm willing to play. My father was very serious about getting it right.*

Q. *Are there specific roles you are pre-cast in?*

A. *No, so far only the ones I am not supposed to be cast in. I'm going to help you out here. No jumping jungle ladies, no prostitutes, no slaves. Regular people—that's what I'm supposed to play. It's written in.*

Q. *And Mr. Mayer said yes?*

A. *He did.*

Q. *I can't wait.*

A. *Me neither.*

Q. *It's all very exciting. How does it feel to meet famous people every day? Out here in Hollywood? And in New York?*

A. *I don't think of it that way. They're just people, like any other people, working, doing a job.*

Q. *Is it true you know Cole Porter?*

A. *Met him socially. Liked the man.*

Q. *Tallulah Bankhead.*

A. *Met her, yes, at a party. Don't know her well.*

Q. *Orson Welles?*

A. *Came to an event when I was singing. Liked the man.*

Q. *Is there a romantic involvement with Orson Welles?*

A. *No, no, nothing like that.*

Q. *Vincente Minnelli? You went to dinner with him.*

A. *A fine fellow. Very fine. I liked him when I talked with him that night.*

Q. *But what about romance these days? All these famous people. Don't they fall in love with you?*

A. *I doubt it. They're just people, doing their jobs.*

Her coffee was cold, so she signaled for another and went back to reading. Minnelli wasn't interested in her, but she had lied about Orson. He was a wild man, crazy and passionate. But why, no matter the subject of the interview, did it always come down to her love life?

Q. *There are several other names you've been linked with. Joe Louis.*
A. *That's just to make articles. People like to imagine.*
Q. *But Louis Jones, your husband, is still in Pittsburgh?*
A. *He has work there. We speak often. We're very cordial. We want the best for our children.*

Did Louis read these articles? Because all that nosy gossip was only going to make her life harder with regard to the divorce.

FIFTEEN

1942

WHAT HAD HAPPENED WITH JOSIAH BEGAN TO RECEDE, FINALLY; George didn't mention it often, and the facts of it came to Marie like bits of a movie she'd once seen but that was fading. Marie had more worries these days about the war. She went to the mailbox each day, in the back of her mind perhaps thinking she might hear from Josiah, but mostly praying that her brother, Freddie, was safe, and praying even more that she would not see a draft notice in George's name.

She was puzzled when a letter appeared in her mailbox from LA. Edwina? Who was Edwina?

Dear Mrs. Elias,

Thank you for your letter. It came to us enclosed in another envelope with other bits of mail which accounts for the delay. Unfortunately, Miss Horne gets a good deal of mail and there is simply no way she can respond to all of it. Even with business matters, she can fall behind. She has been especially taxed in flying coast to coast for engagements, and now she is

busy in Hollywood, thus it falls to me to answer your letter. I'm afraid the
answers are simple and painful. The boy she tried to help has died. She is
sad about that and one day hopes she will tell his story to a reporter who
might at least clear his name.
    With regards,

                                                            Edwina M.

Marie, shaken by the letter, by the puzzle of her promise to Josiah, sat for a long time before she put the letter in the bedroom drawer where she kept things like that. She had her marriage license in there and a few letters from her brother, one of which she reread.

Dear Sis,
    I got your letter. It took a while. Honestly, what do they think is the
secret code in a letter from my sister? So by now you are married. I hope he
is a good man. I hope you are happy. I'm sorry I couldn't be there. I would
have liked to see you in a wedding gown. You are my favorite sister. I guess
you know that. I have nothing to report. I signed up again, but I guess you
know that, too. I'm still in the telegraph office. They think I'm smart. We
ship out soon, no date given. The only thing I really miss about home other
than you is the food, which is way better than what they serve us.
    Your Favorite Brother, because you only have one,

                                                            Freddie

And then, two days later, what she most feared arrived—a draft notice with George's name on it. She presented it, shaking, when he came home.

He held her for a moment. "I felt it. I knew."

"Why couldn't it be Philip?"

"Don't say that." George walked to the kitchen, opened a cupboard, took out a whiskey bottle, and poured a drink. Marie stared at his back. He never took a drink at home.

Just then Philip came down from the second floor as George moved into the living room.

"Say," Philip said, "how about I join you?"

"If you want. I got a draft notice."

"I figured from Marie's face earlier today."

"You too?"

"No, no, they haven't found me yet. I might have to enlist. Thinking about it. When?"

"Two weeks."

Two weeks of torture. Marie hardly slept.

On the day of George's appointment with the draft board, the sun was shining in Pittsburgh. Baseball was in full swing, so the game was the main subject on the radio and on the street and fans even streamed past Marie's house walking to Forbes Field for a home game against the Philadelphia Phillies.

All those people on the street looked happy—how she envied them. She could barely breathe right, waiting for George to come home, which he promised her he would do instead of going to work.

She paced inside and then she went outdoors and paced and then came back in and polished the furniture. The day seemed to last forever, which was one of those tricks time played. Finally at three o'clock George trudged up the sidewalk, looking thoughtful. He didn't see her watching from the window. And she could not tell from his expression what had happened.

"It's okay," he said, as soon as he saw her at the door, and he came in and took her hand. "I won't be going."

Marie couldn't stop wiping her eyes, but even though the news was good, George was not right somehow, not himself. "What did they say? Did they do something to you?"

"Just . . . just tired."

"Should I get you water?"

"No, let's sit in the kitchen. Let's have some tea."

She held onto him until he settled in a kitchen chair. She put on a pot of water to boil.

"They can't use me."

"And that's for sure?"

"Yep." He flashed a piece of paper as she was bringing the bread and butter to the table and it was so quick she hardly saw any detail except a stamp and a circle around 4F.

"What does that mean?"

"My flat feet."

"Your feet aren't flat."

"Apparently they are." He folded the paper and put it back in his jacket pocket.

"We should keep the paper, for proof," she said, unable to quell her nerves.

"I'll put it with the deed for the house and the restaurant. When I go tonight." He kept a metal box at the restaurant with those important papers in it.

Marie supposed that made sense. She broke off a piece of bread and buttered it for him.

"Did they make you do things that were hard on you?"

"Some running, some stomping. They check out endurance and the truth is, I haven't been building mine up. I just stand at work. Flat feet and varicose veins."

"Put your feet up." She turned a second kitchen chair toward him and he did put his feet up, smiling.

"It's funny. I don't want to leave you or the business. But I wish . . . in a way, I wish I were going."

"No!"

"So many men I know will go . . . I don't want to get away with anything."

Marie busied herself at the sink until she could stop crying.

When Philip came home he asked immediately, "How did it go?"

"They don't want me."

"Really?"

"Flat feet and varicose veins," Marie said.

Philip said. "I see." He asked George, "You want a drink?"

"Yes," George said.

Philip studied his brother closely as he brought two glasses of whiskey to the table. "You didn't go to work today?"

"Later. After dinner," George told both of them, "I'll put in a few hours."

"I'm making fried chicken," Marie announced. Did George hear her? He didn't react.

"Good," said George after a beat. "Thank you."

"You ought to make an appointment with Glesman. Get those legs and feet checked," Philip said, narrowing his eyes, which Marie didn't like at all.

"Yeah. I'll do that," George assured his brother.

Why were they shutting her out?

They ate fried chicken and George went to the restaurant and Marie found herself pacing again as if the news had not been wonderful.

IT WAS ALSO a beautiful spring in Hollywood (not surprising). Lena, sitting in the MGM commissary in April, picked at a donut, working to sweeten her spirits. She tried to talk herself into a better mood. It was gorgeous outside, she was making a living, but on the other hand she was the last person to know what she was supposed to *do* at the studio. She assigned herself tasks, studied new songs, sat outdoors when there was no one to talk to, basically waited and waited. It was not unlike being married to Louis. Look nice, stay cheerful, don't ask for anything.

She called her father. "Did we do the right thing?"

"Give it some time. It's a contract. Legally binding."

He'd sounded so tough when he told Mayer it wasn't just prostitutes that were out of the question but that the contract had to stipulate no tramps, no maids, nobody dumb. "She has class. You gotta use it."

Right, they said, and they signed their names. Sometimes she wondered, were they laughing at her father? And her?

On a subsequent day at MGM, doing her best to avoid another donut, she worked on a speech of complaint in her head. Just then a runner found her and told her to go hear a song being recorded in Studio B just in case they might want her to learn it.

She hurried, sun-warmed, over to the studio and listened to another woman sing. Lena would need the lyrics, but pretty much had the melody down. And she felt she would syncopate just slightly if it were hers, to make it more interesting. Jotting notes and singing to herself, she thanked her stars that they had wanted her for something, finally, even if just to learn a song. The piano player stood, thought better of it, sat and told her he was rushed, but he could let her run the song once.

She sang, trying to show where she would hold and interrupt the rhythm. He said, "Fine, you've got it. You can go."

She gathered her handbag and her notebook and the novel she was reading as the piano player and the singing coach buddied up to go to lunch together. She'd thought they might ask her. Dumb. She looked toward where the singer had exited. She was gone too.

It was like high school. She just had to hang around long enough to be included. The whole thing, the contract and the social scene, was a test of will. After all, Walter White of the NAACP said she was doing it for all Negroes, not herself.

She walked, practicing the song she had just learned, trying to keep twenty yards between herself and the two men who hadn't invited her to lunch. She had totally lost track of the woman. In the commissary, she found a table that was not occupied. She sat for a while drinking a Coca-Cola. Then she got up and got herself a tuna salad sandwich.

Out of the blue, three chorus women from *For Me and My Gal* asked if they could sit at her table. "Of course!" she said eagerly. She cut a small piece of her sandwich and ate delicately, only to notice that the three of them were much rowdier than she, all of them with their bacon sandwiches in hand, dripping tomato and mayonnaise. Their antics loosened her up. She picked up her sandwich, grandmother be damned.

One of them noticed enough to say, "There you go. Better, right?"

A dancer with a very thin body and masses of red hair asked her boldly, "Are you still married?"

"Um, yes."

"You have guts. You do. You get around in spite of the marriage."

"Oh, I don't know."

"I want to have a lot of lovers before I die."

Lena winced. "There's a certain amount of gossip. Those guys have to write something to stay employed, you know."

"I'm not blaming you. Seriously. I want to be like you. You have the looks. You ought to have the fun. That's what it's all about, right?"

"Absolutely," said one of the other women.

"I agree," said the third.

At just that point, a man Lena knew to be the studio's big muckety-muck conductor and arranger stopped at their table. He leaned toward the quietest of the chorines, a strawberry blonde with an overbite and a puppy-dog look—her hair came down in two bunches on the sides. He said something about coordinating the music and the dance she was having trouble with and asked, if he held up the beat on the third chorus, would that help.

"Thank you, Mr. Hayton," she said. "Yes, it would help. I'll be there right away."

"You have time to finish your milkshake."

He was such a snob, that Lennie Hayton. Horrible—just one of the worst of Hollywood personalities, Lena thought. She had passed him a hundred times and he never once said hello.

He nodded to the strawberry blonde, turned to look at Lena, and held the gaze too long.

She couldn't breathe. She reminded herself he was a snob and she didn't like him at all. Why had neither of them been able to break the gaze?

The others watched, interested.

AFTER MONTHS HAD passed and Marie and George fully stopped fearing the draft board would somehow reverse its decision, Marie watched as George stirred sugar into his tea and dunked his piece of buttered bread. "I love this," he said. "Doesn't matter the season."

This particular package of bread was a gift from Fran, who could make the thick pita as well as Ummah did, with great butter pits in the squishy bottom section. Marie's bread was coming along, not as good as Fran's. "Thank Fran for this. How is she?"

"She's going to have the baby soon. I met her downtown so she could give me the bread. She's, you know, sometimes embarrassing. Too much, too loud, and . . . I don't know. I mean, she's good to me, but she's so . . . I stay away from her mostly."

George said offhandedly, lightly, "Don't. She needs you."

"For what?"

"To be in her corner. Have her come to dinner and let's give her something significant for the baby. She'll need it."

"Oh, George! Why do you want to support everybody?"

"Not everybody." He gave her a wary look. "Almost everybody, all right. But she's your sister." He dipped the last of his bread and ate it, making a dramatic happy expression.

"I think she's a bit loose. Fran."

"Now, now."

"She might be seeing somebody."

"I hope he's nice."

"She laughs too much. Everything makes her laugh. I thought you noticed that the last time she was here."

"She's trying to make a place for herself, to be pleasant. Surely you can see that."

Marie frowned. She had terrible jealousies. "That's just oily, isn't it? Playing up to people." She was embarrassed by Fran. How could George like her?

He shook his head. "You should give her a chance."

"I'll invite her to dinner. Okay." She did not want to be a terrible person.

But Marie, being practical, wanted to kill two birds while she was being a better person: she asked Fran to come for a whole day, to teach her some cooking tricks *and* make enough of everything to have quite a store of food. It wasn't wrong to make a person sing for her supper, was it?

She climbed into bed beside George that night feeling a twinge of guilt that she was a user, wanting to be a person for whom he would always say, "Give her a chance."

"There you are," he said.

"Here I am. Well, the cooking is getting a bit better these days."

"That first week I thought I wasn't going to make it." He shifted his bulk to put an arm around her.

"The eggs were—"

"Hard. Little baby saucers."

"Philip called them hockey pucks."

He kissed her and sighed happily when her arms went around him.

Every time he made love to her, her body hummed with pleasure, but she also felt, during and after his attentions to her physical self, that nothing she had ever said or thought or done was truly bad, that she was completely acceptable.

Fran, no surprise, came in bright spirits early in the morning on a Saturday bearing ingredients—a special allspice from the old country, a jar of grape leaves, a jar of tahini, a paper bag of bulgur wheat. She always knew where to get things. Short and very pregnant, she moved awkwardly—the baby was killing her back and her leg. Her voice was nervous, rapid and loud, at a higher pitch with each phrase.

Philip, sitting in the living room, examined Fran and dismissed her immediately. He went upstairs.

"Where did he go?" Fran asked.

"Having a drink."

They worked for a whole day. Fran taught Marie how to make the bread squishy inside, brown outside—and they were making two batches, one to use for the spinach pies. They cleaned bunches of spinach, tender, so young and green. Marie had bought so much of it the kitchen looked like a plant store, overtaken as it was by green, but all of it would come down to filling for twenty pies. Late in the afternoon they mixed a tray of kibbee and pounded down some chickpeas to mix with the tahini Fran had brought.

"How much do I owe you for the supplies?"

"Four dollars and maybe thirty cents."

Marie counted it out.

Seven o'clock, George was home, and they sat down to dinner. "Look at this!" he exclaimed. "What a feast."

Even Philip livened up enough to make compliments to the cooks. When they were replete, and the others sat over coffee, Marie packaged up some of each food for her sister to take home. While she was wrapping kibbee she saw Philip go upstairs. George beckoned Fran closer, and she gasped and tears filled her eyes as he pressed the money into her hands, saying, "You're going to need this for the baby."

Marie knew it was fifty dollars. He'd told her he was going to give that much.

Fran's voice came out high and raspy. "I don't know how to thank you."

He dismissed the need for thanks with a wave of his hand. "I'm happy to help. Marie? Let's walk her to the streetcar stop. I *wish* we had a car," he said again.

"A streetcar is okay," Fran insisted. "I like it. I'm used to it."

A FEW DAYS later, Philip doodled with his eggs over easy at the breakfast table while Marie waited to clean up. As she waited, she took the newspaper George had already read to the living room and made her best attempt to catch up on the conflict in Europe.

"What are you doing?" Philip called. "In addition to avoiding me."

"Reading the paper." She made a decision, came back, and sat down hard on the chair opposite him. "Look, Philip. I think it's time you find your own place."

He looked up, surprised, but recovered quickly. "Uh-oh, falling for me, are you?"

"That's not going to happen."

"Why not?"

"I love your brother."

"I'm handsomer."

"Philip. I'm trying to say something. You're a mature man. You should be out on your own."

"He told you to say that?"

"I'm saying it. It's coming from me."

"Well, you have no right."

"I think I do."

"We'll see." He jerked his chair back and just as suddenly went up to his room.

Her head began to pound. After she finished the breakfast dishes she started a batch of bread, kneading hard before reminding herself of Fran's lesson about not being too rough with the dough. An hour later she heard a lot of slamming as Philip left the house. A battle was coming. She looked at the clock, thinking; she didn't have to roll out the dough until noon, so she had a couple of hours.

She bundled the bread in blankets and sheets and tablecloths, the method of keeping it warm she'd learned from her mother and mostly from Fran—and she started to walk. Past the University of Pittsburgh in its big building that looked like an elongated church reaching harder for the heavens than ordinary churches ever did. She kept walking up up the hilly streets, past places for rent, eventually into the Hill and past where she used to live, then up into a poorer section. When she stopped to catch her breath, a little girl approached her. "Can I have your gloves?" the child asked.

"Well, no, sorry, I need them. I only have this pair and another." And alas, this pair was already showing signs of being out in the dirty Pittsburgh air.

The child's hair was dense and almost bigger than she was. She knocked one knee against the other and pointed a toe down, a pose that perfected her bratty image.

"Listen," Marie said, "do you know of a family named Conner? The father is a plumber? I guess you wouldn't know, but I thought I'd ask. You look smart."

The child's eyes darted about. She pointed. "Maybe there."

Marie couldn't help laughing. "And maybe what else?"

The girl pointed to three more places.

"Oh, dear, he lives in a lot of houses." Marie dug in her purse and unearthed a nickel. "Do you like penny candy?"

"Yes."

"Then this is for you."

"What's the problem?" yelled a woman bursting out of a doorway. "What you asking her?"

"Just directions," Marie said, "just if she knows where Mr. Conner lives."

The woman came toward her, then clutched at the plaid dress her daughter wore. "We got more than one Conner. Who you want?"

"There was a young man who got killed in jail—"

"That Conner is three streets back, three houses in when you turn right."

"Do people talk about that person much? Josiah?"

The woman paused, studying her. "How come you want to know? Reporter?"

To be taken for a professional woman—maybe it was the gloves, something about her clothes? Sometimes people gave her credit for being more than she was. Shaking her head, she said, "Just can't help being interested, feeling bad for the family."

"You said it." The woman tugged at her daughter. "What you got there?" She snatched the nickel and probably the promise of candy from her daughter.

Marie walked three blocks back and three houses to the right. A small house.

A man in denim overalls answered.

"Mr. Conner? I . . . my name is Marie Elias. I knew your son a little, from school," she said. "I am the one who—are you alone? I helped him."

He nodded. He did not invite her in. He was frightened, she could tell. It was sad to see how afraid he was. And from no fault of his own.

Mr. Conner did not close the door on her, but he said, "I'm moving out of town. Packing up now."

She saw behind him boxes in the parlor. "Do you know if he's all right?"

He looked at her and behind her, still worried. "Thank you if you tried to help him. And for any kindness." Then he closed the door.

And after standing there for a minute, she decided to deal with her own life, with the reason she had left the house today. She wound back down the hill and the whole way into Oakland, where she went to visit George at the restaurant. The place was crowded, four people waiting for a booth.

George shuffled three or four paper menus, probably looking for the cleanest one. There were so many things to *do* in a business, including updating the menu and going to a print shop. "Sorry, I really shouldn't stop moving right now," he said.

Five minutes later, when he came back to her, she asked, "Did Philip come see you this morning?"

"Yes."

"I've decided. He goes or I go. I can't bear it."

"Oh, please, don't say that. I can't. He's my brother."

"I'm your wife."

George's shoulders slumped. The menus hung at his side. "Did he do something to you?"

"He doesn't have to. He thinks it."

"It could be your imagination."

"It's not."

"I'll talk to him. I can't kick him out."

"Well, I can't tolerate him. So what do we do?" She turned and hurried out. They'd never fought before. It was stupid of her to pick a fight while he was busy.

She made it home in time to roll out the dough.

Philip came into the kitchen. He said, "I know you didn't like what I said. I honestly was joking. Believe me, I know I'm a bad deal." Suddenly he looked extremely sad.

Her hands were floury, a knife in her right and a hunk of bread dough in her left. Sympathy for Philip was not something she wanted to feel, but for a while, she felt it in spite of herself. So. He knew he was awful.

There would be another stack of bills on his dresser. For all the mess in her head, one truth was bigger than everything, bigger than her anger: she still loved George.

ON THE STUDIO lot at MGM, one of the sets was a fake cemetery. It looked so real Lena could hardly believe no one was buried there. She ate a cheese sandwich one day in summer and sat on the fake grass, thinking all kinds of things.

She poked at the fake stone in front of her and turned her thoughts to the power of names in her life. There was a sort of name *chain*. Joe Louis to Louis Jones to Lew Leslie. Lena Horne living on Horn Avenue in LA (strange, wasn't it?) and best friends with Billy Strayhorn.

She had been steeping herself in film when she couldn't kill time with Swee' Pea, who was in and out of town—and at least not in uniform. They'd rejected him as too frail.

It was either war movies or fluff being made by the studios. The war movies helped people to think about bravery as an honorable way to live and maybe die. They helped people to accept death, to mourn. The musicals helped them run away from fear and grief. Both were useful, she supposed. She saw everything the studio made.

At *Joan of Paris* she thought, "Why couldn't I play something like that?" and she wondered how to bring the subject up with Louis Mayer and Arthur Freed. Ditto something like *Casablanca*. She studied acting by watching. She couldn't master the slow, slight smile of Bergman or the awkward exuberance of Garland. *Be yourself*, her father kept saying.

SIXTEEN

1943

A YEAR PASSED AND DURING THAT YEAR THERE WERE CHANGES IN the lives of both Marie and Lena—the latter Marie knew about from reading the papers. Marie got pregnant and had a daughter. She named her daughter Helena—because of the warm-hearted woman who lived next door to her mother and who had married Alberto and also because the dazzling Lena Horne was really named Helena. These were the gifts, dazzle and warmth, she hoped to give her daughter.

And there was change coming from George, too. When she had tried to announce the pregnancy to George, she had to speak second because he came home bursting with his news: He had bought the bar next door to his restaurant and was going to expand and combine the two places. She tried to be happy for him, but all she could think was that she would see him even less (which turned out to be true). When she got around to telling him they were having a baby, he cried with happiness.

Philip enlisted. So when Marie went to the mailbox she now looked for letters from him as well as from Freddie and the odd chance that Jo-

siah would find a way to tell her how he was. George asked her to call
him at work if there was any significant news about any of them.

MGM STARTED PUTTING Lena to work. In 1943, peas began hitting the
window, and she was much in the papers because she made three movies: *Swing Fever, Cabin in the Sky,* and *Stormy Weather.* She was starting
to feel better about her chances. She didn't get to *act* much in the films,
but it was a start. Other actors had begun to sit at her table in the commissary. Now Lennie Hayton even said hello to her. A thought crossed
her mind. LH and LH. Lena and Lennie. Their names were so close.
And names were always . . . No, she told herself. No, never. They worked
in the same place. Get some sense, Lena!

One night at a party Lennie played piano and Lena sang. Without
her noticing, at one point everybody had left and there they were.

"May I take you home?" he asked.

"Yes."

"Would you consider having dinner with me tomorrow?"

"Just dinner?"

"Yes."

"Yes."

And somehow, twenty-four hours later, at two in the morning, she
was lying a little apart from him in his bed. Now she had another rumor
to worry about. She moved a little closer. Arms around her. That's what
she needed. Arms around her.

For a man's dwelling, the place was not bad at all—the sheets, thick
with threads, were a startling white; the cashmere blanket felt luxurious, not at all scratchy.

Lennie had worn a beautiful camel hair coat at dinner. Like her father, he was aware of fabric.

From what she'd seen of his house as they passed through it, the
place was extremely orderly. Lena pulled the blanket up close to her
cheek, thinking how crazy it was that she had ended up here.

The Manhattans had helped, of course. The good food helped. His
arm across the table, his hand taking hers, and the murmur in his voice,
all of that helped. But she knew, and he surely knew, this wouldn't go
down well at the studio.

He got up from the bed and she became aware again of how very pale he was. She could hear him in the bathroom, water running, all those personal sounds. When he returned he had a towel wrapped around his waist and he looked like an actor in costume for some non-white role. He climbed back under the covers and reached an arm around her. He was not gorgeous, not ugly, just regular, as well as very talented, very smart, and somewhat mysterious.

Lying there, she admitted to herself two things: that every time he said hello to her at the studios this last year a tremor went through her, and that when MGM lent her out to make *Stormy Weather* she *missed* being at the commissary, her eyes wandering the room to see if he'd come in.

"I'm embarrassed to say I've never seen you perform in a club," he'd told her earlier that evening when they were at dinner. "Don't ask me how I've managed that."

She made a face, smiled her big smile as she pushed a chocolate mousse across the table to him. "I guess that's a relief, in a way. I don't have to apologize for anything."

"Anyway, I got myself a print of *Stormy Weather*," he'd said then, taking a spoonful and pushing the mousse back. "I've been wanting to watch it. Let's go back to my place and watch it together."

But when they got to his place they began kissing, and she only stopped long enough to call Edwina to say she was staying overnight at a friend's place.

Now it was two in the morning.

He leaned forward, one knee on the bed, kissed her forehead, then her lips. "Are you all right?"

"We had a few Manhattans tonight. I think we might be a little crazy."

He pointed to a wall across from the bed to his left. "See that wall? I project on it sometimes when I want to be in bed. What do you say we watch the movie in here?"

"Now? Aha. Maybe you think it will put you to sleep . . ."

"No. I'm trying to break a spell. I'm a superstitious guy. If we watch it together, it won't be bad luck."

"Huh." She was stuck for words. Luck?

"What I'm saying is, I don't think of this as anything ordinary. Or temporary." He straightened up in his towel sarong and left the room.

She heard clunking noises somewhere down the hall. She knew she could get up, call a car, and go home, but she couldn't make herself move that much, so she burrowed down farther in the bed. He returned, wearing a brocade robe of purples and blues and wheeling a cart with a projector on it, a thing of metal knobs and wheels.

"I work at home a lot. I review things here when I can't stand the studio."

"Where do you keep that?"

"In the room with the piano. I'll show you around later. You haven't even seen the house."

"I guess we were in kind of a hurry."

He started the projector and climbed back into bed.

In her first appearance in the film she was wearing a fez with feathers of about two feet sticking out on each side. The headpiece was considered exotic, glamorous.

"You must have poked out a few eyes with that."

"Tried to."

"You look gorgeous." His voice was warm. "I know they put you in a lot of gold, a lot of white. That makes sense. It really works on you."

She watched the Lena on screen smiling, smiling, smiling, being charming. She heard herself singing, "There's No Two Ways about Love." The song was about how love comes and grabs you even if you don't want it to. *It's over, no escape, you're caught,* said the song.

"Ah," he said, letting out a big breath.

"What?"

"Good. You sounded good."

At one point, when she didn't have a scene, Lennie left in his beautiful robe and came back with two glasses of brandy.

They watched her as she sang "I Can't Give You Anything but Love," and they watched Fats Waller do "Ain't Misbehavin.'" Fats was wonderfully naughty, flirting outrageously by making eyes at everyone in the film audience. They watched Cab Calloway calling out "Hi De Ho." Lena knew she was downright wooden next to him. She said, "How does he get away with it? He's dancing, but his feet are hardly moving!"

"He dances with his hands."

That was right. His feet hardly did anything, but he was so animated you *thought* he was dancing.

The script was building up all the while to her singing "Stormy Weather," the title song. Her character was a woman who gives up love for show business because she loves singing and is ambitious. The phrase *typecasting* had been flung at her more than a few times over the last year.

Neither Lena nor Lennie said anything when the black actors on screen added blackface to make themselves blacker.

Later in the film she wore another extreme headdress while she sang and did what were supposed to be Egyptian shoulder and arm movements.

Lennie groaned.

"What?"

"I can't believe I'm falling in love with someone who sings a song called "Diggy Do.""

"It's 'Diga Diga Doo!'" She pretended affront. "That's the title."

"You were wonderful," he said, when the movie ended.

"No. Just all right. Coming along. I hope one day I'll be really good."

SEVENTEEN

1943, 1944

MARIE COULDN'T BELIEVE HER EYES WHEN SHE SAW THE RETURN address—a letter from Lena, after all this time.

> *Dear Mrs. Elias,*
>
> *I remember you well. I didn't know your new last name. Of course we both knew Josiah. I still live with the tragedy of his loss. I hear there was nothing investigated after all in the murder charge or his death. I have tried to interest reporters from the Courier in writing a tribute to him, explaining that he was wrongfully accused and that his name should be cleared. However, the reporters who see me only want entertainment gossip. I did tell one man that when he found a rookie reporter trying to make his name that he should tell that reporter about Josiah and ask him to contact you. That was all I knew to do. Life is sometimes very disappointing. People are, anyway.*
>
> *My regards,*
>
> *Lena*

Marie tried to imagine a life in which a person could be so far behind in correspondence. More charitably she reminded herself she had been busy, too. Her daughter was six months old.

It was all too late. And Marie was supposed to let things be. They didn't need a reporter to rake things up now.

Nobody called, and after a while she stopped worrying.

Six more months went by and her daughter was one.

Marie was home one afternoon, had just made mujadara, which happened to be one of George's favorite meals, when she heard a knock at the door.

The house smelled like cooked onions; she was carrying her daughter, who was wriggling, wanting to walk, to speak, the usual handful; and she wore the clothes she cleaned house in. She went to open the door, frazzled, with the usual worries about what trouble might be standing there.

A Negro man said, "Hello. I'm James McCoy. I'm from the *Courier*."

"Oh. Yes?"

"I'm trying to write a political piece about that young man who got killed in jail. Maybe they won't even like it. I mean, no guarantee they'll take it. A friend of mine was talking to Miss Lena Horne."

"Yes?"

"Miss Horne told a friend of mine you saw something that would show the guy—"

"Josiah Conner?"

"Yes—was innocent. May I please come in? Something smells fantastic."

"Lentils and rice."

"Yes, ma'am. I'm sorry to come in talking about your food. Forgive me that."

She had to let him in. What she would say, she couldn't imagine or plan ahead for. "Would you like some of the lentils?"

"No, no, no, I didn't mean—"

"I'll get you some. Coffee?"

"Coffee, yes."

Why could this man not have arrived two years ago? What good was he now?

"You have to behave," she whispered to her daughter. "Shh." She put Helena down in the playpen in the dining room, visible from both the living room and the kitchen. "I keep her where I can see her," she called out to Mr. McCoy as she quickly dished out some of her supper and poured a cup of coffee, hands shaking the whole time.

"I understand. I have a daughter 'bout her age. Name of Larette."

"That's a pretty name."

"Yes, ma'am."

"Well, here. I won't give you the name of this. It's just lentils and rice and oil and onions. I call it grub. You might like it."

"Smell goes the whole way out to the street."

He took a bite, then put the dish and spoon down to pick up his notebook, but quickly took the dish up again. "Wow, that's good."

He ate two bites quickly, then slowed down. "I don't get a lot of good assignments, never the really interesting stuff. But I'll try to get this article in. I did read everything I could about the situation before coming here. There wasn't much of a case to make against this young man. Nobody much wants to *talk* about it, either. But you saw something?"

"Yes. But it's done with now. Maybe we should let him rest in peace."

"But Miss Horne said this was the unfairness of the system, that people would always think he did it, that Negroes get blamed for all sorts of things and other people who commit crimes walk away. Shouldn't we say all that? Clear his name?"

"I'm not sure I want to dredge all this up again," she tried.

"I thought you wanted to clear his name. I was told you did."

"Yes. I did." She found herself saying, as she tried to arrange her wrinkled old blouse, "I do." And the thought nudged her that Josiah was far away, with a new name. Why not let justice be done?

"It isn't much," she said. She took a big breath and told him about the car sliding fast past her that January night and the way Josiah (though she didn't recognize him because he was at a distance in the blizzard) appeared to be trying to get help for the wounded man, and she explained how from the start she questioned his immediate arrest by police. "The police didn't even believe he'd been to the movies. I know he must have been. He went often. I think I saw a piece of paper he wrote on but I can't prove it. It was lost in the blizzard."

"Anything else?"

"Well, I read that a gun was never found."

McCoy said, "I read that too." He ate a bite, had a drink of coffee. "You knew this Conner well?"

"I knew him, Josiah, from school, and he came into my family's store."

"That's it?"

"And into the candy store where I worked. We talked about movies. And he was friends with Lena Horne. I knew her a little." She chose her words. "Josiah was smart, polite, and . . . very likable."

"I'm going to try to write that we don't know the real story, may never know the real story, but that if you want to look hard, it looks like Conner was an easy solution to something. The police didn't dig. I wish I knew more, like who might have wanted this Klein dead. I'm going to look into it more, too, before I quit on this."

She didn't dare say what she thought, what she'd been thinking for some time, ever since she'd learned Madeline Klein had a man in her life at the time of the murder. Wasn't there the possibility that the man, the supposed lowlife, might be involved? But she felt as guilty as if she'd said it.

McCoy, folding up his tablet, said, "Interesting case. It's a damn shame the police didn't want to work it."

"I don't want to be quoted. If you write this."

"I'd have to see about that. Thank you for your time, Mrs. Elias. And thank you for the food."

How could she blame him? He was trying to do the right thing and yet she didn't know how to step—left, right, straight ahead. How many people had this one little meeting betrayed? Josiah, Schmidt, Howard, Madeline. Even George. She was making life hard for a number of people.

She told George about the interview as they changed clothes for bed. She put the radio on, music, to mute the emotions being raked up. George sat on the edge of the bed, listening to her. "I tried to come up with something to put off the reporter but I couldn't think of anything that would stop him from doing his job."

They needed a good laugh. It was a shame the comics weren't on the radio tonight.

George told her, "I can't think of a thing you could have said unless you went back on your story completely. Even that would make trouble. Maybe they won't print. It's long after the fact."

She hoped for that.

Months went by.

It seemed it might be so.

She and George got invited to a party at the Kleins' in the summer. She had a small nervousness about being around Madeline, but the party was big enough that they never ended up sitting together and talking.

It got to be November and coming up on Marie's second wedding anniversary. One night George said, "Howard and Madeline want to take us out. I mentioned our anniversary and Howard said, 'Let's do something special.'"

"What?"

"You choose. Something different."

"Jazz at the Crawford Grill?"

"Jazz! All right. What a great idea."

Madeline called the next day. "Let's get our hair and nails done together."

It was going to be all right. Madeline sounded very friendly.

The Tic Toc was crowded and there was a line, but Madeline whispered that she had just tipped the hostess, which was why they were whisked to a good table. "I'm buying," Madeline said.

"Oh, no. You're taking us tonight."

"Oh, yes. I want to."

Marie ordered grilled cheese, which came with a side of fries and coleslaw. Madeline ordered the roast chicken special.

"Out in the Hill for music tonight!" Madeline exclaimed. "I'm so glad you came up with something different to do."

"How's Howard?"

"Good, I guess. Grumpy a lot of the time."

"Well, business is a worry, I'm sure. It is for George. Won't the big lunch kill your appetite for dinner?"

Madeline said, "Oh, no, I won't have dinner. I'll let them have cereal."

Marie tried not to be shocked by the idea of cereal for dinner. "Oh, I just remembered." She removed a package from under her handbag. "I baked bread. I brought you two loaves." She'd given a gift of it before, when she and George went to that party in the summer, and it was apparently a big hit.

"I love your bread!"

"It's getting better. Every batch, better. Now it puffs up and the pocket is distinct. And it's thick."

"Well, there's my dinner. That's all I want."

"Glad to help." People were so different. Marie usually made a salad, a vegetable, and a meat.

Madeline nodded vaguely. "How are you getting your hair done?"

"Just a trim."

"Well, I clipped a picture of Joan Crawford from one of my magazines. *Above Suspicion*. Last year. That was a good film. I want to do that style with the roll on the bangs. A little lower than hers. I have such a high forehead."

Ah, a high forehead, a sign of the ruling class, Marie had read. Madeline was very good-looking, almost porcelain in her beauty. She knew it and carried herself with the confidence of one who knew how desirable her whiteness was. Marie wondered if Madeline had any talents. It wasn't cooking, for sure. Maybe it was being smart, up on things.

"I think you should have them do your hair in rolls," Madeline said, scrutinizing Marie. "You had it kind of like that once. Your hair holds a shape, doesn't it?"

"Holds it and refuses to let it go!"

"You're funny. You're crazy about George, aren't you?"

"Yes. He works too hard, though. I miss him during the day."

"My God, you *are* lucky."

"I guess so." In a rare burst of carelessness, she added, "I worry. He's drinking more than he used to."

"Drink doesn't hurt."

"But it *does*."

Madeline closed her eyes. "I guess you're right. But once you get a taste for the stuff . . ." She opened her eyes and looked at Marie. "It makes things better."

"Does it?"

"Does for me. I had a bad day yesterday. Some guy came asking questions about my husband's death. His idea was the kid didn't do it."

Marie took her hands from the table and put them on her lap. She was trembling now and wouldn't be able to pick up a fork to save her life.

"As far as I'm concerned it's over and done with. Get this: it was a Negro man, stirring up trouble. Not so comfortable on our street, I can tell you. He was a mess, trying to ask this and that. He writes for the Negro newspaper."

Marie had reviewed every possibility for what might have happened that night. Any of the possibilities could have been written up, like something in *Movie Stories* magazine. But as time passed, Marie settled on the suspicion that Madeline's lover did it or paid someone to do it. It chilled her to think that.

Yet Madeline always seemed to her like one of those movie characters, dressed beautifully and always up to something, a woman that a man might kill for.

Marie said, "I'm sorry the guy bothered you."

"Why are you sorry? Let's just eat."

Marie asked, "Do you think people get very dressed up to hear jazz?"

"I think they do."

"I'm wearing my black velvet again."

Madeline shook her head. She said, not unkindly, "A lady of simple pleasures, that's you."

At the end of the afternoon, Marie's hair was smooth and shiny. Madeline's new style was much nicer than the dripping sausage curls, more flattering.

"You seem preoccupied."

"Sorry," Marie said. "My daughter might be getting a cold."

"See you tonight."

Marie fed her daughter mashed potatoes with the littlest bit of mashed meatloaf mixed in. And then she put on the velvet suit, all the while listening to the radio.

George got home at eight. He had borrowed a car again, this time from Krieger, wanting to treat Howard for all his kindnesses.

In a reversal of the first outing with the Kleins, George drove to Squirrel Hill to pick up Howard and Madeline. Then Marie, knowing the Hill, gave directions to the Crawford Grill. Her heart leapt to be back near her old home ground. "There, there, you see it? The Grill." Posters of musicians covered the whole front of the building.

George dropped them off before driving down the street to park. Three women came from around the corner—all of them in hats, gloves, and shoes that matched their dresses. None of them wore coats and neither did Marie or Madeline, since they were going right in. The three women who had just passed Marie told her, "I love your suit!"

She beamed.

As soon as Howard got them inside, Madeline asked a mustachioed man in a full white apron, black pants, and a white shirt, "Is that the entertainment?" She inclined her head toward where a man up high on a platform played a piano covered in mirrors.

"That's the preshow," he explained. "That's Woogie—Woogie Harris—he's doing the warming up tonight. The trio plays in the other room. I can seat you. Three?"

"One more," Howard said. "He'll be right in."

George came in and the host led them to the next room. The Crawford was not what Marie had first imagined, not fancy at all, only Formica tables with the basic salt and pepper and sugar on the tabletops. There were tables in the center of the room, but the host showed them to leather banquette seats. The women took the soft seats. The waitresses looked a little like nurses in their crisp white uniforms and white shoes.

"Ma'am, I love that suit," said their waitress as she handed them menus.

She had been right. The suit was special.

"Gee," Madeline commented as Marie said a thank you. "This is going to go to your head."

The waitress smiled at Marie as if to warn, *Don't let her bother you.* She asked, "What can I get all of you to drink?"

"Two whiskeys straight," Howard answered. "Two with 7-Up. Is that good?"

Marie and Madeline made no argument.

The stage—just a small raised platform—held three musicians who were smoking and setting up. Howard pulled out a pack of Camels. He and his wife each took one and he leaned in and lit hers with a flourish.

"George?"

"All right." He took a cigarette and accepted a light from Howard. He looked tired.

Marie smoothed a hand over his back.

There were posters everywhere. Marie couldn't make out if Madeline was studying posters or was simply uncomfortable, but her attention began to get very scattered.

"We should order food. I'm starved," Howard said as he put on a pair of glasses and studied the menu.

"He only had cereal for dinner," Madeline said with a laugh. "I hid the bread for myself. I suppose I could eat again."

George was first studying the way the room was set up, then, intently, the prices on the menu. "Simple food. It could have been ordinary, but it's not. It's a special place, nothing a person could imitate."

Marie told him, "It kept building up for years. Lots of famous people have played here. Lots."

He got a whimsical expression. "Well, I don't have the music."

And Howard was thinking of business, too. "I never thought to rent machines up here. Maybe I should talk to somebody about it." He put down the menu. "How about I order us fried chicken and greens and cornbread."

Everybody agreed to that, even Madeline, who was tilting a lapel watch toward herself, squinting through the smoke.

When they had their drinks, George and Marie sipped so slowly that neither of them was ready when it was time to order another round. Howard asked, "Are you doing all right? Working too hard, buddy?"

"I'm fine."

"Guitar, huh," Madeline observed, nodding to the trio, now assembled and ready to start. "That's something different."

The other instruments were a bass and a piano. A slip of paper on the table told them the guitarist was Danny Barker and that he was up from New Orleans. The pianist was Sir Charles Thompson from Ohio. The bass player was from Pittsburgh and this was his first job with well-known people. His name was Jonah Barrow.

Marie and the others settled in, getting used to the sounds.

George kissed Marie's ear and put his arm around her. He whispered, "You're great. I'm watching you listening."

About an hour later, just about when they had finished the chicken and sides, Madeline got up and headed toward the ladies' room.

She was gone for a long time. At first the rest of them didn't notice. Then they did.

"She must not like the music," Howard ventured.

"I'd better go check on her. Maybe she doesn't feel well."

Marie made her way down a hallway, stood in line for the lavatory, and when she finally got in there, found no Madeline. Puzzled, she looked around. There was a door to a backyard partway open. She thought perhaps Madeline had gone into the yard for air.

She pressed the heavy door and tried to take in what she saw. Madeline *was* out there, but not alone. She and a man were standing almost nose to nose. He seemed agitated.

Marie tried to tiptoe backward.

Madeline turned. She stared for a moment and then made a gesture that surely meant, *Go away. Shut up.*

Back at the table, Marie said, "She's okay. The line is long."

The rest of the evening, with the jumpy, nervous music, went by in a haze.

The next week she got a letter from McCoy.

Dear Mrs. Elias,

I couldn't do much. They are willing to put a small notice in. That's about it. I did what I could. Thank you for your hospitality.

Sincerely yours,

James McCoy

She bought the *Courier* and read it twice.

A woman has come forward requesting anonymity as she described events on the night of the murder of businessman Joseph Klein five years ago. She was downtown during the blizzard when she saw a car leaving the scene of the shooting, driving recklessly.

Moments later, Josiah Conner was accused of the murder. He insisted he was walking home from the movies.

Police never found a murder weapon, but they believed the blizzard and the deep snow must have concealed it. They surmised that later someone found the weapon and kept it.

The witness avers that she tried to tell police of what she saw but that they never acknowledged the information. Josiah Conner was stabbed to death in jail nearly a year later. The case never came to trial.

The witness believes they did not get the right man. The investigation into the jail killing was never made public. It is very possible the wrong man paid for the crime.

At night she and George were sitting together close on the sofa with the radio playing softly. She handed the paper to him and said, "The guy wrote it after all."

She waited until he read it.

"This is going to upset Howard," George said. "But I can't guess what it will do to Josiah, if he sees it, wherever he is."

But the *Courier* was everywhere. She'd bet he would see it. "He's going to wonder why I'm talking now."

"He'll figure it out. He was a smart kid. Is."

"George, I have to tell you something. The other night at the Crawford Grill . . . I saw Madeline with someone. Remember when she left the table for so long? She was in the backyard with a man. I think they were arguing, but they were close, talking. What if he's the guy Howard was upset about? What if he did it? I mean, killed for her?"

"You saw her?

"Yes."

"With a guy."

"Yes. And something dramatic going on."

"I can think the worst, but let's see if something else fits. Maybe she hadn't seen him in a long time and she was trying to discourage an advance. For one thing, she didn't end up with someone else. She's with Howard."

"Sort of with Howard. I think they're in trouble."

George sighed, "Yes, I think they are."

They sat back. He held her hand. And for a while they were stuck for

words. She was thinking even worse thoughts. What if Madeline wanted it, the killing? Asked for it?

George got up and paced the few steps to the front door and back.
He was knocked out lately. He went to the kitchen and poured himself
a drink. When he came back, he sat heavily.

She said, "I probably shouldn't tell you what I've been thinking."

"I think I hear it even when you don't." He closed his eyes. "I have to
say you are somewhat of a surprise. You keep surprising me. From the
start."

"Are you disappointed? Want to be rid of me?" she tried to joke.

"Not anytime soon." He took a drink and sat forward, choosing his
words. "Everything you think, it's come to me, too. I've just fought it
harder. Everything you did, from the start . . . I probably would have
done it too."

EIGHTEEN

1944, 1945

THE WAR WAS THE WAR AND IT, AT ANY RATE, PUT PEOPLE'S SMALL-er troubles into perspective. If they acknowledged what the soldiers were doing for them they became more generous.

Lena wanted to do something for the troops. They loved her, used her picture as a pinup, and Walter White was always telling her she did *right* when she did something for her race, so Lena signed up for the USO tours.

Lennie asked her to call him every day while she was gone and even though she kept telling him this thing between them had to end (they had to pretend they didn't know each other at lunches in the commissary), she found herself phones in Atlanta and Memphis and other places to tell him the performance went well and she felt she had boosted the morale of the soldiers.

One day she told him, "Next is Little Rock. Such a funny name. They don't have a plane for me. They have to get me to a train."

"God, darling, you must be tired."

"Yes. Sure am."

"Call again."

"If I can." How could she let him down? She didn't have an answer.

As soon as she got to Little Rock, a bad feeling came over her. The officer who'd come to pick her up wouldn't look at her, he balked at carrying her luggage, and then he sat in the jeep with his body inclined so far away from her she thought he was going to fall out the driver's-side door.

After good times, there it was again, the slap of reality.

The voices of the officers who greeted her arrival were distinctly unwelcoming. The captain who showed her the stage couldn't look at her. All this. All over again. "Be ready to sing at seven," he said curtly. "Someone will bring you food from the mess." She felt it in the pit of her stomach, the ugliness again.

She did a few practice runs on the stage in the afternoon, getting the angles right, testing the acoustics—which were bad—and getting the scratch out of her high notes. A few of the young boys perked up when they passed her on some mission or other of theirs and it pleased her to be cheering them.

The piano player they sent her was okay, nice enough, a white guy. He hurried in late, breathless, and she did her practice runs once more.

When seven o'clock came, she sang with mounting puzzlement to a sea of white faces. She was at this base *because* they had Negro soldiers too. Where were they? Her smile wouldn't light up; her face felt frozen. At nearly eight o'clock she stomped off the stage to ask the captain who'd shown her the stage, "Where are the Negro soldiers?"

"We don't mix them in the hall," he said. He kept his eyes on his watch, then on the doorway. When he finally had to look back at her, he said, "They don't come in here."

"Well, I want to sing to them."

"I'm sorry. That's not in our plans." He pivoted and began to walk away.

But she followed. "Huh! Well, *where* are they?"

"Bedding down."

She moved around to face him. "Where are they tomorrow, the other soldiers, the Negroes?" she demanded.

"I beg your pardon?" he said in attempted civility, but his eyes were so wide she thought he was going to hit her.

"Morning? Where are they in the morning?" she persisted.

"Eating breakfast."

"Set me up in the mess hall then. I'll entertain them there."

The captain's face went apoplectic—he had probably never taken orders from a civilian, nor from a woman, nor from a Negro. He was blood red with fury.

"Set up some chairs in the mess," he ordered an underling. "This one's going to do a show in the morning."

She slept badly. She had wished the captain dead. She had hoped his fury would give him a stroke and he would die at her feet. And so although she forced herself out of bed, determined to do what she'd come for, she hardly felt like singing.

But when she entered the mess hall, under the smell of bacon, the colored boys were hooting and hollering and cheering her. Her spirits began to return. She gave them her best smile and blew kisses. Only . . . only they were not moving to sit. They kept standing way in the back and the chairs that had been set up were empty. The piano player started to play. She began her little intros to the songs and gestured to the boys to come and sit down.

But suddenly a bunch of white men trooped in to take up the seats while the Negro men continued to stand in the back.

She sang "Chattanooga Choo Choo," almost mechanically while she attempted to figure out what was going on.

At the back of the hall the soldiers were ecstatic. She was doing what she'd come for. But . . . why were they standing, and who the hell were these men in the front who were not the same men from last night? After the first song was done, and her piano player kept vamping, trying to figure out what she needed, she walked over to an officer, a different one, the captain being nowhere in sight. "Who are these folks, here, in the chairs?"

"Germans."

"Germans?" She really didn't understand right away.

"Prisoners of war."

She stood stock-still for a moment, then walked straight to the back of the hall, a move she knew confused the piano player, not to mention everyone else. After gesturing to the piano player to keep going, she sang straight to the Negro soldiers while the Germans twisted in their seats. The Germans liked her plenty, they didn't care to complain, but the Negro soldiers went crazy for her, not just her beauty, not just her music, or for the fact that she was close up to them, which they clearly appreciated; they were also crazy for her message. *You, you, you. You're who I'm here for.*

An hour later she attempted to arrange passage out of Little Rock. The captain, still choking on his anger, had to let her use his office and his phone. She called the USO for transport, the NAACP to make a report, and then, with everything ragged and unsettled, tears finally coming, she called Lennie. She could hardly get the words out as she tried to explain about the Negro soldiers not being allowed in the hall.

"Thank God the other places weren't like that. The next stop has to be better."

"The next stop is home. I'm done. This has beat me. I'm coming home."

"I will be thrilled to see you."

When her train made it to LA two days later, she stopped at the USO office first, only a cab ride from her home, to make a complaint about what had happened at Little Rock. "You have to do something about camps like that one," she said.

But they were not outraged. They said, "Take a break. It's a rough schedule. Fatiguing, that's clear." She began to cry because they were disappointed in her and because she hadn't been able to make them understand the dismissal the Negroes got in Little Rock.

She thought to call for a cab but instead she called Lennie. "Are you home the rest of the day?"

"Waiting for you."

"I could use a drink."

"It's almost made. How are you?" She could hear music, the piano, one hand, his left, messing around with low chords. She pictured him, waiting for her.

She looked around to be sure no one was listening in, since she was making the call from an office with an open door. "Not good. I've got everybody angry with me. The folks in Little Rock, the whole USO. God, even Edwina and my daughter are going to be angry."

"Are you sure?"

"Edwina knows I spend time with you. She's threatened to quit me if I see you again."

There was a pause. He said, "The soldiers don't hate you."

"True." She sat at the borrowed desk.

"They were crazy about you."

She got flashes of the faces of the German soldiers and the colored boys at Camp Robinson. And then the colored soldiers on the train to LA—fellows who had recognized her and engaged in an awed and hushed conversation about her before asking for autographs.

"And count me in as a soldier. Crazy about you." She could hear a scale, a chord. "If you can stop here before going home, I would be grateful. I've got food."

"Oh, good. Love food."

"And drink."

"That's good, too." Of course she'd go to Lennie, the human tranquilizer.

"Take a cab."

She called for a cab but made one more call while waiting. She had to at least talk to her daughter.

Gail answered the phone, breathless. "Mommy? Are you on the way home now?"

She said, "Well, I'm *almost* in California. I'll be home soon."

"How far are you now?"

"Two hundred miles." She couldn't produce the sound of a train or a station, but Gail was young and would not figure it out.

"Is that far?"

"I'll be home in one day, darling. Put Edwina on." Rattle, crunch, she heard the noises of Edwina putting down pots and silverware.

"How can a train take so long?" Edwina asked.

"I just don't know."

"Where are you now?"

"Forgot the name of the town. I'll be home tomorrow. You've been so great, Edwina. I just want to hug you."

"Your daughter misses you a lot."

"I know. I miss her too. Tomorrow. Meanwhile, call for groceries if you need anything at all. Is the money holding?"

"We have enough."

She hung up. Edwina knew.

She carried her two traveling bags, stumbling, sweat rolling down her back.

How weak she was to need comfort so much. But two hours later, she was fed and drowsy and in Lennie's bed, curled toward him.

"Sleep. I need sleep."

"I'll leave you be." He swung a leg out of bed but she touched his arm to stop him.

"The problem is, now I'm not helping any of the soldiers. I wanted to. I still want to. But what I saw—"

"I get it. It's totally unfair." He took her arm and began massaging lightly, running his finger along the line where muscle meets bone.

"If I could get a list of the black camps . . ." she said.

"Great idea. That's the way! You'd be making a statement."

"I keep seeing the faces of those boys. Scared. I wanted to give them courage."

"I *like* this idea of yours. Listen to yourself. If the camps make a distinction, you're in your rights to do the same."

"Could it be done? I'd have to use my own money."

"If you wake up and still want to do this, I'll call a guy I know. He's very organized. He'd be able to figure it all out. Why don't you rest?"

"That would be nice."

"Sleep." He turned her to her side and massaged her shoulders. There he was, like a whisper approving everything she wanted and needed and was.

NINETEEN

1945

AT THE STUDIO, LENA PASSED LOUIS B. MAYER AT LEAST ONCE every month, and every time she did he walked quickly, got himself into serious conversation with someone, and then at the last minute smiled or reached out his hand just enough to perform the gestures of the busy papa who loved his kid but didn't have time just then to talk.

So, sitting ramrod straight in the commissary, she beckoned to Eddie Mannix, who could get to Arthur Freed, who could get to Mayer. Mannix, with a sandwich in hand, smiled and came to her.

"Could we talk?" she asked.

He looked surprised, but he sat.

"I understand some scripts come over your desk, is that right?"

"Well, sure. I read a dozen a day. Well, I *look at* a dozen a day. Everybody's pushing a script."

"I always heard if it doesn't jump out at you in ten minutes, it hits the trash."

"Don't even need ten."

"Wow. Well, nobody is asking me, of course, but I would happily read scripts. I have a vision of a part—it could be a secretary or a schoolteacher who has to go through something tough. A good story, you know. Or a restaurant owner. Like Mildred Pierce. I read the book."

He hesitated. "Cain is great. He tells an excellent story."

"A part like that."

"That's a . . . they have Joan Crawford in that. Comes out in September." He put his wrapped sandwich down, but thought better of it and took it up again.

"What I mean is, I want to urge you to think like that, because Mildred Pierce could be any woman, any woman with a daughter. She could be Chinese or Mexican."

He frowned. "It's Pierce, though, not Rodriguez or Chin. But yes, I take your point. I assure you they're always looking for a property for you."

"I know they are. I'm just saying to open up the search to things they don't think about."

"But we *do* think. It has to be right. Salable. We had one from some soldier—came in military mail—about a Negro schoolteacher, guy even sent a note saying you'd be great in it, but we couldn't make a picture like that. Unknown writer, quiet story, we could never sell it. I mean, everybody has a script to push."

"Could I read that script?"

"Oh, that one is gone, we can't keep all that paper around. We'd drown."

"I'd like a part like that. Even if it's low budget. Could you be my emissary in that regard, just saying that sort of thing in the right circles at the right time?"

Mannix winced and looked longingly toward his sandwich. "I'm sorry you're unhappy."

"I didn't say that. I'm unused. Wasted." Bah, he was terrified of her. His eyes were red with blushing.

Two days later a woman whose name she wasn't sure of . . . Alice, Agnes . . . who played just about every maid in just about everything, no lines, said to her in the ladies' room, "You think you have it over all of us, but you aren't so smart."

"I'm not sure I understand," Lena said carefully, trying to read the woman.

"Fancy contract you have. But I actually get work."

"I know. They're looking for something, they say."

"Oh, yeah. Good luck."

Lena could guess what other Negroes were saying about her. She badly wanted their friendship, but every time she tried, things got awkward. Her contract separated her from them.

At Lennie's house, while he stirred a sauce for pasta, she said, "There are Negroes who own businesses, who are doctors, who are professors, every kind of thing. Do people not know that?"

"I know that."

"Why are there no stories about any of them?"

She still went to the studio every day, hoping. She read a lot of books at MGM, since they didn't give her scripts to read. *A Tree Grows in Brooklyn* made her think about where she grew up. *Strange Fruit*—she kept that one hidden under a folder. Like *Showboat*, it dealt with black and white together. At home on her table, *The Razor's Edge*. She loved stories, she was full of feeling, and had no place to put all that was inside her.

She tried to avoid Lennie at the commissary since she knew people were talking.

One evening Lennie appeared at Lena's house with a large bouquet of flowers and chocolates and a doll for her daughter.

"Oh my God. You're here. What are you doing here?"

"I hate how much time we have to spend apart." He looked around at her place, just a small house that wasn't as good as his.

"Well, sit, sit, I'll get you something."

She took the flowers to the kitchen. Edwina took them from her and said, "What kind of shame are you bringing on this family?"

"He's nice to me."

Edwina tossed the flowers on the counter. "Are these payment for your body? He got you cheap."

When Lena whispered to Lennie that he should leave, he looked as if he might cry.

The next morning she packed a ham sandwich and an apple and two cookies in a paper bag so she could avoid the commissary and avoid the pretense of avoiding Lennie. After she reported in, she read for hours on a borrowed cushion sitting on a wall that was part of a set for Mexico City.

Freed found her. He said, "My dear, I think we have a hot property for you. Would you like to take a break from the movies and appear on Broadway?"

"Are you kidding? Of course."

"It's a big role. The music is fantastic. If you come to the office, we'll give you a sneak peek of one of the songs. You might ask Hayton or someone to play it for you." He looked aside politely.

Lennie was busy conducting that day, so she actually heard "Come Rain or Come Shine" first with one of the young musicians on staff who did whatever they were asked to do. "Another weather song!" she told the kid. He didn't quite get the joke.

But my God, she was going to be on Broadway again after this drought of years and years!

Lennie said, "Get me some dates as soon as you can. Seems I'm going to be flying to New York every two days just to see you for a couple of hours."

The next week Freed gave her the script at the Mexican wall, where she was reading her Somerset Maugham.

"You like it here."

"I do."

Two birds perched on top of the fake wall, as if it were real.

"The part of Della is what we want you to look at."

He smiled and left.

She looked at the first two pages. The script was an adaptation of a well-known novel by Arna Bontemps, a Negro. She looked away from the script at the birds and then looked back at it.

Yes. Della was a whore.

She kept reading.

All the women characters in the script were tramps. She could hear her father's outrage at the fact of her waiting for years for a script and now this one.

But. She couldn't refuse to do it. They were producing it for her.

She stuffed the script into an oversized bag and took it home and stayed home the next day, calling in that she was fighting off a cold.

When she returned to the studio, she was on her way to the commissary when she ran straight into Freed.

"How's our Della?" he asked.

She blazed her smile at him. "Good character name. I haven't read the script yet."

"Well, get going. I mean, get going."

He passed her. Of course he knew she was lying.

She wanted to talk to Hattie McDaniel, a wonderful woman, one of the few MGM Negroes who treated her warmly.

Pretty soon she was not alone. Freed had turned around and was beside her. "You understand how important this is," he said. "We haven't been able to get a script written by and for a Negro for a long time. This one would open doors. Not just for you. If we get this going on Broadway we might be able to make a picture—this or something else, an all-Negro picture, I'm saying. Do you know how *hard* that is to do?"

"I do know." She'd calculated. A cabaret performance reaches a couple hundred people a night, a stage show reaches a thousand or two, a movie reaches millions. Millions. Thus the calculations about what would sell.

They both walked more slowly.

"And you love the music. We're talking about opening doors."

"Just give me some time. I need to know my own mind."

"Of course. Come with me to lunch. We won't talk about it. We'll just eat and let people see that we're friends."

Her muscles relaxed in the wash of defeat, resignation, whatever you wanted to call it—caving in. She knew defeat made her especially beautiful—the smile not too tight, the moist eyes blinking a little rapidly. It was about the only reward there was for giving up.

"You can't keep stalling Mayer. He's going crazy."

She couldn't decide. Could not. Almost two weeks later she was summoned to Mayer's office.

His assistants sat across from her on a sofa, three wrens on a wire.

Freed began. "This is . . . people don't refuse a role like this."

"It's difficult. I've fought so hard not to play—"

"But this is a starring role."

"It's in my contract."

"Yes, yes, yes, but there is such a thing as creative license. When Shakespeare wrote Mistress Overdone, well, he wrote a prostitute. They existed."

"A man would have played her."

They stared at her. They weren't in a mood for scholarship.

"Well, maybe we don't need to bring Shakespeare into it," a small bespectacled guy told Freed. "Gershwin is much more to the point."

She took a letter from her handbag. "I have a letter here that helps to explain."

"From you?"

"No. Walter White. NAACP." She handed it over.

Freed, sitting in the middle, read the letter aloud, but the other two men leaned over to see it as well as they could. She knew what it said pretty much by heart.

> *Do not take this part. You are an important role model for many people of our race. We have worked tirelessly to wipe out stereotypical representations of our people. All of the women and men in* St. Louis Woman *show Negroes in a bad light. There is nothing redeeming in the story. If someone of your status takes on a role like this, it sends a terrible message to all those who admire you. I realize your career is constantly being measured, but you will be measured best in the future, maybe in the distant future, if you stand up for yourself.*
>
> *Yours very truly,*
>
> *Walter White*

"Of course, his position is extreme," Freed said.

She did know.

She'd called Robeson, who said, "Whatever you do, be confident in your decision." This, too, was Lennie's advice. "Do it or don't do it, darling, I'll stand behind you no matter what."

The problem was, an actor like Robeson could make any role godly—jockey, prostitute, card sharp, anything. She was a novice, and so far they'd only cast her in roles in which she was a singer who fell in love and sang about it. Songs, no real acting to speak of.

The men on the sofa continued to pore over the letter, handing it back and forth.

"I don't think the play is bad," Freed said. "It's corny, maybe, corny-dramatic, love and jealousy and pistols and money-grubbing, but it's entertaining. I *love* knowing what people get up to."

But didn't they all know it was stereotypes like that—pistols and money-grubbing—that got Negroes arrested and killed, not to mention barred from decent places?

Freed slapped his thighs. "Well, we have a line on someone else. The show will happen with or without you. But I'm not going to take your decision just yet. I want you to sleep on it, make sure this is *your* answer and that you're not being pushed by other people." He paused significantly before asking, "There are other people besides White getting into the act, aren't there? I wonder about the Negro actors out here and if they are using you for their own purposes." He raised his eyebrows, baiting her.

She fell for it. "Mary Baltimore has a lot of class. She told me she thought it was a bad, bad script."

"Mary said that?" he asked, smiling. "Ha! *Did* she?"

"Yes. You know her?"

"Met her sister. She sent her sister to audition for it."

Lena was taken off-guard and then she laughed. "Maybe she hates her sister."

That cocky answer only got her out the door and down the hall before she allowed herself to scream about how stupid she was. Damn, she wanted to punch Mary Baltimore in the face.

She didn't sleep on the problem. She paced on it. She drank whiskey on it. And several cups of joe on it.

Not one of the voices in her head that night said a definite, *Yes, do the role.* So, finally . . . there was her decision. She was saying no.

Lennie said, "Okay. Well, now you have to live with it." When she gave him a questioning look, he said, "Grudges hold big here."

She didn't believe it at first. It took a while for the punishment Mayer was exacting to sink in. She told Lennie they were looking at her for *Showboat.*

He tried to talk her down.

She said, "But it's *Showboat.* I'm perfect for it. They always said."

"Don't count on it."

Soon enough she saw *Showboat* would not come through. But she tried to take that in stride. When she asked what else she might do, they said they had nothing at all for her these days. When a request came in for a cabaret appearance, they nixed it.

So this was how it would be. A slow career death. It became more and more difficult to hold her head up.

And, as happens when things are down, who did she run into in the ladies' room but the same damned actress, the small tidy woman with tight hair who had taunted her months ago.

"Still feeling uppity?"

"I don't know your name," Lena said, washing her hands, looking at the woman in the mirror.

"Does it matter?"

"To me, yes."

"My name is Constance Williams."

Lena hid her shaking by tugging hard at the rolling cloth towel. "I want to tell you how it is. If I make one little misstep, the papers write about it. If I say what truly goes on, I get in trouble. I know you think I have it easy, but—"

"You *do* have it easy. The rest of us aren't in the magazines every week. You get the goods. You sit around with white people half the day."

"And *you* have friends. You have a sort of club I never get invited to. If you struck out on your own, you'd see a little bit of what I'm—"

"You're ruining it for us, you know."

"That's exactly what I'm trying not to do. Let's don't be enemies. Constance?"

But the young woman shook her head. "You really don't get it. You have it all." She left the room.

No work. Her son on brief loan again. Edwina was leaving her. She couldn't be seen with Lennie. No, not *all*.

She went home each day despondent.

One day she was sitting in the kitchen, and again, Edwina had brought her a cup of tea, a reminder of the good times, the days when they had been comfortable together, but this time there was a sick feeling in the air, the feeling of breakups of all sorts. Edwina said, "There is so much mail. Do you want me to go through it before I leave?"

"Think about staying for a while," Lena pleaded.

Edwina didn't answer. She had settled a large box full of envelopes on the kitchen table, mostly requests for autographs and photos. "It's terribly expensive, sending photos to everyone who asks. You should cut back."

"I'll try. Edwina, I hope you think some more about it and don't leave us."

They went through the mail for almost an hour before there was a knock at the door. The timing couldn't have been worse. At the door, Lena found Lennie, the cause of the scolding, laden with packages, murmuring that he'd come to win Edwina over. There was a candy box and a bag of something balancing on top of a huge box. "Lobsters for everyone. If you have a big pot, I'll do them," he said happily.

"Lobsters! What's the reason?"

"Just wanted to. And, I think Mayer is softening. My gut tells me he's going to give you something. Singing engagements at a few theaters, I *think*. This is a precelebration."

Edwina walked into the living room to see what was up, dropped her handful of letters, and stomped out of the room.

"Did you buy a lobster for Edwina?"

"She can have two. I brought six."

"Let me go talk to her."

Edwina was huddled in her room, studying train schedules. "Oh, my honey," Lena said. "You have been so fantastic. Can't you stay and try to know him?"

"I cannot bear that man."

"He's a lot nicer than I am."

The look Edwina gave her said, *Anybody is nicer than you are.*

"Come eat with us. You don't have to do a thing. Just let us treat you."

"You'd better get someone for the kids. I told you to do it *weeks* ago and you haven't done it yet. I care about them."

"I know you do."

"But I won't stay."

"Lennie brought you a box of candy."

"I don't want it." Edwina was trembling, looking away from her. She hated white men in general, but this one got the worst of it.

Lena sighed. "I should get back out there—it's only right that I help him in the kitchen."

And when Edwina didn't say one easy or comforting thing, Lena left.

Lennie had already found the lobster pot and had it on the boil.

"What possessed you to do this?" she asked.

"Well, I remembered how you like lobster. And I do. And I thought, why not do something to cheer you up? Those sons of bitches are putting you through it. They want you to suffer. I don't want you to suffer. I want you to remember . . . fun and . . . love."

"Oh. Oh."

He kissed her forehead then, and her eyes. "You're going to make it through this."

"I hope so."

"Oh, I know so. You're a champion."

"Of what?"

"Everything." He looked out to the yard where Gail and Teddy chased each other. She'd had Teddy on loan for three more weeks. It was one of the things that got her through. The children, sensing they were being looked at, stopped running, waved, and then came in to see what was up.

Lennie said, "Here they are. The best kids in the world."

"You want to play catch?" Teddy scratched one leg with the foot of the other.

"Well, okay. Do you throw hard?"

"A little bit," Teddy bragged, and then Gail said, "No, he's easy," and patted Teddy on the back.

Lennie followed the kids outside. He pretended to be bad at catching. Maybe he actually was. The kids were comfortable, easy with him.

She picked up the phone and made a few phone calls.

Out the window Lennie ran around, practically somersaulting to catch the red ball.

It had to be Lennie.

FINALLY THERE WAS something—a song, just a song, not an acting part, but it was in *Ziegfeld Follies* and it was a *good* song. A song that demanded expressivity and . . . something like acting. She practiced on the lot, at home—an angry hiss, a whimper . . .

And then she did it in the music studio for a few people. It was titled "Love," though other people kept calling it "A Moment's Madness."

The way the song kept accelerating with anger was wonderful, just fantastic. It was about how insane love is, how mad, how full of pain. Oh, it was terrific. As she sang she thought about the time she threw chocolates at Lennie. She thought about her father's disapproval of her love life. About Louis and his anger. *Insane* was a really good word for a singer to get hold of. She could hold the *a* and get a nasal buzz on the *n*.

"Good, you got it for sure," they said. They sent her to costumes. She would be wearing a wonderful purple-and-green top, sashed at the waist, and purple flowers with greens in her hair.

The scene she was in was very odd, though. Minnelli ran the principals one day before shooting. He wanted to see what he had—two actresses fighting over a man in a smoky bar, the fight, and then the song. Lena whispered, "Shouldn't I be one of them? Fighting?"

"No, my dear, you can't burst into song after a hair-pulling fight. You get to slink out from behind that curtain and your song is a . . . a *comment* on the fight."

So she went back to the Mexican wall, practicing, reading, having a hot dog and a Coke.

The next day all the extras were there, she was in costume, and they were shooting. The characters in the dark barroom set were all Negroes, the women dressed in sexy clothes, the men looking as if they were all used to having women fight over them. Constance Williams was playing one of the patrons. To make the scene exotic, there was a woman with a bird on her shoulder.

Lena waited and sweated in her beautiful headpiece for four hours while they shot the dances and the fight. And finally they wanted her song. She did her slink from behind the curtain and sang a few bars.

Vincente stopped her. He gave her the direction he often gave Judy Garland, to sort of motor forward with her arms, to swing her hips, to do the same move backward. Lena didn't like it—she felt stiff—and she remembered Lennie often telling her she needed to work on how she moved her arms. But Vincente, a sweet director, wanted those gestures, and so she gave them.

"Break," Vincente said. "And then we shoot the song."

An MGM waiter brought in a whole tray of hot dogs. The costume people set up a clamor but they couldn't stop the ravenous actors from eating. Lena instead practiced the motor movement Vincente wanted.

"You look just fantastic," he said.

"You still want all that hip movement?"

"Absolutely. It's just extra. Everybody is going to be looking at your face."

They took their places, she sang, and Vincente called it done.

She loved the song. Loved it and planned to keep it in her repertoire as Lennie suggested she do. Hugh Martin, the songwriter, knew something about love, that was clear.

Later in the day, the actors crowded into the viewing room to see the rushes. Lena sat apart from them. The actresses who played the fight scene laughed and hugged each other and made plans for dinner. The men who joined them carried the same arrogance about them they'd played in the film. It *did* happen. People fell into their roles and took them on.

The thing that puzzled her as she watched was that the actors in the barroom scene didn't look at her; they seemed bored, sort of frozen in a dream while she moved among them, singing. Why didn't they react to her?

She sought out Vincente. "Are we shooting that again?"

"No. It's perfect."

"Nobody looks at me or reacts . . ."

"Oh! You're not really *there* in the barroom. You're a spirit, a commentator."

TWENTY

1945

ON A HOT DAY IN JUNE MARIE HIRED A BABYSITTER AND WENT downtown to meet McCoy at the candy shop as she had agreed to do in a phone call. He said he had a couple more questions for her. Since the article was already written, it was a little puzzling. George had told her to just tell the truth. He said she should treat herself to a movie afterward. She hoped the meeting would be brief. Anyway, a movie, after so few in the last years, would be a treat.

Dressed in her lightest cotton dress, a simple light blue thing she'd made the summer before, Marie took the streetcar downtown and walked the next half block to the candy shop, where Mr. McCoy was waiting for her, standing with another man. The other man was a tall, sad-looking fellow, relatively young, with beautiful brown eyes.

McCoy said, "This is Detective Marshall."

Marshall put out a hand. "Pleased to meet you."

Marie shook his hand, taken aback. She said to McCoy, "I thought you just had one or two questions for me."

"I want you to show Detective Marshall your movements in the candy shop that night."

A detective. Now her heart sank again and her brain scrambled for meaning. She hurried to say, "Um, I don't have real evidence, you know. It's just that back when it started, I saw something that I thought would help clear him. Could you tell me why now . . ."

Marshall said firmly, "We need to check a few things. Will you show me your movements?" Marie went through it all, opening the door, closing it again, looking up the street. She was aware that the girl behind the counter had been prepared for this meeting and didn't act surprised at all.

She pointed to the place up the street where Klein had sat dying in his car. She even described the piece of paper that flew at her in the blizzard.

"Thank you," Marshall said.

"I should buy something before I leave the shop," she said, glad to be done with it.

"Go right ahead," said McCoy. "We'll wait."

So she was *not* done with it? Was she in trouble? What else did they want?

She ordered a box of chocolates and came back out. The two men flanked her. "We're going to the Stanley theater," Marshall said.

"Oh, I was going to see *Double Indemnity* today. They brought it back."

"Heard of it. Well, all right, but we need to go to the Stanley first. Where Conner said he went. The same ticket clerk is still there."

She walked along with them. Marshall unearthed a photo from his pocket just as they got there. She saw it was a newspaper photo, grainy, and it was of Josiah. Marshall showed his credentials and asked the ancient geezer behind the window, "Sir, do you have a good memory?"

"I'd say so. Excellent memory."

"You remember the night there was a . . . a blizzard and a shooting up the street?"

"Sure do."

"Were you working that night?"

"Yep. Slept in the theater."

"Do you remember this boy coming to the theater? This picture was in the paper."

"Yep. There was only about five people come to the movies that night."

"Did the boy leave early or anything?"

"No, not that I seen."

"Was he with anyone?"

"Not that I seen."

"When the police doubted that he'd been to the movies, you didn't come forward. If you're sure he was in your theater, why didn't you say anything?"

"Didn't figure it was my business. Police know what they're doing."

"And this woman with us . . ." He moved aside to reveal Marie and asked, "Was she one of the five in the theater that night?"

"Don't remember so."

"Thank you." Marshall almost took Marie's arm as he pointed her in the direction of the Nixon. "*Double Indemnity*, did you say? That's where you're headed?"

"Yes. They brought it back."

"You know what it's about? A bad marriage, a murder. It's going to give you nightmares," Marshall said, amused.

"Maybe I shouldn't see it."

"I hear it's thrilling. If you can handle being tense. Mrs. Elias, something else. Will you describe the car that you saw driving away?"

"This was a long time ago."

"I know."

"Gray. I think gray. I don't know cars."

"How many people in it?"

"Two. It felt like two."

"Men? Two men?"

"I think so."

"Was it a police car?"

"Oh, no. I think I would have noticed."

"Okay. So. I have some ideas. I don't like them much, but there they are. You can go see your movie. You did the right thing, coming here. It's up to me to deal with the can of worms you opened up."

She felt breathless. This detective was actually *looking into* the murder of Klein now, years later.

She would never rest again, it seemed, never again. If she'd opened up a can of worms, she was responsible in a new way for Josiah, his safety, and yet she had no way of contacting him. If her worst suspicion about Madeline was true, she was helping to convict a woman who had been an acquaintance.

She fixed her attention on the movie she had so looked forward to as her treat for coming to town to see McCoy. Fred MacMurray—she had liked him in *Alice Adams*—was starring. She watched and ate chocolates, but nothing lifted her spirits during this outing.

That night she told George about meeting with the detective. He got quiet. "Okay," he said firmly. "There is machinery moving that we can't do much about and we're in it, but we're in it together."

"I'm sorry."

"No, no. I admire you. Meantime, let's try to take care of our lives. Let's live the best lives we can."

"What does that mean?"

With a slight shake of his head, he said, "No intentional harm?"

"You sound like a doctor."

"It's a good oath."

She tried to take the position that everything was now out of her hands.

George came home in the afternoon one June day soon after and said, "There's something I want to show you." She'd already seen the new car. What could it be? He looked incredibly happy.

"Right now?" she asked, touching her hair.

"No need to fix your hair. Just bring Helen and come."

They got into their brand-new Buick—she shined it every other day and George hardly ever took it to work because the muddy patch behind the restaurant was not friendly to the tires, which were pristine from her work on them.

"But where are we going?"

"It's a surprise."

She held Helen on her lap and they drove for about fifteen minutes. George was more excited than he had been when he brought the new car home. "I don't know this section," she said.

"Called Dormont."

She'd heard of it, never been there.

George pulled up in front of a house where a man stood on the porch in a shirt and trousers but no suit jacket. "That fellow is selling his house. I had a tip. There is no middleman so it saves a little money."

"Not for us? For us, George?"

"Well, let's see what you think of it."

The brick house was flanked by two pine trees and two lilac bushes. The porch was cement, not wood. When she got inside, she could see the place had more windows than their Oakland house did. And a better backyard with a big cherry tree. There was something called a sunroom and there was a porch in back, too. Yes, it was definitely lighter, and bigger than what they had, but she never did like the idea of leaving what was familiar. "I don't know," she said. "We don't *need* anything more."

"I want you to have something really good. It's a step up and this is a nicer neighborhood." Their daughter was curious, touching everything—counters, refrigerator.

Marie began to feel excited. "All right," she said. "All right."

George was flushed with pleasure. "Then we'll do it. I'll give the guy some time. He wanted some time. We'll move in October."

WHEN THE NEWS came in September that the war was over, Marie went out on the street with her Oakland neighbors, two metal cooking pot lids in hand. The women were all yelling, "The war is over!" while doing their best to make the sound of clashing cymbals. Marie ran back inside to get her daughter. She gave her a pot and spoon as noisemakers. All around the neighborhood children were running and leaping, though most of them didn't know why.

She would be leaving soon, dealing with new neighbors, new streets, new grocers.

She watched children cavort around George's new Buick, worrying all the while that some child would scratch it.

"Your brother-in-law's gonna be coming back!" a neighbor yelled.

"Yes!" And her brother would be coming home too, at some point. He'd made it.

George thought Philip would want to stay in the Oakland house. "But there are finances to figure," she told him. "He buys you out or you buy him out."

"Well, you are a hardheaded woman," George said, amused.

"Somebody has to pay attention to practicality."

On that September day, Marie and her daughter made as much

noise as they could, thrilled, both of them, with raising their voices. When they got back into the house, the phone was ringing.

George said over shouts, "Can you get a sitter tonight?"

"I could try. Why?"

"Howard and Madeline want to go celebrate."

"They want to see us?"

"Howard seemed really happy. I don't think they think you were the anonymous woman. I think it's really all right."

She wasn't sure she believed that. Madeline was pretty unhappy about the time McCoy bothered her. And it could get worse, didn't George know that? "I haven't been around Madeline since—"

"I know. Let's assume the article had no effect on her. Howard has always been very decent to me."

Right. So, they were going to the Pittsburgh Golf Club.

Well, this time it was too hot for velvet. She threw on her fall-weight burgundy dress, got a babysitter, and by eight thirty she and George were seated on elegant sofas with Howard and Madeline. The place was so crowded they couldn't get in to dinner until nine. They'd already had several cocktails in the spirit of the evening. It was quite a night, joyful people all around them.

A waiter brought them glasses of champagne. "This is a gift from an anonymous giver!

Madeline raised her glass, saying, "Here's to benefactors!"

They toasted each other and drank.

"Not bad at all," Madeline said, getting hers down quickly. "I could use another one of those!"

Marie could tell Madeline was pretending something, pretending good spirits.

The men began talking about the economy, whether stocks would go up, whether people would want to spend. "I think the bar was a great move," Howard said. "You did right."

"Aren't they boring?" Madeline whispered to Marie.

"I actually like hearing about the business."

"You shabby girl! You're going to be boring, too. Let's go to the powder room."

The waiter with the tray of champagne stopped them on their way and Madeline took another.

The powder room was breathtaking. There were small upholstered chairs in a mauve brocade and those chairs were lined up to an elongated marble dressing table and a mirror the size of Rhode Island. A tint coming from the rose walls and the mauve lampshades made every woman look her best. Marie wanted to duplicate the colors in her new house.

Madeline plunked her glass on the marble and sat, scrutinizing herself. Marie sat beside her.

Women behind them were taking off gloves and lifting the veils on their hats, and others were putting those things back on.

"I'm so bored," Madeline said. "I'm bored to death."

"It's a long wait."

"I'm not talking about here."

"Oh."

After drinking her flute of champagne, Madeline said, "We should go shopping. Is money tight for you?"

"Not too bad. There are car payments and we're moving in October to the new house, so there is a lot going on." Marie stood, fussing in her purse for a handkerchief, eager to avoid inquisition.

Madeline said, "Or we could go to a movie. My treat." She began to apply lipstick, looking at Marie behind her in the mirror.

"Well, first of all, no need to treat me. There's one with Lena Horne I want to see."

"Or maybe jazz again in the Hill." She continued to study Marie through the mirror.

"Oh. Yes. I loved it."

"Really? All right. Let's go hear jazz again." She capped her lipstick and turned to look Marie in the eye. "I'm not happy."

Marie took a while to think and said, "I always hear sons are a lot of work. Are they getting you down some?"

Madeline took in a large breath. "That's not it. But sixteen and fourteen, they aren't any help either. In a couple of days, boarding school. I talked Howard into it. What was that face you just made?"

"Oh, boarding school," Marie murmured. "I'm curious about it. I don't know anyone who went to one."

"Yes you do. I went. I was *sent away*."

As they walked back to their husbands, Marie could see that Madeline was fairly tipsy, weaving in and out among the chairs.

They had steaks. And wine.

And dessert (cheesecake). And cognac.

At midnight Marie climbed into their Buick and caught her breath as George swung too wide and scraped a tire against a curb. She waited until they were home to say, "You drank too much."

"Howard kept buying."

"You could say no."

George frowned. "You're right. I feel for him. He doesn't know what to do with Madeline. He's sorry he's with her but he's committed to the boys. He's unhappy."

"George. She was involved. I know it. I feel it."

"That's too serious a thing to say without proof."

Granted. He was having trouble driving in a straight line, so she held her tongue.

They stumbled into the house and to bed.

"Please don't become like your brother."

"No. No chance of that." He kissed her softly, eyes, ear, mouth. "I love you with all my heart," he said.

She felt frightened. She could feel there was trouble coming, but she didn't know what it was.

Finally she drifted off, at five in the morning.

When she woke, George was already gone to do the books at the restaurant and her daughter was pulling at her, asking her to read.

The percolator pot was still warm. Bless George. The newspaper on the table announced WAR OVER in huge type, then on the next line, JAPAN SURRENDERS TO END WAR.

She downed two aspirin with a heated cup of coffee as chaser, and began reading the newspaper to her daughter.

AN ENVELOPE WITH no return address arrived in the middle of the next week. The postmark was Chicago. Inside was a certified check for fifty dollars. A little thrill went through her. *Josiah's all right*, she thought. *He's saying he's all right and he's thanking us.*

After that, she dragged George to see *Ziegfeld Follies* at the Nixon—a date, a romantic time together that she insisted upon. When Lena came on screen, she nudged George. "Again. Do I look like her?"

"Maybe. I don't know. Maybe first impressions."

As they walked to the car, George said, as if they'd been having this discussion all along underneath, "Josiah. Not the most usual friendship, but you knew him, liked him. Was it ever more than that?"

George. Oh, George. "Sometimes there are friendship crushes, maybe it was kind of like that. Not like what I feel for you, not a bit like you and me. Josiah was smart and had a lot of spirit. He said he had a really good family. I was interested in that. And his feelings showed. He was nuts about Lena. No, George, I don't know how to explain it. I just always loved seeing him."

Later, when she had plenty of time to think about it, she wondered about what prompted certain feelings and the difference between liking and longing for someone.

THE END OF September came and Madeline called, wanting to go see *Mildred Pierce*.

Marie said, "Maybe in a couple of weeks? I'm still packing for the move."

Outside in Pittsburgh the air was crisp, almost but not quite cold. The leaves were turning already, but the sun shone so brilliantly it hurt.

Marie packed pots and pans while her daughter sat on the floor, occupied with two books. Bread dough wrapped warmly was rising, sending a faint smell to the air.

There was a friendly sounding tap at the door, and Marie went to answer, expecting a neighbor or the meter man. But it was not a neighbor or a meter man. It was Philip standing there, wearing an army uniform, and . . . not looking the same. He was very thin.

"Oh, my God," she said. "You're really here." She stood back to let him in. When he embraced her, she realized his body was not only thin but hard and tense.

"I'm really here," he said.

"Oh, Philip! We kept thinking you'd call—" she began, but left off, looking at him. His skin was tawnier and drier, more lined. She ran back to fetch Helen, who was toddling forward to see what was happening.

"Helena! She's so big. She looks like George."

"I know. We're calling her Helen these days. How did you get here?"

"I've been hopping trains, eating hamburgers and sandwiches. All the time I thought about something you might cook."

"Oh, well, my cooking is a bit better these days."

"It was pretty good when I left. Will you feed me tonight?"

"Of course." She moved aside. "Let's not just stand here. Come to the kitchen. I'm sorry about the mess." She indicated the boxes being packed. "We didn't know when you'd be here."

His eyes widened. "You're moving."

"We wrote to you." He shook his head. "It missed you, I guess. We're going to a house in Dormont."

"Ah."

"Sit down. Let me get you something. What would you like?"

"A cup of coffee?"

"Sure, yes. And what else?"

"Any homemade bread in the house?"

"Yes. There is some from the last batch. And a fresh batch coming tonight. And we were going to have loobyeh with rice."

He pretended to fall to one knee, only slightly sliding off the chair. "Bless you. I thought I might never want rice again, but if it comes with the loobyeh, I want it. I had A rations a couple of times, B rations more than a couple of times, but mostly C."

"I don't know what that means."

"Canned and dried is what it means. Protein in a small package. Protein, meat."

"Oh, sounds awful."

"When you're hungry . . . it's funny what you think you like."

"I want to hear. Let me make the coffee first." Helen was smiling at him and he reached over and touched her hair. Marie watched this new sweetness in him, fascinated. "Did you stop at the restaurant?"

"I didn't. I didn't want to be around strangers. I just thought maybe I could get here and catch my breath."

"Shouldn't we call George?" She pointed to the living room where the phone was. "He'll be so upset if we don't."

She put on a fresh pot of coffee and used the remaining little bit of butter she had on the bread—half a round loaf that she prepared for him.

He was saying, "Yes. Yes. Yes," to George on the phone. Then he came back into the kitchen. "George is going to leave work, come home early."

Philip started on the buttered bread even before the coffee was ready. "So wonderful," he said. "Just bread and butter."

"Of course you know we expanded. George is hopelessly busy."

"The bar, yes. I'll go see the place tomorrow. And a house too. That's a lot going on, but he sounded excited."

"We are. A lot of adjustments."

He looked around. "What about this place?"

"We'll work it out. Wait for George. We'd need to rent if we don't sell, but he said he would charge you as little as possible."

Philip's face tensed a little. "Other news?"

"My brother, Freddie, made it. He's not home yet, though. I'm dying to see him again."

"Good, good."

She was truly glad Philip had made it out of the war alive and that he was sweeter now, but she thought she saw a bit of the old Philip, hidden in his eyes, wanting trouble.

George arrived some forty minutes later, arms outstretched to his hapless brother, still able to love, still George.

THEN IN A blink it was a Sunday in early October—moving day. George had hired a truck and two men to do the heavy lifting. Marie was in the kitchen of the new place, unpacking the dishes she had recently packed, with Helen underfoot watching everything closely.

It occurred to Marie again, and she hoped it was true, that Philip had been cleansed by war. Uncomplaining, he was out in the other room, helping with the heavy furniture. Could his good spirits last?

Howard Klein arrived with a bag of bagels and brought them straight to the kitchen, handing them to Marie. They were still warm, the smell of them intoxicating.

"We should have these right now, before they cool," she said.

"I agree. I brought cream cheese, too. But some people like butter."

George had managed to get butter to bring to the house—not a lot, but she removed it now from the brand-new refrigerator George had put in the place.

"Tell the men to stop, Howard. It's a good time for a break."

"Right."

"Is Madeline here?" she asked cautiously.

"Said she had other things to do. I don't know what. The boys are away. And we have cleaning people." He shrugged.

"Women always find more work," Marie offered, hoping that was true.

She had been sad all morning, on the verge of tears, just . . . just sorrowful all morning. Change. Every time, it got her. How strange to feel sad when everything was new, *because* everything was new.

Howard made the announcement out in the living room. Quickly, she put the bagels on a tray and added knives, butter, and cheese.

The dining table hadn't made it into the house yet, but the coffee table, which would do very well, sat in the middle of the living room. She put the tray down. "Help yourselves."

The men came forward. George had explained that he didn't want to bother friends with moving, so he'd chosen some customers who needed work and promised them a good day's pay. He had cash in an envelope for them in the kitchen, and when Marie questioned the amount, he said, "Now, now."

"They'll spend it on drink, George."

He put an arm around her and squeezed. "A funny thing for a bar owner to discourage. Joking. Joking." He drew in a breath and said, "Okay. I'll call it Thanksgiving money; that way I'll put the idea of their families in their heads."

Two new living room chairs had been delivered yesterday with the refrigerator. Philip sat in one. George indicated that Howard should take the other, but Howard kept standing. The four movers squatted or sat on the floor, eating bagels.

"Never had one of these," said one of the men. "Interesting. I thought they were doughnuts at first."

"Wonderful treat," George said. "I always loved bagels."

Howard brightened, knowing he'd pleased his friend. Like George, he was naturally generous. How miserable he must be with Madeline, who couldn't be pleased by much.

George saluted with his bagel. "I'm in heaven."

"You're working too hard," Marie told him quietly. "You seem out of breath."

"A little."

When the work break ended, the movers wiped their hands on their pants and got started toward the truck again.

George walked toward the front door, stopped, changed direction, and lifted a box that was intended for the second floor, but he stopped again and put it down.

Marie, on her way back to the kitchen, looked back and saw him. Was he deciding something? He looked confused and he was sweating profusely even though cold air blew in through the front door. "George," she said. "George, stop."

"Gotta help." He lifted the box and started for the stairs.

Marie hurried toward him to talk him into resting. His feet were stepping oddly and she thought he was going to stumble.

He managed to climb to the third step. The box fell first, and then he fell, trying to grab at something.

Marie ran to him. "Oh, God."

"I'm sorry," he said. "I'm so sorry."

Philip, who was still in the room, stood suddenly. Howard, still inside as well, cried out, "George, George, what happened? Are you okay?"

Philip shouted, "Let's get him to a hospital. No time to call for anyone. Carry him to a car. It's his heart."

Marie knelt beside George with Philip on the other side of him. George closed his eyes and breathed raggedly.

"Philip, why are you moving him? What happened? What's happening?"

"Heart problem. I told him to tell you. I told him."

George whispered, "Marie. Don't worry."

He could talk. He could tell her. Even though his breathing wasn't right, he spoke. That was a good sign, right? Holding on to him, she asked, "*Is* it your heart?"

"Pain." He pointed toward his chest. His face was strange with surprise and wet with sweat; his shirt, too, was damp.

Howard called the movers. "Hurry," he yelled, then gave them orders to lift and carry George while he helped. "Get him into my car. Back seat. I'll get it running." They lifted George to the back seat of Howard's car. Marie wedged in and put his head on her lap. Philip took the front passenger seat and held Helen. It all happened very fast.

Howard took off as soon as the movers slammed the back doors.

"It's okay, George, we're taking you in," Howard called.

Through the side window Marie could see the movers standing in the street, stunned. The house was wide open behind them.

Howard said, "George, hang on. George, we're getting you help."

George didn't answer, but his hand found Marie's hand.

"Where are we going?" she asked Howard.

"Presbyterian."

"Nothing closer?"

"No. Damn, damn, damn," Howard said. "Of all days to be out here instead of in Oakland."

All these years Marie had heard the names of hospitals, Jewish and Catholic and Protestant names, but she had no idea about their policies. Did they take everyone?

Howard drove fast. "I'm running these stop signs." He pressed the car horn. Helen cried and twisted, trying to look into the back seat.

Like this, Marie thought, *is it going to be like this?*

When the staff at Presbyterian brought a gurney, George's clothes were soaked and his face was white with pallor. Nurses were talking every which direction. Philip was explaining to one who stood still that his brother had a bad heart.

As they wheeled him away Marie tried to follow, but they told her she had to go back out to the waiting room.

Howard found a smaller room, apart from the larger waiting room. There were a couple of tables in there with hard wooden chairs. Maybe it was a meeting room. She didn't care.

Howard lifted Helen and took her to a far table where he did his best to tell her stories he half remembered from his own childhood.

Philip sat next to Marie. She asked him, "How did you know about his heart?" But she meant, of course, how did she not know. The reality of it was making sense now, coming closer and closer.

"A doctor told him when he was eighteen or so. He knew it before they did the draft examination. He thought maybe his heart had somehow healed itself. He'd read about that once, hearts that seemed bad and then they weren't. I told him to tell you. But he kept hoping his heart would fix itself. Honestly, I told him it was not the kind of thing to keep from you."

"Okay. It's okay." She forgave George that. She made every bargain with God she could to get George back. "Philip. I want to see him. Help me find somebody to talk to."

"They won't let us while they're working. I should have gone against him and told you."

She stood and paced. How had she not seen?

Something happened to her body all of a sudden, as if huge scissors had cut into her back, snapping a muscle. She doubled over and couldn't quite stand up.

"What is it?" Howard shouted.

"My back."

"Try to sit down."

"I can't. I can't stand up, either."

"Little by little," he said.

She tried, little by little, gasping.

Philip asked her to point to the spot that was in spasm. She did.

"Excuse me," he said, "but I'm going to rub." He began to massage her back. "Try to relax."

"I can't. I want to see him."

"Try."

After five more minutes of Philip massaging and her working at moving again, she was beginning to stand a little just as a doctor entered the room. They all looked at the doctor and he looked at them. Later, when there were more words passed back and forth, the doctor would explain that a second heart attack had happened at the hospital and that it was massive and that there was nothing they could do for the man with the enlarged heart.

But for several seconds, in the silence that was the first communication, as Marie managed to stand, the doctor allowed the truth to step into the room. Even Marie couldn't deny what she knew before the doctor nodded slightly to say, "I'm sorry."

HAPPINESS, THERE AND gone, thought Lena, as she opened the door to the *Courier* man who came right to the house on Horn Avenue to do the interview. "You want to know if I'm surviving the *Ziegfeld Follies* fiasco," she said grimly while Edwina's replacement, Annmarie, brought glasses of water and tea.

"Well, yes, that's what I'm supposed to write about. It will be small, but just so you know, when you make waves, I get more space. So if you want to make some . . ."

"Egg me on."

"Okay. I need quotes. They cut you right out of the film in the South. Is that right?"

"I was happy to get that role, but some people didn't like it. God help this country. I believed in this country. I believed in democracy. They clipped me right out."

"In some places . . ."

"In a lot of places. Down South." She watched him write. "I'm discouraged. Nothing has changed since I first performed way back at the Cotton Club."

He wrote what she said, murmuring, "Good. You're talking." Then he took up his role as agitator again. "Say something about your contract?"

"Tokenism. My contract salves a few consciences. It doesn't get me much past that."

He said, "Keep going. Angry with? The bosses?"

"I'm angry with everyone. I'm livid. People can say whatever they want about me. I'll never be polite again. If there's a rally, I'm going to be in it. If anyone will listen, I'm going to speak."

"Being blacked out of the film, is that what finally did it?"

She thought seriously. "I been mad at the world for a long time." She heard herself. She'd said, "I been," not "I've been."

"That's gonna get you some print. Personally, I admire you for complaining."

"You do?"

"Say more if you can. For instance, look at all the coverage you get, all kinds of publications, always a big fuss over you? People don't know why you'd be angry."

"Negroes need to be angry. Period. Okay, I was born looking a certain way. It calms some people. They think I'm okay. Other places, I'm not welcome. Oh, there's a lot of pretending. But . . . I'm angry for my people."

"You're marvelous."

"I'm going to keep talking."

"Good. You know how you sent me looking for somebody to talk to that woman in Pittsburgh? You did something there. They printed a story—"

"I know. I saw."

"—and it isn't over. They got a detective interested."

"All the good it does now."

"Some good. Maybe justice. Do you know anything about the boy's father? They can't find him anywhere." He stood and put his things together. "I said I'd ask you."

"Nope. Said a few words to him when I first met him and at the funeral home but never kept track of him. Sad case. The saddest."

She was exhausted. Telling the truth could sap a person who was used to smiling and making do.

TWENTY-ONE

1946

SUNDAY, SIX MONTHS AFTER SHE BURIED GEORGE, MARIE SAT AT the back booth, working on the accounts. She kept looking up, thinking George would come into the restaurant, which she now managed. And at home, the rare hours that she was there, she kept expecting him, too. A few new neighbors, trying to be kind, told her the dead walked among us all the time. They told her to have faith that she would be re-united with him as soon as her time came.

At first Fran brought her things—food, magazines, books. And Fran watched Helen along with her own daughter, Marian, when she could. She had gotten her job at the school back. She was good, and they'd missed her, they said.

Marie began to see that although *she* had often neglected Fran, her sister always came back loving. There were simply good people in the world and she had been graced to have a couple of them in her life.

These days her parents just sat and worked the store. They'd both survived heart attacks, but they were slowed down. Fran moved back in and began to care for them, getting up before dawn, cooking, cleaning, before she went to her job at the school. Then she came and helped Marie.

For the first three months Marie had Philip running the bar, but he started drinking again and she knew she couldn't keep him on. One day she walked in as a Negro man left, and she saw Philip throw the man's glass to the ground, causing two customers to applaud him.

"Don't ever do that again," she told him, not caring who heard. "Not in my place. George would never do that."

Philip's eyes wouldn't focus. "George, George, George," he said. "I'm sick of hearing about him."

One customer said, "I ain't coming back if he *don't* break the glass."

"I see," she said. "Well, that's your decision." She wanted to say something like, *I won't miss you*, but she had a hardheaded business sense about keeping a customer if she could.

Philip said, "Man, it's just a glass. They expect it."

She said, "Come over to the restaurant for a moment. I need to show you something."

Philip looked puzzled, but he followed her from the bar to the restaurant. "What? A stockpile of extra glasses?"

She turned to him. Every part of her was shaking as she said, "This won't work. I'll check on you whenever I can, but I'll find someone else to do the bar."

"You think you can run this place?"

"I'll have to." She went back to the bar and stood ready to serve. Finally she said, "Anybody need anything?" The customers laughed.

What she did over the next three months was fix a schedule. Fran in the kitchen after school hours worked so fast that Marie had her prepare the cooked foods for the next day. And Fran's cooking was good. When Fran was there, Emil worked the counter. While Fran was at school, the stocky waitress worked the counter. Marie added Selma, who was done with school, as a waitress. Selma might be shy but she was also responsible, and she got the orders in correctly. Marie paid both her sisters a salary.

She ordered the food and updated the menus, and she also bartended from ten in the morning until four in the afternoon when a man named Smiley took over and she released Selma to help take care of their parents.

In her first days as bartender, Marie hardly knew a beer from a bottle of whiskey, let alone a blended whiskey from bourbon; the fancier gins and vodkas and liquors were completely foreign to her. She knew those things now. Two of the customers had enjoyed (too much enjoyed) giving her lessons. But they sobered up as she learned the ropes. Howard Klein put in a pinball machine free for three months, just to see if she—or rather her customers—liked it. They did.

She was breaking even, but very hopeful, because each week was better than the last.

One night Fran made some Lebanese foods in the restaurant kitchen and Marie tried them on a few regulars the next day. They were so enthusiastic that she got an excited feeling about slowly, slowly introducing things the customers weren't used to. Maybe she would have a special night—say, Wednesdays—for specialty foods.

She got up at six and went home at ten in the evening, with Helen asleep on both ends of the travel.

She drove now. Better each week. The car was hers.

She was miserable without George. She thought of him almost every minute.

What would he have done about Philip?

Philip had almost instantly found himself a boozy girlfriend; that's all she knew except that he'd come around and tried to apologize to her a month after she fired him. She didn't take him back.

One day last week, Madeline called to ask how she was.

She said she was very busy, but surviving.

Madeline said, "You're like Mildred Pierce."

"I don't know who she is."

"That movie! Joan Crawford. She runs a restaurant. She has several lovers. Very realistic."

"No, I don't know that movie."

"Well, anyway, listen. Are you listening? I hope you know that what you saw a couple of years ago was me making speeches of refusal to a proposition."

Marie felt herself blinking rapidly. "I tried not to think anything."

"You never told anyone about me meeting my policeman that night, did you?"

"Policeman?"

"He was out of uniform."

"Oh. Like I said, I blanked it out."

"Good for you. That's the way. I'll call again."

"Sure."

That conversation gave her nightmares. Oh, how she wanted George to be alive, saying he would stand by her.

Now she was sitting at the back booth, doing accounts. She looked up when the door opened. No, not George. It was Fran, come to check on her.

"Sundays get lonely," Fran said.

ON ANOTHER LONELY Sunday morning, Marie was again sitting at the back booth, with the radio on, polka music. Otherwise silence.

Someone tapped at the door. She moved toward the door a few steps, ready to call out, "We're closed," when she saw a tall figure out there—the detective, Marshall. She felt a little frightened. Why would he come here for her on a Sunday?

She unlocked the door.

"You're in business," the detective said approvingly. "Big job."

"Yes, it is."

"Do you mind if we sit? I have to ask you a few questions."

Marie indicated a front booth, where her bills were not spread around, and they sat. "How did you know I'd be here?"

He smiled. "I had someone watching your patterns."

"Oh, my God. Am I in trouble for something?"

"Probably not. I have to ask a couple things about your friend, this woman Madeline. Madeline Klein."

"Is she. . . . What kind of question?"

"Does she confide in you? Talk to you?"

"I haven't seen her for a long time. Except for the funeral. She's not . . . a close friend. I don't even know if *friend* is the right word. My husband was a friend of her husband."

"Has she ever talked to you about a man named Vickers?"

"Vickers. No."

"Former policeman."

She flinched. "No."

"You hesitated. Why?"

"Oh, I don't know. I don't much like subjects like that." She could feel her face flushing.

"My question made you nervous." Marshall removed a photograph from the breast pocket of his sport coat. "Did you ever see this man?"

It was a cop picture, a man in uniform. Marie studied it longer than she needed to. It had his identity and badge number. "It's hard to see with the uniform. Please tell me what this is about."

"He's an ex-cop. Ex. We had a tip. A cousin of Vickers's told us to look into him. The cousin indicated that Vickers ordered the killing of this boy Josiah in jail. It worked the way he wanted. It made the case go away before it went to trial. But . . . see, you had a bee in your bonnet about the *first* killing. You said maybe this case wasn't done, that maybe somebody else killed Joe Klein. So the bee got in my bonnet and I started sniffing around. At first anything I did was unofficial. Then I got permission to proceed." He took in a deep breath. "Your friend never talked about meeting Vickers in high school? Being sent away because she was so crazy about him?"

"I knew she was sent away for something, not that."

"We have Vickers in custody. Now we need to know about your friend. If you know anything."

"I'm thinking."

"And one other thing."

Marie had begun moving the salt and pepper and sugar into a neat line. Her hand froze.

"One more question. Did you ever hear again from the boy Josiah Conner?"

"Hear from him? Before he died? No, he never wrote to me."

"Did you ever hear from someone named Luke Findlay?"

"Luke Findlay. No."

"Sure about that? No contact?"

"I'm sure."

"I thank you for your time. I know you're busy." He began to stand.

"Who is Luke Findlay?"

He considered her. "I think you know."

"No, I don't." She felt lifted off the ground. She was not used to lying.

He paused, then continued. "Fellow who could be buried in one of the Carolinas. Maybe. Maybe not. Could be the name this Josiah is going by. Maybe I have too big an imagination."

"I'm trying to catch up to what you're saying." But she could feel her face was so hot it must be flushed.

"It's a very complex case. It seems either Luke Findlay or Josiah Conner disappeared. Somewhere, somehow. You know what? I think your Josiah was innocent."

Marie gazed at the man. He was tall and sad and serious-minded. She tried to think what an innocent person would say, then she asked, "Why would he not come back to his family?"

"We're working on that. The person with the answers was the old warden, but he died."

"He *died*?"

"Why? You knew him?"

"No, not really. I met him at the jail once. I don't tend to look at the lists in the papers. Of deaths."

"It's depressing, isn't it?"

"You said . . . this case is complex."

"Very complex. Look at this. It was a cousin of Vickers's who needed a chit to get out of trouble, and he's the one who talked. Where would we be without that? Don't worry. Vickers is beat, at the end of his fight. Next door to making a full confession."

He stood fully and checked his pockets, then frowned and sat down again. "Oh, one more question for you. Do you sense Madeline was in on it? That she had her husband killed by her lover? You must have gotten some idea about that."

Marie shook her head slowly, trying to piece together bits and pieces of conversations with Madeline. "I don't know how she could live with herself if she did that. She never confided in me. Is Vickers saying she knew?"

"He's not saying anything. He completely clams up when we mention any involvement from her. True love, I guess. Do I have to say you don't ever breathe this? I said more than I should, I know that. But then, you seem to be a person who can keep a secret. Even a very big secret." He winked at her, or she thought he did. "To my mind, the basic point is the Conner boy was innocent. Sounds like a nice fellow.

Oh—did I tell you, Vickers had an uncle in the mailroom? That might be an answer to some of our questions."

After Marshall left, Marie sat for a full hour at the same booth before limping back to her bills.

Madeline's lover made the newspapers.

PITTSBURGH SUN-TELEGRAPH
EX-COP ARRESTED IN 1941 MURDER OF BUSINESSMAN

He went free for 5 years but ex-policeman Conrad Vickers is in custody and has confessed to the killing of businessman Joseph Klein. The case was closed nearly a year after the killing when Josiah Conner, a youth who had been charged with the murder, was killed in Allegheny Jail where he was awaiting trial. Conner was mounting a case for his defense when he was knifed to death. Vickers has admitted to hiring another inmate, Luke Findlay, to kill Conner.

City Police Chief James Reilly says he is waiting for more information before he is willing to say his former officer is guilty of the crimes, and he believes that a trial will show this to be the false confession of a man in emotional distress. Police are still trying to put together the sequence of events and to locate Luke Findlay, whose jail records have been expunged and whose location is not known. "Something is missing from the paperwork, but we'll get to the bottom of it," Reilly assured reporters.

Conrad Vickers was a long-time friend of Madeline Klein, the widow of the businessman. According to friends, Vickers wanted her to divorce her husband and marry him. Detective Paul Marshall says that the case is one of a love triangle that had consequences beyond the three people involved.

The case was reawakened when a woman told a Courier reporter that she had been in the city the night of the murder. There was a blizzard that night. She says she saw a car careening down the street after the sound of shots rang out. Immediately after that, police arrested Conner, who stood at the automobile where Klein lay dying. Conner insisted he was trying to help the man, but he was not believed. The gun used in the killing was never found.

PITTSBURGH COURIER

Six years ago Josiah Conner insisted he was arrested for a crime he did not commit. He was accused of shooting Pittsburgh business- man Joseph Klein on a winter night in a blizzard. A year later Conner was killed in jail.

Until now the case has stayed closed. But a new arrest of a for- mer policeman, Conrad Vickers, has yielded a confession to both crimes, the shooting of Klein and the subsequent contract killing in jail of Josiah Conner by another inmate, Luke Findlay, whose jail record is non-existent and who has disappeared.

The motive was apparently jealousy. Vickers was in a relation- ship with the widow of Joseph Klein. She has not been charged with any crime.

No surviving relatives of Conner's can be found to shed light on his side of the story. Police are searching for Findlay. Bulletins have been sent to precincts around the country. The initial crime was of a white man killing a white man but two Negroes became em- broiled in the conflict.

Marie read the articles several times. She had to hope Josiah had a secure new name and had left no trace of the Findlay identity.

On Monday morning, early, when she was sitting in the restaurant kitchen, she watched Emil working. Emil hovered over a large griddle of bacon and squinted at handheld orders for eggs. "Bacon and eggs, sausage and eggs, ham and eggs," he muttered.

She knew what a hard worker he was, how lucky she was to have him in the business, and how out of place he must surely be everywhere else—apartment, neighborhood, even at church. He was one of those people who didn't fit socially. George had wanted to give Emil work and security, but the benefit came back to Marie.

Sometimes she sent Philip money after all. That was the George part of her, the way her husband's spirit invaded her. When she could, she called him, too, to check on him, thinking what a wonder it was that Philip had made it through the war, reckless as he was with his body.

She picked up the phone and made her meat order.

If she hadn't had this work to do, she would have gone out of her mind. George hadn't wanted her to work, but in the long run he made it possible. She liked to think that if he were here, he would beam at her, shake his head in wonder, and say he'd been wrong again, that she was astounding, more than he'd bargained for.

She took up the phone and made another call. "Detective Marshall, please. Yes, I'll wait. Yes, it's important." Emil's eyebrows went up in alarm. *It's okay*, she gestured to him, *it's okay*. And when the detective got on the line, she told him she had three questions.

"Shoot," he said.

"Why do you think Josiah Conner might be alive? In what *way* is he still in danger? Why do the newspapers not say that he might be alive?"

The answers were swift. And so quietly murmured, she understood he didn't want to be overheard.

"My imagination, perhaps, maybe that's all it is. Somebody's body was sent somewhere. Somebody else is free. I talked to a woman— lovely woman, widow of the warden—and I read between some lines. Two: There is one difficult family that had about seven cops on the force, Vickers being one of them. They were reputed to protect each other. There are only three left. And three, the newspapers never got the full story because I didn't *tell* them the full story. I caught your bug."

"Bug?" she asked.

"Believing in the kid."

"Oh."

"Between you and me, tell him, if you get to talk to him, I hope he makes it."

"You're very . . . different," she said.

"I am. Don't get me in trouble, okay? You gotta keep mum. Understand?"

"I promise."

It took most of the morning to recover from that phone call. Then Marie looked in the phone book and made another call. The warden's widow was Enid Schmidt, and she lived in East Liberty.

To an older woman's hello, Marie said, "You don't know me, but I met your husband once. I'm the person the newspaper said was downtown when Josiah Conner was arrested. And I helped him one other time."

"Oh, yes . . . I see."

"Could I talk to you sometime? Just us. I wish I'd called before. I wish I'd seen your husband again. I didn't know what to do, so I was afraid to call. . . . I could come to see you . . ."

"Well, I guess. Yes."

"Good. We have some things in common."

After a pause, Mrs. Schmidt said, "Yes. All right, then."

And so Marie made an appointment for that very evening, when she would leave the place to Fran and Selma, pick up her daughter, and drive to East Liberty.

"Emil. Don't cut into that coconut cream pie. I need it as a gift."

That evening, tapping at the door of the East Liberty house, a small brick structure with a porch, not unlike her own house, she held Helen's hand in one of her hands, and held the pie in her other.

The door opened. A woman with a cloud of white hair but an unlined face peered at Marie and nodded once. She was using a cane. She stepped back to let them in. "Hello. Yes. I'm Enid."

"This is for you. A pie."

"Oh, I love a pie. Should I . . . should I make coffee?"

Marie considered the problems, every which way. Enid was shy. Her daughter should be in bed. "Yes. I won't stay long. I could sit in the kitchen with you while you make the coffee. We can talk that way."

"Oh. All right." Mrs. Schmidt, limping slightly, walked toward an open doorway and Marie followed. She could smell the remnants of dinner, something with tomato sauce, and saw immediately that the dishes hadn't been done yet. She suspected Mrs. Schmidt felt embarrassed by that, so she tried a distraction. "I love your cheerful curtains." She did like them, white with big yellow butterflies. "I see my daughter looking at them."

"I made them."

"I used to sew a lot—all kinds of things. No time now. Do you have children?"

"Two fine sons. Married, both of them. And two children each. I take care of the little ones sometimes. We get along fine. I thank my stars for that." She stooped a little toward Helen. "Aren't you a nice little girl? Are you going to have pie and coffee with us?"

Helen looked at her mother. "Um, milk?"

"What, no coffee?" Mrs. Schmidt teased. She winked at Marie. "I'll get you milk."

Why couldn't she have been my mother? Marie thought. Mrs. Schmidt placed a bottle of milk on the table and paused, taking a breath. "I need to fetch a glass."

Marie said, "Take it easy. I can do that." She went to the cabinets and quickly found a glass. "I don't want to keep you for long. I should get my little girl home to bed. If you want to sit, I can do the rest. I have a restaurant. I do this all day long."

"Thank you. I'll let you help." Mrs. Schmidt held onto the table for stability, then pushed herself off and stood at the stove filling the percolator.

Marie felt herself getting more comfortable as she found plates and cut slices of pie, keeping up a chatter about safe subjects like the weather. She located coffee cups and put them on the table in preparation for the pouring of coffee. Finally, she said, "I was the one who told your husband I was downtown on the day of the murder—the day of the blizzard."

"You saw the car driving away. I read that."

"Yes, and I knew Josiah Conner a little bit from the neighborhood. I couldn't imagine him doing such a thing."

Mrs. Schmidt turned from the stove. "Neither could my husband." Then she said carefully, "I think I'm going to disappoint you. I hate to disappoint you. I don't know anything more."

"Did Marshall the detective talk to you?"

Mrs. Schmidt smiled, came to the table, and sat, looking at the stove as if to encourage faster boiling. She chose her words. "I think my husband was afraid the truth put me in danger. He said he didn't want to tell me certain things because he didn't want me in a position of lying. I asked him once, 'Did you do something criminal?' He didn't answer me. He had taken money out of our metal box that day during all the hubbub, I knew that much. 'I did what I thought was right,' he told me—oh, this was years later, when he was sick."

"I'm sorry. He seemed like a very good person."

"He knew there were some bad police. He was afraid of them a lot of the time. I put an awful lot together from little bits of things he said. He told me, 'Some of the jail officers don't know one Negro from another. All they see is black skin. They put them all in one category.' I was trying to keep him cheerful, you know, when he was sick. 'I think you're quite a guy,' I said. 'You saw that boy you said had something wonderful about him. I remember that.' He . . . I don't know. He got a happy sort of expression. He said, 'Sometimes there's a sweet mess with the paperwork.' I said, 'I think you might have saved a life.' He was dying then, cancer. Oh, I miss him so."

Marie started to cry. Another George. Another good one that left only longing behind.

"Oh!" Mrs. Schmidt said. "What?"

"My husband was like that. Kind. He died in October."

"It's really hard," Mrs. Schmidt said. "Really hard."

"Yes, it is."

After a silence, Mrs. Schmidt said, "That's all I know, honestly."

"So you don't know where the life he saved . . . ended up."

"No. I got a cashier's check—oh, was it almost a year ago. Two hundred dollars. I think maybe that was the person."

"No return address?"

"None."

"Postmark?"

"I didn't notice."

They took delicate bites of the pie before the coffee was ready.

"I'm glad you brought pie. I love a pie."

LENA LOOKED OVER at Lennie, who was driving her to the airport, only ten minutes away, and although both of them were usually talkative, a strange silence had fallen over them.

He knew she'd been bailing her father out financially. He never told her to quit, but he also didn't say much about it. He knew she had jumped at this weekend because Louis would be back in Pittsburgh with her son Teddy—they'd moved to Ohio after the divorce was finalized, making Lena's reach toward her son even more difficult.

"I'd be happy to go with you, last minute," he told her as they drove. "Say the word."

"You don't even have a suitcase with you."

"I could buy things there. I've made last-minute plans before."

After a moment she told him, more kindly, "Louis is difficult enough. Imagine how he'd be if he saw you or even knew you were there."

"I was thinking I'd hide out in a hotel and do some of my work and sleep." He tipped back his captain's hat. His left arm was out the window, a cigarette burning, gracing the highway with ash.

"Your cigarette burns faster that way."

"There's more." He tapped the pack in his pocket. "Also sold in Pittsburgh."

Some people in the world had learned ease. Or maybe they were born with it. Or maybe hangovers helped. Lennie had ease. She didn't. She was always rushing even when there was no place to rush to.

In Pittsburgh, she was supposed to sign papers to finish the sale of the Belmont, which had been held up pending buyer finances. Her father spent his time in Vegas now. He wasn't able to pay back the money she'd lent him two years ago. A gift, then, she told him when his birthday rolled around. He looked embarrassed, so she nudged him and said, "I like to give gifts."

And yet his voice was tight every time she talked to him by phone because he'd heard about Lennie. She saw her father more clearly these days—she could forgive his debt, but he couldn't forgive her need for love. They saw each other only when he hopped a plane or train to ferry Teddy to or away from her as Louis allowed. She'd always said her father adored her, but maybe it was just the other way around. Her love for him had been what sustained her.

That woman Marie, who had stood up for Josiah, had written two letters saying if ever Lena were in town, she would like to talk to her. She would try to fit that in.

"I hate flying," she grumbled, even though Lennie knew perfectly well how she felt. Flying itself frightened her, but it was also hard being the only Negro on the plane most times, wondering if the stewardess would be decent to her.

"Next time I'm coming with you."

"Okay."

She didn't sleep during the flight. She tried to read, but the words wouldn't stay still or make sense. By the time she arrived in Pittsburgh her nerves were frayed in anticipation of dealing with Louis.

The first cab driver pretended not to see her, a second and third stopped and drove away, but finally a fourth accepted her. She gave the old address where she had lived with Louis and his brother—it was where Louis was staying this weekend.

She'd arranged to have the lawyer who was executing the sale of the Belmont come to Louis's brother's house for her signatures so she could maximize her time with her son.

And then she had to get a room. Or . . . she would happily sleep on the couch if Louis would allow her to stay so she could be with Teddy as much as possible. Her watch told her it was seven o'clock. The lawyer was scheduled for eight.

She knew she would get very hungry around midnight—awkward if she got to stay with Louis's relatives, but she didn't want to stop the cabbie to get food to take as an offer. The three candy bars in her handbag would have to do.

She almost fell asleep in the cab. In the strange half sleep, she imagined a dreamy few hours with her son and a good night's sleep.

The cab stopped in front of her former brother-in-law's place. Louis was standing outside the door, stone faced. She paid the cab driver, all the while aware that her heart was sinking with dread.

"You can't come in."

His hair had grown a good bit of gray. That made her sad somehow. And he looked thinner. He was clutching a packet of papers.

"Louis, let's be decent to each other."

"You can't just call and arrange your life around a trip I had to make. You can't do that."

He had said he needed to go to Pittsburgh for the weekend. She had said she had business there so she would make it the same weekend. Why was that a fault? And why did he wait until things were done to show his fury? Vanished was the idea of a place to stay. She would have to go somewhere else.

She tried to think. Her feet hurt and she felt sweaty and rumpled, so she wanted something easy, nearby, but she could not imagine wanting to stay in her father's old Belmont Hotel, now rundown, but also . . . it brought back painful memories. "I just need to see Teddy."

"Well, he's asleep. You can see him tomorrow. In the yard."

"The yard?" The five-foot square in the back where she used to pray for a sliver of sunshine? She remembered it well. "Look, Louis. I'm very tired. I need to get some rest soon. But are you sure Teddy's asleep?"

"He's sleeping. Watkins brought these papers over. He had a dinner he had to be at. He said you can just sign them and he'll come to pick them up."

"Where's Lionel and—"

"They're not here. They didn't want to be here tonight."

She had to go to him to get the packet of papers. She felt the heave of a sob coming. Without thinking, she had been holding her suitcase all this time. She dropped it.

She opened the envelope and tried to study the papers Louis had handed over. The words blurred. Watkins had always been okay, so she simply signed. "I'll need to call a cab again."

"I'll call it for you."

It was starting to rain, speckling her clothes, frizzing her hair, oh, not hard, just a light rain, but it would have been nice to duck inside and miss it.

Minnie came out of the house and stood beside Louis. She looked with naked admiration at the flowered dress, the mauve high heels, the gloves with a light pink tint that Lena wore.

"Hi, Minnie."

"She can stay at my place tonight," Minnie said.

They walked the few blocks in a drizzling rain, trading off the suitcase. "He called me to watch Teddy today. That boy is getting big."

"How was he?"

"Good. Good. Always interested in something."

The evening felt like rolling the film backward to her old days—a lumpy single bed and a crust of bread—literally, toast and butter. But she concentrated on the sounds that came through the open window, the music of nighttime and springtime in Pittsburgh. A shout here and there. The excited voice of a child up too late. Memory. Being young and loving her father's way of life and going to the clubs and being so proud of the famous music and even, way back, loving Louis.

But now she was someone else, famous and infamous and a stranger to a lumpy single bed. She would have to get a good hotel after she spent the day with Teddy tomorrow, one with a dining room and food, things she'd been raising herself up to in these ten years.

She was two people, the old Lena, the girl who lived in the Hill and stayed at the hotel and sat out back with Josiah, just needing to talk to someone, and she was the new Lena, famous, friends with Judy Garland and Ava Gardner and living in a way Minnie and Louis couldn't even comprehend.

In an uncomfortable night of sleep, she had half dreams about Teddy, who at times merged with her father, and she felt a longing to hold and to nurture and to help.

On Sunday morning she gave Minnie her flowered dress and mauve shoes and pink gloves. Minnie was delighted, saying, as she had many times before, "You have an eye," and Lena said, as she had many times, "Got it from my pa."

They carried the suitcase back to Lionel's house. Lena took her place in the backyard and after a while Minnie ushered Teddy out. Oh, he was thin! How were they living? Why wasn't Louis fattening him up? Teddy squirmed when she hugged him but she couldn't let go, and held him tight, trying not to cry. When she finally released him, she tapped him on the nose and said, "I miss you so much."

They had to sit on the chairs that had been the old kitchen chairs from when she lived there. "I wish you could write letters! I wish you could be with me. Is your school okay?"

"It's okay."

"But if you could come out with me for a longer time, you could go to school with your sister. Wouldn't that be great?"

"I don't know."

"Really?"

"She said sometimes the kids weren't nice."

"That's everywhere. That's just people." He was so young. It was his first year in grade school. She didn't want to admit even to herself that it was probably easier for him being in school with Negro kids.

"If you ask to come back out with me, maybe we can look around for a different school?"

He smiled, he nodded, but he didn't say yes.

She could not accept losing him. She had to keep trying. "How about if we go someplace for lunch?"

"Well . . ."

"I'm starving, really really hungry. We could go early! We could have a second breakfast."

Again Teddy hesitated. "Just a minute." He went back into the house.

A few seconds later Louis came out. "We're going back to Ohio today. We'll be leaving in a half hour or so."

"What! Why are you doing this?"

"Doing what?"

"Leaving. You said you'd be here this weekend."

"I didn't say *for* the weekend. There was a quick something I had to do. I said *on* the weekend."

"Can't you stay longer?"

"We can't. We have other things planned in Columbus. You can't just come into town and expect everybody to change everything for you."

"When were you going to tell me what your plans were?"

"When were you going to ask?"

Her son was on the verge of tears. "It's all right," she told him. "I'll come to Ohio in a couple of weeks. I'll send for you, too, for a trip out to see us. Okay?"

Teddy nodded, clenching his jaw hard.

"Don't worry, sweetheart. It's okay to cry."

Louis frowned and grabbed his son by the shoulders.

"It's okay," Lena insisted.

So before she expected to, Lena took a jitney to the William Penn, her one suitcase on the seat beside her. It was only eleven in the morning. Downtown was fairly deserted except for a few knots of people in front of the churches.

Lena dismissed the jitney and went into the William Penn and up to the counter.

She felt it as soon as she walked in, the old problem. There was fear on the face of the young man at the counter; it was a fear that she had seen a million times, but she forged ahead in spite of what her gut was telling her. "I need a room for one night."

"I'm sorry," he said. "We are full."

She stood for a long time, gathering her words. "I doubt if you're full."

He looked down—at the floor, then began rifling through the booking sheets.

"I'll talk to your manager."

"He isn't in. He comes at two today."

"Where are the phones?" She fumbled in her purse, hoping she had change.

He pointed to the bank of phones as if she were too dull to recognize them.

There were four phones, all available because there was nobody around in this reportedly full hotel. She would talk to the manager. She was almost—*almost*—amused by the thought that she should have brought clippings with her because she knew some of the well-known musicians *had* stayed here. She could have Lennie call them, Freed if necessary. But first she skimmed the phone book under *E*, looking for *Elias*. She dialed a number for George Elias, but there was no answer. Her journalist had told her there was a restaurant, George's Place. But it was Sunday. Most were closed. On the other hand, she was extremely hungry. She found an entry for the restaurant and dialed.

A woman's breathless voice said, "Hello?"

"Is this . . . ?"

"The restaurant is closed."

"Is this Marie? Elias?"

"Yes."

"This is Lena Horne. Could we meet? Get something to eat, possibly? And talk? You wanted to talk. I'm in town."

"Oh. Yes! I'm at work now, just doing accounts, but . . . I have my little girl with me. I would have to bring her. She's been asking about food."

"All right, then. I'll try to find out what's open downtown. Can you get to downtown? Or should I come there?"

There was a pause. Lena couldn't tell what it meant, perhaps a worry about money. The girl she'd met, the one she thought of as a pesky little sister, had been poor.

"Tell me where to come," the woman said.

"I'll be standing outside the William Penn."

FINALLY. SHE WOULD finally get to make her report, Marie thought, but relief drifted into sadness. Somehow holding on to a secret had strengthened her.

Marie settled Helen in the back seat to complaints—the child was used to the front seat. "Shh," she said. "We have something we have to do." The rearview mirror told Marie she looked plain, no makeup.

Even though she didn't know what was open for lunch downtown, she couldn't imagine she was dressed appropriately to go somewhere with Lena. She had put on a pair of pants and a light blue sweater she wore to work on Sundays.

They *could* go back to her own restaurant, start up the kitchen, and make . . . something, an egg sandwich. It would be easier than talking at a restaurant.

She checked the back seat. "Helen. Are you okay?"

"Hungry."

"Yes. Soon."

The trip downtown was quick, straight down Fifth Avenue, past the old haunts, past the Hill where she used to live. Soon she was pulling the Buick up in front of the hotel, where Lena, looking like a fashion model, stood patiently with a suitcase beside her. Everyone who passed turned to look at her.

Marie got out of her car, straightening her sweater. "Lena. I'm Marie."

"I remember, yes. Brilliant seamstress."

"I was doing my bills. I'm not dressed to go anywhere very nice, but . . ."

"I've been asking the porter. There's not much open, only the restaurant dining room which . . . isn't very good, he said. I hear there's a coffee shop around the corner." She shrugged. "Pie and coffee. Not lunch."

Marie hesitated. "I could take you to my restaurant. I could see what we have handy, do something quick."

"Oh, no, no, you were leaving there for the day, right?"

"I was just about done, yes." Marie took a good breath and said, a little hesitantly, "I don't know if you would consider it, but I have lots of food at home. It's Arabic food, though. You might not like that."

Lena paused too. "The food is great, I've had it, I love it, but I'm trying not to be any trouble . . ."

"If you like the food, I'd be happy to make us a lunch. I could drive you back here after."

"It's not far?"

"Not far at all. That's my daughter in the car." She did not say, *I kind of named her after you.*

And of course her news would be easier to give now, in a house, in privacy.

"Well, I hope you like what we have," she said. Marie and her daughter had both been looking forward to the homemade bread, grape leaves, and spinach pies, and also to the kibbee she still had to make.

She was puzzled about the suitcase, but perhaps Lena was just leaving the hotel and about to leave town. Lena put her suitcase in the back seat and got into the passenger seat.

"Very kind of you," Lena told her. "You've rescued me."

Marie started up the car. "I hope . . . nothing terrible."

"Terrible enough." Tight smile. And then Lena turned to the back seat. "Well, aren't you wonderful? What a nice smile you have."

Marie could see in the rearview mirror Helen shrugging, grinning. "She likes to read."

"So do I. Thank God for books. Right?" This line was delivered, too, to Helen.

"I don't know how she reads. I think she memorizes the books and figures out what the letters must be spelling. I was never good at that kind of thing."

Lena nodded.

"My house is simple. I hope you won't mind."

"I won't mind. You seem good, strong."

"Do I? Well, I have the restaurant now. I have to be."

"About your husband, you said in one of your letters. I'm sorry."

Marie teared up and said more than she intended. "I'd give anything to have him back. He had a heart condition and I never knew."

"Aw. Aw. Damn, oh damn," Lena said, "the way things happen."

"Mommy?"

"Everything's all right. We'll be home in no time."

"I've never seen this part of the city," Lena said.

"I hadn't either. It's a bit calmer than Oakland. I miss the Hill, though."

"Do you?"

"Grew up there."

"You wanted to talk about Josiah?"

"Yes."

"It's horrible, how he ended."

Marie said, "I have something to tell you, as soon as we sit down. We're almost there. I'm going to first put out some foods to hold us over, but if you can stay for an hour and a half, by then I'll also have the rest of lunch. I hope you like it."

"I love food of all kinds—spicy, exotic, everything."

The road widened at the commercial district. "Just a little bit more." *Soon,* she thought, *I will tell her.* She felt something like stage fright.

"That way," Helen said, pointing right. "Then that way, that way." She pointed left.

"Smart!" Lena said. "I have a daughter a little older than you."

Marie pulled up in front of her house. "She'll know the restaurant business in a year or two. I have her with me so much of the time."

"Are you good at it? The restaurant?"

"Um. Yes. I think so. Give me a job, I do it."

Lena chuckled, but there was a trace of bitterness in her tone when she said, "Give me a song, I sing it."

"I play your recording of 'Stormy Weather' all the time. I love it."

"Can't get away from that one no matter what I do."

As soon as they got into the house, Marie put a pot of coffee on and got out bread and butter.

Lena dove into the bread and butter. "I'm sorry. I haven't eaten in pretty much a day."

Then Marie, gratified to see how freely her guest was eating, brought a tray of spinach pies and a plate of stuffed grape leaves to the table, saying, "Please. Have whatever holds you over. Please."

There was no problem at all. Lena *was eating.*

"I made the bread."

"*Did* you?"

Helen was so entranced watching Lena that she forgot to bring her own spinach pie to her mouth.

"The thing is," Marie said, and made herself sit down. "Josiah wanted us to talk. He told me to tell you something in person. I thought it was strange, and I almost called, but he said no letters or phone calls. . . . He said, if you came to town . . ."

"I don't understand. When? They let you visit him?"

"No. He . . . he was brought here to the house. I know this is going to be hard to take in. We—my husband and I—kept him here and got him out of town. I need to say this carefully. It's the truth. He's not the one who died. He's . . ."

Lena stared at her, then began nodding like an old woman. "I knew something . . . I knew something felt odd. This is crazy."

Marie spelled it out, best she could, explaining the probable mixup in the prison and the heroics of the warden. "My husband and I were told we must never tell anyone. And Josiah said, only you, in person."

"But why didn't he contact me himself?"

Marie was not sure she understood completely, though she guessed it had something to do with healing a heartbreak. So she just said, "He's hiding."

"What about his family, their house?"

"I don't know if he could ever come back. They caught the guy who did it, but there are relatives of the guy."

Lena got up, walked to the window and looked out for some time, then came back and sat down again. Helen watched her, fascinated.

"Where is he now?"

"If I ever hear, I'll find a way to tell you."

"He'll come find me. I want to know everything you know." She looked at Marie expectantly.

Marie told about her visits to the jail, the lawyer, Madeline, and times she suspected Madeline while Lena listened. "I'm going to make the rest of lunch now. Can you stay?"

"Yes."

"Good."

Lena shifted restlessly in her chair. "What if he can't make it?"

"I think he is somehow figuring out how to live. He sent me money, a cashier's check, a while ago, wanting to pay me back, but there was no return address. The postmark was Chicago. That's a big city."

"It sure is. Which is good. I can work to get a booking in Chicago."

Marie began soaking bulgur wheat. "Look. I promised the detective I would never talk, so no matter how much you want to do something, you have to stop yourself. No talking to newspapers. You can't do anything reckless. He asked me to tell you in person. So it's done. I'll never tell anyone else."

It was frightening that Lena did not look convinced.

"He loved you. I saw him going to the fundraiser for *The Duke Is Tops*. And he was dressed in a suit, so . . . grown-up, so . . . in love."

"He went to it?"

"Yes."

"He never said."

"He always worried about hurting you. Or bothering you."

Finally Lena nodded agreement. "I won't talk . . . but he might need money or connections. If I could find him, I could help."

Marie looked at her steadily. "I think it has to be up to him to make contact."

"I don't get it."

"The guy they caught has a lot of relatives. They're cops, but not the good kind."

Lena pursed her lips as if to seal them, and nodded.

"I have to finish mixing the kibbee," Marie said. "It won't take long. Please, relax."

Lena went into the living room with Helen. Marie could hear them talking about Helen's books. She could hear Helen explaining that the photos on the mantel were of her father. How funny and sort of sad to see that Lena, a famous person, could wolf down spinach pies and talk about children's books and be ordinary.

Ten minutes later Marie had the kibbee mixed. She tasted it and approved it. She patted it into a sineeya and poured oil over it and precut pieces, then slid the baking dish into the oven, calling out, "Only thirty-five minutes and we'll have the rest of lunch."

"I'll be ready," Lena called back. "Your daughter is showing me the house."

Not only showing but bragging about the house. It was embarrassing, but it seemed Lena had a store of patience with the child.

While the house tour was in progress, Marie tossed a salad and set the dining room table. She had decided to use her best dishes and silverware, things she hadn't bothered to take out since the Christmas before George died.

At lunch, Lena sat, posture erect. "Can you stand more questions?"

"Yes."

"What was he like when he was here?"

"Sad, very sad. Scared, of course."

"Why did he never take my help when he was in jail? I wrote to him several times. Was he angry?"

"I didn't know you offered help because he didn't know. According to the warden, someone in the mailroom was keeping mail from him."

"Are you sure?"

"Yes. He never got my letters either. If you wrote, he never knew."

Marie served her guest two squares of kibbee and a large helping of salad, letting herself think aloud. "I'm sure his father left town to be with him. Maybe they started a plumbing and handyman business somewhere. Maybe he's just a plain guy living in some city—Denver, say, or Chicago, married, even."

"He could never give up the movies," Lena said. "I picture him trying to work his way to California. That was his dream."

"But . . . it might be something he doesn't want anymore."

Lena's eyes widened. Was she angry or surprised? "I'm going to look at the tech credits for every movie made. I'll figure it out. The man I'm going to marry will help me."

The last sentence sat there for a little while, surprising both of them.

"You're going to get married?"

"Maybe. Now that's what *you* can't talk about. I could be in such trouble at the studio."

"Why?"

"He's white."

"Oh."

"I never thought I would or could."

"Is he a movie star?"

"No. Oh, Lord, that would be totally impossible. He's a musician. It still could ruin both of us."

"I'm sorry you have to hide the marriage." How one hid such a thing, Marie wasn't sure.

When lunch ended, Marie understood she'd taken something away from Lena. "He worshipped you, you know."

Lena said, "Maybe not as he got older. Let me help with the dishes."

"Oh, no. I can do it."

"I'll dry. I insist. It's funny. I haven't done a dish for a long time. I used to like it."

"Really?"

"Thinking time."

"I use very hot water," Marie explained, as she filled the sink. "My hands get red but my nails never break. Isn't that strange?"

"Strange and interesting. Do you need clothes? I keep giving things away. I'd like to send you some things."

Marie looked down at her outfit. "I put this outfit on when I do bills and otherwise I wear dresses or skirts to work. Nothing . . . dress-up like yours. I would never have anywhere to wear it." She nodded toward Lena's beautiful gray suit.

"I'll see if I have things you might like."

To change the subject, Marie said, "Tell me about your children. They get mentioned in articles sometimes."

"My daughter is with me. She's very smart. Very loyal to me through everything. She accepts the man I'm seeing."

"And you have a son. I read it in the *Courier*."

Lena's face told Marie she had asked the wrong question. "I have a son I almost never see. Even this weekend. His father has found the perfect way to punish me." Lena was suddenly close to tears, so Marie just whispered, "Awful," and went silent.

Lena had dried half the dishes when she said, "I didn't eat much last night and I didn't sleep much last night. Would you mind terribly if I go lie down for a few minutes?"

"No. Of course. Whatever you want." Marie assumed her guest meant the sofa but she heard Lena climbing the stairs.

The nap was longer than a few minutes, much longer. Marie had to quiet Helen and read to her, book after book.

Almost two hours later, when Marie tiptoed upstairs, she saw Lena in the spare room, asleep, her suitcase at her side. In that moment, Marie understood what Josiah had said about Lena's life being tougher than it looked. The woman standing outside the William Penn with her suitcase was standing there because they wouldn't let her in. Lena would need a place to stay the night and Marie had to make her feel easy about it, as if it were the most natural thing in the world.

When Marie drove Lena to the airport the next morning, Lena looked straight ahead at the road and said, "You turned out okay."

Marie said, "I hope you'll let me know if Josiah contacts you. I came this far in the story. I'd want to know."

"It's strange to think he's out there somewhere. To me he seems lost. You seem to be used to the idea."

"I always like to think it could be Idaho or Nebraska or Oregon. It could be anywhere. It kind of thrills me."

"Taking a course in film at night, maybe," Lena tried joking, but her tone said she couldn't let go of the idea completely.

"Working as a plumber during the day."

"Going by some other name."

"I know. I try to guess the name, but God knows it could be anything."

"I'm going to be looking at film credits. That boy. He wanted to be somebody. *Be* somebody," Lena said.

Marie thought, *Didn't we all?*

2016

LENA SENT SOME CLOTHES RIGHT AFTER THE PITTSBURGH MEET-ing but after that they lost track of each other again. Of course, Marie knew a great deal about what was happening with Lena because she was still in the papers and magazines, in all kinds of publications.

By the 1960s she was almost as well known for talking about civil rights as she was for singing.

It was a horrible time for the country. It started with deaths: Medgar Evers, then John Kennedy, Malcolm X, Martin Luther King—and then Bobby Kennedy. There were photos of Lena consulting with Bobby Kennedy, who had vowed to improve the racial situation in America.

Cities erupted. There was violence everywhere, buildings razed, people hurt. And Pittsburgh was one of the worst.

One day in late April 1968, Marie said to her daughter, who was visiting, "Go with me to the Hill. I need to see." She and Helen had been watching the news, catching a street name here, a storefront there. But the old Hill was long gone now because years ago urban renewal had wiped out a whole neighborhood; the people who stayed had to move up to the Upper Hill. Marie's parents were dead by then but they wouldn't have been able to survive the move. Now the rest of the Hill was a war zone—Molotov cocktails blowing up everywhere, stores looted. The National Guard had to be called in.

Helen had a Volkswagen bug at this point—she was a graduate student—and offered to drive her mother. They went into Oakland first, then up to Centre Avenue and then up, up into the Hill.

"Oh," Marie said. "Oh, dear God, I can't stand it. Everything is gone."

"Should I keep going?"

"Yes."

Helen stopped the car in front of what had been a whole row of houses, gone but for some timbers and soggy furniture, one piece of which was a green sofa out on the street. It *looked* wet. A boy of about five was sitting on it, picking with his fingers at something that might have been dry cereal in a bowl.

"I see. Keep going."

Helen kept going. Marie told her daughter about places that used to be. "Mike's Barber Shop. Lite Printing. Hilltop Sandwich Shop. Ellie's Hair Salon." Soon there would be no one who even remembered that wonderful life, and now, clearly, the Upper Hill was not wonderful—it was a place of terrible poverty.

Helen stopped the car again in front of what used to be a grocery store. "Reminds me of Grandma's."

"Kind of."

"At least nobody burned it down."

They parked, got out of the car, and tried the front door. But even from outside they could see it was empty, not a can of beans on the shelves. Through the dark windows they saw a man coming forward, wielding a baseball bat and stepping over cartons that had once held takeout food.

He opened the door. "I'd get out of here, I was you," he said.

"I used to live in the Hill. I wanted to see."

He looked them up and down. "It's bad. And whites not welcome."

"My mother had a store like this. She had a wonderful garden in back."

"So? So what? Like I said, whites not welcome."

"We used to get along," she said.

He looked as if he didn't believe her or didn't care.

LENA, DURING THAT decade and right after, having reacted to the national losses, having been public about it, and strong, a very strong speaker, went through her own losses. She didn't speak publicly about those, but the journalists connected the dots. They saw her falling apart and that was news.

First Swee' Pea had cancer. Lena was one of his visitors, as was Ellington, but love couldn't keep Swee' Pea alive. At his funeral, people said things like they hoped he heard music at the end. Lena told *Time* magazine he was possibly the only man she ever really loved. She was to lose all the men in her life in a sort of barrage.

She had bought her father a motel to run and then a house to live in, so he could be in the California sun. In April 1970 he died of emphysema.

A couple of months later her son, rejecting the dialysis machine she'd bought him, decided he'd rather be dead than be an invalid, so he went, too.

Then something killed her husband, Lennie Hayton. Drink, some speculated; her abandonment of him, others thought.

She told one journalist the sorrows had come in battalions. She had to explain it was a quote from Shakespeare.

Marie wrote her a note expressing her sympathy.

Lena wrote back that she treasured the note. She sent clothes, which were too fancy for Marie, who gave them to her daughter, who loved them.

AND THAT WASN'T quite that. More than a decade later, Marie was glad to see Lena had bounced back. Age was like that—people found a way. Helen took Marie to New York to see her first Broadway show, Lena's show, which was getting rave reviews. There she was, as beautiful as ever, but now free, making jokes, flirting with the audience, letting all the anger out. She sang "Stormy Weather" and of course people went wild. That was her story. Then she sang a whole lot of other songs, interspersed with commentary about some of the things she'd put up with in her career. She laughed at some of what she'd endured, spat out her anger at other times. She sounded black now; Marie wasn't sure of all the reasons, but she sounded different. And then she sang "Stormy Weather" again, bringing it up from the gut, belting it out so hard she had people crying.

"She is fantastic," Helen said.

Marie felt a moment's jealousy and then realized how absolutely silly that was. During the standing ovation she applauded as hard as anyone in the theater.

*   *   *   *   *   *   *   *   *   *   *   *   *

I AM HELEN, of course, Helena at birth. I got it down as well as I could. Both my mother and Lena are gone. Probably Josiah is too, by now.

They all wanted to be somebody.

I, for one, think they were.